SECOND LIFE

www.**transworldbooks**.co.uk

Also by S J Watson

BEFORE I GO TO SLEEP

For more information on S J Watson and his books,
see his website at www.sjwatson-books.com

SECOND LIFE

S J Watson

Doubleday

LONDON · TORONTO · SYDNEY · AUCKLAND · JOHANNESBURG

TRANSWORLD PUBLISHERS
61–63 Uxbridge Road, London W5 5SA
www.transworldbooks.co.uk

Transworld is part of the Penguin Random House group of companies
whose addresses can be found at global.penguinrandomhouse.com

Penguin
Random House
UK

First published in Great Britain in 2015 by Doubleday
an imprint of Transworld Publishers

A CIP catalogue record for this book
is available from the British Library.

ISBNs 9780857520197 (cased)
9780857520203 (tpb)

Typeset in 11/14pt Sabon by Falcon Oast Graphic Art Ltd.
Printed and bound by Clays Ltd, Bungay, Suffolk

Penguin Random House is committed to a sustainable
future for our business, our readers and our planet. This book
is made from Forest Stewardship Council® certified paper.

MIX
Paper from
responsible sources
FSC® C016897
FSC
www.fsc.org

1 3 5 7 9 10 8 6 4 2

For Alistair Peacock,
and for Jenny Hill

If repression has indeed been the fundamental link between power, knowledge, and sexuality since the classical age, it stands to reason that we will not be able to free ourselves from it except at a considerable cost.

Michel Foucault

God guard me from those thoughts men think
In the mind alone

W. B. Yeats

Part One

Chapter One

I climb the stairs but the door is closed. I hesitate outside it.
Now I'm here, I don't want to go in. I want to turn round,
go home. Try again later.

But this is my last chance. The exhibition has been on for
weeks and closes tomorrow. It's now or never.

I close my eyes and breathe as deeply as I can. I concentrate on filling my lungs, I straighten my shoulders, I feel
the tension in my body evaporate as I breathe out. I tell
myself there's nothing to be worried about, I come here
regularly – to meet friends for lunch, to catch the latest
exhibitions, to attend lectures. This time is no different.
Nothing here can hurt me. It's not a trap.

Finally I feel ready. I push open the door and go in.

The place looks exactly as it always does – off-white walls, a
polished wooden floor, spots in the ceiling that hang off
tracks – and though it's early there are already a few people
wandering around. I watch for a minute as they pause in
front of the pictures, some standing further back to get a
better view, others nodding at a companion's murmured
comment or examining the printed sheet they've picked up
downstairs. The atmosphere is one of hushed reverence,
of calm contemplation. These people will look at the
photographs. They will like them, or not, then they will go

11

back outside, back to their lives, and in all likelihood they will forget them.

At first I allow myself only a glance at the walls. There are a dozen or so large photos hung at intervals, plus a few smaller ones between them. I tell myself I could wander around, pretend to be interested in them all, but today there's only one photograph I've come to see.

It takes me a moment to find it. It's hung on the far wall, at the back of the gallery, not quite in the centre. It's next to a couple of other shots – a full-length colour portrait of a young girl in a torn dress, a close-up of a woman with kohl-rimmed eyes smoking a cigarette. Even from this distance it looks impressive. It's in colour, though it was taken in natural light and its palette is mostly blues and greys, and blown up to this size it's imposing. The exhibition is called 'Partied Out', and even though I don't look at it properly until I'm just a few feet away I can see why this picture is in such a prominent position.

I haven't looked at it in over a decade. Not properly. I've *seen* it, yes – even though it wasn't a particularly well-used photograph back then it had been featured in a couple of magazines and even a book – but I haven't looked at it in all this time. Not close up.

I approach it obliquely, and examine the label first. 'Julia Plummer', it says. '*Marcus in the Mirror*, 1997, Cibachrome print'. There's nothing else, no biographical information, and I'm glad. I allow myself to look up at the picture.

It's of a man; he looks about twenty. He's naked, shot from the waist up, looking at his reflection. The image in front of him is in focus, but he isn't, and his face is thin. His eyes are narrowed and his mouth hangs slightly open, as if he's about to speak, or sigh. There's something melancholy in the photograph, but what you can't see is that up until the moment before it was taken the guy in it – Marcus – had been laughing. He'd spent the afternoon in bed with his girlfriend, someone he was in love with as much as she was with him. They'd been reading to each other – Isherwood's *Goodbye to Berlin*, or maybe *Gatsby*, which she'd read and he hadn't – and eating ice cream from the tub. They were warm, they were happy, they were safe. A radio was playing rhythm and blues in their bedroom across the hall, and in the shot his mouth is open because his girlfriend, the woman taking the shot, was humming along and he was about to join in.

Originally the picture had been different. The girlfriend was in the frame, reflected in the mirror just over the man's shoulder, her camera raised to her eye. She was naked, blurred out of focus. It was a portrait of the two of them, back when photographs taken in mirrors were still unusual.

I'd liked the shot like that. Preferred it, almost. But at some point – I don't remember when, exactly, but certainly before I first exhibited it – I changed my mind. I decided it looked better without me in it. I took myself out of the picture.

I regret it now. It was dishonest of me, the first time I used my art to lie, and I want to tell Marcus I'm sorry. For everything. I'm sorry for following him to Berlin, and for leaving him there, alone in that photograph, and for not being the person he thought I was.

Even after all this time, I'm still sorry.

It's a long time before I turn away from my picture. I don't take portraits like that any more. It's families now, Connor's friends, sitting with their parents and younger siblings, jobs I pick up at the school gate. Pin money. Not that there's anything wrong with that: I put my best effort into it, I have a reputation, I'm good. People will invite me to their children's parties to take shots of the guests to be emailed as souvenirs; I've even taken the pictures at a kids' party arranged to raise money for the hospital Hugh works at. I enjoy it, but the skill is technical; it's not the same as making portraits like this one – it's not art, for want of a better word, and sometimes I miss making art. I wonder if I still could, whether I still have the eye, the instinct to know when exactly to trip the shutter. The decisive moment. It's been a long time since I really tried.

Hugh thinks I should get back into it. Connor's older now, he's starting to live his own life. Because of his difficult start we both threw ourselves into looking after him, but he needs us less than he once did. There's more space for me now.

I look briefly at the other pictures on the walls. Maybe I will, soon. I could concentrate a little more on my career and still look after Connor. It's possible.

I go downstairs to wait for Adrienne. Originally she'd wanted to come with me, to see the exhibition, but I'd told her no, I wanted to see the picture alone. She hadn't minded. 'I'll just meet you in the café,' she'd said. 'Maybe we can grab a bite to eat.'

She's early, sitting at a table by the window with a glass of white wine. She stands up as I approach and we hug. She's already talking as we sit.

'How was it?'

I pull my chair under the table. 'A bit weird, to be honest.' Adrienne has already ordered a bottle of sparkling water for me and I pour a glass. 'It doesn't feel like my picture any more.'

She nods. She knows how anxious I've been about coming here. 'There're some interesting photos up there. Will you go and take a look? Later?'

She raises her wine. 'Maybe.' I know she won't, but I'm not offended. She's seen my picture before and isn't bothered about the others. 'Cheers,' she says. We drink. 'You didn't bring Connor?'

I shake my head. 'Definitely too weird.' I laugh. 'He's busy, anyway.'

'Out with his mates?'

'No. Hugh's taken him swimming. They've gone to Ironmonger Row.'

She smiles. Connor is her godson and she's known my husband for almost as long as I have. 'Swimming?'

'It's a new thing. Hugh's idea. He's realized his fiftieth is next year and he's dreading it. He's trying to get fit.' I pause. 'Have you heard from Kate?'

I look down at my drink. I hadn't wanted to ask the question, not so soon, but it's out now. I'm not sure which answer I'd prefer. Yes, or no.

She sips her wine. 'Not for a while. Have you?'

'About three weeks ago.'

'And . . . ?'

I shrug. 'The usual.'

'Middle of the night?'

'Yep,' I sigh. I think back to my sister's last call. Two in the morning, even later for her, over there in Paris. She'd sounded out of it. Drunk, I guessed. She wants Connor back. She doesn't know why I won't let her have him. It isn't fair and, by the way, she isn't the only person who thinks Hugh and I are being selfish and impossible.

'She was just saying the same old thing.'

'Maybe you need to talk to her. Again, I mean. When she's not so—'

'Angry?' I smile. 'You know as well as I do how much good that's likely to do and, anyway, I can't get hold of her. She won't answer her mobile and if I ring the landline I just get her flatmate, who tells me nothing. No, she's made her

15

mind up. Suddenly, after all this time, all she wants in the world is to look after Connor. And she thinks Hugh and I are stopping her for our own selfish reasons. She hasn't paused, even for a moment, to wonder how Connor might feel, what he might want. She certainly hasn't asked him. Once again, it's all about her.'

I stop talking. Adrienne knows the rest; I don't need to carry on. She knows the reasons Hugh and I took my sister's son, that for all these years Kate has been happy with the situation. What neither of us knows is why that has changed.

'Will you talk to her?' I say.

She takes a deep breath, closes her eyes. For a moment I think she's going to tell me I have to sort it out myself, I can't come running to her every time I argue with my sister; it's the sort of thing my father used to say to me. But she doesn't, she just smiles. 'I'll try.'

We order and eat our lunch. We discuss our mutual friends – she asks me if I've seen Fatima recently, did I know Ali has a new job, she wonders whether I'm planning on going to Dee's drinks party at the weekend – then she says it's time she left, she has a meeting. I tell her I'll catch up with her on Saturday.

I can't resist going through the gift shop on my way out. They'd wanted to use my picture of Marcus on the cover of the brochure but I never replied to the email and instead there's a picture of an androgynous-looking guy sucking on a lollipop. I didn't reply to the requests for interviews either, though that didn't stop one of the magazines – *Time Out*, I think – running a piece about me. I was 'reclusive', they said, and my picture was one of the highlights of the exhibition, an 'intimate portrait', both 'touching and fragile'. Bullshit, I wanted to reply, but I didn't. If they want 'reclusive', I'll give it to them.

I look again at the lollipop guy. He reminds me of Frosty, and I flick through the book before moving over to the post-cards arranged on the display rack. Normally I'd buy a few, but today I just get one, *Marcus in the Mirror*. For a moment I want to tell the cashier that it's mine, that I took it for myself, and that, though for years I've actively avoided it, I'm still glad they used it in the exhibition and I've had the chance to own it again.

But I don't. I say nothing, just murmur a 'Thanks' then put the card in my bag and leave the gallery. Despite the February chill I walk most of the way home – through Covent Garden and Holborn, down Theobald's Road in the direction of Gray's Inn Road – and at first I can think of nothing but Marcus and our time in Berlin all those years ago. But by the time I reach Roseberry Avenue I've managed to move on from the past and instead I'm thinking about what's happening here, now. I'm thinking about my sister, and hoping against hope that Adrienne can make her see sense, even though I know she won't be able to. I'm going to have to talk to Kate myself. I'll be firm, but kind. I'll remind her that I love her, and want her to be happy, but I'll also tell her that Connor is almost fourteen now, that Hugh and I have worked hard to give him a stable life and it's important it isn't upset. My priority has to be to make her realize that things are best left as they are. For the first time I allow myself to consider that Hugh and I probably ought to see a lawyer.

I turn the corner into our road. There's a police car parked a few doors from the house, but it's our front door that's open. I begin to run; my mind empties of everything but the need to see my son. I don't stop until I'm in the house, in the kitchen, and I see Hugh standing in front of me, talking to a woman in a uniform. I take in Connor's towel and trunks, drying on the radiator, then Hugh and the officer

17

turn to look at me. She's wearing an expression of perfect, studied neutrality, and I know it's the way Hugh looks when he's delivering bad news. My chest tightens, I hear myself shout, as if in a dream. '*Where's Connor?*' I'm saying. '*Hugh! Where's our son?*' But he doesn't answer. He's all I can see in the room. His eyes are wide; I can tell that something terrible has happened, something indescribable. *Tell me!* I want to shout, but I don't. I can't move; my lips won't form words. My mouth opens, then closes. I swallow. I'm underwater, I can't breathe. I watch as Hugh steps towards me, try to shake him off when he takes my arm, then find my voice. 'Tell me!' I say, over and over, and a moment later he opens his mouth and speaks.

'It's not Connor,' he says, but there's barely enough time for the relief that floods my blood to register before he says, 'I'm sorry, darling. It's Kate.'

Chapter Two

I'm sitting at the kitchen table. I don't know how I got here. We're alone; the police officer has left, her job done. The room is cold. Hugh is holding my hand.

'When?' I say.

'Last night.'

There's a mug of sweet tea in front of me and I watch it steam. It has nothing to do with me. I can't work out why it's there. All I can think of is my baby sister, lying in a Parisian alleyway, rain-soaked and alone.

'Last night?'

'That's what they said.'

He's speaking softly. He knows I'll remember only a fraction of what he tells me.

'What was she doing there?'

'They don't know. Taking a short cut?'

'A short cut?'

I try to picture it. Kate, on her way home. Drunk, probably. Wanting to shave a few minutes off her journey.

'What happened?'

'They think she'd just left a bar. She was attacked.'

I remember. A mugging, the officer had said, though they don't know yet if anything was taken. She'd looked away from me, then. She lowered both her gaze and her voice, and turned to Hugh. I heard her, though. 'She doesn't appear to have been raped.'

Something within me collapses as I think of it. I fold inwards; I become tiny, diminished. I'm eleven years old, Kate's four, and I have to tell her that our mother isn't coming back from the hospital this time. Our father thinks I'm old enough to talk to her, he can't face it, not this time, it's my job. Kate is crying, even though I'm not sure she understands what I've told her, and I'm holding her. 'We'll be fine,' I'm saying, even though part of me already knows what will happen. Our father won't cope, his friends will be no help. We're on our own. But I can't say this, I must be strong for Kate. For my sister. 'You and me,' I tell her. 'I promise. I'll look after you. Always.'

But I hadn't, had I? I'd run away to Berlin. I'd taken her son. I'd left her to die.

'What happened?' I say again.

Hugh is patient. 'Darling, we don't know. But they're doing everything in their power to find out.'

At first I'd thought it would be better for Connor to stay away from Kate's funeral. He was too young, he wouldn't cope. Hugh disagreed. He reminded me that our father hadn't let me and Kate go to our mother's and I'd resented him for the rest of his life.

I had to concede he was right, but it was the counsellor who decided the matter. 'He can't be protected,' she said. 'He has to deal with his grief.' She hesitated. We were sitting in her office, the two of us. She had her hands folded on the desk in front of her. I was looking at the marks on her hands, tiny abrasions. I wondered if she was a gardener. I pictured her, kneeling beside flower beds with pruning shears, deadheading roses. A life she can return to, when this is over. Unlike us.

'Julia?'

I looked up. I'd missed something.

'Does he *want* to go?'

When we got home we asked him. He thought about it for a while, then said he'd like to, yes.

We bought him a suit, a black tie, a new shirt. He looks much older, wearing them, and walks between me and Hugh as we go into the crematorium. 'Are you all right?' I say, once we've sat down.

He nods, but says nothing. The place feels drenched with pain, but most people are silent. In shock. Kate's death was violent, senseless, incomprehensible. People have retreated within themselves, for protection.

Yet I'm not crying, neither is Connor, and neither is his father. Only Hugh has looked at the coffin. I put my arm around our son. 'It's all right,' I say.

People continue to file in behind us and take their seats. There is shuffling, voices are hushed. I close my eyes. I'm thinking of Kate, of our childhood. Things were simple, then, though that is not to say they were easy. After our mother died our father began drinking heavily. His friends – mostly artists, painters, people from the theatre – started spending more and more time with us, and we watched our house become the venue for a kind of rolling party that sputtered and faltered but never quite stopped. Every few days new people would arrive just as others left; they would be carrying more bottles and more cigarettes, there would be more music, sometimes drugs. Now I can see that this was all part of our father's grief, but back then it had felt like a celebration of freedom, a binge that lasted a decade. Kate and I felt like unwelcome reminders of his past, and though he kept the drugs away from us and told us he loved us, he was neither inclined nor able to be a parent and so it'd fallen to me to look after us both. I would prepare our meals, I'd put a squirt of paste on Kate's toothbrush and leave it out at bedtime, I'd read to her when she woke up crying and made sure she did her homework and was ready for school every day. I held her and told her that Daddy loved us and everything would be all right. I discovered I adored my sister, and despite the years between us we became as close as twins, the connection between us almost psychic.

Yet she's there, in that box, and I'm here, in front of it, unable even to cry. It's beyond belief and, somewhere, I know I let her down.

There's a tap on my shoulder. I turn round. It's a stranger, a woman. 'I just wanted to say hello,' she says. She introduces herself as Anna. It takes me a moment to place her; Kate's flatmate, we'd asked her to do a reading. 'I wanted to tell you how sorry I am.'

She's crying, but there's a kind of stoicism there. A resilience. 'Thank you,' I say, and a moment later she opens the bag on her lap. She hands me a sheet of paper. 'The poem I picked . . . d'you think it's okay?'

I scan the poem, even though I've already read it in the order of service. 'To the angry,' it begins, 'I was cheated, but to the happy I am at peace.' I'd thought it an odd choice, when surely anger is the only response possible, but I say nothing. I hand the sheet back. 'It's great. Thank you.'

'It's one I thought Kate might like.' I tell her I'm sure she's right. Her hands are shaking and, even though the reading isn't long, I wonder how she's going to get through it.

She does, in the end. Though upset, she draws on some inner reserve of strength and her words are clear and strong. Connor watches her, and I see him wipe a tear away with the back of his hand. Hugh's crying, too, and I tell myself I'm being strong for them both, I have to keep myself together, I can't let them see me fall apart. Yet I can't help wondering whether I'm kidding myself and the truth is I can't feel any pain at all.

Afterwards I go over to Anna. 'It was perfect,' I say. We're standing outside the chapel. Connor looks visibly relieved that it's over.

She smiles. I think of Kate's phone calls over the last few weeks and wonder what Anna thinks of me, what my sister had told her.

'Thank you,' she says.

'This is my husband, Hugh. And this is my very dear friend, Adrienne.'

Anna turns to my son. 'And you must be Connor?' she says. He nods. He holds out his hand for her to shake it, and for a moment I'm struck again by how grown up he seems.

'Pleased to meet you,' he says. He seems totally lost, unsure how he's supposed to behave. The carefree boy of just a few weeks ago, the child who would race into the house, pursued by three or four friends, to pick up his football or his bike, seems suddenly to have gone. The boy who would spend hours with his sketch pad and some pencils has disappeared. I tell myself it's temporary, my little boy will be back, but I wonder if that's true.

We carry on talking, for a while, but then Hugh must sense Connor's distress and suggests they make their way over to the cars. Adrienne says she'll go with them, and Hugh turns to Anna. 'Thank you for everything,' he says, and he shakes her hand again before putting his arm around Connor's shoulders. 'Come on, darling,' he says, and the three of them turn away.

'He seems a nice lad,' says Anna, once they're out of

earshot. The wind has whipped up; there'll be rain soon. She smooths her hair away from her mouth.

'He is,' I say.

'How's he coping?'

'I don't think it's really sunk in yet.' We turn and walk towards the flowers that have been arranged in the courtyard outside the chapel.

'It must be hard for him.'

I wonder how much she knows about Connor. She and my sister were old friends; Kate told me they'd known each other at school, though only vaguely, through other people. A few years ago they'd reconnected through Facebook and quickly realized they'd both moved to Paris. They met for drinks and a few months later Anna's flatmate moved out of her apartment and Kate moved in. I'd been pleased; my sister hadn't always found it easy to keep friends. They must have talked a great deal, yet Kate could be secretive, and I imagine the painful subject of Connor was something she might not find easy to raise.

'He's okay,' I say. 'I think.'

We've reached the south-west wall of the crematorium, the wreaths, the white chrysanthemums and pink roses, the sprays of white lilies pinned with handwritten cards. I bend down to read them, still not quite understanding why it's Kate's name I see everywhere. Just then the sun breaks through the clouds and for the briefest of moments we're lit by its brilliance.

'I bet he's quite a handful,' says Anna, and I stand up. Connor's a good lad, no trouble at all. We decided to tell him the truth about his background as soon as he was old enough to understand it.

'He's fine,' I say. 'So far . . .'

'He gets on well with his dad?'

'Very.' I don't tell her that it's how well he gets on with me that I worry about. I try to be as good a mother as I can, yet sometimes it doesn't come easily. Certainly not in the same way that fatherhood comes to Hugh.

I remember I talked to Adrienne about it once. Hugh was busy with work, and Connor and I were on holiday with her twins. She had been amazing, all day, with all three children. They were much younger, there were tantrums, Connor was whining about everything and refusing to eat. I hadn't been able to cope, and felt bad. 'I worry it's because he's not mine,' I said, once the children had gone to bed and she was sitting with a glass of wine, me with a soda. 'You know?' She told me I was being hard on myself. 'He *is* yours. You're his mum. And you're a good one. You have to remember that everyone's different, and your mother wasn't around to set an example. No one finds it easy.'

'Maybe,' I said. I couldn't help wondering what Kate would have said.

'That's good,' says Anna now, and I smile. 'Yes,' I say. 'We're very lucky to have him.' We carry on looking at the flowers. We make small talk, avoiding the subject of Kate. After a few minutes we walk back out, towards the car park. Adrienne is waving to me, and I tell Anna I'd better go over.

'It's been good to meet you,' I say.

She turns to me and takes my hands in hers. Her grief has broken through again, she's begun to cry. 'I miss her,' she says simply.

I hold her hands. I want to cry, too, but I don't. The numbness pervades everything. It's a defence, Hugh has said. I'm blocking everything. Adrienne agrees: 'There's no right way of grieving Kate,' she says. I haven't told any of my other friends how I feel in case they think I'm unconcerned about my sister's murder. I feel bad.

'I know,' I say. 'I miss her, too.'

She looks up at me. She wants to say something. The words tumble out. 'Can we stay in touch? I mean, I'd like that. If you would? You could come and visit me in Paris, or I could come and see you. I mean, only if you want to, I guess you're very busy—'

'Anna, please.' I put my hand on her arm to silence her. Busy doing what? I think. I had a few jobs in my diary – a couple wanted pictures of them with their eight-week-old baby, the mother of a friend of Connor's wanted the family and their Labrador – but I've cancelled those. Right now I'm doing nothing except existing, thinking of Kate, wondering whether it can really be coincidence that the day I went to look at the picture of Marcus is also the day that claimed her.

I manage to smile. I don't want to seem rude. 'I'd like that very much.'

Chapter Three

Hugh is eating breakfast. Muesli. I watch as he pours milk into his coffee and adds half a spoonful of sugar.

'Are you sure it's not too soon?'

But that's precisely why I want to go, I think. Because it's been two months and, according to my husband, I'm still in denial. I need to make it real.

'I want to go there. I want to meet up with Anna. I want to talk to her.'

As I say it I realize how much it means to me. Anna and I are getting on. She seems warm, funny. Understanding. She doesn't seem to judge. And it was Anna who was closer to Kate than all of us – closer than me, closer than Hugh, or Adrienne – so it's Anna who can help me, in a way that my other friends can't. And perhaps I can help her, too.

'I think it'll do me good.'

'But what are you hoping to achieve?'

I pause. Perhaps part of me also wants to be sure she doesn't think badly of me and Hugh, for taking Connor. 'I don't know. It just feels like something I want to do.'

He's silent. It's been nine weeks, I think. Nine weeks, and I still haven't cried. Not properly. Again I think of the post-card that's still in my bag, where I put it the day Kate died. *Marcus in the Mirror.*

'Kate died. I have to face it.' Whatever *it* is.

He finishes his drink. 'I'm not convinced, but . . .' His voice softens. 'If you're sure, then you should go.'

I'm nervous as I step off the train, but Anna's waiting for me at the end of the platform. She's wearing a dress in pale lemon and standing in the sunlight that arcs in from the high windows. She looks younger than I remember, and she has a quiet, simple prettiness I hadn't noticed at the funeral. Her face is one I'd have once wanted to photograph; it's warm and open. She smiles when she sees me, and I wonder if she's already shedding her grief, while mine is only just beginning to grip.

She waves as I approach. 'Julia!' She runs forward to greet me. We kiss on both cheeks then hold each other for a few moments. 'Thanks so much for coming! It's so good to see you . . .'

'You too,' I say.

'You must be exhausted! Let's get a drink.'

We go to a café, not far from the station. She orders us both a coffee. 'Any news?'

I sigh. What's there to say? She knows most of it already. The police have made little progress; Kate had been drinking in a bar on the night she was attacked, apparently alone. A few people remember seeing her; she seemed in good spirits, was chatting to the barman. Her phone records haven't helped, and she was definitely by herself when she left. It's irrational, but I can't shake the feeling that I'm responsible for what happened.

'Not really.'

'I'm sorry. How're you doing?'

'I just keep thinking of her. Of Kate. Sometimes it's like nothing's happened at all. I just think I could pick up the phone and call her and everything would be all right.'

28

'You're in denial. That's normal. After all, it hasn't been that long.'

I sigh. I don't want to tell her how Kate has been haunting me, that I've been dialling her number over and over again only to hear a pre-recorded voice, speaking in French, informing me that her number hasn't been recognized. I don't want her to know I bought Kate a card, that I wrote out a message and sealed the envelope, then hid it in the bureau underneath a pile of paperwork. I don't want to admit that the worst thing, the hardest thing, is that some small part of me, a part of me I hate but can't deny, is glad she's gone, because at least now she's not ringing me up in the middle of the night to demand I return her son.

'Two months,' I say. 'Hugh says that's hardly any time at all.'

She smiles sadly, but says nothing. In a way I'm relieved; there's nothing anyone can say that might help, everything is irrelevant. Sometimes silence is better and I admire her for braving it.

'How about you?' I say.

'Oh, you know. I'm really busy with work, which helps.' I remember that she's a lawyer, working in compliance for a big pharmaceutical company, though she hasn't told me which one. I wait for her to say more but she doesn't.

'How's Connor?' she asks. She seems genuinely concerned; I can't believe it had once crossed my mind that it'd been her trying to help my sister to get him back.

'He's all right. I suppose . . .'

Our coffees arrive. Two espressos, sachets of sugar in each saucer, a single foil-wrapped chocolate.

'Actually, I'm not sure he is. All right, I mean. He seems angry all the time, slamming doors for no reason, and I know he's crying a lot. I hear him, but he denies it.'

She doesn't respond. Part of me wants to tell her I'm worried I'm losing my son. For so many years we've been so close, more like friends than mother and child. I've encouraged him in his art, taken him out sketching. He's always turned to me when he's been upset, as much as he has to Hugh. He's always told me everything. So why does he now feel that he has to suffer alone?

'He keeps asking if they've caught anyone yet.'

'It's understandable,' she says. 'He's young. He's lost an aunt.'

I hesitate. She'd known, surely?

'You know Kate was Connor's mother?'

She nods.

'How much did she tell you?'

'Everything, I think. I know you took Connor when he was a baby.'

There's a tightening in my throat, a defensiveness. It's that word. 'Took'. I feel the same familiar spasm of irritation – the rewritten story, the buried truth – and I try to swallow it down.

'We didn't *take* him, exactly. Back then, Kate wanted us to have him.'

Even if she didn't later, I think. I wonder what Kate's version of the story became. I imagine she told her friends that we'd swooped in, that we snatched Connor when she was managing perfectly well, that we only wanted her baby because we couldn't have one of our own.

Again the tiny part of me that's relieved she's gone bubbles up. I can't help it, even though it makes me feel wretched. Connor is mine.

'It was complicated. I loved her. But Kate could have a very distorted sense of how well she was coping.'

Anna smiles, as if to reassure me. I go on. 'I know it wasn't easy for her. Giving him up, I mean. She was very young, when he was born. Just a child herself, really. Sixteen. Only a little bit older than Connor is now.'

I look down at my coffee cup. I remember the day Connor was born. It had only been a few months since I got back from Berlin, and I'd been at a meeting. I was back in the programme, and I was glad. Things were going well. When I got home Hugh had packed an overnight bag. 'Where are we going?' I said, and he told me. Kate was in hospital. In labour. 'I've called your father,' he added. 'But he isn't answering.'

I couldn't process what I was hearing, yet at the same time part of me knew it was true.

'In *labour*?' I said. 'But—?'

'That's what they said.'

But she's *sixteen*, I wanted to say. She has no job. She's living at home, our father is supposed to be looking after her.

'She can't be.'

'Well, apparently she is. We need to go.'

By the time we arrived Connor had been born. 'Don't be angry,' said Hugh, before we went in. 'She needs our support.'

She was sitting in bed, holding him. She passed him to me as soon as I walked in, and the love I felt for him was instant and shocking in its intensity. I couldn't have been angry with her, even if I'd wanted to.

'He's beautiful,' I said. Kate closed her eyes, suddenly exhausted, then looked away.

Later, we talked about what had happened. She claimed she hadn't even known she was pregnant. Hugh said it wasn't that uncommon. 'Particularly with teenage girls,' he said. 'Their hormones might not have stabilized, so their periods can be irregular anyway. It's surprising, perhaps, but it does happen.' I tried to imagine it. It was possible, I suppose; Kate was a plump child, faced with a body that was now unfamiliar. She might have missed the fact she was carrying a baby.

'She tried to manage,' I say to Anna now. 'For a couple of years. But . . .'

I shrug. She had nothing. By the time Connor was three she'd taken him to Bristol – without telling anyone why – and was living in a tiny bedsit with a shared bathroom and no kitchen. She had an electric hob plugged in next to the sink and there was a travel kettle balanced on an upturned washing-up bowl. The only time I visited, the place smelt of urine and soiled nappies, and Kate was in bed while her son sat strapped into a car seat on the floor, naked and hungry.

I look up at Anna. 'She asked me to take him. Just for a few months. Until she got on her feet. She loved Connor but couldn't look after him. Mum wasn't around, of course, and Dad had no interest. Six months turned into a year, and then two. You know how it is. Connor needed some stability. When he was about five we decided – all of us – that it'd be better if we formally adopted him.'

She nods. 'You didn't try to contact the father?'

'It was all a bit of a mess. Kate never told us who he was.' There's a pause. I feel a sense of great shame, on Kate's behalf, plus sadness for Connor. 'I don't think she really knew.'

'Or maybe he wasn't someone whose help she wanted . . .'

'No.' I look out of the window at the traffic, the taxis, the bikes wheeling by. The atmosphere is heavy. I want to brighten it. 'But he has Hugh, now. They're incredibly close. They're actually very similar.'

I say it in a kind of rush. It's ironic, I think. Hugh is the one person that Connor has no blood relationship to, yet it's Hugh who Connor looks up to.

'You know,' says Anna, 'Kate always told me that although it was very painful she was relieved when you offered to look after Connor. She said that, in a way, you saved her life.'

I wonder if she's just trying to make me feel better. 'She said that?'

'Yes. She said if it hadn't been for you and Hugh she'd have had to move back in with your father . . .'

She rolls her eyes, she thinks it's a joke. I keep quiet. I'm not sure I'm ready to let her into the family story. Not that far, not yet. She senses my discomfort and reaches across the table to take my hand.

'Kate loved you, you know?'

I feel a flush of relief, but then it's replaced with a sadness so profound it's physical, a beat within me. I look at my hand, in Anna's, and think of the way I'd held Kate's in mine. When she was a baby I'd take each tiny finger and marvel at its delicacy, its perfection. She was born early, so fragile, and yet so full of energy and desire for life. I wasn't yet seven, but already my love for my sister was fierce.

And yet it wasn't enough to save her.

'She said that?'

Anna nods. 'Often.'

'I wish she'd told me that when she was alive. But then I guess she wouldn't, would she?'

She smiles. 'Nope . . .' she says, laughing. 'Never. That wouldn't have been her style.'

We finish our drinks then take the Métro as far as Rue Saint-Maur. We walk to Anna's apartment. She lives in a mansion block, above a laundrette. There's a communal door and Anna tries the handle before punching the code into the entry lock. 'It's broken, half the time,' she says. We go up to the first floor. There's a writing desk on the landing, littered with post, and she pulls out one of its drawers and feels underneath it. 'There's a spare key here,' she says. 'It was Kate's idea. She was always forgetting her keys. It's handy for my boyfriend, too, if he gets here before me.'

So, there's a boyfriend, I think, but I don't ask questions. As with any new friendship, these are the details I'll discover gradually. We go in, and she takes my bag, dropping it by the door. 'You're sure you won't stay here?' she says, but I tell her it's fine, I'll stay at the hotel I've booked, a few streets away. We've talked about it; I'd be in Kate's room, surrounded by her things. It's too early. 'We'll have a drink, then you can check in on the way to dinner. I know a great place. Anyway, come through . . .'

It's a nice flat, big, with high ceilings and windows to the floor. The furniture in the living room is tasteful, if bland. There are framed posters on the walls, the Folies Bergère, the Chat Noir; the prints anyone might pick in a hurry. It hasn't been decorated with love.

'You rent this place?' She nods. 'It's very nice.'

'It'll do for a while. Would you like a drink? Some wine? Or I might have beer.'

So there are some things Kate hasn't told her. 'Do you have any juice? Or some water?'

'Sure.' I follow her into the kitchen. It's at the back of the flat, neat and clean – unlike mine when I left this morning – but still Anna apologizes. She quickly puts away a loaf of bread that's been left out, a jar of peanut butter. I laugh and go over to the window. 'I live with a teenager. This is nothing.'

I think of my family. I wonder how Hugh's coping with Connor. He said he'd take him out tonight – to the cinema – or maybe they'd play chess. They'll get a takeaway, or maybe eat out. I know that I ought to give them a call, but right now it's a relief to have only myself to think about.

Anna grins and hands me a glass of apple juice. 'You sure that's all you want?'

'Yes, thanks.' She takes a bottle of wine out of the fridge. 'I can't tempt you? Last chance!'

I smile, tell her again that I'm fine. I could tell her I don't drink, but I don't want to. She might have questions, and it's not something I want to talk about. Not right now. I don't want to be judged.

Anna sits opposite me and holds up her glass. 'To Kate.'

'To Kate,' I say. I take a sip of juice. I register the briefest wish that my glass was filled with wine, too, and then, like every other time, I let the thought go.

'Do you want to see her room?'

I hesitate. I don't want to, but there's no avoiding it. It's one of the things I came here to do. To confront the reality of her life, and therefore also of her death.

'Yes,' I say. 'Let's.'

It isn't as bad as I thought it would be. There's a window leading on to a little balcony, a double bed with a cream duvet cover, a CD player on the dressing table next to the perfumes. It's tidy; everything is neatly arranged. Not how I imagined Kate living at all.

'The police have searched the room,' says Anna. 'They left things pretty much as they found them.'

The police. I picture them dusting for fingerprints, picking up her things, cataloguing her life. My skin is white-hot, a thousand tiny detonations of shock. It's the first time I've connected the place I stand with my sister's death.

I inhale deeply, as if I can breathe her in, but she's gone, not even her ghost remains. The room could be anybody's. I turn away from Anna and go over to the bed. I sit down. There's a book on the dressing table.

'That's for you.'

It's a photo album, the kind with stiff pages and sheets of adhesive plastic to keep the pictures in place. Even before I open it I sense what'll be inside.

'Kate used to show these to people,' says Anna. '"That's my sister," she'd say. She was so proud, I swear.'

My photographs. Anna sits on the bed beside me. 'Kate told me your father kept these. She found them when he died.'

'My father?' I say. I never suspected he was even remotely interested in my work.

'That's what she said . . .'

On the first page is that picture. *Marcus in the Mirror.*

'My God . . .' I say. I have to swallow my shock. It's the full picture, unedited, uncropped. I'm there, standing behind Marcus, the camera raised to my eye. Naked.

'That's you?'

'Yes.'

'And who's the guy? I see him everywhere at the moment.'

I feel an unexpected flush of pride. 'The photo's been used in an exhibition. It's become quite popular.'

'So who is he?'

I look back at the picture. 'An ex. Marcus.' I stumble over his name; I wonder when I last said it out loud. I carry on. 'We lived together, for a while. Years ago. I was . . . what . . . ? Twenty? Maybe not even that. He was an artist. He gave me my first camera. I took this in our flat. Well, it was a squat, really. In Berlin. We shared it with a few others. Artists, mostly. They came and went.'

'Berlin?'

'Yes. Marcus wanted to go there. It was the mid-nineties.

The Wall was down, the place felt new. Like it'd been wiped clean. You know?' She nods. I'm not sure she's that interested, but I carry on. 'We lived in Kreuzberg. Marcus's choice. I think it was a Bowie thing.' She looks puzzled. Maybe she's too young. 'David Bowie. He lived there. Or recorded there, I'm not sure . . .'

I put my fingers to the photograph. I remember how I used to take my camera with me everywhere, just as Marcus would take his sketchbook and our friend Johan his notebook. These objects weren't just tools, they were part of who we were, they were how we made sense of the world. I developed an obsession with taking portraits of people as they got ready, got dressed, put make-up on, checked their hair in the mirror.

Anna looks from me to the picture. 'He looks . . .' she begins, but then she stops herself. It's as if she's seen something in the picture, something upsetting, that she can't quite define. I look at it again. It has this effect on people. It creeps up on them.

I finish her sentence. 'Unhappy? He was. Not all the time, I mean, he was singing along to some song on the radio just after this picture was taken, but yes. Yes, he was sometimes.'

'Why?'

I don't want to tell her the truth. Not all of it.

'He was just . . . he was a little bit lost, I think, by this point.'

'Didn't he have family?'

'Yes. They were very close, but . . . you know? Drugs make things like that difficult.'

She looks up at me. 'Drugs?'

I nod. Surely she can see it?

'Did you love him?'

'I loved him very much.' I find myself willing her with a

fierce hope not to ask what happened, just like I hope that she won't ask how we met.

She must sense my reluctance. 'It's an amazing photo,' she says. She puts her hand on my arm. 'They all are. You're very talented. Shall we look at some more?'

I turn to the first page. Here Kate has pasted a picture taken much earlier; black and white and deliberately bleeding at the edges. Frosty, made-up, but not wearing her wig, putting her heels on. She was sitting on our couch, an overflowing ashtray at her feet, next to a packet of cigarettes and a lighter. It was always one of my favourite photographs.

'Who's that?'

'That's Frosty. A friend.'

'Frosty?'

'I can't remember her real name. She hated having to use it, anyway.'

'She?' Anna looks shocked, and I understand why, I suppose. In the picture Frosty's hair is cropped short; even with the make-up she looks more male than female.

'Yes. She was a woman.' I laugh. 'Actually, she was sort of neither, but she always called herself she. She used to say, "You gotta decide, in this world. There's only two bathrooms in the bars. There's only two boxes on the forms. Male or female." She decided she was a woman.'

Anna looks again at the picture. I don't expect her to understand. People like Frosty – or even people like Marcus – aren't part of her world. They aren't even part of mine any more.

'What happened to her?'

'I don't know,' I say. 'None of us thought Frosty would last long. She was too fragile for this world . . . But that might have just been our own melodramatic nonsense. The truth is, I left Berlin in a hurry. I left them behind. I have no idea what happened after I'd gone.'

'You didn't look back?'

It's an odd phrase. I think of Lot's wife, the pillar of salt. 'I couldn't.' It was too painful, I want to say, but I don't. I close the photo album and pass it back to her.

'No. They're yours.'

I hesitate.

'Keep them. This, too.'

She hands me a box that was on the floor next to Kate's bed. It's a biscuit tin. On the lid are the words *Huile d'Olive*, a picture of a woman in a red dress.

'It's for you.'

'What is it?'

'It's just some personal stuff of Kate's. I thought you should have it.'

So this is what's left of my sister. This is what I've come to take home. Back to her son.

I'm nervous, as if the tin might contain a trap, a rat or a poisonous spider.

I take off the lid. The box is full of notebooks, photos, paperwork. Her passport is on the top and I open it to her photograph. It's recent, one I haven't seen before. Her hair is shorter and I can see she'd lost weight. She looks almost like someone else.

I look at the expiry date. It's valid for eight more years. Eight years she'll never need. I snap it shut and put it back, then close the box.

'I'll look at the rest later,' I say. I realize I've begun to cry, for the first time since she died. I'm exposed, raw. It's as if I've been slit open like one of Hugh's patients, neck to groin. I am flayed, my heart a jagged slash.

I put the box down. I want to get away, to find somewhere quiet and warm where I can stay for ever and not have to think about anything at all.

But isn't this what I came for? To mine the memory of my sister, to make sure there is a tiny part of her that survives for Connor? To feel something, to say sorry, to say goodbye?

Yes, I think. That's why I'm here. I'm doing the right thing. So why do I hate myself?

'It's okay,' says Anna. 'You go ahead and cry. It's okay.'

Chapter Four

We take a cab to the restaurant. We're shown to our table, outside on the pavement. White tablecloth, held down with plastic clips, a basket of bread. The evening is warm and pleasant, the air still, loaded with promise.

We chat. Once I recovered we told ourselves we must spend the evening celebrating Kate's life as well as mourning her death. We laugh, there's an ease between us; Anna even takes out her phone and takes a snap of the two of us with the river in the background. She tells me she likes this area of the city and wants to live here, one day. 'It's very central,' she says. 'By the river . . .' She orders a carafe of wine. As the waiter begins to pour I put my hand over the top of my glass and shake my head.

'You're not drinking?'

'No,' I say. I think of the excuses I've made in the past – I'm on antibiotics, I'm dieting, or driving – but then the inevitable happens. Other excuses begin to crowd in, the ones that tell me why this time, this one time, I can take a sip. It's been a difficult day, I'm stressed, it's been fifteen years and it won't do any harm.

My sister has been killed.

'I'm fine.'

I think back to what I've learned. I can't avoid the temptation to drink, I have to recognize the urge. I have to know that it's normal, and temporary. I have to challenge it, or ride it out.

'To be honest, I don't drink. I haven't for a while.' Anna nods and sips her wine while I ask for some sparkling water. She looks interested but asks no questions, and I'm relieved. When she puts her glass down I see that she's distracted, restless. She shifts in her seat, rearranges her napkin.

'I wanted to talk to you about something.'

'Go on.'

She hesitates. I wonder what she's going to say. I know the police have interviewed her extensively; the bar Kate was in that evening is one she goes to. I brace myself for a revelation.

'It's about the money . . .'

I smile. Kate's will must have surprised her, and Hugh warned me she'd probably mention it.

'The money Kate left to you?'

'Yes. It was a shock . . .' She picks off some bread. 'I really wasn't expecting it. To be honest, I had no idea she had any money to leave, let alone that she'd leave some of it to me . . . And I didn't ask her for it. I do want you to know that.'

I nod. I remember it'd been Hugh who had persuaded Kate to write a will in the first place, and we'd both been relieved when she'd later changed it to include Anna. It meant she had friends, she was putting down roots.

'I know. It's okay.'

'Were you surprised? That she left money to me?'

'No. It makes sense. You were her best friend. Kate was a generous person. She must have wanted you to have it.'

She looks relieved. I wonder whether it's because of the money, or the fact that this conversation isn't proving as awkward as she'd feared.

'Where did it come from?'

'Our father. He died a couple of years ago and left his money to Kate. Just what was in the bank, plus the proceeds from the sale of his house. It came to a lot more than anyone expected.'

A lot more, I think. Almost a million pounds. But I don't say it.

'Did he leave some to you?'

I shake my head. 'He thought I didn't need it, I guess.'

Or maybe it was guilt. He knew he'd neglected his younger daughter. He was trying to make it up to her.

Anna sighs.

'Oh, it's okay,' I say quickly. 'Hugh has money in the family and Kate was struggling.'

'But she didn't spend it.'

'No. Hugh suggested she put some of it away, save it for a rainy day. But neither of us thought she would actually listen to him.'

'I would happily give my share to you. If you want?'

She's being serious. I put my hand on her arm. 'Absolutely not. Besides, she left the rest to Connor. It came to quite a lot.' A lot more than she left to you, I think, though again I don't say it. 'I'm his trustee, though I'm not giving it to him until I'm sure he won't spend it all on computer games and new trainers.'

She says nothing. She looks unconvinced.

'Kate clearly wanted you to have that money. Enjoy it . . .'

Her face breaks into a smile of relief. She thanks me, and a moment later the waiter comes over and for a minute we're lost in the choosing and ordering of our food. Once he's retreated, there's silence. The sun pours its golden light over the river. People stroll, arm in arm. The veil of my grief lifts, briefly, and I glimpse peace. I feel myself almost capable of relaxing.

'This is so lovely,' I say. 'I can see why Kate came to Paris.'

Anna smiles. I think how things might've been, if my sister and I had somehow managed to reconcile our differences and found a way back to the closeness we'd shared until the last few years. Perhaps then I could've visited them both. It might've been the three of us sitting here, chatting, gossiping, having fun. Were we really that different, Kate and I?

I turn to Anna. For the first time I feel able to ask her. 'I wish I knew what happened,' I say quietly. 'That night . . .'

She sips her wine then pours herself more.

'Normally we'd have gone out together,' she says. Something in her tone makes me think I'm not the only one who feels guilty. 'But I was busy that day. She was on her own.'

I sigh. I don't want to imagine it.

'Is it a bad area? Where she was found?'

'No. Not particularly.'

'What happened, Anna?'

'What've the police said? Do you talk to them?'

'Yes. Not as much as Hugh. The Foreign Office said they'd prefer to liaise with just one of us. It keeps it simple, I suppose, and he volunteered. But I speak to them, too.'

'And you discuss what they say?'

'Oh, he tells me everything. But none of it's very helpful.'

'Really?'

'No. It's all dead ends. There's no motive. They said they'd talked to her friends, but—'

'But none of us knew anything . . .'

'No. So they just keep drawing blanks. The only thing they're puzzled about is her earring.'

I close my eyes. This is hard. I can't help but visualize my sister's body. She was found wearing one earring. It looked as though the other had been torn off.

'They asked me about that.'

'You don't remember anything?'

She shakes her head. 'No. Was it expensive?'

'It was cheap. Costume jewellery. Cheap gold, I think. A funny kind of dreamcatcher design with turquoise feathers. I suppose in the dark it might've looked expensive, but why take only one? And, as far as they can tell, nothing else was missing. She still had her phone, her purse.' I hesitate. 'I think that's why I find it so hard. It seems so senseless. Hugh keeps suggesting I have some therapy.'

'And do you think you should?'

I pick up my glass. 'I'm just not sure what good it would do. It's typical of Hugh, though. He's a wonderful man, but he's a surgeon. If something's broken he just wants to fix it and then move on. Sometimes I think he's secretly angry that I'm not getting back to normal quickly enough. You know? He thinks I'm over-obsessing about knowing who killed her.'

'And are you?'

'Of course not. I know it won't bring her back. It's just . . . we used to be as close as two people can be, you know? We used to finish each other's sentences. How could I have not known when she was in trouble?'

'You're not to blame—' she begins, but I interrupt her.

'You knew her, Anna. What was she even doing there, in that bar, alone?'

She takes a deep breath. 'I'm not sure.' She looks out, towards the river. The coaches on the bridge are silvered in the last of the evening sun, the buildings on the right bank glisten.

'What? What is it? Anna?'

'I think she might've been seeing someone . . .'

'A boyfriend?'

'Kind of . . .'

I feel a surge of energy. A Pavlovian response to the promise of progress.

'What d'you mean? Who was she seeing? Did the police know?'

'It's not that simple.' She looks uncomfortable. 'She . . . she had boyfriends. Boyfriends, plural.'

I take a deep breath and put down my fork. 'You mean more than one at the same time?'

She nods.

'You think one of them found out about the others? Did you tell the police?'

'I told them as much as I knew. I presume they looked into it, I think they still are looking into it. The thing is . . . it wasn't as straightforward as that.' She hesitates but doesn't lower her voice, even though there are people at the surrounding tables. 'They weren't really boyfriends as such. Kate had fun. You know? She liked meeting guys and having a good time. We both did, occasionally.'

'In bars?'

'No. Online.'

'Okay . . .' I say. 'So she dated people off the internet?'

'Not just dating.'

'She was meeting men for sex.'

She looks defensive. 'It happens! But, anyway, I know she didn't meet them all. She was more into it than me, but still a lot of it was just sex talk, you know? Fantasy.'

I try to picture Kate, alone in her room, in front of her laptop. For some reason I think of Connor sitting at his computer, his face illuminated by the screen, then of Hugh doing the same thing.

I dismiss the thought. Hugh isn't that sort of person.

'We both used to go online together. This is before I met my boyfriend, of course. We'd chat to people, compare notes, sometimes go on dates. You know?'

'But the police said she left alone.'

'Maybe she'd been stood up?'

'Promise me the police know this? They didn't say anything . . . She might have put herself in real danger.'

'Oh, yes. I told them. They questioned me for hours. They asked about everything. Her friends. People she knew. Even you and Hugh.' She looks at me then down at the table. Anger prickles. Have we been investigated? Do they think I'm capable of hurting my sister? 'They took away her computer, her phone. I guess they didn't find anything . . .'

'Maybe they didn't look hard enough?'

She smiles sadly. 'Well, I suppose we have to trust that they know what they're doing. Surely?' She pauses. 'I'm sorry. If I've upset you.'

I look out over the city. It's dark now, the sky is lit, Notre Dame sits in front of us, owning its own ghostly history. I'm overwhelmed with sadness. All these questions that lead nowhere.

I begin to cry again. It's as if it's a new skill; now I've started, I can't stop. 'How can someone do this to my sister – to anyone – and get away with it?'

'I know. I know.' She hands me a tissue from her bag then puts her hand on mine. 'You need closure.'

I shut my eyes. 'I know,' I say. 'But everything I try to do just opens it all up further. It's like a cut that won't heal.'

In my mind I see Kate as a toddler: we're ready to go to a party, she's wearing a dress in lemon that had once been mine and a band in her hair with a yellow bow. She's just pulled herself up on a chair but has let go. She wobbles then looks at me. She's hesitant, determined, and after a couple of false starts she lifts one foot, then the other. She takes a few steps, her arms out wide, then begins to fall. I remember I'd caught her, swooped her up – already she was giggling – and carried her through to where our mother stood, putting on her gloves. 'She walked,' I said. 'Katie walked!' And our mother hugged us both to her, all three of us laughing, delighted.

The weight of my grief presses down and I blink the image away. She puts down her wine. 'Might it help to go there?'

'Where?'

'To the place it happened.' I shake my head, but she goes on. 'I went. The other week. I had to see it for myself.' She squeezes my hand. 'It's just an alleyway. Nothing special. Next to a train line.'

I don't speak. I can't tell her how many times I've seen it, how many times I've imagined my sister there.

'I left some flowers there. I think it helped.'

Still I say nothing. I'm not ready. I'm not ready to stare Kate's death in the face. I'm not strong enough.

'You just need more time . . .'

Time. The thing I have plenty of, the thing Kate ran out of.

'Come with me?'

I close my eyes. Kate is there, I want to say. Her ghost. She's trapped there, screaming. She can't escape, and I can't help her.

'No. No. I can't.'

Something snaps. I feel it give, then there's a release. I reach for the carafe. The gesture is automatic, I'm barely aware I've moved. I'm thinking of Kate, of her sitting at her computer, chatting to strangers, telling them her secrets. I'm thinking of Anna. I'm thinking of Hugh, and of Connor, and of Frosty and Marcus, and before I know what I'm doing my glass is in my hand, and it's full of wine, and I'm thinking, It can't hurt now, surely? and, Haven't I waited long enough?

The answers will come, if I'm not quick. I raise the glass to my lips, I push all thought away, and then, for the first time in fifteen years, I'm drinking, and drinking, and drinking.

Chapter Five

I sit on the train. I'm thirsty, my lips are dry, but my head is remarkably clear. I remember hangovers, and this isn't one. I didn't drink that much. I can't have done, or I'd know it.

I think back to last night. The drink slid down my throat as if it were something that belonged, a key in a lock, something that completed me, and as I swallowed I felt myself relax, the unclenching of muscles I didn't know I'd been tensing. It felt a little too much like coming home.

This isn't good. I know that, I tell myself that, over and over. Unless I'm careful I'll forget that there are no halfway houses, I'll convince myself that I can handle one drink, here and there, or that I'm fine as long as I only drink wine, or don't drink before the evening, or drink only with a meal. One excuse will bleed into another.

I know I have to do something. I know I have to do it now.

When I get home I call Adrienne. She's the person I always ring, when I need help. She understands, though she's never been in the programme. Her addiction is to work, if it's to anything. She answers straight away.

'Darling, you're home. How was it?'

I'm silent. I don't know what to say. So many years of

vigilance, all wasted, all gone in one night. I should confess everything, yet part of me doesn't want to.

'I just . . .'

'What is it?'

'Can I talk to you about something?'

'Of course.'

I can't say it. Not yet.

'Did you know Kate was using websites? To meet men, I mean?'

'Well, I know she used dating sites. Like everyone else. Is that what you mean?'

'Yes. But she wasn't just dating. Anna said she was having fantasy sex.'

'Cybersex?'

'Yes. And she'd meet up with people, apparently.'

I hesitate. I'm aware this isn't why I called her, this isn't the reason I wanted to speak to her. But it seems easier. It's a build-up, a preparation. Adrienne says nothing.

'Did you know?'

'Yes. She told me.'

Jealousy prickles my skin.

'She never told *me*.'

Adrienne sighs. 'Darling, she was having fun. It wasn't a big thing, just something she did occasionally. And, anyway, you hadn't really been talking for a while.'

She's right. Not about anything that really mattered, I guess. There's another wave of nausea.

'What if the man who killed her was someone she met online?'

'The police know what she was doing. I'm sure they're looking into it.'

Are they? I think. I can't focus on it, now. I close my eyes.

I take a deep breath. I open my mouth to speak, but the words still won't come.

'Darling, are you all right?'

She knows, I think. She's my oldest friend and she can just tell. I lower my voice, even though the house is empty.

'Julia, what is it?'

'I had a drink.'

I hear her sigh. I can't bear her disapproval, but I hear her sigh.

'I didn't mean to. I mean, I wasn't going to, but . . .'

I stop myself. I'm making excuses. Not taking responsibility. Not admitting that I'm powerless over alcohol. Basic stuff.

I take a deep breath. I say it again.

'I had a drink.'

'Okay. Just one?'

'No.'

Please don't tell me it's a slippery slope. I know that. Please don't make me feel worse than I already do.

'Oh, darling,' she says.

'I feel pretty bad. Awful, in fact.'

Another pause. Please don't tell me it's nothing and I ought to forget it.

'Adrienne?'

'You're going through a lot,' she says. 'It happened. It's a slip, a relapse, but you need to forgive yourself . . . Have you thought about what we talked about?'

She means therapy. She agrees with Hugh, and like everyone in therapy she thinks I should go too, or see a counsellor. She's even recommended someone. Martin Somebody-or-other.

But the truth is, I don't want it. Not now, not yet. Not

while I'm like this. I think it would fail, and then it would no longer be something I can have in reserve.

'No,' I say.

'Okay, well, I won't say any more, but I wish you would. Think about it at least.'

I tell her I have, and I will. But I'm beginning to wonder if I deserve this pain, if somehow I owe it to my sister to live through it. I couldn't save her. I took her son.

'Have you told Hugh?'

I don't answer.

'About having a drink. Have you told him?'

I close my eyes. I don't want to. I can't.

'Julia—?'

'Not yet,' I say. 'There's no need. It won't happen again—'

She interrupts me. 'Darling. Listen. You're my oldest, dearest friend. I love you. Unconditionally. But I think you need to tell Hugh.' She waits for me to speak, but I don't. 'I know it's entirely up to you, but I'm sure it's the right thing to do.'

She's being tender, kind-hearted; yet still it feels brutal. I tell her I'll do it tonight.

Hugh is out for the evening. He's playing squash, then there'll be drinks afterwards. He isn't late, though, and Connor has only just gone to bed when he gets in. Almost straight away I decide I'm going to tell him.

I wait until we're sitting in the living room, watching television. At the first ad break I pause the screen then turn to him, as if I'm going to ask if he wants a cup of tea.

'Darling?'

'Uh-huh?'

I stumble over the words.

'I've had a relapse.'

I don't say any more. I don't have to. He knows what it means. He hasn't been through the programme, or even to a meeting, but he's read the literature. He knows enough. He knows what a relapse is, just like he knows he mustn't try to control my behaviour by modifying his own, that he can't stop me drinking by never drinking himself.

He also knows better than to ask how many drinks I had, or when, or why. It's pointless. The answers are irrelevant. I had a drink. Whether it was the tiniest sip or a whole bottle makes no difference at all.

He takes my hand. I thought he was going to be angry, but he's not. It's worse. He's disappointed. I can tell, from his eyes.

'I'm sorry.'

'You don't have to apologize to me.'

It's not what I want to hear. But what do I want to hear? What *can* he say? Addiction is a sickness unlike those Hugh is used to facing. He's someone who cuts the bad parts out, sends them to the incinerator. The patient is cured, or not.

I look at him. I want him to tell me he loves me. I don't want him to tell me he knows what I'm going through. I want him to remind me that a lapse doesn't have to be a relapse, or tell me that I can start going to meetings again, or make me feel that we're in it together.

'I won't drink again,' I say.

He smiles, and tells me he hopes not, for my sake, and for Connor's. He tells me he's here for me, always, but it's too late. He layered the guilt on first, and now I'm hardly listening. Instead, I'm thinking of my sponsor, Rachel. I wish I could ring her, but she's moved away, it's been too long. And I'm thinking of Kate.

Finally he's silent. I wait for a moment then thank him. We

sit for a few more minutes, then I tell him I need to go to bed. He kisses me, and says he'll be up in a minute.

I'm on my own, but I won't let this happen again, I tell myself. I'll be vigilant. Whatever happens, whatever it takes, I won't drink again.

Chapter Six

I wake early. My eyes flick open. Another bad night. It's June, two months since I went to Paris, four since Kate died. It's still dark. It's the middle of the night.

The room is hot and airless, the sheets soaked. Hugh has kicked the duvet off and lies next to me, snoring gently. The clock on my side of the bed ticks, too loud. Four forty. The same time I woke up last night, and the night before that.

I've been dreaming of Kate. This time she was about four, it was summer, we were in the garden. She was wearing a yellow dress, angel wings made out of yellow paper, black tights. She wanted me to chase her; she was making a buzzing sound, pretending to be a bee. 'Come on!' she was saying, over and over, but I was bored, I wanted to stop. I wanted to get back to my book. 'Come on, Julia!' she was saying, 'Come on!' then she turned and ran, towards a wood. I wanted to tell her not to go in there, but I didn't. I was too hot, too lazy. I just let her run away from me, and then turned to go back to the house. As I did the dream morphed, we were adults now, something terrible was happening, and suddenly it was me who was running, running after her, calling her name, and she who was disappearing into an alleyway. It was dark, I was desperate to catch up with her, to save her. I ran round a corner and she was there, slumped on the floor. I was too late.

I sit on the edge of the bed. Every night it's the same, a dream of Kate, bleeding to death, and then in a dream behind a dream there's Marcus, always Marcus, his mouth open and accusing. I know I won't sleep again, I never do.

Tonight I'm weak. I can't help it. And so I let myself think of him. Of Marcus. For the first time in years I think of the day we met. I close my eyes and I can see it. I'm back there. Marcus is sitting opposite me, the other side of the circle. It's his first meeting. We're in a church hall, it's draughty, a tea urn fizzes in one of the corners. The chair – a guy called Keith – has already outlined the programme and introduced the first speaker, a woman whose name I've forgotten. I barely listen as she speaks; I've been coming for a while, ever since I caved in and admitted I've been drinking too much for too long. Plus, I'm watching Marcus. He's the same age as me, and we're both much younger than the others in the group. He sits forward in his chair. He looks eager, attentive, yet at the same time he doesn't seem wholly interested. Something about him is wrong. I wonder if he's here for himself, or for someone else. I picture a girlfriend, someone who he'd hoped to persuade here tonight but who refused to come. Perhaps he wants to go home, back to her, and tell her what he's learned. It's not so bad, he might say. These people want to help. Next week come with me.

I wanted to find out. I don't know why; maybe he looked like someone I thought I could get on with. I went up to him, during the break. I introduced myself, and he said his name was Marcus. 'Hi,' I said, and he smiled, and in that moment I realized just how attracted I was to him. It was a desire that felt solid, had a shape, a pull that felt physical. I'd never experienced it before, not like this. I wanted to reach out, to touch his neck, his hair, his lips. Just to be sure he existed, was real. 'First time?' I said, and he said yes, yes it was. We chatted for a while. Somehow – I don't remember how, or even whether he volunteered the information himself – I learned that the girlfriend didn't exist. He was single. When it was time to go back to our seats he came and sat next to me, and after the meeting we went outside. We paused to say goodbye, about to head off in different directions.

'Are you here next week?'

He shrugged, kicked the kerb. 'Probably.' He turned to leave, but then he pulled a scrap of paper out of his wallet.

'Got a pen?' he said.

Was that it? I wonder now. Was that the moment my life slipped out of one track – recovery, stability, sobriety – and into another? Or did that come later?

I open my eyes. I can't think of him any more. He belongs in the past; my family is here, now. My family is Hugh, and Connor.

And Kate.

I get up. This can't go on, this waking up in the middle of the night. This *avoiding* of things. I'm haunted by the place she lost her life; I should've gone to see it when I had the chance, but there are other ways.

I go downstairs and sit at the kitchen table. I'm determined, I have to do this. In Paris I was a coward, but now I can put it right. I open my laptop and log on to the map programme. I type in the address.

I press enter. A map appears on the screen, criss-crossed with roads, scattered with points of interest. There's an arrow dropped into it and when I click on Street View the map disappears, replaced by a photo of the road. It looks broad, lined with trees, with shops and banks and a stack of prefabs covered in graffiti. The photo has been taken during the day and the place looks busy; passers-by frozen as they walk along it, their faces blurred inexpertly by the software.

I stare at the screen. It looks ordinary. How could my sister have lost her life here? How could it have left no trace?

I steel myself, then navigate along the road. I see the alleyway, cutting down between a building and the raised railway line that crosses the road.

I'm here, I think. The place she died.

I zoom in. It seems anodyne, harmless. At one end there's a kiosk, painted blue with a sign advertising *Cosmétiques Antilles*, and there are two rows of bollards dotting the pavement. The alleyway curves after what looks like four or five yards, and I can't see down it.

I wonder where it leads, what's at the other end. I wonder why there was no one there to save her and, for the millionth time, what she was doing there.

I need answers. I fetch the box that Anna gave me from under my bed and take it back downstairs. I look at the picture on the front, the woman in the red dress. For two months I've tried to ignore this, terrified of what I might find, but I can't any longer. How bad can it be? I ask myself. Didn't Anna say it was just some paperwork? That's all.

Yet still I'm afraid. But what of? Evidence of how far she'd come, perhaps. Proof that she was right, that Connor would have been better back with her?

I take out her passport and hold it for a moment before putting it to one side. Underneath it there are some letters, and beneath them her birth certificate and driving licence, along with her medical card and a note with what I assume is her National Insurance number.

It calms me, somehow. I'm facing something that's been waiting for me. I'm doing well. I feel surprisingly okay.

I dig further in. It's more difficult; there are photos, taken at parties, one of Connor that I'd sent her, another of some friends on a boat trip along the Seine. I tell myself I'll look at them properly later. Further down there's a pink Filofax, pocket-sized. This seems hardest of all, but when I flick through its pages I see she seems to have stopped using it when she got an iPhone last summer. Tucked into it is a single sheet of paper. I take that out and unfold it.

Straight away I see a name I recognize. Written at the top is 'Jasper1234'. It's the name of the Labrador we had when we were little, followed by four digits, and next to it she's written 'KatieB', and then a Web address, encountrz.com. The rest of the page is filled with a list of odd words – 'Eastdude'; 'Athletique27'; 'Kolm'; 'Ourcq' – all written at different times, in different inks and with different pens. It takes me only a moment to piece it together. Encountrz is the site Anna told me about, the one they both used. Kate used our dog's name as a password, KatieB as her username.

I refold the page and put it back. The guilt I've told myself I shouldn't feel rolls again in my stomach. I should've looked at this sooner, I think. It might be important, something the police have missed. I've let her down; there was something I could've done to save her, something I could still do to make it all right.

I dial Anna's number. It's early, but this feels urgent. And it's an hour later in Paris. Nearly six.

She answers almost immediately. Sleepy, anxious. 'Hello?'

'Anna? It's me. Julia.'

'Julia. Is everything okay?'

'Yes, fine. I'm sorry to call so early. I didn't mean to wake you, but that box you gave me? You're sure the police have gone through it?'

'Box? You mean Kate's things?'

'Yes. The police have definitely looked at it?'

'Yes, I'm certain. Why?'

'I'm just looking at it all now—'

'Now? It's very early . . .'

'I know, but I couldn't sleep. The thing is, there's a list of names. I think they might be people she was talking to. Online, I mean. I thought the police should see them . . .'

'They did, I think. They had everything in that box. They said they'd kept everything they might need.'

'You're sure?'

'I think so, yes. Give me a second.'

She's quiet for a moment; I imagine her shaking herself awake. 'Sorry. What names are they?'

I read the first couple out. 'Do any of them sound familiar? Did she mention any of them to you?'

'No—'

I carry on reading. After a few more names she stops me. She's wide awake now.

'Wait. Did you say "Ourcq"? That's not a username. It's a Métro station.'

I know what she's going to say.

'It's near where they found her body.'

'So that's what she was doing there? Meeting someone off this list?'

'I don't know,' she says. But already I'm feeling a curious surge of energy. 'But I guess it's possible.'

I end the call. I look again at the list of usernames in her Filofax. It's as if I've found a weak spot in the wall of my grief, something that might lead me first in and then through, on to the other side. To peace.

I wake my laptop. I type quickly: encountrz.com. I tell myself I just want to have a look. I can't do any harm. I'm about to press enter when I hear a noise. A cough, then a voice.

'Darling?' It's Hugh. 'It's half five in the morning. What on earth are you doing?'

I close the browser window and turn to face him. He's wearing his gown, tied around his waist, and yawns as he rubs his eyes. 'Are you okay?'

'Yes. I couldn't sleep.'

'Again? What's wrong?'

'I just keep thinking the police must've missed something.'

He sighs. I say the same thing to him every single day.

'I think they're being incredibly thorough.' He comes over and sits next to me. I know he can see what's on my screen.

'If I hear anything new I always tell you straight away. You know that.'

'Yes. But do you think they're still investigating what happened?'

'I'm sure they're doing everything—' he began, but I interrupted him.

'I mean, *really* investigating it?'

He smiles. It's his sad smile, full of compassion. His surgeon's smile. I used to imagine him practising it in the mirror, determined not to be one of those doctors accused of having a poor bedside manner.

'I'm *sure* they are. We've discussed it with them. They've interviewed all her friends, all the people she worked with. They've been through her phone records, they've taken the information off her computer. They've followed up every lead. But something like that? It can't be easy. Random, unprovoked . . .'

'You told them about the dating sites?'

'Yes. I rang them as soon as you told me. But they already knew. Anna told them. They said Kate didn't have a boyfriend . . .'

'But they're not just about dating. Anna implied she was using them for sex. Casual sex.' He shakes his head but I go on. 'You know. One-night stands. Anna says it wasn't that often, but she did it. And she didn't always tell her where she was going, or who she was meeting.'

A look of disapproval flashes on his face. I wonder for a moment whether he thinks she deserves what she got, and then instantly I dismiss the thought.

'D'you think that's who killed her?'

'Who?'

'Someone she went to meet. To have sex with, I mean. Or someone she was messaging, at least?'

'I'm sure the police are looking into that—'

'They haven't told us they are.'

'Look, we've been through all this, Julia. They're looking into it. The truth is, I think she talked to a lot of people online but only met up with one or two.'

I hesitate. I need to push him; I'm almost certain he knows more than he's telling me, that there might be a tiny fragment that's been overlooked, a detail that will unlock the rest and make it all fit into place.

'But—'

He interrupts me. 'Julia, we've been through all this a thousand times. They've kept her laptop; they're doing everything they can. But if she was doing that and keeping it secret then it would be almost impossible to find everyone she might have been in contact with. There might be sites she used that we don't know about, any number of people she was talking to . . . What's that?'

At first I don't know what he means, but then I see that he's looking at my screen.

'It's a photograph.' He isn't wearing his glasses and has to lean forward to get a better view. 'It's where Kate died.'

He puts his hand on my shoulder. It feels heavy, meant to reassure. 'Are you sure it's a good idea to look at that, darling?'

'No,' I say. I'm not desperate, but I'd like him to approve. But why would he? He thinks the police are doing their best and that's the end of it.

'I'm not sure it's a good idea at all, but what else am I supposed to do?'

'Come back to bed?'

'Soon . . .'

'Come on.' He squeezes my shoulder then gently closes the lid of my machine. 'Come and get some rest. You'll feel better. I promise. Doctor's orders.'

I stand up. I won't feel better, I want to say, I never do. He turns to go back upstairs.

'I'll be up in a minute,' I say. 'I'm just going to make myself a cup of tea. I might read for a bit. Until I feel sleepy.'

'Okay,' he says. He knows I have no intention of following him. 'You haven't forgotten we've got people coming for supper? Have you?'

'No,' I say, even though I had.

'Maria and Paddy . . .'

Of course. We've known the Renoufs for years, ever since Maria joined Hugh's department as a registrar. Hugh tipped her for success even then, said she was going places, was someone he mustn't let go. I like them both, but this is the first time he's invited them – invited anyone, in fact – since Kate died. I suppose he thought cooking would do me good.

Maybe he's right. Following a recipe. Chopping, weighing, measuring. I used to enjoy it, before Kate. I went on courses, I was proud of the fact that I'd gone from someone who knew nothing about cooking to someone who could make their own pasta.

But, now? Now, I don't want to see anyone.

'Can't we cancel?'

He comes over. 'Darling. It'll do you good, I promise.' He kisses the top of my head. It's a tender kiss, warm. For a moment I want to climb inside him, have him protect me. 'We'll have fun. We always do. Maria will talk endlessly about work and Paddy will flirt with you, and then when they've gone we'll laugh about it. I promise.'

He's right. I know he is. I can't keep running.

'I'll go shopping this morning,' I say.

He goes back upstairs. I sit in the chair. I leave my machine closed. I don't want to log on to encountrz. I'm afraid of what I might see.

I make tea, I sit with my book. An hour passes, two. Hugh comes downstairs, showered now, ready for work, then a little while later, Connor.

'Hi, Mum,' he says. He's dressed, wearing his uniform, the grey jumper, the white shirt with a maroon tie. I watch as he gets himself a bowl of cereal, pours himself some juice. He's looking older every day, I think.

'Are you all right, darling?' I say, and he replies, 'Yep,' with a friendly shrug, as if there's no reason at all he might not be.

Maybe he really is fine, but I doubt it. He's stopped crying now, but if anything that's more worrying. The only time he ever talks about Kate's death is to ask if there's 'any news', by which he means, 'Have they got them yet?' I'd felt angry at first – it's all he can focus on – but now I see that it's the only prism through which he can process his grief. After all, he's just turned fourteen. How else is he supposed to respond?

He sits down with his breakfast and I watch as he begins to eat.

The counsellor we've taken him to says all this is normal. He's doing as well as can be expected, working through his grief in his own way, and we should try not to worry. But how can I not? He won't talk to me. He's slipping away. Now, I need him to know how much I love him, that there's nothing I wouldn't do for him, but it's almost as if he's decided he no longer cares.

I clear my throat. 'It's okay, if you want to talk.'

'I'm fine.' He eats his cereal quickly as I make myself a coffee. For a moment I'm back with Kate, it's her getting ready for school, not her son, but then a moment later Connor is standing, gathering his things. Don't go, I want to say. Sit with me. Talk to me. But of course I can't. 'See you later!' I say, and before I know it he's almost out of the door. From nowhere comes an almost overwhelming urge to hug him.

I would have done, once, yet now I don't. These days he's as likely as not to respond to a hug with indifference, as if what I'm doing is of no concern to him, and today I couldn't bear that. 'Love you!' I shout instead, and he says, 'Bye, Mum!' as he leaves. It's almost enough.

He's growing up. I know that. He's becoming a man; it would be a tough time even if he didn't have Kate's death to wrestle with. I have to remember that, no matter what happens, how hard it gets, how distant he becomes, he's in pain. I might feel like I've already failed him a million times but still I have to look after him, to protect him, like I looked after and protected his mother when she was a child.

I turn away from the window. I'm photographing a family next week – a colleague of Adrienne's, her husband, her two little girls – and I need to think about that. It's the first time I've felt able to work since Kate died and I want it to go well. Plus, I have a dinner party to prepare. Things must get done.

Chapter Seven

I call Adrienne to get her friend's details. I want to make arrangements. I have my studio at the bottom of the garden in which I keep my tripods and lights, a couple of backdrops I can suspend from the ceiling. I have a desk there, though usually I do my editing on my laptop in the house, at the kitchen table, or in the living room. 'It would be good if they could come to me,' I say. 'It'll make it easier.'

She can hear the lack of enthusiasm in my voice.

'What's wrong?'

'You can tell.'

'Of course. Talk to me.'

I don't want to, but I can't work out why. Is it because I'm worried she'll just tell me to leave things alone, to stop meddling, to stop worrying?

'I looked through Kate's things. The stuff Anna gave to me.'

'Darling—'

'I found her login details. For the website she was using.'

'For what?'

'Meeting men. There was a list of names. Of people she was talking to – or meeting, I guess.'

'Have you given them to the police?'

'Hugh said they already had them.'

'Good. Then there's nothing more you can do.'

But there is, though.

'I could log on. As her, I mean. I have her password. I could find out if there was anyone else.'

For a long time she's silent.

'Adrienne?'

'Wouldn't the police have done that?'

'I don't know. Maybe they don't realize what encountrz.com is? Or that Jasper1234 is her password? I thought I could go online and just look at her chat history. See if there are any other names on there.'

'I don't know . . . it sounds risky.'

Her reservation strengthens my resolve.

'I'm just talking about getting a list of names.'

There's a long pause, as if she's trying to weigh something up. The wisdom of me having something to do, perhaps, versus the chance, the likelihood, it will just lead to more disappointment.

After all, she's right. In all probability the police have done all this already.

'I suppose it can't hurt,' she says. 'As long as you're only talking about getting the list. But why not double-check with them first?'

Suddenly I'm not sure it's a good idea at all. A list of names. What would the police even do with it?

'I probably won't even bother.'

She sighs. 'Just be careful, Julia. Whatever you do. And keep in touch.'

I spend the afternoon shopping, cooking. For a while I lose myself in the rhythm of the recipe. Just for a moment. But the evening gets off to a bad start. Connor announces that he's doing homework and wants to eat in his room, which means that Hugh and I bicker about whether we should let him.

Tensions fester, and things don't pick up until our guests arrive.

After that the evening follows its usual pattern, yet the atmosphere is undeniably different. Kate's death casts its now-familiar shadow – Paddy mentions it almost as soon as they arrive, and they both say how sorry they are – but it's more than that. I'm detached, I can't engage. They talk a lot about Geneva, where Hugh's been invited to deliver a keynote speech at a conference next week. Maria's going to present her work, too, and even though I've been there I don't contribute. I feel outside of it all, observing from a great distance. I watch as Hugh pours wine and nod as they all sip it appreciatively, I eat the beef Wellington I've cooked and accept their compliments graciously, but it's an act, I'm pretending to be a normal person. It's not me.

When we've finished Paddy says he'd like to pop outside for a cigarette. 'I didn't know you smoked,' I say.

'Filthy habit,' he says, 'but . . .' He shrugs his shoulders. I tell him we're happy for him to smoke in the house near one of the open windows but Maria protests.

'No way! Make him go outside!'

He pretends to be upset, but it's good-natured, humorous. He takes his cigarettes out of his jacket and looks at me. 'Keep me company?'

I say I will. Hugh looks at me but says nothing. We go outside, closing the patio door behind us. It's almost dark, still warm. We sit on the wall, at the edge of the pool of light that shines from the kitchen; behind us sits my studio. He holds a cigarette out to me. 'You don't, do you?'

I take it. 'Very occasionally,' I say. He lights his cigarette and hands me the lighter. I inhale deeply, feeling the draw of the smoke, the instant hit. We sit in silence for a moment, then he asks me how I'm coping.

'Really, I mean.'

I swallow hard. 'It's tough. You know . . .'

'I do. My brother died. Years ago. Cancer. He was older than me . . .'

'Oh, God,' I say. 'I had no idea.'

'No reason you should.' There's silence. A beat. 'The end wasn't unexpected, but it was still awful. I can't even begin to imagine what you're going through.'

We sit for a few moments.

'How's Connor?' he says.

I sigh. There's nothing to say, yet still I'm glad he's bothered to ask. 'He's all right, I think. He's not really talked about it. I'm not sure that's a good thing, though . . .'

'He will, I guess. When he's ready.'

'I suppose so. I just wish I knew what he was thinking. What was going on in his mind. He spends hours in his room, though that's nothing new, I suppose. It's as if he's avoiding me.'

'He's at that age, I suppose. Plus, he's a boy.'

I look at him, at his profile, silhouetted against the light in the house. Is it as simple as that? I lost my mother when I was young; I have no idea what's normal. Maybe he's right, it's just the fact that he's a boy, and I'm a woman, and that's why he's slipping away from me. I find the thought curiously reassuring. Maybe it has nothing to do with the fact that I'm not his birth mother.

'Have you and Maria ever thought about children?'

He looks over at his wife, visible in the kitchen, helping my husband to prepare the dessert. Connor has joined them, they're laughing at something.

'Not really,' says Paddy, looking back to me. 'Maria's career . . . you know? And I'm not that bothered. I'm from a big family. We have a lot of nieces and nephews . . .'

71

He sounds disappointed, but I don't know him well enough to probe further. Not really.

'That's good,' I say. I grind my cigarette out.

'Shall we go back in?'

'Sure!' He wipes his hands on his jeans, then stands up and holds out his hand for me to take. 'Are you going to Carla's party?'

I'd completely forgotten. Another colleague of Hugh's, with a big house in Surrey, a large garden, a gas-fired barbecue. She throws a party every July and invites everyone. Last year had been fun, but now I'm not looking forward to it at all. I'm trapped, though; she sends the invites out in April. There's no way we can get out of going.

'I guess,' I say, standing up. He smiles, and says he's glad. It's a fraction of a second before he lets go of my hand, not long enough to be sure it means anything at all. I'm not certain whether I'm holding on to him, or him to me.

They leave. Hugh goes into the kitchen, without saying a word. I follow him. He begins to tidy up, scraping each plate before rinsing it and putting it in the sink. He doesn't smile, or even look at me as I speak.

'What's up with you?'

Still no eye contact. A plate clunks into the sink. Is this because I went outside to sit with Paddy?

'It's Connor,' he says.

'Connor?' I pick up a cloth and begin to wipe down the worktop. 'What about him? Are we still arguing because I said he could eat in his room?'

'Among other things.'

I choose to ignore him. If he wants to bring anything else into this, then he'll have to talk about it rather than make me guess.

'He's been really upset recently,' I say instead. 'I don't think we should force him to do something he doesn't want to do. I think we need to cut him some slack.'

He puts down the plate he's holding and turns to face me. 'Yes, well, I think we've been cutting him far too much slack lately. We shouldn't indulge him. It's really important we keep things normal, Julia.'

'Meaning?'

He turns his palms upwards. 'The grief counsellor said we mustn't make too many allowances. He has to realize that life goes on.'

Life goes on? My anger ratchets up another notch. Life didn't go on for Kate, did it? I take a deep breath. 'I'm just worried about him.'

'And I'm not? He comes in, smelling of cigarettes—'

'Cigarettes?'

'Hadn't you noticed? On his clothes . . .'

I shake my head. I haven't noticed any such thing. Either I've become neglectful, or Hugh is imagining things, and I suspect it's the latter. 'Maybe his friends smoke? Have you thought about that?'

His eyes narrow in accusation.

'What next? Drinking?'

'Hugh—'

'Fighting at school—'

'What?'

'He told me. He got involved in some scrap.'

'*He* told you?'

'Yes. He was upset. He wouldn't tell me what it was about, but it's not like him, Julia. He's never fought at school before.'

He's never lost his mother before, I think, but I don't say it.

'Maybe we need to let him make his own mistakes? He has to grow up. He has to let off steam, especially given what's happened.'

'I just think we need to keep a closer eye on him.'

'Me, you mean. You think *I* should be keeping a closer eye on him. You know, it seems to me that you're a perfect father whenever it just involves playing chess or ordering takeaways when I go away. Yet whenever he needs some kind of discipline that's suddenly my job?' He ignores me. 'Well?'

'I don't mean that. Look, I'm just not sure you're—'

'I'm *what*?'

I know exactly what he means. *Setting a good example.* This is about what happened in Paris.

'I'm not sure you're there for Connor at the moment like he might need you to be.'

I can't help but laugh, but it's a reflex. At some level he might be right.

'Meaning what, exactly?'

He lowers his voice. 'Julia, please calm down. Be reasonable.'

I go back to the table, to finish clearing it, to turn my back on him. It's then that it happens. In front of me is the glass I'd been drinking from and as I pick it up a sudden and almost irresistible urge bubbles up from nowhere. I imagine filling it from the bottle of red wine they hadn't quite finished, drinking it down. I can feel it, heavy in my mouth. I can taste it, peppery and warm. I want it, more than anything.

I hold the glass in my hand. I tell myself this is the first time since Paris, the first time I've even been tempted. It isn't a relapse. It only means what I let it mean.

'Julia?'

I ignore him. Ride it out, I tell myself. Ride it out. The

desire will crest like an ocean wave and then subside. I just have to wait. Hugh is here, anyway, and whatever happens I won't drink in front of him.

Yet I managed to drink in Paris, and that was weeks ago. I haven't even been tempted since. Even if I were to drink now it wouldn't have to signify the beginning of the end.

I think back to the programme. The first step. This isn't something I can control; the fact I've gone for weeks without being tempted again doesn't mean I'm over it. All control is an illusion.

I think of my sponsor, Rachel. 'Addiction is a patient disease,' she said to me, once. 'It'll wait for your whole life, if it has to. Never forget that.'

I haven't, I tell myself. I won't.

'Julia?' says Hugh. He sounds annoyed. I've missed something; he's been talking to me.

I turn round. 'Yes?'

'I know he's upset about his mother's death—'

His choice of words stings, but my anger forces the desire to drink to slip down another notch.

'He's never thought of Kate as his mother.'

'You know what I mean. Kate's death is bound to bother him, but—'

'But what?'

'But he's still not really talking about it, and I find that worrying. He should be, by now.'

His comment enrages me. 'Has it ever occurred to you that it's a process? There isn't a timetable. Not everyone can deal with Kate's death in the same way that you have.'

'Meaning?'

'It's going to take Connor a good deal longer to get over Kate's death than it's taken you, that's all.'

I think of what Adrienne has told me. 'Don't ever think

Hugh doesn't care. It's just his prissiness. Grief is messy, and he doesn't like mess. Plus, don't forget he has to deal with life and death at work. All the time. It must harden you, a little bit.'

He looks shocked. 'I'm not *over* her death. Kate and I were close once. I miss her, too. What makes you say that? It's hurtful.'

'Are you still talking to the Foreign Office? Or are you leaving it all to me—?'

'I talk to them all the time, Julia—'

'You don't think I should go online and look at the place she was killed—'

'I just think you're in a bad enough state as it is. You need to concentrate on Connor, on your work. On the future, not the past.'

'What is *that* supposed to mean?'

He opens his mouth to speak, but then seems to think better of it. A moment later he turns and throws down the tea towel that he'd hooked over his shoulder.

'Julia, I'm really worried about you.'

'About *me*?'

'Yes, believe it or not. I think you need to go and see somebody. You're not coping. I'm going to Geneva on Monday and you'll be here on your own—'

'Oh, I'll be fine,' I say, but he's still talking, he doesn't seem to have heard me.

'—and I just wish you'd at least consider going to see someone—'

My fury surges, doubled in strength. Something breaks. I can't take it any more. 'Oh, just piss off, Hugh.' The glass I hadn't realized I was still holding smashes on the floor. I don't remember throwing it.

He takes a step towards me, then seems to think better of

it and turns as if to leave. He's finally angry, and so am I, and it almost feels better. It's something other than numbness, or pain.

'Where are you going?'

'Out. I'm going for a walk. I need to cool off.'

He leaves. The whole house shudders, then falls silent, and I'm alone.

Chapter Eight

I sit on the edge of the bed for a while. I stroke the duvet cover. Egyptian cotton, duck-egg blue. Our bed, I think. What happened?

We bought it when we moved in here four years ago and it's nothing particularly special. It's a place we sleep, talk, read. Occasionally we make love, and when we do it's still tender, slow. Enjoyable, usually, if not exciting.

Was it ever exciting? I think so, for a while, but the frenzy of a relationship's early days is unsustainable; it has to burn out, become something else. It's not his fault, or mine. It happens to everyone.

Maybe it happened sooner, with us. Hugh is the son of my father's best friend; he's known me since I was at school. Though he was older than me, we always got on, and as his father tried to look after mine, Hugh looked after me, and helped me to look after Kate. Our passion, when it eventually came, was muted. It was already accompanied by a history. Sometimes I think it's as if we missed out a stage, as if we went from being friends straight to being companions.

I hear Hugh come back home. He goes into the living room. I stand up. I have to go downstairs, to talk to him, to sort things out. If I don't he'll sleep on the couch in his office and I'll spend another night lying in bed, alone, trying to sleep while my brain fizzes with images, with thoughts that won't subside. I'll turn the events of the evening over and over, and always at the centre will be Kate. Walking down the alleyway, looking up to see a figure in the shadows in front of her, smiling a greeting but then, as she steps forward, he raises his hand and her smile turns to terror as she realizes that things have gone wrong, this time she's made a mistake. The man she's come to meet isn't who she thought he was.

I know that if I were to close my eyes I'd see it, as clearly as if it were happening in front of me. A fist in the face, a booted foot. Why didn't I know, somehow? That psychic connection I always thought we had; why did it let us down, when it really mattered? Was it severed when we took Connor? I'd see her blood, spilled on to the concrete. I'd see her nose, broken. I'd hear her cry out. I'd wonder if she knew, if she sensed this was it. I'd wonder how much pain there was. I'd wonder if she thought about me, and if so whether it was with love. I'd wonder if, at the end, she forgave me.

I go downstairs. 'Hugh?'

He's sitting in the living room with a glass of whisky. I sit down opposite him.

'You should go to bed.'

'I'm sorry.'

He looks at me, for the first time since I came into the room. He sighs, sips his whisky.

'It hurts.'

'I know.'

There's nothing else to say. We go to bed.

In the morning I talk to Connor.

'I don't know what you heard last night,' I say. 'But your father and I love you very much.'

He's sloshing milk into his cereal bowl and some spills on the table. I resist the urge to dab it dry. 'I just heard you arguing.'

It feels like a slap. It's the very opposite of what I want for my son, of what I promised Kate. Stability. Loving parents. A home free of conflict.

'All couples argue. It's normal.'

'Are you going to split up?'

'No! No, of course not.'

He goes back to his cereal. 'What were you arguing about?'

I don't want to tell him.

'It's difficult. The last few months have been tough. On all of us. With Auntie Kate, and everything.' I know I'm stating the obvious, but it feels true, and necessary. A shadow crosses his face and for an instant I see how he'll look when he's much older, but then it passes, leaving a kind of sadness. I think he's going to say something, but he doesn't.

'Do you miss her?'

He freezes, his spoon midway between the bowl and his mouth. He puts it back. Again he looks thoughtful, much older. For some reason he reminds me of Marcus – it's the same expression he had when on those rare occasions he was worried or pensive – but then he speaks and becomes a teenager once again.

'I don't know.' His face collapses, tears come. It's unexpected and I'm swept to my feet in an urge to soothe and comfort.

'It's okay. Whatever you feel, or even if you don't know, it's okay.'

He hesitates. 'I suppose I do miss her. A bit. Do you?'

'Yes. Every day.'

'I mean,' he goes on, 'we didn't see her that often, but still . . .'

'It's different, isn't it?'

'Yes. When someone is alive you might not see them very much, but you know you can. If you want.'

'Yes.'

'And now I can't.'

I remain silent. I want to give him the time to speak, but also I'm wondering whether he really had felt that he could see his mother. Hugh and I may have given him permission if he'd asked – to do that, to go and stay with her – but we had never really encouraged it. Maybe I was too frightened that she wouldn't let him come back.

'You know,' I say eventually, 'whatever you're feeling, you can ask me about anything. Anything at all.'

Even though I mean it, my words sound hollow. Because the truth is, there are secrets, things I won't tell him, even if he asks.

There's a long pause, then he asks, 'Do you think they'll get them? The people who killed Kate.'

It stops me in my tracks. He hasn't called her Auntie. I wonder if it's the first step on the path to calling her Mum. The air between us crackles.

'I hope so, darling. But it's difficult.'

There's a silence between us.

'Dad says she was a nice person who fell in with a bad crowd.'

I press some bread down into the toaster and look up. I smile. That's exactly what Hugh used to think of me. A nice person, over-influenced by those around me. He would tell me, while I was in Berlin, 'Look after yourself,' he'd say, 'We all miss you . . .', and I knew he meant, *Those people aren't your friends*. He was trying to save me, even then; I just wasn't ready to be saved.

'She was a really lovely person. Full stop.'

He hesitates.

'So, why didn't she want me?'

'Connor,' I begin. 'It's complicated—'

'Dad says I shouldn't worry about it. He says that Auntie Kate loved me very much but she wasn't coping, that she couldn't afford a baby, but you could, so it made sense.'

'Well, that's really a very simplistic way of looking at it . . .'

I wonder when Hugh's been telling Connor all this. I didn't even know they'd talked. I tell myself we need to make more of an effort, to be upfront with Connor, to be united. Like we'd decided years ago.

'If you wanted children, why didn't you have one?'

'We couldn't.' I'm trying to keep my voice even; I don't want it to crack, to betray how much loss I contain. 'We'd been trying. For several years. But one of us . . .' I stop. He doesn't need the details. 'We just couldn't.' It comes to me, then. The clinic: white walls and rubber floors, boxes spilling blue gloves, posters advertising helplines and charities that I knew I'd never call. I remember the stirrups, the cold metal between my legs. It felt like a punishment.

I realize I've still never told anyone about that, certainly not Hugh. He doesn't know anything about that baby I could have had but didn't.

'Who couldn't?'

I look at my son. At Kate's son. 'I don't know.' The familiar sense of shame comes, then. I thought I'd conquered it, years ago. I was mistaken. 'We don't know. But it doesn't matter. It makes no difference. We love you, Connor. You're our son.'

The toaster pings, the bread pops up. I'm startled, briefly, then I begin to butter his toast.

'Thanks, Mum,' he says, and I'm not sure what he's thanking me for.

I take the key from my bag and unlock the padlock. The shed door swings inwards with a creak and I wait for a few moments to let some of the heat out before stepping in. Even though the walls are lined and painted and I light scented candles in here when I work, it still smells vaguely of wood. Yet it's comforting; my own space, a refuge.

I close the door behind me and sit at the desk. I put the biscuit tin in front of me, the one Anna gave me. I feel calmer, now. I know what I have to do.

I take Kate's Filofax out of the tin and put it on the desk, next to my laptop. The light that streams into my studio through the window behind me reflects off its surface and I adjust my chair and change the angle of the screen. Finally I press a key.

My background picture is an old photo of me, sitting on a bench on the Heath with Connor on my lap. In the photo he's four, maybe five. A decade ago, and I look so happy, so excited finally to be a parent, yet now it feels as if it belongs to a different time completely. I realize once again how Kate's death has sliced my life in two.

I press another key and the picture of Connor disappears, replaced by the last window I'd had open. It's a video.

I press play. It's a film of the two of us, me and Connor, on a beach. Hugh took it, years ago, back when he still used his camcorder. Connor is about five, dressed in red trunks and slathered in sunblock, and the two of us are running away from the camera, into the sea, laughing as we do.

It was a glorious summer; we'd hired a villa in Portugal.

We spent the days by the pool, or on the beach. We had lunch in a restaurant in the village, or we'd take a drive into the hills. We sat on the terrace and watched the sun go down after we'd put Connor to bed. We'd sit, and talk, and then we'd go to bed ourselves, where, quietly, carefully, we made love. We were happy. So very, very happy.

The video is almost over when I get a call; it's Anna, on Skype. I don't want to talk to her now. I click ignore. I'll call her back later. What I have to do won't take long.

The video finishes; Connor is frozen in the distance.

I'm ready.

I open my browser and begin to type the web address: encountrz. I only have to type the first few letters; the rest autofills from the night before last, the time I hadn't got as far as pressing enter.

I press it now. I have a sense of weightlessness; it's inexplicable, but real. My body has become unmoored. I'm floating. The window loads. A photo appears, a couple, walking along a beach, laughing. It looks somehow banal, but what had I expected?

At the top of the screen is a box marked 'Username', and another headed 'Password'. I type in 'KatieB', then 'Jasper1234'. I select enter.

I'm not sure what will happen. The machine seems to hang, to take an age, but then the screen changes and a message appears across its centre.

'Welcome back, Katie. It's been a while!'

It feels as if something has struck me, slammed me back to earth. I'm winded, I can't breathe, but then I realize the message is automated. I breathe deeply, try to calm down. Next to it there's a button marked 'Enter'. I press it.

I'm not ready for what I see; there's a picture of my sister, in the top-left corner of the screen beneath the website's logo. It jolts me again. It's like she's there, sitting at her computer. It's as if all I have to do is type a message and press send – just like I can with Anna, and Adrienne, and Dee and Fatima – and then I'll be able to talk to her again, tell her I'm sorry, that Connor is safe. That I miss her.

But I can't. She's gone. I focus on why I've logged on here, I make myself look at the photo she used. It looks like it was taken on a holiday. It's a close-up. She's lying on a beach towel, on her front, reading a book. Her sunglasses are pushed back on her head, her skin is tanned. She's wearing a bikini and has hoisted herself up on her elbows. Her breasts push up against the fabric of the towel, yet it looks unposed, natural.

She's smiling. Happy. I stare at the picture. I wonder when it was taken, and by whom. She looks so relaxed. I can't believe the little girl I'd once held, once bathed, once read to, is gone. I can't believe I'll never speak to her again.

I begin to cry. I'm sliding, backwards, towards pain. I can't do this, I think. Not alone.

I call Anna back.

'There should be a tab at the top for recent activity. You could look there. It lists the last few people who have looked at her profile.'

She's already asked me if I'm all right, what I'm up to. She's already questioned whether this is a good idea and I told her the half-lie that Adrienne had suggested it. 'I just want to see if there's anything the police might've missed.'

'Right. Got it.'

'Then you should see the rooms. On the right?'

I minimize the chat window and Anna's face disappears. Behind it is the dating site, the list of chatrooms. Looking for Love? Something Extra. A Bit on the Side. Couples and

Groups. I wonder which one Kate would have gravitated towards.

'Okay.'

'Kate and I used to go to Casual Chat,' says Anna. 'But there should be a tab, at the top. Friends and Favourites.'

'I see it.'

'They're the people Kate was chatting to. The ones she's connected with, linked her profile to.'

I click on the tab and the page changes. A list of names appears, with thumbnail photographs. I freeze. My right hand begins to shake. Robbie676, Lutture, SteveXXX . . . this list goes on.

I scroll down; there are about fifteen names in total.

'Anything?' says Anna.

My hope floods away and I'm suddenly empty. Hollowed out. This is futile, and I'm an idiot. What did I think I'd see? A message from one of her friends, telling me he killed my sister? A message to her: 'I got you in the end'?

'I don't know. Just a list of names. They could be anyone.'

She says nothing.

I realize for the first time that she might be scared. She's been on the same site, possibly even talking to the same people. She must be thinking how easily it might have been her in that alleyway instead of Kate.

For a moment I wish it had been, but then I push that thought away. I don't wish that, not on her, not on anyone.

'Maybe you should look at some of them?' she says. 'Their profiles? Find out if any live nearby.'

I'm surprised. 'Won't they all?'

'Not necessarily. Don't forget, Kate wasn't only interested in meeting up with people in the real world. With some of them it was all virtual. They might be anywhere, on the other side of the planet.'

She's right, of course. I select a couple of the profiles to look at in detail. SexyLG, whose profile picture is of a sunset, lives in Connecticut; CRM1976, it turns out, is a woman. I click on a few more and find that most seem to live abroad – in Europe, the States, Australia. Some are much older than Kate, a couple younger. None looks like the kind of person I imagine Kate being interested in, sexually or otherwise.

'Anyone?'

'Not yet. I need to look in more detail.'

I scan through the rest. I can see only one who fits the bill. Harenglish.

'Here's one. Male, lives in Paris.' I click on his profile. He's used a head-and-shoulders photo, and is bald. He wears glasses and a leather motorcycle jacket. He's hidden his age but looks as though he's in his mid- to late thirties. He's a Pisces, he says, single, looking for love or 'fun along the way'.

'What's he called?' says Anna. I tell her, and then hear her typing. I guess she's logging on to the same site, searching for his profile.

I stare at his picture as if it's a puzzle I need to solve. He looks nice enough, sort of innocent, but then what does that even mean? Anyone can find a decent picture of themselves, anyone can present themselves in the best light. Isn't that what we're all trying to do, on some level? Show our best face to the world, leave the darkness within? The screen of the internet just makes it easier.

If only there were some way I could find out how well he'd known my sister. If they'd been close enough that she'd listed him as a friend, why hasn't he messaged her, why hasn't he expressed shock, or at least surprise, when she disappeared?

'I don't recognize him.'

I imagine doing what Adrienne suggested. Taking down

his name, along with any more that look as if they might be people Kate had met, then handing the information over to the police. But maybe they'll have looked at these names already.

'I'm going to message him.'

'Wait!' There's an edge in her voice; it's alarming, surprising. I open her Skype window; her eyes are narrowed as if she's concentrating, she looks anxious.

'What is it?'

'That might be dangerous. I mean, think about it. You're logged on with Kate's profile. If it is him who killed her he'll know you must be someone else, pretending to be her. It'll just drive him underground. We have to be clever about this.' She hesitates. 'Maybe I should send him a message? Say hi. See if I can find anything out.'

I hear her begin to type. 'Sent,' she says after a few seconds, and as she does my machine pings with a message. It's not from her, though, and neither is it from Harenglish. Someone else has messaged Kate. Eastdude.

There's a peculiar rush of excitement, one I wasn't expecting.

'I've got a message!'

'Who from?'

I tell her. The name's familiar. I open the list of usernames Kate had tucked into her Filofax and see that I'm right. It's there.

'This guy's on Kate's list. It's him.'

'Julia, we don't know that.'

She's right. Even as I begin to argue, I realize my logic is flawed. If he's killed my sister, why would he be messaging her now?

I stare at the message as if it's dangerous, poisonous.

'Maybe he just wonders why Kate's been so quiet.'

88

'I'm going to read it.'

I click on Eastdude's message and it opens in a new window. It looks as though it's been typed hurriedly. 'Hey katie. You're back! Missed u! If u fancy another hook up – I'm still up 4 it!'

I try to imagine what Kate would've done. Would she have just sent a reply, a yes? And after that? They'd arrange a date, I suppose, they'd meet up. Drinks and dinner? Or would she have just gone to his place, or had him round to hers? Would it be simpler just to cut out the preliminaries?

'He wants to know if she wants to hook up.'

'Hook up where?'

'He doesn't say.' I click on his profile. He's in his early thirties, he says, though the photo suggests an extra ten years at least. Under 'Location' he's written 'New York'.

'New York.'

'But that doesn't make sense.'

I read it again. ' "Another hook up". I don't remember Kate ever going to New York. Did she?'

'No. He must mean cybersex.'

Cybersex. Just endless descriptions of who's doing what to who. What they're wearing, how it's making them feel. Adrienne has always joked that the reality is lots of people sitting around in jogging bottoms, covered in baby puke.

'But would they call that a hook up?' I say.

'I guess they might.'

'There's no message history.'

'Then you should forget it, Julia.'

'I could answer his message. He thinks I'm Kate.'

'And achieve what?'

'Just to find out what he knows . . .'

I look at the picture again. This Eastdude. He looks

innocent, harmless. His hair is receding, and in the picture he's chosen he has his arms around a woman who's been inexpertly cropped out of the shot. Just as I'd removed myself from the picture of Marcus.

I wonder what he and Kate had talked about. I wonder how well he knew her, if at all.

Isn't that why I came on here? To find out?

'I'm not sure it's going to help,' says Anna.

'Trust me,' I say. 'I'll talk to you later.'

Our messages scroll up the screen. Eastdude thinks he's talking to Kate.

– You don't remember how hot it was? I'm upset.

On the next line is a symbol, a round face, yellow, winking. He's joking.

I feel uncomfortable. Is this how a sex chat begins? A reference to *hotness*?

– I've had a lot on, lately.

His reply is almost instantaneous.

– Work?

I'm not sure what he means. Kate had had only temporary jobs, I thought; bar work, waitressing, office admin. Again I wonder what she's told him.

I need to keep it vague.

– Sort of.

– Too bad. Anyway, would love to carry on where we left off. Are you okay? I thought something had happened to you.

– Why's that?

– You went quiet. Then I had a visit from the police. Asking me what we'd been talking about. If I'd been to Paris recently. I guessed it might be something to do with you.

I freeze.

– Did you tell them?

His reply takes a moment.

– What do you think?

What does he mean? Yes, he has, or no, he hasn't?

I remind myself he can't have killed my sister. He thinks he's talking to her.

Unless he's lying.

– Nothing's happened to me, I say. I'm fine.

– Better than fine if you ask me!

There's another icon; this one a red face with horns.

– Thanks, I say. I realize I need to be careful if I'm going to draw him out. So, you said you wanted to carry on where we left off.

– Tell me what you're wearing, first.

I hesitate. This is wrong, and I feel awful. I'm impersonating my sister – my dead sister – and for what end?

I try to persuade myself. I want to find out who killed her. I'm doing this for the right reasons, for the sake of Kate and her son.

So why do I want to throw up?

– What was I wearing last time? I type.

– You don't remember?

– No, I say. Why don't you tell me?

– Not much, by the end.

There's another smiling face, this one with its tongue hanging out.

I hesitate. The cursor blinks, waiting for me to decide what to type, how far to take this. It feels surreal; me in London, him in New York, separated simultaneously by thousands of miles and nothing at all.

– I'm imagining that's what you're wearing now.

I don't reply.

– I'm thinking of you wearing nothing at all . . .

Still I don't say anything. This isn't what I wanted to happen.

– I'm getting hard here.

I close my eyes. I shouldn't be doing this. I'm a voyeur, I am sampling my sister's virtual life, my dead sister's private life. I'm a tourist.

I should stop, but I can't. Not now. Not until I know for certain that it isn't him.

Another message arrives.

– How about you? You want me?

I hesitate. Kate would forgive me, wouldn't she? I type:

– I do.

– Good, he says. Tell me you remember. Tell me you remember how hot it was. The way you described your body. The things you did.

– I remember.

– Tell me what you want, right now.

– You.

– I'm kissing you. All over. Your lips, your face. I'm going down. Your breasts, your stomach.

Again something within me tells me this is wrong. He thinks he's talking to Kate. He's imagining having sex with my dead sister.

– You like that?

My hands hover over the keyboard. I wish I knew what to say.

– You like feeling my tongue on your body? You taste so good . . .

What would Kate have said?

– You want me to go lower?

What can I say? Yes? Yes, I do? I can tell him I want him to go lower, I don't want him to stop, or I can ask him what he's told the police, where he was in February on the night of

Kate's death, whether he murdered my sister. Even as I say it in my head it sounds ridiculous.

I grab my machine and stand up. I don't know what to do.

– Are you ready for me?

The ground beneath me opens. I begin to sink. My heart is beating too hard, and I can't breathe. I want to stop my mind from spinning, but I keep thinking about what Kate might've said, what she might've done.

I look at the machine in my hand. For a moment I hate it; it's as if it contains all the answers and I want to shake them loose, to demand the truth.

Yet it won't. It can't. It's just a tool, it can tell me nothing. I slam it closed.

Hugh comes home from work and we eat dinner, the three of us, at the table. Afterwards he packs his suitcase, occasionally asking me where a shirt is, or if I've seen his aftershave, then goes upstairs to finish off his speech while Connor and I sit in the living room with a DVD. *The Bourne Identity.* I can't really concentrate; I'm thinking about this afternoon, wondering whether the guy Anna messaged – Harenglish – had got back to her. I'm thinking about cybersex, too, which I guess is really no different to phone sex. It makes me think of Marcus; there were no texts back then, no emails, no instant messaging services, unless you include pagers, which almost no one had. Just the voice.

Connor leans forward and grabs a handful of the popcorn I've made for him. My mind drifts.

I remember the first time Marcus and I had sex. We'd known each other a few weeks, we spoke on the phone, we hung around after the meetings drinking coffee. He'd started to tell me his story. He came from a good family, his parents were alive, he had a sister who was nice, normal, stable. Yet there was always alcohol in the house, forbidden to him, and he was drawn to it. The first time he got drunk was on whisky; he didn't remember anything about it, other than the fact that he felt some part of himself open up, then, and that one day he would want to do it again.

'How old were you?' I'd asked.

He'd shrugged. 'Dunno. Ten?'

I'd thought he was exaggerating, but he told me he wasn't. He started drinking. He'd always been good at art, he said, but the drink made him feel he was better. His painting improved. The two became intertwined. He painted, he drank, he painted. He dropped out of college, his parents kicked him out of their home. Only his sister stood by him, but she was much younger, she didn't understand.

'And after that I was on my own. I tried to cope, but . . .'

'What happened?'

He made light of it. 'One too many times waking up with no idea where I was or how I got there. One too many times wondering why I was bleeding. I rang my mother. I said I needed help. She got a friend to take me to my first meeting in the fellowship.'

'And here we are.'

'Yes. Here we are.' He paused. 'I'm glad I met you.'

It was a couple of weeks later that he called me. Kate was watching television with a friend and I took the call on the extension in the kitchen. He sounded upset.

'What's wrong?' I said.

'I've had a drink.'

I sighed, closed my eyes. 'Have you called Keith?'

'I don't want to speak to Keith. I don't want to see him. I want to see you.'

I felt both awful and thrilled at the same time. He'd had a drink, but it was me he'd turned to. He asked me round to his flat, and I said of course I'd go. When I arrived he was sitting on his threadbare sofa, a bottle at his feet. I sat next to him and took his hand. Had I known we were going to kiss? Probably. Did I know it was almost certainly a mistake? Probably not.

The film ends and Connor goes upstairs, then a little while later so do I. I listen at his door on the way up, but I hear nothing except the rhythmic tap of his fingers on the keyboard. I run myself a bath and lie in the water for a long time, my eyes closed, drifting in and out of an exhausted sleep, occasionally topping up with hot water. When I get out Hugh's in bed already.

'Come,' he says. He pats the bed next to him, and I smile. 'In a minute.' I've wrapped a towel round my chest and I tuck it tighter, then sit at the dressing table and apply my moisturizer. By the time I've finished Hugh is snoring and I turn off the light. It's hot, but there's a light breeze and I go over to the window to adjust the curtains. Outside, there's a figure, barely visible in the shadows, an image as thin as smoke. It looks like a man, and I turn to wake Hugh, to ask him if he can see it, or whether he thinks it's my imagination. But he's fast asleep, and when I look back the man has gone, and I wonder whether he'd ever been there at all.

Chapter Nine

I drive Hugh to the airport then return home. It's Monday, the traffic is bad, the air thick with heat. I've been determined to keep busy during his absence – to get on with jobs, sort out Connor's room, go through the files on the computer, make sure everything is charged and ready for the shoot on Wednesday – but by the time I get home it's early afternoon and far too hot to do anything much at all.

I'm restless, unsettled. I change into a summer dress and decide I'll sit in the garden. I go to the fridge to get a lemonade, but when I open the door I see the bottle of wine Hugh opened last night. Desire swells again, just as it had after the dinner party. I get the lemonade, then close the door, but there's no point in pretending I'm not feeling it.

Rachel used to tell me that. 'Take a step back and hold it up to the light,' she said. 'Consider it.'

I do just that. First, I'd like a glass. Second, I'm alone, Hugh's away, Connor at school. There's no logical reason I shouldn't.

Except there is. There's every reason.

This time the desire builds. I acknowledge it, feel it, yet it doesn't go away. It's growing, it starts to feel more powerful than me, it's an animal, a ruthless predator, something with teeth, something that wants to destroy.

I won't let it win. Not this time. I tell myself I'm strong,

I'm bigger than this thing that wants to claim me. I ride it out, stare it down and eventually it begins to retreat. I put ice in my drink and find the novel I'm reading, pick up my laptop and go outside. I sit at the table on the patio. My heart beats hard, as if the fight had been physical, but once again I'm pleased with my vigilance.

I sip my lemonade, listening to the sounds of summer, the traffic, the planes overhead, a conversation in a distant garden. My book is in front of me but I ignore it. I know I won't be able to concentrate; I'll read the same page, over and over. It's futile.

I open my laptop. I wonder whether the guy from yesterday – Harenglish – replied to Anna, or whether Eastdude, the one I'd been chatting to, has messaged me again.

I navigate to the messages page. He has. I open it. 'What happened? I hope you're all right.'

Anxiety courses through me. It's electric. Anxiety, and also excitement; even though he thinks he's talking to Kate, part of me is flattered at his disappointment.

I try to focus on what's important. I have to be more methodical. I tell myself it's unlikely he had anything to do with Kate's death: assuming what he told me is true, the police have interviewed him as a suspect and eliminated him from their investigation. Plus, he lives in New York.

There's no point in answering his message. I click delete. Part of me feels bad, but he's a stranger, someone I'll never meet. I don't care what he thinks. I have more important things to do.

I navigate to Kate's Friends and Favourites page and go down the list. I'm careful this time, I check each one, finding out where they live. They're scattered all over. Not counting Eastdude, there are eleven people she used to chat with. Of those, only three live in France, and only one, the guy from yesterday – Harenglish, the one Anna messaged – is in Paris.

I hesitate. I open Skype but Anna isn't online. I send her a note asking if she's had a reply, yet at the same time know that she'd have told me if she had.

I remind myself that his silence doesn't mean that Harenglish is the guy who killed Kate. Not at all. Maybe they hardly chatted, barely knew each other. Maybe he rarely logs on to his messages, or doesn't respond to things straight away. There are a million reasons for his silence. It doesn't have to be because he knows exactly where she ended up.

But I need to be sure. I sit, for a moment. I sip my drink. I think about my sister, and what I can do to help her. As I do, the idea that's been forming all night is finally birthed.

I call Anna. 'I've been thinking,' she says.

'Yes?'

'About your suggestion. You know, chatting to that guy. It might not be such a bad idea.'

I tell her.

'I'm thinking of setting up a profile of my own. I thought, if I can chat to people . . . if they think I'm someone new . . . they're more likely to tell me things.'

She talks me through it. I work quickly, and it doesn't take long. I hesitate when it asks me to select a username, but then settle on JayneB. It's close enough to my own name, but not too close. The photo I choose is one that Hugh took a few years ago on holiday. In it, bright sun behind my head is throwing my face into partial shadow. I haven't chosen randomly; Kate and I don't look that similar generally, but in this photo we do. If someone had known Kate, they might mention a resemblance; it might give me a way in. I enter my details – date of birth, height, weight. Finally I press save.

'I'm done,' I say.

She tells me to be careful. I go back online. I'm excited, at last I'm doing something. The guy from yesterday – Harenglish – might talk to me, thinking I'm someone new. Maybe then I can find out who he is and how well he might've known my sister.

I message him. 'Hi,' I say. 'How you doing?' I know he won't reply straight away, if he replies at all, and so I go inside to refill my glass. I grab myself an apple from the bowl. I wonder what this guy might do when he sees my message. Whether he gets lots, or just a few. Whether he answers them all, or just the ones that take his fancy. I wonder what normally happens, if there's such a thing as *normally*.

I go back outside. There's a breeze, it's getting cooler now. I have another sip of my drink then sit back down. I bite into my apple; it's crisp but slightly sour. I put it on the table and, as I do, my computer pings.

I have another message, but it's not from him. This one is from someone new. As I open it I get the strangest feeling. A plunging, a descent. A door has been nudged open. Something is coming.

PART TWO

Chapter Ten

I sat in the garden for hours that day, my laptop humming in front of me. I was exploring the site, clicking on profiles, opening photographs. It was as if I believed I could stumble on Kate's killer accidentally, that somehow I'd just be drawn to him. The ice in my glass melted, the dregs of my lemonade began to attract flies. I was still there when Connor came home from school, though by now the battery on my computer had run down and I was just sitting, in silence, thinking about Kate, and who she might have been talking to, and what they might've said.

'Hi, Mum,' he said, and I closed my machine. I said hello and patted the chair next to me. 'Just doing some editing,' I said as he sat down. The lie slid off my tongue so easily I barely noticed it.

The following night, he's due to go to Dylan's party. His best friend, a nice enough lad, if a bit quiet. They spend a fair bit of time together, here mostly, playing on the computer or on Connor's Xbox. I tend to stay out of their way, listening in from time to time. There's usually a lot of laughter, or there certainly used to be, before Kate. Dylan will come in occasionally and ask me for more juice or a biscuit, terribly polite. Last Christmas I took them sledging on the Heath with another couple of boys from school I didn't know. We had a good time; it was nice to see Connor with people his own age, to get a glimpse of what kind of man he'll turn into. Still, I can't think that he and Dylan discuss feelings. I can't picture him as someone Connor goes to for support.

It's Dylan's birthday and he's celebrating at his house; just pizzas and bottles of cola, some music, maybe karaoke. A few of them are staying over in a tent in his garden and I imagine late-night DVDs and a final snack before torches and sleeping bags are handed out. They'll go out on to the lawn, spend the night laughing, chatting, playing video games on their phones, and the next day, when their parents pick them up, they'll tell us nothing except that it'd been all right.

I drive him there. We pull up outside the house and I see the balloons tied to the gateposts, the cards in the lounge windows. Connor opens the car door and at the same time Dylan's mother, Sally, comes out into the porch. She's someone I know quite well, we've gone for coffee after school, though always with other people, and I haven't seen her for a while. I wave, and she waves back. Behind her I can see streamers, the flash of children running upstairs. She raises her eyebrows and I smile in sympathy.

'Have fun,' I say to Connor.

'I will.'

He lets me kiss him on the cheek then picks up his bag and races into the house.

When I get back home the place seems cavernously empty. Hugh is still in Geneva and has sent me a text message – the flight was okay, the hotel is nice, he's heading for dinner soon and wonders how I'm feeling – and I tap out a reply. 'I'm fine, thanks. Missing you.'

I press send. I make some dinner, then sit in front of the television. I ought to call my friends, I know that. But it's difficult, I don't want to inflict myself upon them, and I can sense that when they hear my voice the energy drops as the shadow of Kate's death falls on all of us.

I'm not me, any more, I realize. I carry something else now. The stigma of pain. And I don't want it.

I think of Marcus. We'd been seeing each other for less than a year when he said he wanted to move. 'Where?' I asked, and he said, 'Berlin.'

He seemed so certain, and so desperate. I thought he was trying to get away from me, even though until that moment we'd been happy. He could see it in my eyes. The flash of disappointment, suppressed a moment too late.

'No,' he said. 'You don't understand. I want you to come with me.'

'But—'

He shook his head. He was determined.

'You have to. I want to go with you. I don't want to go by myself.'

But you will, I thought. If I don't come. You've already decided.

'Please come. What's keeping you here?' I shook my head. 'Is it the meetings? We've been clean for ages now. We don't need to go any more.'

'I know, but . . .'

'Is it Kate?'

I nodded. 'She's only twelve.'

He stroked my arm, kissed me. 'She's in school now. You can't look after her for ever.'

I thought of all the fun we'd had, Kate and I, despite how hard it'd been at times. We used to make popcorn and sit watching videos, or we'd play in the long grass at the bottom of our garden, pretending to be chased by dinosaurs. Dressing up in our mother's clothes, wearing her shoes, spraying ourselves with her perfume.

'How long have you been looking after her?'

'Eight years.'

'Exactly. And now it's time your father started doing his bit. Besides, she's nearly a teenager now. You have your own life to live.'

I told him I'd need to think about it, but really I already knew. Kate was nearly thirteen, older than I'd been when I started looking after her. She'd had enough years of my life. Kate would be fine.

Except she wasn't. I open my eyes. I reach for my laptop. Anna's online. I message her.

'Any luck?' she asks.

I think of the few people who have messaged me. There's been nothing interesting.

'Not yet,' I reply.

Hugh comes back from his conference. He takes the train from the airport, then a cab, and arrives carrying a huge bunch of flowers. He kisses me then hands them over. 'What have I done to deserve this?' I say, and he shrugs. 'Nothing. I love you, that's all. I missed you.' I find a vase. 'I missed you, too,' I say, a little too automatically.

I take the scissors out of the kitchen drawer and begin to trim the stems.

'How's Connor?'

'Good, I think.'

'And you?'

I tell him I'm fine. 'I had a job,' I say, thinking back to the day before. 'A friend of Fatima's. Her daughter wants to be a model and needed some pictures for her portfolio.'

'That's good,' he says. 'Have you seen Adrienne?'

'No. But she called. She's in York, with work. But we've arranged dinner.'

He smiles and says he thinks that will do me good. I didn't tell him Adrienne has asked if I'd decided about going online and I'd said no, not yet.

Another lie. I've logged on a few times, and now it's Friday night. Hugh's upstairs, catching up with admin, and Connor is at a friend's house working on a homework project. I've already edited the pictures I took on Wednesday, and now I'm half watching the television. It's a drama. Undercover cops, a series of brutal murders, duct tape, revenge and rape. Every victim beautiful, of course, as if we wouldn't care otherwise; plus, we're supposed to envy them their lives right until the moment the blade slices into their flesh.

It's no use, I can't focus. I switch it off. I can't help thinking of Kate. She was pretty, but not beautiful, and she wasn't raped. Kate was killed because she happened to be walking down the wrong alleyway in the wrong part of town at the wrong time, or so Hugh and everybody else tells me. It's as simple as that.

Except it isn't. It can't be.

I log back on to encountrz. I know I should leave it alone, do something else instead, but I can't. My message to Harenglish is now a week old and he still hasn't responded.

He isn't online, but there is something in my inbox, something new.

Largos86. I click on his profile and see that he's younger than me – he claims to be thirty-one, though if anything he doesn't even look as old as that – and is attractive, with curly hair, cut short. I imagine he could be a model, or an actor, though I remind myself he'll have chosen one of the more flattering photos of himself. If he were in the drama I've just switched off he'd be playing a kindly doctor, or a lover. He's too attractive to be the husband. I open his message.

'Hi,' it says. 'I'd love to talk. You remind me of someone.'

I flinch; it's like being punched. *I remind you of someone.* For an instant there's only one thing, one *person*, he can mean. I'd deliberately chosen my profile photo to be one that looks like Kate, after all.

I have to know. Beneath his message is a link, an invitation to a private chat. Largos86 knows I'm online. I click on accept, then type.

– Hi. Who do I remind you of?

His reply comes almost instantaneously.

– Someone I liked a lot.

Liked, I think. Past tense. Someone who isn't around any more, one way or another.

– But let's not talk about her. How're you?

No! It's her I want to talk about.

– Good, I say.

A moment later he replies:

– I'm Lukas. Fancy a chat?

I stop. Since I've been going online I've learned it's unusual for someone to give away their name so quickly. I wonder if he's lying.

– I'm Jayne.

I pause.

– Where are you?

– In Milan. How about you?

I think of his first message. *You remind me of someone.*

I want to find out if he might've talked to Kate. I decide to tell a lie of my own.

– I'm in Paris.

– A beautiful place!

– How do you know the city?

– I work there. Occasionally.

My skin prickles with sweat. I try to take a breath but there's no oxygen in the room.

Could he have chatted to my sister, even met her? Could it be him who killed her? It seems unlikely; he looks too innocent, too trustworthy. Yet I know I'm basing that impression on nothing, just a feeling, and feelings can be misleading.

What to do? I'm shaking, I can't take in any air. I want to end the chat, but then I'll never know.

– Really? I say. How often?

– Oh, not that often. A couple of times a year.

I want to ask if he was there in February, but I can't risk it. I have to be careful. If he did know Kate and has something to hide then he might work out I'm on to him.

I have to keep this light, breezy. If things become sexual there'll be no way of finding anything out, nothing I can do but end the conversation as quickly as possible. I want to look for clues, but I can't let things tip over.

– Where do you stay when you're over here?

I wait. A message flashes. I can't decide whether I want him to tell me he has a flat in the nineteenth, or that his office put him up in a hotel near Ourcq Métro, or not. If they do and he does, then it's him. I'm sure of it. Hugh and I can tell the police what I've found. I can move on.

But if he doesn't? What then? I still won't know.

His message arrives.

– I'm not there often. I tend to stay in hotels.

– Where?

– It varies. Usually pretty central. Or else I stay near Gare du Nord.

I don't need to pull up a map of Paris to know that Gare du Nord is nowhere near the area Kate's body was found. I'm curiously relieved.

– Why do you ask?

– No reason.

– You think maybe it's near you?

He's added a smiley face. I wonder if the flirting has moved to the next level. Part of me wants to end it, but another part of me doesn't. He might be lying.

I hesitate for a moment, then type:

– I'm in the north-east. The nearest Métro is Ourcq.

It's a risk. If it's him he'll know I'm linked to Kate. It can't be a coincidence.

But what will he do? Just end the conversation, log off? Or would he stick around to try and find out exactly what I know? It occurs to me he might already have guessed who I am and why I'm chatting to him. He might've worked it out from the start.

I press send, then wait. Largos86 is typing. Time stretches; it seems to take for ever.

– Is it a nice area?

– It's okay. You don't know it?

– No. Should I?

– Not necessarily.

– So are you up to much? Have you had a good day today?

I hesitate. Last time, at this point, I was being asked what I was wearing, or whether I'd like fantasy role play or straight cyber. It's a relief that this conversation is unthreatening.

– Not bad, I say.

I wonder why I'm relieved. Is it that in these few brief moments I'm not in mourning?

– Tell me what you've been up to.

– You don't want to hear about me.

– I do. Tell me everything!

– Why don't you tell me something about you, first?

– Okay, let me think.

He's added a cartoon, another face. This one looks puzzled. A few moments later his next message arrives.

– Okay. You ready?

– Yes.

– I really adore dogs. And cheesy love songs. The cheesier the better. And I'm really scared of spiders.

I smile. I can't help it. I look back at his photo. I try to imagine what Kate might've thought, looking at him. He's certainly attractive, and around her age.

His next message arrives.

– Your turn. You owe me two facts.

I run through a list of what I might tell him. I'm looking for something that will draw him out, some fact that might lead him to tell me whether he was in Paris in February, or might have chatted to Kate.

I lean forward and begin to type.

– Okay. My favourite season is winter. I love Paris, in February especially.

I press send and a moment later he replies.

– That's fact number one.

– And – I begin, but then I freeze. There's a sound, a key in the lock. The real world is intruding, too loud. It's Connor, coming home. As he opens the door I'm still adjusting, to the living room in which I'm sitting, to my own home. I switch on the television and the credits roll silently. Connor comes in.

'Oh, I didn't know you were in here.'

I close my machine and put it to one side. My heart thuds, as if I've been caught taking drugs. He's wearing a baseball cap I haven't seen before and a black sweatshirt; he's chewing gum.

'What've you been up to?'

'Just studying.'

I force a smile. 'How's it going?'

'Okay. What're you up to?'

I feel dizzy. It's as if domesticity is crashing in around me in an inrush of banality, of making meals, of ferrying to school and back, of worrying about what to cook for dinner and whether the surfaces in the kitchen are clean.

I adjust my necklace. 'Just reading emails.'

He asks for a snack. I make one for him, then he goes upstairs and I go back to my machine. Largos86 is no longer online, so I message Anna.

– He says he's called Lukas.

– And?

What to say? I have a feeling, a suspicion. Based on what?

– I don't know. There's something about him. He seems really keen.

I hesitate, but continue.

– I just wonder if he knew Kate.

– It's unlikely, don't you think?

I agree.

– But yes, it is possible he talked to her.

– You think?

– Well, there aren't that many people who use that site.

– So you think it might be worth talking to him some more?

– Well, don't get your hopes up. But maybe. We might be able to find out who else Kate was talking to. Or at least prove one way or the other whether he knew her.

The next day I take my laptop into my studio. The same guy is online. Largos86.

– You disappeared, he says. I wondered what I'd done.

It's his fourth or fifth message. At first I wasn't sure I'd reply, but they keep coming.

I can't forget what he'd said. *You remind me of someone. Someone I liked a lot.*

– I'm sorry, I say.

I resist the urge to make an excuse. I can't tell him about
Connor coming home. It wouldn't be right. It would take the
conversation in the wrong direction. I wonder who's watching whom. I wonder who's the cat, and who's the mouse?

– Are you alone?

I hesitate. Connor's in the house, doing his homework, he
said, and Hugh's out at a concert with a friend, so I might as
well be. I certainly feel alone.

Plus, I've realized I'm going to have to give something if
I'm going to get something back.

– Yes. Yes I am.

A moment later his message appears:

– I enjoyed chatting to you yesterday . . .

I wonder if there's going to be a *but* . . .

– Thanks.

– But we never really got on to talking about you.

– What d'you want to know?

– Everything! But maybe start by telling me what it is you
do.

I decide I don't want to tell the truth.

– I'm in the arts. I curate exhibitions.

– Wow! Sounds interesting.

– It can be. So how about you? I know you travel.

– Oh, let's not talk about me. It's boring.

Maybe it is, but I'm trying to find out why he's so keen to
chat to me again tonight.

– No. I'm sure it's not. Go on.

– I'm in the media. I buy advertising space for big
campaigns.

– So what are you doing in Milan? Are you on holiday?

– No, he says. I'm living out here, temporarily. Doing some
work. Staying in a hotel. I'm thinking about going out for
dinner, then maybe to a bar. But it's no fun on your own . . .

The ellipsis suggests he's inviting a compliment. I remind myself I still need to find out if he meets people he chats to, and what he does with them if so.

I try to imagine how Jayne might reply. At the very least she'd have to make a reference to what he'd said.

– I bet you wouldn't be lonely for long, I say.

– Thanks, he replies, and then another message comes through.

– Can I ask what you're wearing?

So polite, I think. It's not what I might've expected.

But then what did I expect? This is the way it goes, apparently. *What are you wearing? Describe it to me. I want to take it off, tell me how it feels.* But much sooner, within a few messages, not over a couple of days.

– Why do you want to know?

I wonder if I ought to add a winking face. Is that what Kate would've done?

– I just want to be able to picture you.

I feel myself tense. I'm not sure I want him to picture me. It leaves an unpleasant taste. I remind myself I'm doing this for Kate's sake, and for Connor's. For all of us.

– If you must know, I type, I'm wearing jeans. And a shirt. Your turn.

– Well, I'm just lying here on the bed.

I look again at his photo and picture him. I see the hotel room, bland and corporate. I wonder if he's taken his clothes off. I imagine he has a good body, strong and muscular. He'll have got himself a drink; for some reason I picture him with a beer, drinking straight from the bottle. Something within me begins to open up, but I don't know what it is. Is it because finally I might be getting somewhere, unlocking the riddle of my sister's murder? Or because a good-looking man has chosen to send a message to me?

114

– If you're busy that's cool. I'll leave you alone.

– No. I'm not busy.

– Okay. So I'm here, and you're there. What're you up for? What're you into?

I try to imagine what Kate would've said.

I can't.

– I'm not sure.

– Are you okay?

I decide it's easier to tell the truth.

– I've never done this before.

– No problem. We can chat another time, if you're uncomfortable?

– No. I'm not uncomfortable. I just don't want to disappoint you.

– You're beautiful. How could you disappoint me?

Deep down, but unmistakably there, there's a weak throb of excitement. A distant signal from the remotest star.

– Thank you.

A moment, then he replies:

– It's a pleasure. You *are* beautiful. I'm enjoying talking to you.

– I'm enjoying talking to you, too.

– Why don't you tell me what you're doing this evening?

I stop to think. Soon I'll cook our evening meal, then I might sit with a book. But I don't want to tell him that.

– I might go out, with friends. Or maybe catch a film.

– Nice.

We talk for a little while longer. He asks me what movies I've seen recently, we talk about books and music. It turns out we both love Edward Hopper and have tried but failed to finish *Finnegans Wake*. It's pleasurable, but I seem to be getting further and further from finding out whether he's ever chatted to my sister, or was in Paris in February, or even

115

who I remind him of. After a few more minutes he says:
 – Well I'd better get ready, go for dinner.
 – And then go on to your bar?
 – Possibly. Though I'm not sure I can be bothered now.
 – How come?
 – I might just come back to the room and see if you're still
online.
There's another tiny shock of pleasure.
 – Would you like that?
 – I might.
 – I'd like to chat again.
I don't reply.
 – Would you?
I stare at the blinking cursor. For some reason I'm thinking
of my time in Berlin, in the squat with Marcus and Frosty
and the rest; the sensation of both wanting and not wanting
something at the same time.
Again I remind myself who I'm doing this for.
 – I would.

We end the conversation. I log off and call Anna.
 'How did it go?'
 'I'm not sure.'
 'Did it get sexual?'
 'Not really. No.'
 'It will,' she says.
 'Listen, will you look at his profile online? Let me know if
you recognize him?'
 She hesitates. I hear her stand up; she's moving around her
apartment. 'Of course. But I don't recognize his name. I don't
think he can be one of the ones Kate met. I suppose it's pos-
sible he's someone she chatted to.'
 'I need to find out.'

'Just don't get your hopes up.'

I won't, I tell her. We talk some more. After we've said goodbye I go back online. I can't help it. I look at Lukas's profile, at the photographs he's uploaded. They look completely ordinary. He's wearing a checked shirt, open at the neck, his face is broad and handsome, his eyes dark. Did he know my sister? Is it possible?

I read the rest of his profile. He describes himself as athletic, he's a lover of fun, he enjoys reading, music, eating out. When I scroll down I see there's a link to his Facebook page. I click on it.

He's used the same picture there, but I hardly look at it. I navigate straight to his timeline and begin to scroll backwards. I go back as far as February. I have to be sure.

There's a photo of him, standing in the desert next to a man. They have their arms round each other's shoulders, in triumph. Uluru is in the background. 'We finally made it!' says the caption. When Kate was killed he was in Australia.

It doesn't mean he didn't know her, though. I think again of what he said. *You remind me of someone.*

I send a message to Anna: 'Checked Facebook. He was in Australia.'

I go to bed. It's later than I think; Hugh's turned out the light and is already asleep. He's left the curtains open for me to undress in the light from the street outside. Before I do I check if anyone's there, but tonight the street is empty, other than a couple walking arm in arm, looking either drunk or in love, it's hard to tell. I'm naked when I get into bed; I turn on to my side and look at Hugh, silhouetted in the half-light. My husband, I tell myself, as if I need to be reminded of the fact.

I kiss him gently, on his brow. The night is hot and sticky

and I can taste the sweat that's formed there. I turn on to my other side, away from him. My hand goes beneath the covers, between my legs. I can't help it. It's the talk, this afternoon. The chat with the guy online. Lukas. Something has been aroused, some desire that is complicated yet undeniable.

I let it come. I'm thinking of Lukas. I can't help it, even if it does feel like a betrayal. *You're beautiful*, he'd said, and the excitement I'd felt had been instant and pure. I imagine him now, he's saying it over and over, *You're beautiful, you're gorgeous, I want you*, yet for some reason he changes, becomes Marcus. He's leading me upstairs, we're in the squat, we're going to the room we shared, to the mattress on the floor, to the tangle of bedclothes unmade from the night before. I've spent the day here alone, he's been out. But now he's back, there's only the two of us. He's argued with his family, his mother is distraught, she wants him home. Even just for a few weeks, she'd said, but he knows she means for ever. I tell him I'll support him, if he goes, if he decides he wants to, but I know he won't. Not now he's here, and happy. He kisses me. I imagine the smell of him, his smooth skin, the fuzz of hair on his chest. These details – things that I know are half remembrances and half imaginings, a mixture of fantasy and memory – come, and they lead me somewhere, somewhere where I am strong and in control and Kate is alive and everything will be all right.

My hand, my fingers, move in circles. I try to think of Hugh, a version of Hugh, an idealized Hugh who has never existed. I imagine the way he'd look at me, the way he used to look at me, his eyes leaving my face, travelling down, pausing first at my neck and then again at my breasts before flashing lower for just the briefest of moments before coming back to my face. His appraisal would take three seconds, maybe four. I imagine letting my eyes follow the same path his had taken, taking in his unshaven chin, the black hair that pokes from under his shirt, his chest, the buckle on his belt. I imagine him leaning in to speak to me, the smell of his after-shave, the faint scent of his breath, like chewed leather. I imagine him kissing me, this idealized Hugh, who is really Lukas, who is really Marcus.

My hand moves faster, my body lifts then falls away. I'm free. I've become lightness and air, nothing but energy.

Chapter Eleven

I sit with a glass of sparkling water. Adrienne is late.

The restaurant is brand new. Even Bob had found it difficult to get us a table, according to Adrienne, and as someone who writes restaurant reviews he rarely struggles. I hadn't been able to decide what to wear and in the end had gone for a simple sleeveless dress with a check print, plus the necklace Hugh bought me for Christmas and perfume from my favourite bottle. It's been so long since I've been out for dinner it'd felt like getting ready for a date, and now I'm beginning to feel like I've been stood up.

Eventually I see her coming in. She waves then comes over to the table.

'Darling!' She kisses me on both cheeks then we sit down. She puts her bag under her chair. 'Right . . .' She grabs the menu, still talking as she reads. 'Sorry I'm late. The tube was delayed. "Passenger action", they call it.' She looks up. 'Some selfish prick who'd had enough and decided to ruin everyone else's day.' I smile. It's a black humour that we can share; I know she doesn't mean it. How can she, after what happened to Kate? 'You don't mind if I have a drink?'

I shake my head and she orders a glass of Chablis, then tells me I ought to have the lobster. She's always been a whirl-wind, but tonight she seems almost in too much of a rush. I wonder if she's trying to compensate for being late, or maybe she's anxious about something.

'Now,' she says, once her drink has arrived. Her voice becomes relaxed and reassuring. 'How are you?' I shrug, but she holds up her hand. 'And don't give me any of that "I'm fine" crap. How are you really?'

'I *am* fine. Honestly.' She looks at me, an expression of exaggerated disappointment on her face. 'Mostly,' I add.

She pushes the bread that's arrived towards me, but I ignore it. 'How long has it been, now? It must be four months?'

For the first time I don't know immediately, I have to work it out. I've stopped counting the days and weeks; perhaps it's the first evidence of progress. I'm strangely pleased.

'Almost five.'

She smiles sadly. I know she understands how I feel, more than most. A few years ago her stepfather died suddenly, a heart attack, while he was driving. They'd been close; the intensity of her grief had shocked her.

'Are they any nearer to working out what happened?' For a moment her expression seems to change; she looks almost hungry, unless I'm imagining it. I've seen it before, it's the journalist in her; she can't help herself. She wants the details.

'You mean, who did it? Not yet. They're not really telling us very much . . .' I let the conversation evaporate. It feels like every week that goes by makes it less likely they'll catch them, but I don't want to put that into words.

'How's Hugh?'

'He's okay, you know?' I think for a moment. I can be honest with her. 'Actually, sometimes I think he's almost glad.'

Do I? Or am I just saying that because sometimes I still worry that I am?

She tilts her head. 'Glad?'

'Oh, I don't mean glad that she's dead. It's just . . . sometimes I think he just likes the fact that it makes things simpler, I guess. With Connor.' I hesitate. 'Maybe he's right. They've certainly seemed much closer, recently.'

I look up at Adrienne. She knows that I'd been worried that if it ever went to the courts they'd uphold Connor's right to choose.

'I've known Hugh since for ever, Julia. He's always liked things to be neat and tidy. But he's not glad. Don't be too hard on him.'

I feel empty, like I want to share everything with Adrienne, to offload it, to hand it over and find some peace.

'He's not even there most of the time.'

'Darling, hasn't he always been like that?' She drinks some of her wine. A wave of desire hits me, the first for weeks. I tell myself to ride it out. She carries on speaking, but I have to struggle to concentrate. 'They all are. We marry them because they're successful, ambitious, whatever. Then that's the very thing that takes them away from us. It was the same with Steve, and now it's the same with Bob. I barely see him, he's so busy . . .'

I centre myself. It's different for her. She has a challenging career of her own. She can take herself away from her husband as easily as he takes himself away from her. But I don't want to argue.

'You're seeing someone?'

I feel myself recoil. She knows, I think. About Lukas. Even though there's nothing to know. We're still chatting regularly, and though I try to tell myself there's no reason to think so, I keep thinking he must've known Kate. I can't work him out, and so I keep going back.

'What—?' I say to Adrienne now, but she interrupts.

122

'A therapist, I mean?'

Of course. My panic recedes. 'Oh, right. No, I'm not.'

There's a moment of silence. She doesn't take her eyes off me; she's appraising me, trying to work out why I'd reacted as I had.

'Julia? If you don't want to talk about it . . .'

I do, though. I do want to talk about it, and she's my oldest friend.

'You remember I said I might go online? To get the list of people Kate was talking to?'

'Yes. You said you'd changed your mind.'

I'm silent.

'Julia?'

'There was someone I wasn't sure about.'

She puts down her glass and raises her eyebrows. 'Go on . . .'

'He visits Paris. He messaged me. I convinced myself he might be someone Kate was talking to. Someone the police don't know about.'

'So you gave his details to the authorities?'

Still I say nothing.

'Julia . . . ?'

'Not yet.'

'Why?'

'I need to be sure . . . I'm just talking to him. I'm trying to find out what he knows.'

'Darling, are you sure that's a good idea?'

'What's the alternative? Give his name to the police—?'

'Yes! That's exactly what you should do!'

'I don't want to frighten him off and, besides, they'd probably just ignore it.'

'Of course they wouldn't ignore it! Why would they do that, Julia? They have a duty to investigate it. He lives in Paris, it should be easy enough.'

I don't tell her he lives in Milan. 'I know what I'm doing. We've only chatted once or twice.'

It's a lie, an understatement. I'm trying to backtrack. Things have developed. He turns his video on now and has asked me to turn mine on, though I haven't, yet. He tells me I'm beautiful. He tells me he wishes there could be a way I could be there with him, and even though I feel guilty for lying to him, I tell him I wish that, too. Our conversations end with him telling me he's loved talking to me, that he can't wait until we can chat again. He tells me to look after myself, to be careful. And because it would be impolite not to, because I just can't figure him out, I say the same things to him.

It feels cruel, sometimes. I don't mean it, and yet he clearly likes me, or likes the person he thinks I am.

'He knows where you live?'

I shake my head. The other day I made a mistake and mentioned the tube. I'd had to confess that I was in London, not Paris, but he knows no more than that.

'No, of course not.'

There's a long pause. 'So, what do you talk about?'

I don't reply, which is an answer in itself.

'You are very vulnerable right now, Julia. You're sure you know what you're doing?'

I nod. 'Of course.' But she doesn't look convinced.

'You like him.'

I shake my head again. 'No. It's not like that. It's just . . . there seems to be a connection there. And I wonder whether that connection has anything to do with Kate.'

'In what way?'

'You know how close we used to be. It felt almost psychic. And, well—'

'You think if you feel a connection with this man then it must be relevant?'

I don't answer. It's exactly what I think. She has no idea what a difference it makes, this feeling that I'm at least doing something useful, something that might lead Connor and me to resolution and a place of safety.

'Julia.' She looks stern. 'You look like a teenager who's got a massive crush on a boy in the next year up.'

'That's ridiculous.' I mean it, but I don't sound convincing, even to myself. Is it really how I feel? I can't deny I've looked forward to Lukas's messages.

Maybe it's not about the investigation at all. Maybe it's because now I know how Kate must have felt, chatting to those men; I can feel closer to her. I know her world.

'You know,' I say, 'even if it is futile, a waste of time, so what? I'm just trying to do something to get over the death of my sister.'

'So you told this guy about her?'

I say no, but I'm lying. The other day I'd had a bad morning after a sleepless night and I couldn't stop thinking about Kate. He could tell something was wrong. He kept asking me if everything was all right, whether there was anything he could do. I couldn't help myself. I told him.

He said he was so sorry to hear my sister had died, and asked me how. I was about to tell him the truth when I realized it would be a mistake. I told him it was suicide. There was a long moment when I wondered what he was going to say, and then he said again how sorry he was, and that he wished he could put his arms around me, be there for me.

He said he understood, and it'd felt good. For a moment I almost felt bad for wondering whether he might be somehow involved in my sister's death. Almost.

'Well, that's something, at least. Are you having sex?'

'Of course not!' I say, but I'm thinking about how it makes me feel when he turns his camera on, when I can see him respond to my messages, smile at me, wave at me when he says goodbye. Do I want him?

I think about the other night, in bed. Hugh and I had made love, for the first time in months, but it'd been Lukas I was thinking about.

Yet at the same time it wasn't him. The man I was imagining, dreaming about, was a fantasy. My own construction, almost completely divorced from the Lukas I chat to, the one I see on camera.

'He knows about Hugh?'

'Of course not.'

'Why?'

'Because I want him to think I'm available. Otherwise, how will I find out whether he is who he says he is?'

'Right.' She looks at me, dead in the eye. 'And what do you think Hugh would say? If he found out?'

It's not the first time I've considered it, of course. 'But I'm just trying to find out what happened. If nothing else, to help Connor.'

She looks properly exasperated, now. It's as if she thinks I'm stupid. Possibly she does. Possibly I am.

Our food arrives. I'm grateful. There a diffusion of tension as we arrange our napkins and begin to eat. 'Look,' I say. 'It's not like there're any feelings attached to any of this. It's just words on a screen . . .'

She forks her salad. 'I think you're being naive. You're getting sucked in.'

'Can we change the subject?'

She puts her fork down. 'You know I love you, and support you. But—'

Here we go, I think. 'What?'

'It's just . . . it's surprising what people give away online, without knowing it. How easily it can feel real.'

'Adrienne. I'm not an idiot, you know.'

'I just hope you know what you're doing.'

We finish our meal and have coffee before we leave. It's another warm night; couples meander through the city, arm in arm. The air is full of laughter, of possibility. I feel unsteady, almost as if I've had a drink. I decide to take the tube home.

'It's been great to see you.'

'You, too.' We kiss, but I'm disappointed. I thought she'd see my chats with Lukas for what they are, even give me support. But she hadn't. She doesn't. 'You be careful,' she says, and I tell her I will.

I reach the platform just as a train pulls in. It's pretty full, but I sit down on one of the few remaining seats and, a moment too late, realize it's sticky with spilled beer. I take my book out of my bag, but it's a defence. I don't open it.

At Holborn there's a commotion. A group of lads get on, teenagers, or early twenties; they're wearing shorts, T-shirts, carrying beers. One of them says something – I don't hear what – and the others laugh. 'Fuck!' says one; another says, 'What a cunt!' It's loud, they're making no effort to tone it down; there are children around, despite the time. I catch the eye of the man sitting opposite me and he smiles and raises his eyebrows. For a moment we're united in our disapproval. He has a long face, cropped hair, glasses. He holds a brief-case on his lap, in soft leather, but is wearing jeans and a shirt. The train pulls away. He smiles, then goes back to his paper and I open my book.

I can't concentrate. I read the same paragraph, over and over. I can't pretend I'm not hoping I'll have a message from Lukas when I get home. I keep thinking about the man sitting opposite me.

I sigh, look up. He's looking at me again, and now he smiles and holds my gaze for a long moment. This time it's me who looks away first, to the advert above his head. I pretend to find it fascinating; it's a poster for one of the universities. BE WHO YOU WANT TO BE, it says. A woman wears a mortar board, clutches a scroll, her grin wide. Next to it is a poster for a dating agency. WHAT IF YOU KNEW THAT EVERYONE IN THIS CARRIAGE YOU FANCY IS SINGLE? What if I did? I think. What would I do? Nothing, I don't suppose. I'm married, I have a child. I glance down, just briefly, away from the poster; he's reading his paper again. I find myself looking at his body, at his chest, which is broader than his narrow face would suggest, at his legs, his thighs. Although he looks nothing like him, I start to see him as Lukas. I picture him, looking up at me, smiling the way I've seen Lukas smile on Skype so many times over the last few days. I imagine kissing him, letting him kiss me. I imagine dragging him into one of the stairwells at the next station, unzipping his jeans, feeling him grow erect in my hand.

Suddenly I see myself as others see me. I'm shocked at what I'm thinking. It isn't right. It isn't me. I look down at my book and pretend to read.

Chapter Twelve

I think he's there again. Standing not quite under the light.
Watching my window.

There, yet not there. When I look directly into the shadows
I can convince myself it's nothing, a trick of the light, an
optical illusion. Just my brain, seeking order in chaos, trying
to make sense of the random. Yet, as I look away, the figure
seems about to come into focus. To declare itself as real.

This time, I don't turn away. This time, I tell myself he's
real. I'm not imagining it. I stay where I am, watching him.
Last time I'd told Hugh and he said it was nothing, a trick of
the light, and so tonight I want to burn his image on to my
retina, take it again to my husband, show him. Look, I want
to say. This time, I'm not being absurd, I'm not imagining it.
He was there.

The figure doesn't move. It's utterly still. I watch, and as I
do it seems to recede somehow, into the shadows. There, yet
not there.

I turn and wake my husband. 'Hugh. Come here. Look.
He's here again.'

Reluctantly he gets up. The street is empty.

Maybe Hugh's right. Maybe I am being paranoid.

'Hugh thinks I've lost my mind,' I tell Anna. We're on Skype,
I've finished adding some images to my website, tidying

things up. Her face is in the window in the corner of my screen.

'Could it just be someone walking their dog?'

'There's no dog.' She begins to say something, but the video freezes and I don't hear it. A moment or so later it resumes and I carry on. 'He's standing outside my house. It creeps me out. If I turn away, to fetch Hugh or whatever, he's always disappeared when I turn back.'

'It might just be some weirdo.'

'It might, I guess.'

'Have you talked to Adrienne?'

'No,' I say. I'd meant to the other night, but was worried she already thought I was crazy.

'What are you going to do?'

I tell her I don't know. 'But it feels so real. I swear. I'm not crazy.'

'Of course not,' she says. 'I didn't think that for a second. Also, it's a pretty logical response to what's happened.'

I'm relieved. Even if Anna is humouring me, at least she's doing that rather than trying to convince me I'm mistaken, or insane.

'How're things with that guy? The one you've been messaging. The one you think might have something to do with Kate.'

'Lukas?'

Should I tell her? Or will she just tell me to give the information to the police and then walk away?

'Not sure,' I say. I give her some details. More than I gave Adrienne, but not everything. 'We're messaging occasionally. There's something about him. Something I can't quite put my finger on. It's probably nothing . . .'

Is it, though? He's still pursuing me. Or I'm pursuing him; I can't tell. Either way, I've turned my camera on, too, now.

Last night. Just for a moment, less than a minute. But I've let him see me.

Yet I don't tell her that.

'Well, I heard back from that guy I messaged. The one from Kate's list? Harenglish.'

'You did?'

And you didn't tell me? I think, I guess he must have had nothing to do with it.

'What did he say?'

'Nothing much. But he said he isn't looking to meet people, not in real life. He's online for a bit of fun. Sexy chats, he said. But online only. He loves his wife too much to risk anything else.'

'You believe him?'

'Yes. Yes I do.'

It's the day of Carla's party. She lives miles away, halfway to Guildford. Hugh drives, Connor sits behind me, listening to music on his iPod, far too loud. Last year we'd all enjoyed the day; I'd taken a salad I'd made – grilled aubergines, a salmon with preserved lemons – and even bought a new dress. Connor had got on well with the neighbour's children, Hugh had enjoyed relaxing with his colleagues. Now, I don't want to be here; I'd had to be persuaded. 'It'll be fun,' said Hugh. 'Connor will get to see his friends, and it'll be a chance for you to show him how well you're coping.'

Am I coping, though? I think about Lukas. He's at a wedding today, and last night I gave him my number, after we'd talked, after I'd told him about the man I thought I'd seen outside my window, after he'd given me his.

Now I wish I hadn't. I feel bad enough about leading him on.

I turn to look at Hugh. Lukas had said he wished he could

protect me, that he'd never let anyone hurt me. I'd felt safe. But my husband? He's sitting forward, his eyes fixed on the road. It's how I imagine he looks in theatre. Scalpel in hand, crouching over a body that's been split like a gutted fish. Would he protect me? Of course not. He thinks I'm making it up.

Carla greets us with a flurry of smiles and kisses then takes us through the house to the patio. Hugh goes over to Carla's husband, Connor towards a picnic blanket where the other kids are clustered. I spot Maria and Paddy standing with a few others and join them.

Maria embraces me, then her husband does. They're talking about work; Maria mentions the conference in Geneva. She begins to describe the work she presented – she mentions anterior descending arteries, calcification, ischaemia – and the others either nod or look confused. There's an older man standing next to Paddy and I remember him from last year, a barrister, from Dunfermline, and when Maria finishes he says, 'Sounds utterly impenetrable!' and everyone laughs. A moment later he turns to me.

'And how do you fit in? Do you butcher people for a living, too?'

There's a moment of silence. Kate hadn't been butchered, but still the word stings. An image of my sister comes and I can't shake it away. I open my mouth to answer but no words come.

Paddy tries to rescue me.

'Julia's a photographer.' He smiles and turns to me. 'Very talented.'

I try to smile, but I can't. I'm still looking at Kate, her flesh torn, exposed, dying. The man I'm being introduced to has his hand out, he's smiling.

'Will you excuse me?' I say. 'I'm just going to the bathroom.'

I lock the door behind me and lean against it. I inhale deeply then step forward. The window is open; laughter drifts up from the patio below.

I shouldn't have come here, I should've made an excuse. I'm sick of pretending everything's normal, when it isn't. I take out my phone. It's automatic, instinctive, I'm not sure why I do it, but I'm glad. I've had a message from Lukas.

'The wedding's fun. I'm drunk already. Thinking of you.'

Despite the blackness I'm feeling, joy rushes in, as if to disinfect a wound. It's not because the message is from him, I tell myself. It's the simple thrill of being wanted.

By now I know how Kate would've replied. 'I'm at a dreadful party,' I type. 'Wish you were here . . .'

I press send. I rinse my hands in cold water then splash some on my face and my neck. It trickles down, under my dress to the small of my back, lighting up my skin. I look out of the window.

Connor is outside. He's sitting on the grass with another boy and a girl. They're laughing at something; he seems particularly close to the girl. I realize it won't be long until he's dating, then having sex, and then part of him will be lost to me for ever. It's necessary, but it fills me with sadness.

He lifts his hand to wave at his father. It strikes me how much he looks like Kate, when she was his age. They have the same slight roundness to their face, the same half-grin that can disappear and reappear in an instant.

He looks like his mother. It shouldn't be a surprise. Yet it is, and it hurts.

*

I rejoin the group, but I can't tune into the conversation. Why had I been so excited to get Lukas's message? Why had I replied to him? The questions circle and after a minute or two I excuse myself and go to say hello to Connor. He's with his friends, I'm interrupting him, and I feel bad. I move on, to the summer house tucked away at the side of the garden, between the house and the gate that leads to where the cars are parked. It's octagonal and painted mint green, filled with cushions. When I get there I see that the doors are open, and that it's empty.

I sit down and lean back against the wood. The babble of conversation continues. I close my eyes. The smell is of recently varnished wood; it reminds me of the only childhood holiday I can remember from when my mother was alive, a chalet we rented in the Forest of Dean. I can picture her, standing at the stove, boiling water for my father's coffee while I fed Kate. She's singing along to a radio, humming to herself, and Kate is giggling at something. We were all alive, then, and mostly happy. But that was before the slow process of dislocation that ended only when my sister's death left me totally alone.

I want a drink. Right now. I want a drink and, worse, more dangerous, I think I deserve one.

A shadow falls across my face. I open my eyes; there's a figure in the doorway in front of me, silhouetted against the afternoon light. It takes me only a moment to realize it's Paddy.

'Hi!' He sounds bright but his enthusiasm is slightly forced. 'May I join you?'

'Of course.' He steps forward. He stumbles on the low step. He's drunker than I'd thought.

'How's it going?' He holds out one of the two glasses of wine he's brought from the house. 'I thought you might want this.'

I do, I think. I do.

But I know I have to ignore it.

He puts the glass on the floor, where I can reach it. Ride it out, I tell myself. Ride it out. He sits down on the bench. He's right next to me, so close we're touching.

'They're still talking shop. Do they ever stop?'

I shrug. I don't want to be drawn into this. Us versus them. The surgeons and their spouses, who are almost always wives.

'It's their job.'

'Why do we do it?'

'Do what?'

'These parties? D'you enjoy them?'

I decide to be honest. 'Not altogether. I don't like being around drunk people. Not with my addiction.'

He looks surprised, yet he must know. We've talked about the fact I don't drink, albeit obliquely. 'Your addiction?'

'Alcohol.'

'I didn't know.'

We're silent for a while, then he slides his hand into the pocket of his jeans, his movements slow and uncoordinated. 'Smoke?'

I reach to take a cigarette from him. 'Thanks.' The air between us feels solid. Loaded. Something has to happen, or something will break. A resolve, or a defence. One of us has to speak.

'Listen—' I begin, but at the exact same moment he speaks, too. I don't catch what he says and ask him to repeat it.

'It's just . . .' he begins. His head lowers, he falters again.

'What? What is it?' I realize I know what he's about to say. 'It's just . . . what?'

From nowhere, I see Lukas. I imagine him kissing me. I think of my fantasy, I want it to be lust, pure lust, that threatens to crack my head against the wall behind me. I want his hands on me, desperate, pushing up my dress. I want to feel the desire to give in, to let him do what he likes.

I want to feel longing so strong that it turns into need, unstoppable need.

'Paddy—?' I begin, but he interrupts me.

'I just wanted to say I think you're very beautiful.' He takes my hand quickly, and I let him. I'm both shocked and not shocked at the same time. Part of me had known he'd say this to me, sooner or later.

Again I think of Lukas. His words, in someone else's mouth. It occurs that if Paddy were to look up, take the back of my neck with his hand, kiss me, I wouldn't stop him. Not if he does it now. This is the moment when I'm weak enough, but it won't last.

An absurd thought comes. It's you, I think. You standing outside my bedroom window, both there and not there . . .

And then he does it. He kisses me. There's no groping, no urgent pushing into my clothes. It's almost juvenile. It lasts for a few moments, and then we separate. I look at him. The world is still, the chatter from the party a distant murmur. This is the moment when we will either kiss again – this time with more urgency, more passion – or else one of us will look away and the moment will be over, lost for ever.

His eyes narrow. Something's wrong. He was looking at me, but now he's not. He's looking over my shoulder.

I turn round to follow his gaze. Someone's there.

Connor.

I stand up. The glass of wine that Paddy had been holding spills, soaking my dress, but I barely notice it. 'Stay here!' I hiss, forcing the door open. I begin to run. Paddy calls after me, but I ignore him, too.

'Connor!' I shout, once I'm outside. He's walking away, back towards his father. 'Connor!'

He stops, then turns to face me. His face is inscrutable. 'Mum! You're there! I couldn't find you.'

I catch up with him. I can't tell if he's being sarcastic, or whether I'm imagining it.

'What's up?'

'Dad sent me to look for you. He's making a speech or something.'

'Right.' I feel terrible, worse than if he'd just come out and said it. *I saw you kissing that guy. I'm telling Dad you're cheating on him.* At least then I'd know.

But he says nothing. He's impassive and unreadable. This is it, I think. I've screwed up. One indiscretion, in all this time, and my son has to be there to see it. It seems unfair, yet at the same time I deserve it.

'I'll be there in a second,' I say.

Once he's gone I go back to Paddy. 'Fuck!'

'Did he see us?'

I don't answer. I need to think.

'Did he say anything?'

'No. But that doesn't mean he didn't see us.' I run my fingers through my hair. 'Shit . . . !'

He moves towards me. I'm not sure what he's going to do, but then he takes my hand. 'It'll be fine.' His hand goes to my face, as if to stroke it.

'Paddy, no!'

'What's the problem . . . ?'

The problem? I want to say. My husband. My son. My dead sister.

'I like you. You like me. Come on . . .'

I remind myself he's drunk.

'No.'

'Julia—'

'No,' I say. 'Paddy, I'll never sleep with you. Ever.'

He looks wounded, as though I've slapped him.

'Paddy—' I begin, but he interrupts me.

'You really think you're something special, don't you?'

I try to stay calm.

'Paddy. You've had a lot to drink. Let's just go back and forget all about this. Okay?'

He looks at me. His eyes are cold.

'Fuck you,' he says.

Chapter Thirteen

It's three in the morning. It must be, maybe later. It's too hot, my skin is heavy. I can hear the soft sound of summer rain against the window. I'm exhausted, yet sleep has never felt further away.

My mind will not be still. I can't stop thinking about Paddy. What I should've done, and what I shouldn't. And I can't stop thinking about what my son might've seen. Or might not.

Hugh thought I'd had a drink. He asked me, on the way home. Casually, without looking in my direction. Hoping to ambush me, trick me into telling him the truth.

He spoke quietly. Connor was in the back, listening to his iPod. 'Darling. Have you . . . ?'

'What?'

'Did you have a drink?'

I was indignant. 'No!'

It took him a moment to work out whether to believe me. How far to push things.

'Okay. I just thought I saw Paddy take one for you.'

'He did. But I didn't drink any of it.'

I held my breath, but Hugh just shrugged. I looked over my shoulder; Connor was oblivious, a time bomb.

'I've already told you I won't drink again,' I said, looking back to my husband. 'I promise.'

*

Now, I throw back the covers. I go downstairs and pour myself a glass of water. My laptop's where I left it this morning, on the island unit in the kitchen.

I ought to leave it alone. It's the middle of the night; Lukas won't be online. No one will. Plus, haven't I done enough damage today? I rinse my glass and put it back on the drainer, then step over to the window. It's dark outside. I look out, at the garden. My own reflection hovers above the patio.

He hasn't been in touch since yesterday afternoon; he was drunk even then. Who knows what kind of state he'll have been in by the time he went to bed? I imagine him, lying face down in his hotel room, half undressed, one shoe kicked off.

Or maybe he's not alone. People pair off at weddings; romance is in the air, alcohol on tap, hotel rooms never very far away. What if some woman has attached herself to him? Or he to her? What if . . .

I stop myself. Why am I even thinking like this? It's not as if I have any reason to be jealous.

I sit down. I can't help myself.

He's online. At first I think maybe he's just left his computer switched on, but then he sends me a message.

– You're there! Can't sleep either?

I smile. It's as if we're connected somehow.

– No. Had a good time?

– I only got in about an hour ago. I didn't want to go to bed.

– Why?

– Hoping I'd get the chance to speak to you, I suppose. I was going to ring, but didn't want to wake you.

I feel a mix of emotions. I'm flattered, yet relieved. Hugh

would have heard the call, and who knows what he might have thought?

It would have been an irresponsible thing to do, but then I remind myself that Lukas thinks I'm single. Available.

– I wasn't asleep.

– I couldn't stop thinking of you. All day today. I wished there was some way you could've been there. Some way I could show you off to people.

I smile to myself. Not for the first time I wonder how he always manages to say the right thing.

After a moment his next message arrives.

– I have a confession.

I try to keep it light.

– Sounds ominous! Good or bad?

– I don't know.

Is this it, I think?

– Then you'd better tell me.

I wonder how I'd feel if he were to type, 'I was in Paris in February and I did a terrible thing.'

I remember the Facebook page I've looked at. It's not that.

– It's good, I think. I didn't tell you before because I wasn't sure, but now I am.

There's a pause.

– But I want to tell you face to face. I want to meet you.

Whatever is growing inside me swells further. I realize part of me wants that, too, but another part wants just to look him in the eye. To appraise him, weigh him up. To assess what he knows, or might have done.

I shake the image away. I'm getting too close to the edge. I'm married. He's in Milan, I'm in London. I can't see it happening. It's a fantasy. That's all. Preposterous. I'm only imagining it because I know it's impossible. Lukas must exist in a box; there has to be a protective barrier between him and my real life.

Another message arrives.

– We *can* meet, he says. I didn't want to tell you in case it freaked you out, but the wedding was in London.

I freeze.

– I'm here. Now.

Fear ripples through me, but it's mixed with something else. Excitement; my stomach knots and tips, I can taste the metallic kick of adrenalin on my tongue. My excuses have vanished. He's here, we're in the same city. It's as if he's standing right in front of me. The things I'd thought about, the things he'd described doing to me, could really happen. If I want them to. But, more importantly, I could meet him, on my terms, my own turf. I could find out what he knows. Whether he knew my sister.

I try to calm myself. I type.

– Why didn't you tell me?

I'm relieved that he can't see me, can't see the anxiety written on my face.

– I don't know. I wasn't sure you'd want to meet me. I wasn't sure it was a good idea. But something happened today. I missed you, in a weird way. Maybe because I had your number. Anyway, I know it's what I want. You're what I want.

His words sit there, on the screen.

You're what I want.

– Tell me you want to meet me, too.

Do I? Yes, I think. For Kate. If he knew her she might have told him about others, people she'd met. She might've told him all kinds of things, things she told no one else. He might be able to help me.

I think of what both Adrienne and Anna have both told me. *Be careful.*

I wish I'd told him about Hugh. I wish he knew I was married, that I have a son. That things are not as simple as they seem. I could be honest then. I could tell him how impossible it is for me to meet him, no matter how much I might want to. I wouldn't have to invent an excuse.

– You do want to meet me, don't you?

I hesitate. I should tell him I'm busy. I have something I can't get out of. A meeting, I could say. An appointment. I could even tell him I'm about to take a flight, off on holiday. I could be vague. 'Such a pity,' I'd tell him. 'Maybe next time.'

But he'd know what that means, really. *Next time*, meaning, *never*. And then I'd lose everything, all the progress I've already made. And for the rest of my life I would wonder if he might have held the key to unlocking what happened that cold February night in Paris, and I'd just let him slip through my fingers.

I think back to his first words to me. *You remind me of someone.*

I make my decision.

– Of course! How long are you here for?

– Until Tuesday evening. We could meet that day. Around lunchtime.

I know what Adrienne would say. She's made it clear. Talk to Hugh. Give his details to the police and then walk away.

But I can't do that. They'll do nothing. My hands hover over the keyboard. It's getting light outside; soon my husband will get up, then Connor. Another day will begin, another week. Everything will be exactly the same.

I have to do something.

Chapter Fourteen

Morning. Hugh and Connor have left, for work and school. I don't know what to do with myself.

I call Anna. She doesn't answer, but a minute later I get a text message. 'Everything OK?'

I tell her it's urgent and she says she'll make an excuse. A few minutes later she rings back. Her voice echoes; I guess she is in one of the bathrooms at work.

'Well, we didn't see that coming!' she says, once I've explained what happened last night. 'You've told him you'll meet him?'

I think back to my final message.

'Yes.'

'Okay . . .'

'You think it's a bad idea.'

'No,' she says. 'No. It's just . . . you really need to be careful. You're sure he's who he says he is?'

Yes, I think. I'm as sure as I can be about someone I've never met.

'He could be anyone,' she says.

I know what she's trying to tell me but I want someone on my side. 'You think I shouldn't go.'

'I didn't say that.'

'I just have to know. One way or the other.'

'But—'

'For Connor, as much as for me.'

She doesn't answer. I hear something in the background, running water, voices, a door closing, then she speaks.

She sounds anxious, yet somehow excited, too, as if she senses that we're edging closer to the truth.

'You'll meet him somewhere in public?'

We've arranged to meet in his hotel, at St Pancras.

'Of course.'

'Promise me.'

'I promise.'

'Could you take a friend? Adrienne?'

'He thinks we're meeting for . . . well, he thinks it's a date.'

'So, she can sit in a corner. You don't have to introduce her.'

She's right. But I already know what Adrienne would say if I asked her, and there's no one else I can go to.

'I'll think about it.'

'Ask her!'

'Okay . . .'

I wish she weren't so far away.

'I'll be fine.'

'I know,' she says. 'Just promise me you'll be careful.'

'I will.'

I get ready. I shower, moisturize. I shave my legs with a fresh razor, the same number of strokes on each leg. An absurd need for symmetry I haven't experienced in years.

I talk to Hugh over breakfast. I toy with the idea of telling him the truth, but I know what he'll think, what he'll say. He'll make me feel absurd. He'll stop me from going through with it. And so I need an excuse, an alibi, in case he rings and

I don't answer, or comes home unexpectedly. 'Darling,' I say, as we sit down with our coffee. 'I've got something to tell you.'

'What is it? What's wrong?'

He looks so worried. I feel a sharp stab of guilt.

'Oh, it's nothing serious. It's just that I've been thinking about your idea. About seeing someone. A counsellor. And I've decided you're right.'

He takes my hand. 'Julia,' he says. 'That's great. I really don't think you'll regret it. I can ask a colleague, if you like, see if they can recommend someone—'

'No,' I say, a little too hurriedly. 'No, it's okay. I've found someone. I'm seeing them later.'

He nods. 'Who? You know their name?'

'Yes, of course.'

There's a silence. He's waiting.

'Who is it?'

I hesitate. I don't want to tell him, but I have no choice. And, really, it can't hurt. He'll observe the Hippocratic oath. He might look him up, but he'll never try to contact him. 'Martin Green.'

'You're sure he's good? I know plenty of people who could recommend—'

'Hugh, I'm not one of your patients. This is something I have to do, by myself. Okay?' He begins to protest, but I silence him. 'Hugh! It's fine. Adrienne says he's very good and, anyway, it's just an initial consultation. Just to see how we get on. Trust me. Please?'

I see him relax. I smile, to show him any anger has vanished. He returns my smile, then kisses me. 'I'm proud of you,' he says. I feel guilt wash over me, but ride it out. 'Well done.'

*

Now, I go over to my wardrobe. I must choose my clothes carefully. I have to convince Lukas I am who he thinks I am, that I want what he thinks I want.

I try my jeans with a white blouse, then a dress with tights and boots. I stand in front of the mirror. Better, I think. I choose a necklace and make up my face – not too much, it's the middle of the day, after all – but enough for me not to feel like me any more.

Maybe that's what I'm doing, really. Choosing the clothes that will turn me from Julia into that other person, the one Lukas has met online. Into Jayne.

I sit at the dressing table and spray my perfume, a squirt behind each ear, one more on each wrist. It smells buttery and sweet. It's expensive, something Hugh bought me for Christmas a couple of years ago. Fracas. My mother used to wear it, and it was always Kate's favourite, too. Its fragrance makes me feel closer to them both.

Finally, I'm ready. I look in the mirror. At my reflection. I think of my photo. *Marcus in the Mirror.* I remember that first time we had sex. I've never lacked confidence, but that night, even as he kissed me, I thought he might pull away. Even as he undressed me, I thought, this is the first time, and it will also be the last. Even as he entered me, I thought, I can't possibly be good enough for this man.

And yet I was. We started seeing each other. We started missing meetings, now and again at first, then more often than not. And then we moved to Berlin. It was cold; I remember we slept rough that first night, and then hooked up with friends he had out there. A week of sleeping on floors turned into a month, and then we found a place of our own, and—

And I don't want to think about it now. About how happy we were.

*

I stand up. I check my phone for messages. Part of me hopes he's cancelled. I could undress then, take off the make-up, put on the jeans and shirt I was wearing when I said goodbye to Hugh this morning. I could make myself a cup of tea and sit in front of the television, or with a novel. This afternoon I could do some work, ring some people. Along with my relief I could nurse a quiet resentment, I could vow never to message him again and then go back to Hugh and spend the rest of my life wondering whether Lukas knew Kate, whether he might have led me to the man who killed her.

But there are no messages; he hasn't changed his mind, and I'm not disappointed. For the first time in months I get the sense that something will happen, one way or another. I feel a kind of elasticity; the future is unknown, but it seems malleable, pliable. It has a softness, where before it'd felt as hard and unyielding as glass.

I take a taxi. It's sticky with the heat, even with the window open. The sweat trickles down my back. In the cab there's the same advert I saw on my way home from dinner with Adrienne. BE WHO YOU WANT TO BE.

We reach St Pancras. The car sweeps up the cobbled drive, the door is opened for me. I feel a breeze on my neck as I get out and go into the hotel. The doors slide open and marble stairs lead into the relief of the air-conditioned interior. The roof above us is glass, with iron girders, part of the old station, I guess. It's all elegance here, cut flowers, the smell of lemon and leather and wealth. I look around the lobby; two men sit side by side on a green sofa; a woman in a suit reads the paper. There are signs: RESTAURANT, SPA, MEETING ROOMS. Behind the reception desk all is busy and efficient; I look at my watch and see that I'm early.

I take out my phone. No messages.

I wait for my breathing to slow, my heart to stop its insistent alarm, its attempts to warn. I slip off my wedding ring and put it in my purse. My hand feels naked now, as does the rest of me, but without my ring what I'm about to do feels less of a betrayal, somehow.

At the reception desk I ask for the bar. The guy is young and impossibly good-looking. He points me in the right direction and wishes me a nice day. I thank him and step away. His eyes burn into me as I retreat, as if he knows why I'm here. I want to turn round and tell him it's not what he thinks, I'm not going to go through with it.

I'm only pretending.

Lukas is sitting at the bar, his back to me. I'd worried I wouldn't recognize him, but he's unmistakable. He's wearing a tailored suit, though as I get closer I see he hasn't bothered with the tie. Some effort, but not too much. Like me, I guess. I'm surprised to see a glass of champagne in front of him, another in front of the empty seat at his side. I remind myself I'm here for Kate.

Her face floats in front of me. She's a little girl, seven or eight. Our father has told us he's sending us to boarding school, just for a couple of years, though we both know it'll be until Kate leaves home. She looks terrified, and once again I'm telling her it'll work out. 'You'll have me,' I say, 'and you'll make loads of other friends. I promise!'

I didn't know whether she would, back then. She had a temper, was developing a wild streak. She could take things to heart and get herself in trouble. But she did make friends, eventually. One of them must have been Anna, but there were others. Life was difficult for her, but she wasn't unhappy, not always. And I looked after her. I did my best. Until . . .

No, I think. I can't think of that now. I can't bring Marcus into the room. And so I push the image away and walk over.

Lukas hasn't seen me yet, and I'm glad. I want to arrive suddenly, to be there before he's had the chance to appraise me from a distance. He's ten years younger than me, and looks it. I'm nervous enough, I don't want to risk seeing a flash of disappointment as he sees me approach.

'Hi!' I say, when I reach him.

He looks up. His eyes are deep blue, even more striking in real life. For the briefest of moments his face is expressionless, his gaze invading, as if he's unpicking me, learning me from within. He looks as if he has no idea who I am, or why I'm there, but then he breaks into a broad smile and stands up.

'Jayne!' I don't correct him. There's a momentary flicker of surprise and I realize he thought I wouldn't come.

'You made it!' He's grinning with relief, which makes me feel relieved, too. I sense we're both nervous, which means neither of us has all the power.

'Of course I did!' I say. There's an awkward moment. Should we kiss? Shake hands? He pushes my drink towards me.

'Well, I'm glad.' There's another pause. 'I got you some champagne. I wasn't sure what you'd want.'

'Thanks. I might just get some sparkling water.'

I slide into my seat and he orders my drink. I look at him, at this unshaven, blue-eyed man, and again ask myself why I'm here. I've been telling myself it's to find out whether he knew my sister, but there's more, of course there is.

I wonder whether I'm being naive. Whether it might be him she was going to meet that night. The thought assaults me. It's brutal. The man in front of me looks incapable of violence, but that means nothing. It's not only those who have shaved their heads or inked their bodies that are capable of wielding weapons.

I remind myself of what I've seen. Of where he was in February. I begin to calm down as my water arrives.

'There you go. You're not drinking?'

'No. I don't.'

I see the familiar readjustment that people make when I tell them. I know they're trying to figure out whether I'm a puritan, possibly religious, or an addict.

As usual, I say nothing. I don't need to make excuses. Instead I look around the bar. It used to be the ticket office; people would queue here before boarding their train, and many of the old features – the wood panelling, the huge clock on the wall above us – have been retained. It's busy; people sit with their suitcases, or newspapers. They're eating lunch, or afternoon tea. They're in transit, or else staying in the hotel above. For a moment I wish I were one of them. I wish the reason I find myself here could be that uncomplicated.

As if for the first time, I realize Lukas has a room, just a few floors above. The reason he thinks I'm here swims into focus.

'Are you okay?' he says. There's a tension in the air; we're hesitant. I remind myself that he thinks we're both single and that even if his path has crossed with Kate's there's still no reason I should be finding this difficult.

'Fine. Thanks.' I pick up the glass as if to prove it. 'Cheers!'

We chink our glasses. I try to imagine him with my sister. I can't.

I wonder what would usually happen now. I imagine Kate, or Anna – I know she's done this kind of thing, too. I see kissing, tearing at each other's clothes. I see people being pushed on to a bed in fevered lust. I see naked bodies, flesh.

I sip my water. When I put my glass down there's lipstick on the rim and I'm shocked, momentarily, by its colour. It seems bright, as if it's in Technicolor, plus it's not what I wear, not in the middle of the day. It's not me. Which was the point of wearing it, of course.

I feel lost. I'd thought this would be easy. I'd thought I'd meet him and the answers would spill out, the path to the truth about what happened to Kate instantly become clear. But it's never felt more muddied, and I don't know what to do.

'You look beautiful,' he says. I grin and thank him. I look at him. He looks solid, more solid than anything has looked for a long time. I can hardly believe he's here, that with almost no effort at all I could reach out and touch his flesh.

He smiles. I hold his gaze, but still, somehow, it's me that feels naked. I look away. I think of Hugh, at work, a body under the sheets in front of him, flesh parted, wet and glistening. I think of Connor in the classroom, his head bent over his desk at the end of another school year, the long holidays in front of him. And then Lukas smiles and I put these feelings back, lock them away. He puts down his glass and my eyes catch on something glinting on his left hand.

I'm almost relieved. It's a shock, but the awkwardness that has built between us is broken.

'You're married.'

'I'm not.'

'But your ring . . .'

He looks at his own hand, as if to check what I've seen, then at me. 'I never told you?'

I shake my head. I remind myself that I can't accuse him of deception, with the lies I've told.

'I *was* married . . .' He takes a deep breath, then sighs heavily. 'Cancer. Four years ago.'

'Oh.' I'm shocked. It's brutal. I search his eyes and see only pain. Pain, and innocence. I reach out my hand as if to take his. I do it automatically, without thinking. A moment later he reaches and takes hold of mine. There's no crackle of electricity, no spark of energy jumping from one to the other. Even so, I'm dimly aware that this is the first time we've touched, and the moment therefore has significance no matter what happens next.

'I'm so sorry.' It feels inadequate, as it always does.

'Thank you. I loved her very much. But life goes on. It's a cliché, but it's true.' He smiles. He's still holding my hand. Our eyes lock. I blink, slowly, but I don't look away. I feel something, something I've not felt for a long time, so long I can't quite work out what it is.

Desire? Power? A mixture of both? I can't tell.

Once again I try to visualize him with Kate. I'd know, surely? All through our childhood I'd known what she was thinking, when she was in trouble. If this man had anything to do with her death then wouldn't I just know?

'I can't bear this any more. Shall we go upstairs?'

This isn't right. This isn't why I came.

'I'm sorry. Can we just talk, for a while?'

He smiles and says, 'Of course.' He takes off his jacket and hangs it over the back of the chair, then takes my hand once again. I let him. We speak for a while, but it's small talk, we're avoiding things, though what we're avoiding is different for each of us. For me it's Kate, but for him? The fact he wants to take me upstairs, I guess. After a few minutes there's a moment of decision. He's finished his drink, mine is gone already. We can get more and carry on talking, or we can leave. There's a hesitation, a drawing in, then he says, 'I'm sorry. For not telling you I was married, I mean.' I don't reply. 'Can I ask you something?'

'Of course.'

'Why did you say you were in Paris? When we first talked, I mean.'

We're skirting the edges now, circling in.

'I was. I was on holiday out there.'

'Alone?'

I think of Anna. 'With a friend.' I see my chance. 'Why? When were you last there?'

He thinks for a moment. 'September last year, I think it was.'

'Not since?'

His head tilts. 'No, why?'

'No reason.' I try a different tack.

'You have friends there?'

'Not really. No.'

'No one?'

He laughs. 'Not that I can think of!'

I pretend to look wistful. 'I've always wanted to be there in winter. February. Valentine's day in Paris, you know?' I smile, as if dreaming. 'Must be beautiful.'

'So romantic.'

I sigh. 'I guess. You've never been in winter?'

He shakes his head. 'It's funny, I can't imagine it snowing there. I guess I associate it with the summer. You're right, though. It must be beautiful.'

I look at my glass. Why would he lie? He doesn't know who I am. Why would he tell me he'd never been to Paris in winter if he had?

'So who's your friend over there?'

I look puzzled.

'The one you were visiting?'

'Oh, just a friend.' I hesitate, but I've already decided what I have to do. 'I thought you might know her actually.'

154

'Know her?'

'She sometimes uses encountrz.'

He smiles. 'I don't know many people off that site, believe it or not.'

I force myself to laugh. 'No?'

'No. You're the first person I've met.'

'Really?'

'I swear.'

I realize I believe him. He never talked to Kate. Disappointment begins to build.

'But you talk to people on there?'

'A few. Not that many.'

I know what I have to do. I take out my phone and unlock the screen. I'm smiling, trying to keep it light. 'Wouldn't it be funny . . .' I'm saying '. . . such a coincidence . . . She'd love it if . . .'

I hold my phone out to him. I've opened a picture of Kate. I force myself to speak.

'This is her. My friend.'

Silence. I look straight at him as he takes my phone in his hand.

'Have you chatted to her?'

His face is expressionless. I'm aware that the next emotion that flashes in his eyes will tell me the truth. I've sprung the photo on him, he's unprepared. If he's ever seen Kate before he'll give himself away. He has to.

There's a long moment, then his face breaks into a grin. He looks at me. He's shaking his head, laughing. 'Never seen her online, no. But she looks like fun.'

I can see that he's telling the truth. I'm certain of it. More disappointment slides in, yet it's muted, and mixed with relief. 'She is!' I say. I force myself to smile and put my phone away. I begin to babble. 'To be honest, she doesn't go online that much. Not any more . . . in fact, I'm not sure she ever did, really . . .'

Lukas is laughing. I worry that he can tell something's wrong. 'It would have been quite a coincidence! Shall we get another drink?'

I say no. 'I'm fine, thanks.'

I try to calm down.

'So how about you? Do you meet up with many people you speak to online?'

'No, not really. No.'

'But you met with me.'

'Yes. Yes I did.'

He takes my hand again. He's looking me in the eye.

I can hardly breathe. He didn't know my sister. He never met her.

'Why?'

I should stand up. I know that. I should walk away, tell him I'm going to the bathroom, never come back. It'd be easy enough; he doesn't know where I live.

I will, I tell myself. Soon.

'I like you, I guess.'

'And I like you.'

He leans towards me. He sighs. I can feel his breath on my cheek.

'I like you a great deal.'

I can feel the warmth of his skin, I can smell his aftershave, mingled with sweat. He's opened me. Something I've been holding in check for weeks, months, years, is flooding me.

'Let's go upstairs.'

'No. No, I'm sorry—'

'Jayne . . .' He's almost whispering. 'Beautiful Jayne . . . I'll be gone tomorrow. This is our one chance. You want it, don't you? You want me?'

I look back at him. I feel more alive than I can remember.
I don't want it to stop. Not yet. It can't be over.

I nod.

'Yes.'

He's kissing me, his hands are around my waist, he's pulling
me towards him and yet at the same time pushing me back,
back, back towards the bed. I fall backwards on to it and
then he's on top of me and I'm pulling the shirt from his
trousers, unbuttoning it blindly and with clumsy hands, and
his hands are on my chest, and then his mouth, and it's all
sweat and fury and I don't resist, because there's no point,
that line is already crossed, it was crossed when I walked up
to him in the bar, crossed when I left the house to come here,
crossed when I said, 'Yes, yes, yes, I'll come and meet you,'
and there's no point in pretending otherwise. My betrayal
has been gradual but inexorable, the sweep of the hand on a
clock, and it's led me here, to this afternoon. And right now,
with his hands on my naked flesh, and mine on his, with his
prick stiffening between my legs, I'm not sorry. I have no
regrets at all. I realize how stupid I've been. All along, from
the very beginning, this is what it'd been about.

When we finish we lie on our backs, side by side. The after-
glow. But it's awkward somehow; I understand now why it's
called the little death, but even if that's true at least it means
I was alive before.

He turns to face me. He props his head on his arm, and
again I'm aware of the years between us, the fact that he's
Kate's age, more or less. His skin is taut and firm, his
muscles flex when he moves, visible, alive. As we made love
I'd been shocked by this, and now I wonder if it's something
I ever had with Hugh. I can't quite remember; it's as if my

memories of a younger him have somehow been overwritten by all that's happened since.

I remind myself that being ten years younger than me makes Lukas twenty younger than my husband.

He reaches out to stroke my arm. 'Thank you . . .' I feel it should be me thanking him, but I don't. We say nothing for a while. I look at his body, now that it's still. I look at his stomach, which is firm, and at the hairs on his chest, none of which are grey. I examine his mouth, his lips, which are moist. I look into his eyes and see he's looking at me in the same way.

He kisses me. 'You hungry? Shall we get something to eat?'

'In the restaurant?'

'We could get something sent up.'

It must be nearly three, I think, possibly even later. Connor will be back soon. And even if he weren't, even if I had all the time in the world, having lunch with this man seems somehow like a step too far. It would be a sharing of more than just our bodies, would imply a greater intimacy than what we've already done, which was just lust, and flesh.

I smile.

'What's funny?'

'Nothing.'

I realize a part of me wants to get away. I need to be on my own, to find solitude and process what I've just done, and the reasons I did it. I didn't mean to, when I came here, yet here I am. 'I'd love some lunch, but I probably ought to get going. Soon.'

He strokes my shoulder. 'Have you got to go?'

'Yes.' I search for an excuse. 'I'm meeting someone. A friend.'

He nods his head. I realize I'd like him to ask me to stay, I'd like him to beg me to cancel my friend, I'd like to see disappointment when I tell him I can't.

But I know he won't ask. Spending the rest of the day together was never part of the deal he thought he'd struck with me; it's against the terms of our engagement. And so the silence between us extends, becomes almost uncomfortable. The schizophrenia of lust; it's hard to believe the intimacy we shared just a few moments ago can evaporate almost in an instant. I become aware of the details in the room, the clock on the TV that's mounted on the wall opposite, the fireplace, the stack of old hardback books on the mantelpiece that surely no one reads. I hadn't noticed them before.

'When's your flight?'

He sighs. 'Not till tonight. Eight o'clock, I think.' He kisses me. I wonder dimly why he hasn't checked out, then realize I'm the reason. 'I have all afternoon.' He kisses me again. Harder, this time. 'Stay . . .'

I think of him getting on his flight, going back home. I think of never seeing him again. I remember when I'd thought the same thing about Marcus, when I believed that he'd meet someone else in Berlin, someone more interesting, and I would end up coming home, back to Kate and my father, my old life. But he hadn't. Our love had deepened, intensified. In winter we would open the window of our apartment and crawl out on to the cold ledge. We'd wrap ourselves in a blanket and look at the Fernsehturm glowing in the bright blue sky, talking about our future, all the places we'd go and the things we'd see. Or else we'd take a bottle of cheap wine, or vodka, to Tiergarten, or hang out at Zoo Station. I had my camera; I took pictures of the rent boys, the dropouts and runaways. We met people, our lives expanded, opened out. I missed Kate dreadfully, but I didn't regret leaving her behind.

But that was the old me. I can't behave like that any more.

'I'm sorry,' I begin. I have the distinct impression that I'm slipping away, that Jayne – the me, the version of me, that is able to do what I've just done – is disappearing. Soon it will be replaced by Julia – mother, wife and, once upon a time, daughter. I'm not sure I want her to go.

'I really have to—'

'Please don't.' He's fierce now, and for a moment he looks so desperate, so alive with desire, that I feel a sudden rush which takes me by surprise. It's happiness, I think. I'd forgotten what it was like, this pure, uncomplicated happiness, more powerful than any drug. It's not what I just did, what I realize I'm about to do again. It's not that I've deceived my husband and got away with it. It's me. I have something, now, something that's mine. A private thing, a secret. I can keep it hidden, in a box, and take it out occasionally, like a treasure. I have something that belongs to no one else.

'Stay,' he says. 'For a while at least.' And I do.

Chapter Fifteen

I go home. When I open the door I find a handful of post-cards pushed through the letterbox. I bend down to pick them up and with a gasp of shock see that they're the post-cards that prostitutes leave in phone boxes. On each there's a picture of a woman, a different woman, wearing lingerie, or nothing at all, and posing next to a phone number. 'Hot Young Slut', says one, 'Spanking fun', reads another. Straight away my mind goes to the last thing Paddy had said to me – *Fuck you* – and straight away I tell myself they're from him. He's pushed them through the door in a fit of childish, spiteful anger.

I try to calm myself down. I'm being paranoid. They can't be from him, surely. It's as ridiculous as me thinking it was him standing outside my window. The simpler the explanation, the more likely it is to be true, and Paddy would've had to travel across town, on a day when he's supposed to be at work, during a time when he knew I wouldn't be in the house. It's much more likely it was kids. Just kids, messing about.

Yet still I can taste fear in my mouth as I tear them into little pieces and put them in the bin. I ignore it. I won't let it get to me. It's nothing, nothing to worry about, a stupid prank. I must stop being paranoid.

I go upstairs and step out of my boots. I take off the

make-up I'd put on earlier, then the clothes. It's hard to imagine that just a few hours ago I was putting all this stuff on; it's as if a film's playing backwards, a life spooling in reverse. By the end it's a different me standing here, in front of the mirror. Julia. Not better, not worse. Just different.

I put my jeans on, a shirt, then go back downstairs. My phone rings. It sounds alien, too loud. I'm annoyed; I'd wanted more time with my own thoughts before the real world crashed back in, but when I pick it up I see it's Anna and am pleased. She's someone I can talk to, someone I can be honest with.

'How did it go? Did you find anything?'

'He knows nothing. I'm certain of it.'

She hesitates, then says, 'I'm sorry.'

Her voice is soft. She knows how much I need answers.

'It's okay.'

'I really thought—' she begins, but I'm gripped with an urge to tell the truth and she's the one person who might understand.

'We had sex.'

'What?'

I say it again. I consider telling her I thought it might help, but I don't. It's not true, no matter how much I might want to believe it. We had sex because I wanted to.

'Are you all right?'

I wonder if I'm supposed to feel bad. I don't.

'Yes. Fine. I enjoyed it.'

'Is this because of Kate?'

Is it? I don't know. Did I want to have sex with Lukas so that I could walk in her shoes?

Either way, I understand her better now.

'Maybe.'

'Will you see him again?'

Her question shocks me. I search for a hint of condemnation in it, but there's none. I know she understands.

'No. No, I won't. In any case, he leaves tonight.'

'You're all right about that?'

'I don't have any choice,' I say. 'But yes, yes I am.'

I'm trying to sound light, unconcerned. I'm not sure she believes me. 'If you're sure,' she says, and then I change the subject. We talk some more, about her, and her boyfriend, Ryan, and how well it's going. She says I ought to come and visit her again, when I get the chance, and tells me that she'll be over with work in the next few weeks but hasn't been given the dates yet. 'We could catch up then,' she says. 'Go for dinner, maybe. Have a bit of fun.'

Fun. I wonder what kind of fun she means. I remember she's younger than me, but not by that much.

'That'd be great,' I say. I know I must sound distracted. I'm still thinking of Lukas, imagining meeting him again, wondering what it might be like to be able to introduce him to my friends one day, wondering if the reason I never will is what makes the thought so appealing.

I remind myself that this is my real life. Anna is my real friend. Not Lukas. 'I'd like that a lot,' I say.

Connor gets in. I make him a sandwich and tell him to make sure he remembers to put his PE kit in the laundry, then a while later I hear Hugh's key in the lock. He comes into the kitchen as I'm cooking dinner. I kiss him, as usual, and watch as he gets a drink, then takes off his tie and hangs his jacket carefully over the back of the chair. The guilt I feel is predictable, but surprisingly short-lived. What I did this afternoon has nothing to do with the love I feel for my husband. Lukas in one box, Hugh in another.

'How was your day?' I say.

He doesn't answer, which I know means *not good*. He asks how my session of therapy went.

'Okay.' I'm aware I sound unconvincing. 'Good, I think.'

He comes over, puts a hand on my arm. 'Don't give up on it. It takes time. I know you're doing the right thing.'

I smile, then go back to the dinner. Hugh says he's going up to his office, and I'm glad, but as he turns to leave I can't bear it any more. He's not himself. His voice is flat, he's moving as if the air is thick. Something is wrong.

'Darling?'

He turns round.

'What is it?'

'Bad day,' he says. 'That's all.'

I put down the knife I'd been using to chop vegetables. 'Want to talk about it?'

He shakes his head. The disappointment slices into me and I realize how much I want to feel connected with my husband. Right now, after what happened this afternoon – after what I did – I need him to confide in me. His reticence feels like a rejection.

'Hugh?'

'It's nothing,' he says. 'Honestly. We'll talk later.'

We eat our dinner, the three of us, then sit at the table in the kitchen. Connor is opposite me, his computer open in front of him, a notepad and a stack of biology textbooks next to it. He's studying the valves of the heart, his father's subject, and leans into the screen, clicking his trackpad regularly. He has a look of intense concentration. Hugh sits next to him with a paper, making notes of his own, occasionally glancing at Connor's work, making a comment when he's asked a question. He seems back to normal now; whatever was bothering him earlier is forgotten, or pushed below the surface. It was probably nothing. Just my imagination. My phone buzzes as another message arrives.

– I wish I'd bought you flowers this afternoon. You deserve a little romance.

I put my phone back, face down. I look up at my family. They haven't noticed, and couldn't possibly see what it says, yet still I feel guilty. I shouldn't be doing this, not here, not now.

But I'm not doing anything. Not really. It buzzes again.

– You're amazing. In a weird way it feels like I've known you for ages.

This time I have to reply.

– Really? You think so?

– Yes.

His reply is instant. I picture him, at his keyboard, waiting for my next response.

– You're not so bad yourself.

I press send, then type another message.

– And you did buy me champagne.

– Which you didn't drink.

– But you bought it for me. That's the main thing.

– It's the least you deserve.

Hugh coughs and I look up. He's looking at me, at the phone in my hand. 'Is everything all right?'

'Oh, yes.' I'm trying to keep my voice steady. 'It's just Anna. She's thinking of coming over.'

'To stay here?' says Connor, looking up expectantly. I wonder if he's thinking about Kate, about what he might find out about his mother from her oldest friend.

'No. No, I don't think so. She's coming for work. I imagine they'd put her up in a hotel.'

He says nothing. It crosses my mind that it might do him

good, to get to know Anna a little better. I tell myself I'll make sure they meet, when she comes.

I look back at my phone. Another message.

– What are you up to?

The question is undeniably sexual. Yet when he's asked me that before, back when we were first chatting, the same words had been entirely innocent.

Or maybe I'd just chosen not to see them for what they were.

Hugh stands up. 'I'll make a coffee,' he says. 'Julia?'

I tell him I don't want one. He goes over to the machine and switches it on before filling its tank from the tap behind me. I hold my phone closer to my chest. Just slightly.

'How is she?'

'Fine,' I say. 'I think.'

'I hadn't realized you were still in touch.'

I'm surprised. He must know we've been talking. It crosses my mind that he suspects, somehow, that I'm lying.

'Oh, yes.'

He doesn't answer. As he sits back down my phone buzzes once more.

– Are you there?

Hugh notices. He looks annoyed, or upset. I can't tell.

'Sorry, darling.'

'It's fine.' He picks up his pen, as if he's about to go back to his paper. His annoyance has lasted only for a moment. 'Message your friend. We'll talk later.'

'I'm sorry.' I switch my phone off, but Connor has already started asking his father something about arteries and in a moment Hugh will be busy with an explanation. I'm hurting no one.

'I'm just going to go and do some work,' I say.

*

I cross the garden and go into the shed that is my office. I put my phone down and open my laptop.

– Sorry, I type. I was out. I'm at home now.

– Doing?

– Nothing.

– Wearing?

– What do you think?

There's a pause, then:

– I need to see you again. Say you want to see me, too.

Yes, I think. I do. Funny how much less ambiguous my desires are now that they can't be fulfilled.

– Of course I do.

– I'm imagining you. Naked. It's all I can think about . . .

I'm sitting on the stool. I can feel the metal footrest under my feet, the hard acrylic of the seat beneath my buttocks. I close my eyes. I can see him, here in the room with me. He seems real. More real than anything else.

I don't reply for a moment. I see my family, in the kitchen, Connor puzzled, Hugh helping him, sipping his coffee, but I push it down and instead imagine what Lukas is describing. I imagine what he wants to do.

I begin to type. I picture him as I write. He's standing behind me. I can smell his aftershave, the faint aroma of his sweat.

– I want to be naked for you.

– I want you so badly.

I think of his urgency this afternoon, his desperate need. The shock of his desire. I let it course through my body. I feel alive.

– I want you, too.

– I'm imagining it. I'm reaching over to you. Running my hand through your hair.

Again I flash on my husband, my son. This is wrong, I

think. I shouldn't be doing this. I should protest. But I can feel his hands on my scalp, both rough and gentle at the same time. Lukas is drawing it out of me, bit by bit he's making me feel safe, moment by moment encouraging abandonment. He coaxes out my fantasies and they're unfurling in front of him.

– Tell me what you want.

My hand goes to my throat. I imagine it's him, touching me.

– Tell me your desires.

I turn round. I slide the bolt that locks the door from the inside. I take a deep breath. Can I do this? I never have before.

– Tell me your fantasies.

There are lots of things I've never done before. I undo a button on my shirt.

I begin to type.

– I'm alone. In a bar. There's a stranger.

– Go on . . .

I let the images come.

– I can't take my eyes off him.

– He's dangerous . . .

– Someone I won't be able to say no to.

– Won't be able to say no to? Or who won't take no for an answer?

I hesitate, briefly. I know what he wants. I know what I want, too.

It's words on a screen, I tell myself. That's all.

– Who won't take no for an answer.

– What happens?

I breathe in deeply. I fill myself with possibility. I undo another button on my shirt. I'm hurting no one.

– Tell me, he says, and I do.

*

168

When we finish I'm not embarrassed. Not quite. I haven't described rape – it'd been more complicated than that, more nuanced – yet still I'm uneasy, as if I've somehow betrayed my sex.

It'd been a fantasy, I tell myself, and not an uncommon one, from what I've read. But not something I'd wish on anyone. Not in real life.

He sends me a message.

– Wow! You really are something.

Am I? I think. I don't feel it. In this moment, now it's over, I want to tell him everything. I want to explain about Hugh, the husband he doesn't know I have. I want to tell him about my gentle, caring, solicitous Hugh.

I also want to tell him that sometimes Hugh isn't enough. My need is raw and animal, and yes, yes, very occasionally I just want to feel used, like I'm nothing, just sex, just pure light and air.

And I want to explain that one person can't be everything, not all the time.

But how can I, when he doesn't even know Hugh exists?

– You, too, I say.

I look at the time. It's almost nine; I've been in here for nearly forty-five minutes.

– I have to go, I say, but then I hear the quiet roar of a plane flying overhead and something strikes me.

– Shouldn't you be in the air, now?

– I should.

– You missed your flight?

– Not missed. I cancelled it. I thought I'd have one more day in London.

– Why? I say. I'm hoping I already know the answer.

– To see you.

I'm not sure what to feel. I'm excited, yes, but underneath

it is something else. At the moment I can almost convince myself I haven't been unfaithful, haven't betrayed my husband. But if I see him again?

I tell myself I wouldn't have to sleep with him.

Another message arrives. It's not quite what I'm expecting.

– The truth is, he says, I have something I need to tell you.

Chapter Sixteen

We arrange to meet back at the hotel the following day. I arrive early; I want time to collect myself, to calm down. I'm nervous, I can't work out what this thing is he wants to tell me. It can't be something good, otherwise surely he'd have told me yesterday, as we lay in bed together, or last night as we chatted online. It's hard to prepare yourself for the worst, when you don't know what the worst will look like.

I'm distracted enough as it is. This morning Hugh has finally told me what was on his mind. He'd had a letter, a complaint. It had been copied to the head of the surgical directorate and the chief executive. 'A complaint?' I said. 'What happened?'

He poured the tea he'd made. 'Nothing, really. I did a bypass on a patient a few weeks ago. Pretty standard. Nothing unusual. He's fine, but has pumphead.'

I waited, but he didn't go on. He does this a lot. I'm expected to know.

'Which is?'

'Postperfusion syndrome. Poor attention, impaired fine motor skills, some short-term-memory problems. It's pretty common. Usually it gets better.'

'So why the complaint?'

He put his cup down. 'The family are claiming I didn't warn them it was a possibility pre-operatively. They're claiming it might've affected their decision if they'd known.'

'Did you?'

He looked at me. I couldn't tell if he was angry. 'Of course. I always do.'

'So what's the problem?'

'I pulled the notes from my consultation yesterday and went through them. I didn't make a note specifying that I'd warned the family that this was a possibility.' He sighed. 'And, apparently, if I didn't write it down then, legally, I might as well have said nothing. The fact that I *always* tell *every* patient makes no difference.'

I put my hand on his shoulder. 'Will it go further?'

'Well, the complaint is official.' He shook his head. 'It's pathetic. I mean, what would they have done, anyway? No one ever turns round and says they won't go through with a bypass because there's the danger they'll forget what's on their bloody shopping list for a few weeks! I mean . . .'

I watched as he fought to get his anger under control. He's grumbled to me before – about how unreasonable some patients can be, how determined they are to find something to complain about, however trivial – but this time he looks furious.

'There'll have to be an investigation. I'll write a letter of apology, I guess. But I know the type. They're after compensation. I didn't do anything wrong, but they'll take it as far as they can.'

'Oh, darling—'

'And right now that's the last thing I bloody need.'

I felt guilty. I've been wrapped up in Kate's death, forgetting that he's had a job, a life to continue, too. I told him we were in it together, we'd be fine. I almost forgot about Lukas.

*

Now, though, he's all I'm thinking about. I go through the station, up the stairs, on to the concourse by the platforms. I think of yesterday, and of the time I was here on my way to see Anna, to visit her in Paris. Back then, the only thing I'd been able to think about was Kate.

Lukas is waiting for me. Although we'd arranged to meet in the hotel lobby, he's just outside the bar, standing underneath the huge statue that sits at the end of the platforms – a man and a woman, embracing, he with his hands around her waist, she with hers held to his face and neck – holding a bunch of flowers. As I approach, I notice he hasn't seen me arrive. He's shuffling from foot to foot, nervous, but when he sees me he breaks into a grin. We kiss. To anyone watching it must look like we're trying to replicate the bronze statue that towers above us.

'It's called *The Meeting Place*,' he says, when we've separated. 'I thought I'd wait here, instead. Seemed appropriate.'

I smile. He's holding the flowers out to me. They're roses, deep lilac and very beautiful. 'These are for you.'

I take them from him. He leans in and kisses me again, but my hand goes to his shoulder as if to push him away. I feel so exposed; it's as if the whole world is in the station, watching us. I'm nervous, I seem to want everything at once: for him to get to the point quickly and leave, for him to invite me to stay for lunch, for him to tell me yesterday was a mistake, for him to confess to having no regrets at all.

But at first he's silent as we walk through the darkened bar towards the brightness of the lobby. 'It *is* you,' he says, once we've emerged into the light. I ask him what he means.

'That perfume. You were wearing it yesterday . . .'

'You don't like it?'

He shakes his head. He laughs. 'Not really.'

There's a momentary shock of disappointment. He must see it. He apologizes. 'It's fine. Just a bit too strong. For me, at least . . .'

I smile, and briefly look away. His comment hurts, just for an instant, but I tell myself it doesn't matter. There are more important things to worry about.

'I guess it is a bit overpowering. For the middle of the day.'

'Sorry,' he says. 'I shouldn't have mentioned it.' He opens the door and stands aside for me to go through.

'What was it you wanted to tell me?'

'I'll tell you in a little while. Let's get a drink?'

We sit, then order coffees. I put the flowers on top of the bag at my feet. It's as if I'm trying to hide them, and I hope he doesn't notice.

I ask him again why we're here. He sighs, then runs his fingers through his hair. I don't think it's nerves. He looks lost. And scared.

'Don't be mad, but I lied to you.'

'Okay.' It's the wife, I think. She's alive, and believes he's still out here because he missed his flight. 'Go on . . .'

'I know we started this only as an internet fling, but the thing is, I really want to see you again.'

I smile. I don't know what to think. I'm flattered, relieved, but I don't understand why there's been a build-up. *Something I need to tell you. Don't be mad.* There must be a *but . . .*

'Do you want to see me again?' He sounds hopeful, unsure.

I hesitate. I don't know what I want. I still can't quite shake the thought that he might help me find the answers I need.

Yet that's not the whole story. There's part of me that wants to see him again for reasons that have nothing to do with Kate at all.

'Yes,' I say. 'Yes, I do. But it's not that easy. You're going home today, and I live here, and—'

'I'm not going home today. Or not back to Italy, at least.'

'Okay . . .' Now we're getting to the point. My mind races ahead. *Where then?* I want to say. *Where?* But instead I just nod. Part of me already knows what he's going to say.

'I live here.'

The reaction is instant. My skin crawls; I'm hyper-sensitized. I can feel the sun on my shoulder, the roughness of the fabric of the seat, the weight of the wristwatch on my arm. It's as if everything that has been out of focus has snapped sharp.

'Here?'

He nods.

'In London?'

'No. But, not far away. I live just outside Cambridge.'

So that's why we're meeting here. At the station.

'Okay . . .' I'm still processing what he's told me. It's too intimate, too close. Perversely, the news makes me want to get away from him, so that I can sit with it for a moment and work out how I feel.

'You seem very . . . quiet.'

'It's nothing. It's just a surprise. You told me you lived in Milan.'

'I know, I'm sorry. You're not angry with me?' Suddenly he sounds so young, so naive. Somehow he reminds me of myself, when I was eighteen, nineteen, back when I was falling in love with Marcus.

He goes on. 'For lying, I mean. It was just one of those things you say when you think you're just chatting online and it's not going to lead anywhere. You know how it is—'

'I'm married.' It comes out abruptly, as if I weren't expecting it myself, and as soon as I've spoken I look away, over his shoulder. I don't know what his reaction will be, but whether it's anger, or disappointment, or something else entirely, I don't want to see it.

For a long moment he says nothing, but then he speaks.

'Married?'

'Yes. I'm sorry I never told you. I thought it didn't matter. I thought this was just an internet thing. Just like you.'

He sighs. 'I thought so.'

'You did?'

He nods towards my hand. 'Your ring. It leaves a mark.'

I look down at my hand. It's true. Around my finger there's an indentation, the inverse of the ring I normally wear, its negative.

He smiles but is clearly upset.

'What's he called?'

'Harvey.' The lie trips off my tongue easily, as if I'd known all along I'd have to tell it.

'What does he do?'

'He works in a hospital.'

'A doctor?'

I hesitate. I don't want to tell the truth. 'Sort of.'

'Do you love him?'

The question surprises me, but my answer comes instantly.

'Yes. I can't imagine life without him.'

'Sometimes that's just a lack of imagination, though . . .'

I smile. I could choose to be offended, but I don't. As it turns out, we've each had our lies. 'Maybe . . .' Our coffees arrive: a cappuccino for me, an espresso for him. I wait while he adds sugar, then say, 'But not for me and Harvey. I don't think it's a lack of imagination.'

I stir my coffee. Maybe he's right, and it is. Perhaps I can't imagine a life without Hugh because it's been so long since I've had one. Maybe he's become like a limb, something I take for granted, until it's missing. Or maybe he's like a scar. Part of me, no longer something I even notice, yet nevertheless indelible.

'So is this it, then?' His face is flushed; he looks childishly defiant. I look away, over to the desk. A couple are checking in; they're older, excited. They're American, asking lots of questions. Their first trip to Europe, I guess.

I realize that, while I might not know what Lukas and I have, I don't want it to be over. I've felt better, these last few days and weeks, and now I know it wasn't all to do with trying to find the person who murdered Kate.

'I don't want it to be. But my husband, he's the—' I stop myself. The father of my son, I was going to say, yet not only is that something I don't want to tell him, it's another lie. He looks at me expectantly. I need to say something.

'He's the person that saved me.'

'Saved you? From what?'

I pick up my coffee then put it down. I really want a drink. Ride it out. Ride it out.

'Another time, perhaps.'

'Shall we go upstairs?' he says. There's an urgency to his voice, as if he wants to finish his sentence before I can say no. 'I still have a room.'

I shake my head, even though I want to. I want to so much, but I know I mustn't. Not now. Now I know what might be possible. Ride it out, I tell myself again. Ride it out.

'No,' I say. 'I can't.'

He puts his hand on the table between us. I can't help myself. I put mine on top of it. 'I'm sorry.'

He looks up, into my eyes. He seems nervous, hesitant. 'Jayne. I get that we hardly know each other, but meeting you feels like the best thing that's happened since my wife died. I can't just let you go.'

'I'm afraid . . .'

'Are you saying yesterday was a mistake?'

'No. No, not at all. It's just . . .'

It's just more complicated than that, I want to say. It's not just about me, and Hugh. There's Connor, too, and what's happening in our lives. Kate's death. Hugh's case. It's not an easy time. Nothing is straightforward.

I find I want to tell him the truth about Kate. Maybe he can be there for me. Impartial. Supportive. He's lost his wife, after all. He might understand in a way that Hugh, that Anna and Adrienne and the others can't.

'Just what?'

Something stops me.

'I don't want to jeopardize my marriage.'

'I'm not asking you to leave your husband. I'm asking you to come upstairs. Just one more time.'

I close my eyes. How do I know it'll be one more time? I remember telling myself that once before, as the needle bit into my flesh for the second time, and then again when it did for the third.

'No.' And yet, even as I say it, I'm thinking of afterwards, as we lie together, the two of us wrapped in the sheets. I can picture the room, the high ceiling, the gentle draught of the air conditioning. I can see Lukas, sleeping. There's the tiniest sound as his chest rises and then falls. For some reason, despite the path that's brought me to him, I realize I feel safe.

Soon I will go home – back to my real life, back to Hugh and to Connor, back to Adrienne and Anna, back to a life without my sister – but perhaps if I do this first it'll be different. The pain of her death will not have faded, but it will be blunted. I won't care quite so much that the person who took her life is still free. Instead I'll be thinking about this moment, when everything feels so alive and uncomplicated, when all my pain and sorrow have shrunk down, condensed and transformed to this one thing, this one need, this one desire. Me and him, him and me. If I sleep with him again there'll at least be one more brief moment when there's no past and no future and nothing else exists in the world except for us, and it will be a tiny moment of peace.

He takes my hand. He speaks softly.

'Come on. Come upstairs.'

PART THREE

Chapter Seventeen

My new camera arrives. It's a Canon, a single-lens reflex, not quite top of the range but smaller and lighter than the one I've been using for the last few years. I researched it online and ordered it a few days ago. I don't need it, it's an extravagance, but I want to get out more, take more photographs on the street, like I used to. It was Hugh's suggestion that he buy it for my birthday and he looked delighted with himself when he handed me the package on Saturday.

I opened it later that day, upstairs, and alone, and then took it out, on Upper Street, around Chapel Market and the Angel. I tried a few test shots, and as I brought it to my eye the action felt intuitive, instinctive. When I looked through the viewfinder it felt almost as if this is how I prefer to see the world. Framed.

I take it out again now, slung round my neck, with a zoom lens I ordered at the same time. It's very different taking pictures on the move. I have to spot a potential shot among the chaos, and then wait for the perfect moment, all while trying to stay inconspicuous and unobserved. My shots on Saturday were poor; I was indiscriminate. I felt rusty, like a singer who's spent years in enforced silence.

I tried not to be disappointed, though. I told myself that once I'd regained my confidence I'd find my subject; for now I just need to take photos and develop my eye. The joy of these shots is in their taking, less so in how they end up.

But then, that's how it always was. I think back to the pictures I took in Berlin. It was easy, there. The friendships we forged were deep, people were drawn to us, our place quickly became a refuge for the rootless and abandoned. It was filled with artists and performers, with drag queens, junkies and prostitutes; they came for a few hours, or a few days, or months. I found I wanted to document them all. They fascinated me: they were people for whom identity was fluid, shifting, something they chose themselves, without being constrained by the expectations of others. At first some treated me with suspicion, but they soon realized that, far from trying to pin them down, I was attempting to understand and document their fluidity. They began to trust me. They became my family.

And always, in the centre, was Marcus. I photographed him obsessively. I took pictures of him as he slept, as he ate, as he sat in a bath full of cool water that ended up looking like sludge, as he worked at a canvas or sketched on the war-scarred streets of what used to be the East. We cooked dinners for everyone, huge pans filled with pasta, served with tomatoes and bread, and I took photos. We went to the Love Parade and took ecstasy and danced to techno with the other freaks, and still I took photos. All the time. It was as if I didn't consider a life lived unless it was also documented.

Today I've come to the Millennium Bridge. It's mid-afternoon and very hot – on the walk here the city steam seemed to rise from the streets – but at least here on the bridge there's a breeze.

I crouch down to make myself as small as possible and set up my equipment. I drink some of the bottled water I picked up on the way here, then my hand goes back to my camera. I'm scanning faces, looking for the shot, waiting.

For what? A feeling of otherness, of the extraordinary that resides in the mundane. For a long time I see nothing that interests me. Half the people on the bridge are tourists wearing shorts and T-shirts, while the rest sweat in suits. I take a few shots anyway. I change position. And then I see someone interesting. A man, walking towards me. He's in his late thirties, I guess, wearing a shirt, a jacket but no tie. At first he seems unremarkable, but then I pick up on something. It's intangible, but unmistakable. I feel a tingle, my senses are heightened. This man is different from the others. It's as if he has a gravity, is disturbing the air as he moves through it. I bring my camera to my eye, frame him in my viewfinder, zoom in close. I focus, wait, refocus as he comes towards me. He looks right at me, right down the lens, and although his expression doesn't change, something seems to connect. It's as if he both sees and doesn't see me at the same time. I'm a ghost, shimmering and translucent. I squeeze the shutter release, then wait a second before squeezing it again, and then once more.

He doesn't even notice. He looks away, over my shoulder towards Tower Bridge, and keeps on walking. A moment later he's gone.

I stay for a while longer, but even without looking at the pictures I've taken I know it. I have my shot. It's time to leave.

I go through the lobby and up to the room. Lukas comes to the door in a towel; as usual, he's poured us both a drink – a beer for him, a sparkling water for me – and once we've kissed he hands me mine. I breathe him in, the deep, woody smell of his aftershave, the faint trace of the real him underneath, and smile. I put my camera down on the table. It's the first time I've brought it with me.

'You took my advice.'

'I did. An early birthday present to myself,' I lie.

'It's your birthday?'

'Next week. Next Tuesday, in fact.'

He kisses me again. Tuesday. It's become our day. We haven't missed one yet, and in between we chat online. It's almost as good, but not quite. We share each other's lives. We describe the things we'd like to do to each other, with each other. We tell each other our most private fantasies. But Tuesday is the day we meet.

'I should've known that. I should know when your birthday is.'

I smile. How could he? It's something else I haven't told him, something I've kept for myself, along with my husband's real name, and the fact that I have a son.

But I have told him the truth about Kate.

I hadn't intended to, but last week he was telling me how he'd known from the moment we first began chatting that he wanted to meet me. I felt guilty.

How could I reply? I only met you because I thought you might have some connection to my dead sister.

'It's not that simple,' I said, instead. I decided to be honest, to tell him the truth. There'd been enough lies. 'I have something to tell you. My sister, the one I told you about? She didn't kill herself. She was murdered.'

That familiar look of shock. He reached out to touch me, then hesitated. 'But . . . ?'

I told him what had happened, that the only thing taken was an earring. I even described it to him. Gold drop, with a tiny dreamcatcher design with turquoise feathers. I told him about going to see Anna, the list of names I found in Kate's things, the first time I'd logged on to the website. Encountrz.

'And that's why you came to meet me?'

'I'm sorry. Yes.'

He held me close. 'Jayne, I understand. Maybe I can help.'

'Help? How?'

'There are other sites. Your sister might have been on those, too. I could try to find her.'

It was tempting, but it felt futile, and I wasn't sure I could go through it all again. I told him I'd think about it.

And now he's here, in front of me. Talking about how he hadn't known when my birthday was. 'We'll do something special,' he says. He picks up my camera. 'You've been taking photos?'

Special? I wonder what he means. Go out for a meal, take in a show? It sounds ridiculous.

'I thought it was time. See if I've still got it.'

'And do you?'

I shrug, though I'm being modest. Today, on the bridge, I'd felt like the old me, back when I was in Berlin and taking pictures all the time. I can already feel myself slipping back into my talent. It's like going home.

He holds up the camera. 'May I?'

I sip my drink. 'If you like.'

He turns it on and flicks through the pictures, nodding as he does. 'They're good.'

'I brought you some of my old shots. Like you asked?'

He puts the camera down and takes a step towards me.

'Want to see them now?'

He kisses me. 'Later,' he says, then kisses me again. 'God, I've missed you.' He slips the towel from his waist and I glance down.

'I've missed you, too.' And even though it's only been a week since the last time I was in a room like this – and we've talked online every day – I mean it.

We kiss again. I feel him stiffen between us and know that

in a moment he'll be on top of me, and then inside me, and then once again everything will be all right.

Afterwards, he stands at the window. A gust of wind lifts the curtains and I catch a glimpse of the street outside. We're on the first floor; I see the sky, wisps of cloud, I hear the murmur of the street, the traffic, the voices. It's hot in the room, sticky.

I let my eyes travel the curve of his body, his neck, his back, his behind. I notice his blemishes, the details I don't see on the camera and forget every time we meet. The mole on his neck, the vaccination scar on his shoulder that matches Hugh's, the red flush of a birthmark on his upper thigh. It's been a month now, and these details still surprise me. I grab my camera; he turns as I click the shutter, and when he sees I've taken a picture of him his face breaks into the same half-smile I used to see on Marcus.

'Come back to bed. Let's look at these pictures.'

We lie, side by side. The envelope I've brought with me is between us, its contents spilled out. My work, my past. A pile of glossy ten-by-eights.

He holds up a picture of Marcus.

'And this one?'

It's *Marcus in the Mirror*, and I tell him the same story that I told Anna, more or less. 'An ex. That was taken in the bathroom of the flat we lived in.'

'Also in Berlin?'

'Yes.' I've told him about my time there. About what I used to be like, who I was before I became the person I am now.

'You were happy there?'

I shrug. It's not an answer.

'Some of the time.'

'Why did you leave?'

I sigh and turn on to my back. I look at the ceiling, at the curlicues in the plasterwork. When I don't answer he puts the photo down and moves closer, so that he's right next to me. I feel the warmth of his body. He must sense my struggle.

'When did you leave?'

It's an easier question, and I answer straight away. 'I went over there in the mid-nineties, and stayed for three or four years.'

He laughs. 'When I was at school . . .'

I laugh, too. 'You were.'

He kisses me. My shoulder. 'It's a good job I love older women,' he says.

And there's that word again. *Love*. We haven't used it. It's something we've approached only obliquely. *I love it when you . . . I love the way you . . .*

We haven't yet lost the verb, the qualifier. We haven't gone as far as *I love you*.

'So, I was hanging out, you know. Bars and clubs. Living in a squat.'

'East Berlin?'

I shake my head. 'Kreuzberg.'

He smiles. 'Bowie . . . Iggy Pop.'

'Yes, though that was years before. I was taking pictures. It started off small, but people liked my stuff. Y'know? I met this guy who ran a gallery. The picture editor at this magazine heard about me, wanted to use me for some pictures. From there it kind of went crazy. Exhibitions, even fashion shoots.' I pause. I'm approaching it now, this thing I want to tell him, this thing he might not like. 'This was the mid-nineties. Heroin chic.'

He says nothing.

'And, well, there was a lot of it about.'

A beat.

'Heroin?'

I want my silence to be answer enough, but it isn't. I have to tell him.

'Yes.'

'*You* took heroin?'

I look at him. His expression is unreadable. Is it that hard to believe? A part of me wants to rise up, to defend myself. Plenty of people did, I want to say. Still do. What's the big deal?

But I don't. I force myself to take a deep breath. I want to respond, rather than react. 'We all did.' I turn back to face him. 'I mean, I didn't at first. I went over there with Marcus. He was an artist. A painter. Very good, very talented. A bit older than me. I met him when he was at art school. It was him who encouraged me to take up photography. When he moved to Berlin, I went with him.' I nod towards the pictures between us. 'We fell in with that group—'

Or they fell in with us.

'A bad crowd?'

'No.' Again that urge to defend. 'No. I wouldn't say that. They were my friends. They looked after me.' I'm thinking of Frosty, and the others. They weren't junkies. Or even addicts, not in the way that he probably thinks of the word. 'They weren't a bad crowd. They were just . . . we were just . . . *different*, I guess. We didn't fit in. We all just gravitated to each other.'

I hesitate. It's easier than you think, I want to say. Taking heroin every weekend becomes every other day becomes every day. It's frightening, going back there. Though not all of my memories are bad, it still feels raw. I'm being dragged back, and down. It's not a place I can stay too long.

'The drugs were only part of that.'

'So, what happened?'

190

'When I left?'

'Yes. The other week, you said your husband "saved you"?'

'It got too much.' I'm being careful. I don't want to tell him everything, yet I know I must not lie. 'I needed to get out. Quickly.' I hesitate, stumbling over the name I've given my husband. 'Harvey was there for me.'

My mind goes back to that time. Me in the kitchen, with Frosty. She was making coffee for me, sipping red wine from a mug. I don't think she'd been to bed, it was festival time; the day before we'd been marching with friends of Johan, partying in the bars, and then a group had come back here. Now the place was quiet; most people had left to carry on, or were asleep.

Marcus was upstairs, playing a guitar someone had left months ago. 'There you go,' said Frosty, handing me my drink. 'We don't have any milk.' I was used to that. We never did.

'Thanks.'

'How's Marky?'

'He's good,' I said. 'I think. Although his family are freaking out.'

'Again?'

'They want him to go home.'

Frosty gasped in mock-horror. 'What? Away from all *this*? But why?' She laughed. 'I guess they don't understand.'

I shook my head. 'No. I guess they don't.'

'Have you met them?'

I put my coffee down.

'No. Not yet. He thinks his dad might come over. He wants the three of us to go out. Says we should insist. He wants to show them he's cleaned up.'

Frosty tilted her head. 'Has he?'

'Yes,' I said. I was only telling half the truth. We'd kicked together, gone through cold turkey. It'd been a hell of sweating, of vomiting and diarrhoea and stomach cramps so severe we'd both moan with the pain. Our bones ached, and neither of us could find relief in sleep. I felt like I was burning up, nothing helped, and all the time the knowledge that just one more hit would make all the pain go away shone in front of us. But we were both strong, we helped each other when it threatened to get too much, and we'd been clean for a few weeks. Now Marcus's father was on his way and Marcus had begged me for one last hit. Eventually I'd agreed. One, and then no more. Ever. We were going to do it later that day, or the following morning as the sun came up. A final farewell.

I didn't tell Frosty all that, though.

'We both have,' I said. She said nothing, then smiled. 'That's good,' she said, then changed the subject. We finished our drinks, talking about the partying we were planning for the weekend. 'You'll help me get ready?' she said, and I said, yes, yes of course I would.

'Good,' she said, but then it happened. Something passed through Frosty; she looked as if she were somewhere else entirely. It lasted only for a moment, and then she looked up at me.

'Honeybunch,' she said. 'Where's Marky?'

I said nothing. The room was silent, and had been for a while. The guitar playing had stopped.

Now, I look at the picture on the bed – *Marcus in the Mirror* – and then up at Lukas. He's shaking his head. I worry that he disapproves, that this conversation will mark the beginning of our disconnection, yet he deserves my honesty, in this at least. He takes my hand. 'What happened?'

I don't want to go back there; I can't. Sometimes I think

what I did that night was the catalyst for what happened to Kate. If I'd behaved differently she'd still be around. 'I had a wake-up call, I guess. I left. I knew I had to. But I had nowhere to go. Not until Harvey rescued me.'

'You knew him already?'

'Yes. He was the son of my father's best friend. The two of us met when I was still at school and we became friends. He was just about the only person who stayed in contact with me while I was in Berlin, and when it all came to an end it was him I called. I asked whether he'd speak to my father for me. You know, smooth the way . . .'

'And he did?'

'He paid for my ticket. He was waiting for me when I got off the plane. He said I could stay with him, for a few days, until I got myself sorted out . . .'

'And you're still there . . .'

I feel a momentary anger. 'Yes, but you make it sound like an accident. I'm there because we fell in love.'

He nods, and I calm down. I'm glad when he doesn't ask the next logical question: whether that's still the case. The answer isn't straightforward. Where once our love was deep and clear, now it's more complex. We've shared good times, and bad. We've argued, I've been angry, I've hated him as well as loved him. We're there for each other, but it's not un-complicated. Things settle, over the years. They become something else. I can't summarize it with a simple *Yes, I still love him*, or *No, I don't*.

'And then you met me.'

I hold my breath. 'Yes.'

The room is silent. From somewhere, way off, I hear the sounds of the hotel, the other guests, doors banging, laughter, and from outside comes the steady buzz of traffic. But inside all is still.

I turn on to my side. I face him. 'Tell me about your wife.'

He closes his eyes, breathes deeply, then opens them again. 'Her name was Kim. We met through work. She worked for a client. I loved her very much.'

'How long were you married?'

'She was diagnosed just before our first anniversary. They gave her a year to eighteen months. She died about seven months later.'

There's a silence. There's nothing to say. I tell him I'm sorry.

He looks at me. 'Thank you.' He reaches out to take my hand. 'I miss her. It's been years, but I miss her.' He smiles, then kisses me. 'She'd have liked you.'

I smile. I don't know how that makes me feel. It's meaningless, we'd never have met. If she'd still been around, Lukas wouldn't be here with me now. For a long time I'm silent, and then I ask him.

'You said you'd help me to find my sister online?'

'Of course. Do you want me to?'

It's been a week since his offer, but I've thought about it since. It might be painful, but it's worth a try. And I won't be on my own. 'Yes. If you think you can.'

He says he'll see what he can do. I give him her name, the name she'd used on encountrz, her date of birth, anything he might find useful. He taps them into his phone, then says he'll do his best.

'Leave it with me,' he says. The room feels claustrophobic, full of ghosts. He must feel it, too; he suggests we go out. 'We can get some lunch. Or a coffee.'

We get dressed and go downstairs, out of the hotel and down to the station. The concourse is busy but we find a table in one of the coffee shops. It's near the window and I feel on display, yet somehow, right now, it doesn't seem to matter. People's gazes slide across me. I'm invisible. Lukas gets our drinks.

'That's better.' He sits down. 'Are you okay? With me talking about Kim back there, I mean?'

'Yes. Yes, of course.'

He smiles. 'I'm glad we can talk about real things. Things that matter. I've never had that before.'

'What do you normally do, then?'

'With people I chat to online?'

I nod. He looks down and scratches his shoulder absent-mindedly. He's still smiling. I think of the fantasies we've been sharing.

'The same thing we do?'

'Yes. But nothing's been as crazy as it is with you.' He pauses. 'How about you?'

He knows I've never done anything like this. I've already told him.

'My husband and I . . .' I begin, but then my sentence evaporates. 'We've been married for a long time.'

'Meaning?'

'I guess I mean I love him. I want to be there for him. But . . .'

'But it's not always that exciting?'

I don't answer. Is that what I mean?

I look at Lukas. It's easier with you, I think. We want to impress, we save the best for each other. We don't share the stresses of everyday life, not yet, even if we have shared our big losses. I haven't had to sit with you as you vent your frustration at the family who've complained about you, as you've moaned that you've had to write a letter, a 'grovelling apology', even though you know damn well you'd warned them of the possible side effects of surgery. I haven't had to try to support you, knowing that you won't be supported, that there's nothing I can say or do that will make any difference.

'Not always,' I say.

'But you've always been faithful?'

I think of Paddy, in the summer house. 'Pretty much.'

He grins. It's lascivious.

'It's not that exciting, really.'

'Tell me.'

'There was this guy. Quite recently—'

He shifts forward in his seat and I pick up my coffee.

'He's a friend of my husband.' I think back to the dinner party. I want to give Lukas a story. 'His name's Paddy. He's been flirting with me for a while.'

'Flirting? In what way?'

'Oh, you know. When we get together he always laughs at my jokes, compliments me on my clothes. That sort of thing.' He nods, and I hear myself say it. 'I even thought he might be stalking me.'

'Stalking you? How?'

'There was this guy one night. As I was getting ready for bed.'

'You told me.'

I did, I think. He told me he wished he could protect me.

'You really think it's him?'

Even though I know it was never Paddy out there on the street – was almost certainly no one at all, just my vivid imagination combining with a lack of sleep – I hear myself say it. 'Yes.'

His eyes flash wide. He looks almost pleased. I think back to what he'd said. *I'd never let anyone hurt you.*

I'd felt protected. Safe.

Is that why I've told him I thought it was Paddy? Because I want to feel like that again?

'Someone put some cards through the letterbox, too.'

'What cards?'

I tell him. 'The ones the prostitutes put up in phone boxes.'

He holds my gaze. Is this turning him on?

'You think it's him?'

My mind goes to Paddy and his clumsy attempt to kiss me. He'd hate to know the lies I'm telling about him. But he never will.

'Maybe. He tried to kiss me, and—'

'When?'

'You remember the party? When you were at your wedding? He tried to kiss me. I told him I'd never sleep with him. I think it was his way of getting back at me.'

'Did you kiss him back?'

I remember all the times we've been chatting online, talking about our fantasies. Isn't this just the same?

'No. I didn't want to. He forced himself on me.'

'Bastard. Why didn't you tell me?'

'I felt ashamed . . .'

'Ashamed? Why?'

'I could've said no.'

'Didn't you?'

'Yes. Yes, I did.' I look at the table top. 'I dunno. Maybe I could've fought harder.'

He takes my hand. 'Tell me where he lives.'

'Why?'

'He shouldn't get away with shit like that. No one should. I'll have a word with him.'

'And say what?'

'I'll think of something.'

I think of him, knocking on Paddy's door, but then the vision shifts, like a dream that's twisted back on itself and become horrific. I see him standing over Kate's body.

'No,' I say. I try to clear the image, but it persists.

'You're scared.'

'No. No. I'm fine.'

He lifts my hand to his lips, kisses it. 'I want to protect you.' He looks into my eyes. 'I'll look after you. If you're scared.'

Something in the room clicks over. I think of the things I've told him. The things I've wanted to do and have never done. The things I've wanted to have done to me. The air thickens with desire.

'I know.'

'Are you scared?'

I look up at him. The cord between us tightens. The skin of his hand seems to hum with energy, his flesh melds into mine, and I realize I want him, and he wants me, and he wants me to be frightened and if it's what he wants then it's what I want, too.

'Yes,' I say. I'm whispering. He shifts still further forward in his seat. 'I'm very frightened.'

He lowers his voice, too, even though there's now only one other person in the café. A lone traveller, with a suitcase, reading.

'This man. Paddy. What do you think he wants to do to you? If he could?'

My own arousal begins to pulse and grow. It's within me, something physical, something I can touch, I can feel. Something begins to open.

I open my mouth to answer but I have no words. There's only desire left. He pushes himself away from me, still holding my hand. 'Come on.'

He pushes me into the cubicle and locks the door. He's a blur of activity, kissing me, shoving me, holding me. I abandon myself to his will, to whatever is happening. He's tearing at my clothes, our limbs flail, and I realize, as if from a distance, I'm tearing at his. There's the smell of disinfectant, or soap, and beneath it urine.

'Lukas . . .' I say, but he silences me with his mouth, then twists me round, pushes me up against the wall. 'What do you think he might do?' he's saying. 'This?'

I try to nod my head. He has his arm around my throat; it's not rough, he's not holding tight, but it's far from gentle. He pulls down my jeans. I help him. I can feel his cock pushing into me as he separates my legs with his knee. I arch my back, to let him. Somewhere a decision is made; I will let him do what he wants. Whatever he wants. To a point.

Is this what it was like for Kate? I think. Is this how it felt for my sister?

'Tell me,' he whispers. 'You want me to teach him a lesson? Tell me how scared you are . . .'

Chapter Eighteen

I'm sore, when I wake up. I can still feel his fingers on me, his hands.

Yet it's a pain that makes me feel alive. It's something, at least, something better than that other pain, the pain that makes me want to die.

I get up to go to the bathroom. Outside Connor's door I stop to listen. There's the faint sound of music, his radio alarm. I'm about to knock when I decide against it. It's early. He's fine. We're all fine.

In the bathroom, I think of Lukas. Something special, he'd said. For my birthday. I can hardly wait, yet it's the delicious anticipation of pleasure deferred. I think of him as I look in the mirror. I examine my arms, my thighs. I turn round, try to look at my back. There are marks: one in the shape of a hand, another like a bird. They are red, and look angry. The skin on their periphery is purpling.

I'm beginning to bruise.

Six days pass. Almost a week. I catch up with Adrienne, Hugh and I go to the theatre, and then it's Tuesday again, the day of my birthday. Thirty-seven. I sleep late and for once get up last. I go downstairs and my family is already there. There's a pile of cards on the table, a wrapped present. It's the school holidays; the atmosphere is unhurried. Hugh's made a pot of coffee and there's a plate of croissants I hadn't seen him buy.

'Darling!' He hands me a huge bunch of flowers from the worktop, red and green, chrysanthemums and roses. He's still in his dressing gown. It's plain, slate grey. 'Happy birthday!'

I sit down. Connor pushes a card over to me and I open it.

'That's lovely!' It's a picture of the three of us, printed out from a photo on his computer, glued to some card. On the inside he's printed 'Happy Birthday, Mum'. I kiss the top of his head. It smells of shampoo and for a moment I think of him as a little boy and feel a tug of guilt. I'm here, with my family, yet also thinking of later, of my visit to my lover.

I can call him that, now. I turn the word over in my head. *Lover*. I turn to Hugh.

'Aren't you going to be late for work?'

He's grinning – it almost looks like an effort, as if he's having to force himself to forget about the case at work; the family weren't satisfied with the letter and are considering legal action – but Connor is sharing the joke. He hands me his gift.

'Open this, first. Then we'll talk.'

I take it; it's wrapped beautifully. 'Happy birthday, darling.'

Some part of me knows what it is, even before I've opened it.

'My favourite perfume! Fracas!'

My voice sounds overly enthusiastic, even to me. There's an edge of insincerity. I hope he doesn't think I'm ungrateful.

'I noticed you'd run out.'

'Yes. Nearly.'

It's the perfume Lukas hates.

'And I know it was Kate's favourite, too.'

I smile. 'That's very thoughtful, darling.'

'Put some on, why don't you?'

'I don't want to waste it.'

'Please.' He looks disappointed. For an instant his face is lined with worry, but then he smiles again. 'You smell so lovely when you wear it.' He kisses me. 'Wear it today . . .'

'Hugh . . .'

'You do still like it?'

'Yes. I love it.' I open the box, slide out the bottle. Pleasing one man, not pleasing another. Just a squirt, I think. I can wash it off before I meet Lukas. For a moment I feel his fingers tighten around my wrist. I smile to myself as I spray some behind each ear.

'That's not your real present, though.'

'No?'

'Dad's taking you out!' says Connor. His face lights up with glee. I can see they've hatched some plan together.

'When?'

Hugh speaks. 'Today. I've taken the day off.'

They both look at me, now. Expectant.

'Great!' I concentrate on not letting the panic show in my face. 'What time?'

'All day,' says Connor. 'And I'm going out with Dylan.'

'Lovely!' I'm really starting to worry now. I picture Lukas, sitting there, wondering where I am. He'll think I've let him down. He'll think I've lost interest and couldn't even be bothered to tell him.

I'm not like that, and I don't want him to think I am.

I think fast. 'You've remembered it's my therapy today?'

He winces; he had forgotten. 'I didn't, no.' He waits for me to make a suggestion, but I say nothing. 'It's not ideal, but could you cancel it? Just this once?'

I feel myself tense, slipping into anger.

'I don't want to miss one. Martin thinks we're making real progress.'

Martin. Is that the name I've used before? For a moment I can't remember.

He looks to Connor, then back to me. I wonder if he's looking for support, or thinks that we shouldn't be having this conversation in front of our son.

'I know—' he begins.

'I mean, I'm finally starting to feel better. You know?'

'Yes. And I'm really glad. Of course I am. But can't you reschedule?'

Connor puts his spoon down. He's waiting for me to answer.

'For later this week?'

No, I think. No, I can't.

'He's pretty busy . . .' I think fast. 'He charges the full amount for cancellations.'

Hugh's chin tilts downwards. He's getting annoyed, I can tell. 'I think we can afford it, darling. And, anyway, I've booked something for us. There's a cancellation fee on that as well.'

'What've you booked?' I say.

'It's a surprise. An all-day thing. I thought we'd get there around eleven.'

'Let me think.' I stand up. I feel torn. My husband – my lover. I can't have both, just like I could never drink and not drink, or both reach for the syringe and leave it alone. I have to choose one or the other.

Unless . . .

I pick up my phone.

'I'll just see if I can move my session earlier,' I say to Hugh. 'Then I can meet you at about eleven thirty?'

He begins to protest, but I silence him. 'I don't like being unreliable,' I say. 'And it's important to me that I go.' I'm trying to keep my voice even, reasonable, but I've raised it slightly. I smile. 'I'm sure half an hour won't make a difference?' I step out of the room, into the hall and close the door behind me. I press call. A few moments later Lukas answers.

'Hi,' I say, and without thinking I add, 'It's me. Julia Plummer.'

'Julia?' he says. He's confused; it's the first time I've used my real name. 'Jayne,' he says quietly. 'Is that you?'

I feel a sudden fear. I'm aware Hugh is just a few feet away, on the other side of the door. I try to keep myself calm. With my thumb I turn the volume down on my phone until I'm certain I'm the only one who can hear his replies.

'Yes, I'm fine,' I say evenly. I wait a moment, then continue. 'No, no . . .' I laugh. 'Not at all!'

'You can't talk.'

'That's right. Anyway, I was just wondering if we could meet an hour earlier today? It's my birthday and my husband's taking me out!'

I try to sound enthusiastic, for the sake of Hugh and Connor, yet I can't. Lukas will think I mean it, that I'm genuinely excited to be seeing my husband rather than him. That would never do.

He's silent for a moment. I can't tell if he's playing the game, or genuinely hasn't worked out what's going on.

Finally he speaks. 'The usual place, but an hour earlier?'

He sounds odd. I'm not sure if it's disappointment, or anger.

'Yes, if that's okay.'

'That's great.' He laughs. 'For an awful moment I thought you were ringing to cancel.'

'Not at all,' I say. 'I'll see you then.'

I end the call and go back in to Hugh. 'There. Sorted.'

'It was my present,' I say. 'From Harvey.'

He doesn't like it. I can tell.

'Did he make you wear it?'

'Not exactly.'

'Does he make you do many things?'

'Not like you do.'

He doesn't smile. He hasn't relaxed since I arrived a few minutes ago. Something is different.

'It's not that bad, is it?'

'I suppose not.'

I smile. I'm trying to keep it light, make it sound unimportant. Which it is, as far as I'm concerned, at least. I kiss him again.

'Sorry,' I say. I try to withdraw from his embrace, but then he kisses me, pushing back against me as he does. It's urgent, almost violent. His hand goes to my neck and for a moment I wonder if he'll grip me around the throat, but then he cups the back of my head. He begins to push me towards the bed.

'Please forgive me,' I say. Though not real, my fear is somehow addictive. He lets me go, with a tiny shove, then raises his hand, as if to hit me.

'Don't punish me,' I say. 'Please?' For a moment he looks genuinely enraged and I flinch and take a step backwards. Kate's face flashes in front of me, wide-eyed and terrified. I try to fix on what I know: that he never had anything to do with my sister.

'Don't—' I say, but he interrupts.

'Why not?' He starts laughing. His fist is still raised. 'Give me one good reason why I shouldn't. I told you not to wear that fucking perfume,' he says, and for the briefest instant

I'm walking in my sister's shoes. A pure, genuine terror hits, and then his face relaxes. He lowers his hand, but takes hold of me.

'You really are joking,' I say.

'You think?'

'Aren't you?'

He smiles, then kisses me, hard.

'That depends.'

Afterwards, we lie on the floor together. I'm still half in and half out of my clothes. I'm worried my shirt is ripped – I'd heard a tear as he unbuttoned it furiously, and instantly thought about how I might explain it to Hugh – and I've hit my head on the corner of the bed.

He turns to me. 'You're bruised.'

'I know.'

'It was me?'

I smile. 'Yes.' I'm almost proud.

'You know I'd never hurt you for real, don't you?'

'Yes. Yes, I know that.'

I wonder if I do. I wonder what I'm getting myself into, and how deep.

Yet I can't deny it's coming from me as much as him. Everything is reciprocated, every fantasy I share with him is encouraged, taken further. I can't pretend I'm not enjoying it.

'Yes. I trust you.'

'Good.' He kisses me, and it's so tender, so slow, with none of the urgency of just a few moments ago, and none of the ordinariness, the practicality, the perfunctoriness, of Hugh.

'So where's he taking you?'

'Who?' I can't work out if it's jealousy I hear. 'My husband? I don't know.'

'Where are you hoping?'

I sit up. It's uncomfortable, this bringing of Hugh into the room. I've managed so far because I've been able to keep him out, just like I've been able to keep Connor out.

An image of him swims into view. He'll be with Dylan, now. Playing on the computer, or maybe at the park.

I wonder why I'm still glad Lukas doesn't know I have a son.

'I don't know. It'll probably be for lunch, or to the theatre. A couple of years ago he bought me tickets to the opera, but then couldn't come. I went with Adrienne.'

'Who's Adrienne?'

'Just a friend. I've known her for years. Since I moved to London, pretty much.'

'Will you and your husband have sex?'

I look at him. 'That's not fair.'

He knows I'm right. 'You know, you sound like you don't much care where your husband is taking you, or what you're going to do.'

I stand up and begin to gather my clothes. It's not true, quite, but we're playing a game, and I know what I have to say. 'I don't, really. I'd much rather spend the day here, with you.'

'That's what I want, too.'

I take a deep breath. I've been putting it off, but I have to ask, before I leave.

'Did you find anything out? About Kate?'

He stands up and begins to get dressed.

'Not yet. I'm working on it.'

Are you? I think. For some reason I'm not sure I believe him.

'I was thinking about the earring. The one you said was missing.'

'Yes?'

'Are you sure the police are looking into that? I mean, it's looking like it might be a more fruitful lead than looking at her internet friends?'

'Well, they say they are, but I'm not sure.'

He kisses me. 'Leave it with me. I'm sure something will come up. We'll just have to keep digging.'

'Thanks.'

'Don't mention it.' He kisses me goodbye. 'By the way, you haven't had your present from me, yet.'

I smile.

'You'll get it later. It's a surprise.'

I leave one hotel to go straight to another. My head is throbbing, there's a rip in my shirt that I try to cover up by buttoning up my jacket. When I arrive, I see Hugh across the lobby. He's sitting in an armchair; across the room from him there's a piano, above hangs a huge chandelier. I go over to my husband and he stands as I approach. He looks tired, and I feel guilty.

'Darling!' he says. 'How was it?'

I tell him it was fine. I see he's got a beach bag with him, one of mine. It must've been the first one he found. We sit and he pours me a tea.

'Here you go.' I take it from him. I look around the room at the other guests: an older couple eating scones, two women having lunch and discussing something in hushed voices, a man with a newspaper. I wonder what kind of person stays in the hotel, whether it's the kind of place Lukas might one day invite me.

'It's going well,' says Hugh suddenly. 'Your therapy, I mean. You seem much . . .'

'Better?'

'No. Relaxed? At peace? You seem to be much clearer about Kate's death.'

He waits, as if I'm going to say more. When I don't, he says, 'You can talk to me, you know.'

'I know that.'

'We did our best, you know? To help her. To be there for her.'

I look away. I want to change the subject. 'It's just . . . well . . . it's complicated.'

'Connor, you mean?'

'Yes.'

'It wouldn't have turned out better, you know. If he'd stayed with her. It would have been exactly the same . . . or worse. We had to get him out of there. It wasn't a good place for him.'

I shrug, then say, 'Maybe. D'you think he's all right?'

'I think so. I mean, he's struggling a little. With the Kate thing. It must be very confusing for him.'

'I guess,' I say. 'I'm going to take him out next week. We're spending the day together. The cinema, or something. I'll talk to him then.'

He nods. I feel guilty. I should've discussed this with him already. We should be united when it comes to Connor, as we always have been before.

'Good idea,' he says. 'He'll be fine, you know. He's a good lad. He has his head screwed on.'

'I hope so.'

'You know, I think he has a girlfriend.'

He smiles. A pleasant complicity between a father and his son.

'Really?' I'm surprised, even though I shouldn't be, and I feel the heat of jealousy. I always thought I'd be the one he came to, confided in.

'Haven't you noticed? He keeps mentioning this girl – Evie.'

I smile. I don't know why I'm so relieved.

'I think I've met her.'

'Really?'

I think back to Carla's party. The girl I'd seen Connor with; I'm sure that was her name.

'Yes. She seems okay.'

'That's good.' He drinks some of his tea. 'He's seeing a lot of Dylan, too. He's popular. He'll be fine.'

He pauses.

'And tonight we have the house to ourselves. I thought we could get some dinner, and then . . .'

The sentence peters out. I think of the marks on my back, my thighs. For a week I've been going to bed early, undressing in the dark, grabbing my robe as soon as I wake up. I can't let him see the bruises.

I commit myself to nothing. 'That'd be lovely.'

He smiles.

'So, what're we doing here?'

He grins, then puts down his cup. He shifts forward in his seat, as if he's about to stand, to make a presentation, or an announcement. 'Well, I thought we needed to relax . . .' He beams. He hands me my bag; inside it I can see the dark blue of my swimming costume, my shampoo and conditioner.

'They have a spa here.' He points to the sign by the lobby. 'Now, I've booked you a pedicure, and we're both having a massage. I had arranged that for midday, but it's okay, they've moved it to the afternoon . . .'

'A spa?'

'Yes. We can spend all day here. They've got steam rooms and a sauna, and a pool . . .'

'Great,' I say. Anxiety begins to roll in my stomach, to swell into panic. My costume is cut low at the back.

'Shall we go? Unless you'd like lunch here, first?'

I shake my head. I don't know what I'm going to do. 'It's fine.'

'This is your day . . .'

'I know.' I'm desperately trying to think of an excuse, a way out of it. But there isn't one; we're already heading back through the lobby, towards the spa. I think of when I got dressed, just an hour or so ago, in the room with Lukas. I'd looked over my shoulder at my reflection in the full-length mirror. The bruises were dark and purpling, unmistakable.

He's sitting by the pool, where he said he'd be. He's ordered a juice for both of us – it's green, and looks organic – and is sipping his. He's wearing his shorts, the pair I bought for him just before our last holiday, to Turkey. Dimly, beneath the layers of worry, I'm aware that he looks good. He's lost weight.

I sit down next to him. I've wrapped my towel around my chest.

'Fancy a swim?'

I lie back on the lounger. 'In a while.' He puts his paper down.

'Come on.' He stands up. 'There's a jacuzzi. I'm going in now.'

He holds out his hand and I have no option but to take it. I feel a sense of dread, of inexorable momentum. And also guilt; only a couple of hours ago it'd been another man holding his hand out to me.

We go over and sit in the pool. The water is warm and clear. Hugh activates the jacuzzi and it begins to bubble. I lie back, staring at the light dancing on the ceiling, reflected from the thrashing water. The bruises on my back sting, as if I've been branded.

For a moment I want to tell him everything. About Lukas,

and what I've been doing. It wasn't my fault, I want to say. Kate died and I went off the rails, and . . .

And what? And it doesn't mean anything? I genuinely thought I was trying to find out who killed her, for me, for her son? I thought I was doing the right thing?

But who am I trying to kid?

'Hugh—' I say, but he cuts me dead.

'I want to talk to you.'

I look at him. This is it, I think.

It hits me. Connor saw it all, in the summer house at Carla's party. He's finally told his father.

Or someone has seen me, on the street, in a hotel lobby, kissing someone who is not my husband.

'What is it?'

He reaches out, under the water, and takes my hand.

'It's about your drinking.'

Relief mixes with confusion. 'What? What drinking?'

'Julia, I'm worried.' He looks uncomfortable, but not as uncomfortable as he should. I find myself wishing this were difficult for him, a tricky subject, but it's not. Not really. He's in his professional mode.

'Hugh, you've nothing to worry about. I haven't touched a drop.'

'Julia, please don't insult my intelligence. You told me. When you came back from Paris.'

'I know, but I was letting off steam. It wasn't an easy trip.'

'I know. But I think you should start going to your meetings again. It's been a few months . . .'

I think about the visits to the clinic when I got back from Berlin, the seats in a circle, being back on the twelve-step programme. I think about the days and weeks of cramps and sickness and feeling like I had the worst hangover, the worst morning sickness, and nothing, nothing would ever make me feel better. I think about the months of begging Hugh to help me, when in fact he already was.

'Look, if either of us is an expert on addiction, I'd have thought it would be me.'

He's silent.

'My sister died. In case you've forgotten?'

'Of course I haven't forgotten,' he snaps. This isn't going as well as he'd thought. 'You ask me all the time how the investigation is going. How can I have forgotten?'

'Bringing that up now is low, Hugh. I care, that's all.'

He hesitates. Why don't you go to some meetings of your own, I want to say. To Al-Anon. Sort your own stuff out before you start on mine.

'I'm sorry,' he says eventually. 'It's just, I'm not sure it's healthy for you. I wish you'd just trust me to handle it.'

'I do,' I say. 'I will.' I consider telling him it's not just me who can't find peace, who won't rest until the person who killed Kate is caught. It's Connor, too.

'I just worry, that's all.'

'I haven't had anything since then. Not a drop.'

He squeezes my hand. I'd forgotten he was holding it.

'At Carla's party . . .'

'That was Paddy! He brought me a drink but I didn't touch it. And then we were chatting, he spilled his drink on me.'

I look at him. Does he believe me?

His voice softens. 'I just don't want to see you go back there. I can't. I won't.'

'I'm not going back anywhere—'

'Then please tell me the truth.'

'What?'

'Did you fall?'

'Sorry? Fall where?'

'Did you have a fall? Did you have a drink with Adrienne?'

'Hugh, what on earth are you—?'

'Those bruises. I noticed them the other day. I saw how you were trying to cover them up today, too. So, what happened?'

The relief is almost overwhelming. He thinks a few too many glasses of wine is all he has to worry about.

'Drunk, were you?'

'Hugh,' I say. 'I fell. I wasn't *drunk*.' I see a way out. He's seen the bruises, I can't deny their existence. But I can explain why I've been hiding them.

I sigh. 'I'd had a glass of wine. That's all. I guess it doesn't take much.' I hesitate, then say, 'I slipped on the escalator in the tube station.'

'You didn't tell me.'

I try to smile. 'No. It was bloody mortifying, if you must know.' Another pause. 'Ask Adrienne, if you don't believe me . . .'

Even as I say it I know it's a mistake. There's a chance he will. I'm trying too hard, adding extra details.

'I'm sorry,' I say. 'I'm embarrassed. I made a mistake.'

'Another mistake.'

Fury rises within me. 'Yes. *Another* mistake. Look, I feel bad enough as it is. I've said sorry. Can we just forget it?'

'It's not me you need to apologize to.'

'Then who?'

'Like I said, I think you should start going to your meetings.'

No, I think. No. I won't. I'm not ready.

I shake my head.

'Promise me you'll at least think about it.'

No. I can't stand the thought. I'd have to confess everything, all over again. I'd have to admit I'm back where I started.

'I can't.'

'Why?'

'I just . . .'

'Just tell me you'll think about it?'

I sigh. 'Okay. I'll think about it.'

'Or at least talk to your therapist about it?'

'I will . . .'

The anger melts from his face. He lets go of my hand and pats my thigh. 'Darling, I just don't want to see you go through it again . . .'

'I won't. And, anyway, that was a *long* time ago. I know better, now. And besides,' I say lightly, 'I've got you. Keeping me safe.'

I look him straight in the eye. I hold his gaze; it's easier than I think, yet still I hate myself for doing it. It reminds me of the years I spent convincing people I didn't have a problem, but the difference is, this time I don't. I'm just pretending to.

'I know,' he says. His hand is still on my thigh. 'I know.' He's quiet for a moment and I begin to relax. I realize I'm going to have to do something. Next time I might not be so lucky, and whatever is happening between me and Lukas, I can't let it destroy what I have with Hugh.

I tip my head back, close my eyes. Am I being naive in thinking I can keep Lukas separate from my family? Do secrets always come out in the end?

We're both silent for a while, and then, without warning, Hugh speaks.

'Oh, God,' he says. 'I haven't told you about Paddy.'

My eyes flick open. The name is unexpected and it jolts me. I hope it doesn't show.

'Maria rang me yesterday. I completely forgot to tell you. He's been mugged.'

I hear myself echo him. It sounds like my own voice, but coming from a long way away.

'Mugged?'

It's too hot in here, suddenly. I'm sweating. The water is oily and viscous.

'Yes. Over the weekend. I think Maria said it was Friday.'

'Where? By who? Is he all right?'

An awful thought is forming. Last week I told Lukas what Paddy had done. I'd let him think it was worse than it was. Much worse.

He'd said he wanted to protect me.

'He's bruised and battered, and his nose is broken, but he'll be fine. It happened right near where they live, apparently. He was coming home late. He can't remember much . . .'

I think of Lukas. He said I'd be getting my present later. Is this what he meant?

My mind goes to Kate. I see her, lying there in her own blood, her nose broken, her eyes swollen shut.

I look over at my husband. It's as if I know what he's going to say next.

'Funny thing is, they didn't take anything.'

Something within me begins to collapse. I find myself standing up, though I don't know why, or where I'm going. The water slides off me and for a moment I think it's blood. 'Like Kate,' I'm saying. 'Just like Kate.'

Hugh stands, too. 'Julia? Julia, I'm sorry. I shouldn't have told you. I wasn't thinking. Julia, sit down. Please?'

It can't be, I tell myself. It can't be him.

Tell me you want me to teach him a lesson, he'd said, when we were right in the middle. And I think I said yes. Had I said yes?

But he hadn't meant anything. Surely? He hadn't taken me

seriously? It's just a coincidence, it must be. It must be, it has to be.

I think of his hands on me, the bruises, the things he'd done. The things he's told me he'd like to do.

'I'm an idiot,' says Hugh. 'Julia, I'm sorry.'

I turn round. I shiver, I'm freezing, yet the sweat is pouring off me. I run out, into the changing rooms. I make it as far as the bathroom, just.

Chapter Nineteen

Connor arrives home late the next morning. Dylan's with him and the two of them crash in, talking non-stop. I'm waiting for the kettle to boil when they land in the kitchen.

My son. I've missed him; he's all I'd wanted when I got in last night, the only thing in my life I still think I have a chance of getting right.

'Hi, Mum!' he says. He seems surprised that I'm there, and for a moment I think he's going to ask me if I'm okay. I'm not sure what I'll say if he does. Dylan stands behind him, and when I smile at him says, 'Hi, Mrs Wilding.'

'We might go upstairs?' says Connor.

I force a smile. 'Okay. Did you have fun?'

'Yeah.' He doesn't elaborate.

'Want anything to eat?'

'No, thanks.'

'Dylan?'

The other boy shakes his head and mumbles something. He's even skinnier than I remember.

'We had something earlier,' says Connor. 'Can we watch a DVD?'

'Sure. Let me know if you want anything,' I say as they disappear upstairs. I turn back to the kettle and make my drink.

I know what I have to do. I've been putting it off all morning. I sit down at the table and phone Lukas.

'Morning, beautiful. I was just thinking about you, too.'

Normally that comment would thrill me, but today I barely notice it. I'm too wound up, too anxious. I've run out of energy. I've spent all night thinking about him and Paddy, about what he might've done. What *I* might have done. I'm exhausted.

'Lukas. We need to talk.'

I sense him shift a gear. I imagine him lying in bed, then abruptly sitting upright. I try to picture it, but fail. I've never seen his bedroom, never seen his house. It's nice, he's told me, semi-detached, with three bedrooms. 'Modern, but with some character.' He's always sounded proud of it, so why haven't I been there?

I wonder if he keeps it tidy. A man, living alone; I wonder if he even makes his bed. Connor wouldn't, if I didn't insist.

'What is it? Is everything okay?'

I feel a sudden rush. I want to shout, scream. I want to tell him, No, no, it isn't!

I take a deep breath and try to calm myself.

'Paddy was attacked.'

Even saying the words hurts. It reminds me too much of Kate.

'Who?'

'Paddy.' I'm annoyed, and at the same time frightened. Has he forgotten? Or is this all part of some game? 'The person I told you about. The friend I told you had kissed me.' I hesitate. My voice wavers. 'He's been beaten up.'

'Jesus . . .' He sounds concerned. It's genuine, I think, but how do I know? I don't know anything. 'Are you all right, Julia?'

I don't want to ask the question, but it's a weight, pressing down on me, and I have no choice. It's the reason I called him, after all.

'Did you have anything to do with it?'

There's silence. Saying it out loud has made it seem real. The suspicion has become a certainty.

I picture him, shaking his head in disbelief. Every muscle in my body is tensed, then he speaks.

'Me? What on earth—?'

I interrupt. I don't want to, but I can't help it. I say it again, louder this time. 'Did you have anything to do with it?'

His reply comes more quickly this time. He's rushing to his own defence.

'No, of course I didn't.' I can't decide whether he sounds angry or just emphatic. 'Is he going to be all right?'

The words rush out, tumbling over each other. 'It just seems a coincidence, that's all. I mean, I tell you last week, and then this week—'

'Listen. Calm down—'

'—this week,' I continue, 'this week, this happens.'

I stop speaking. My body is suddenly alive. I can feel his hands on me, my skin sings with the rough urgency of the sex in the toilet cubicle, my wrists carry a dull ache where he'd gripped them. I think back to what he'd said.

'You asked me if I wanted you to teach him a lesson.'

'I know,' he says. 'And, if you remember, you said yes.'

I collapse inwards. I'm almost breathless, with panic, and rage.

'I didn't mean it, though! We were just messing around. It was play-acting!'

'Was it?' His voice has taken on an edge; he sounds different. Not like him at all. 'You know,' he says, 'you have to be careful what you wish for, Julia. Very careful . . .'

Fear hits me. Terror. It's real, physical. I'm on fire, my phone is alive, dangerous. I want to hurl it across the room. I wish I'd never met him. I don't know who he is, this man, this person I've let into my life. I want everything to go back to how it was before.

'Lukas!' My voice is pleading, I'm almost shouting, only vaguely aware that Connor is upstairs. Right now I'd sacrifice anything to be certain that what happened to Paddy had nothing to do with Lukas. Almost anything. 'Please . . .'

I stop. He's making a noise; at first I can't tell what it is, but then I realize. He's laughing, almost to himself. I'm flooded with light, with air.

'Lukas?'

'Relax. I'm joking . . .'

'Joking? What's so funny?'

'Julia, I think you need to calm down. Think about it. Aren't you being a little paranoid here? I mean, you only told me about this guy last week. Do you think I marched straight round there and beat him up? How could I? You didn't tell me where he lives. You didn't even tell me his full name. For God's sake, I only found out *your* real name yesterday.'

He's right. It can't have been him. But can it really be coincidence?

'I don't know. I'm sorry.'

'I'm sorry, too. For laughing. For not taking it seriously.' There's a pause. He sounds contrite. 'When did it happen?'

'On Friday night, I think.'

'I was in Cambridge on Friday. Out with a bunch of mates.' He hesitates. 'You can check on Facebook, if you like. Ade has put shitloads of pictures up.'

My computer's in front of me. I open it up.

'Julia, this man, you're sure he's going to be okay?'

'Yes,' I say. 'I think so.' I open Facebook and navigate to

his timeline. Friday night. It's true. There are photos of him.

I feel awful. Guilty. Filled with an overwhelming desire to make everything better. 'I've been really stupid. I'm sorry.'

'You do trust me, don't you?' His voice is calm, now. Kind. Soothing. The voice I'm used to. Yet from nowhere I flash on a vision. Him saying exactly the same thing, but to Kate.

'Julia? Are you there?'

I realize I haven't answered him.

'Yes. I'm sorry. I just panicked, that's all.' Relief floods my veins as I realize the truth of what I'm saying. A brightness returns to the world, one I hadn't noticed had disappeared. I go on. 'I'm sorry. All this fantasy talk, I suppose I was worried . . .'

'It's okay . . .'

'I should never have accused you.' Pleasure floods my veins. The pleasure of tension released. 'I don't know what came over me.'

'It's *okay*. Calm down, Julia. It's all going to be okay.'

Is it? I want it to be. I think of all the good times we've had, all the support he's given me over Kate. I get the sense that if anyone can make it okay, then it's him.

It's his voice. He does that. He makes me feel better, calmer.

'Listen,' he says. 'I might've found out something. About Kate.'

My heart surges. 'What? What is it?'

His answer seems to take for ever.

'I'm not sure.'

'What? What is it?'

'It's probably nothing.'

'What have you found?'

Again I hear him hesitate. He doesn't want to raise my hopes.

'There's a site—'

'What site?'

'I don't remember. But I found someone on there. She's using the name Julia.'

'Julia?'

'Yes. It's why I looked twice. There's no photo, but she's about twenty-eight or twenty-nine. She lives in Paris. And . . .'

'And?'

'Well, the thing is, she hasn't logged on since the end of January.'

'What's the name of the site?'

'Why?'

'Because I want to try the login details that worked with encountrz. I want to know if it's her.'

'Why don't you leave it to me?'

Because I want to know.

'Please, Lukas. Just tell me what it's called. I'll take a look . . .'

He sighs, loudly. I can almost hear him try to decide what's for the best.

'I'm not sure it's a good idea,' he begins. 'You'll just get upset, and—'

'Lukas!'

'Hear me out. Here's what I think we should do. I'll send this person a message. If they reply we'll know it's not Kate.'

'But they haven't even logged on since January . . .'

'Okay. Well, why don't you give me Kate's login details? I'll try them for you.'

So this is it, I think. I have to decide now. Do I trust him, or not?

What choice do I have, really? I give him the password. Jasper1234.

'It's the name of our dog, growing up. Promise me you'll try it.'

*

He calls me back an hour later. I haven't been able to settle. I've just been pacing, sitting at my computer, trying to work, failing. When my phone rings I snatch at it.

'Hello?'

'I'm sorry.'

'You didn't get in.'

'No—'

'She might have used a different password—'

'Julia, wait. This woman responded to my message. I asked her for a picture and she sent me one. It's not Kate.'

'Can I see the picture? It might be someone impersonating her . . .'

'It's not,' he says. 'This woman's black.'

I feel utterly flat. It's not worth it, this false raising of my hopes, when it leads only to crushing disappointment. Anything feels better. Even emptiness.

'I'll keep looking. If you want me to?'

I tell him. 'I'm just disappointed.'

'Try not to be. Will I see you next week? Tuesday?'

I hesitate. Everything is too bright, too intense. I want normality, stability. I think back to the visceral love I feel for my son, the way in which I missed him last night after finding out about Paddy's attack. As if for the first time, I realize this love isn't compatible with what I'm doing.

I remind myself why I chatted to Lukas in the first place, why I first met him. To find my sister's killer, for the sake of Connor, for the family.

But that's got me nowhere, and now Connor needs something else from me. A trip to the cinema. A burger. Mother and son. I make my decision.

'I can't. Not Tuesday. I'm busy.'

I have the sense of a grip suddenly relaxed. I'm relieved. It's a good feeling. I've been selfish; now, I'm doing the right thing.

'Busy?'

'Yes. I'm sorry.'

I realize I'm holding my breath. Part of me wants him to argue, to protest, the rest hopes he'll just suggest another day. I want to make sure I can last a week without seeing him.

Silence. I need an excuse. 'It's just that I have a friend. Anna. She wants me to help her look for a wedding dress.'

'She can't do a different day?'

'No. I'm sorry . . .'

'Okay.' I want him to argue some more. I want him to try and persuade me, to ask me who's more important, him or Anna.

But he doesn't. He's saying goodbye and a moment later the call is over.

Chapter Twenty

Tuesday comes. It's Connor's day, and I decide we'll do whatever he wants. I owe it to him; he deserves it. He seems more cheerful, is talking more now, more like his old self.

At the weekend we went to see Paddy. Hugh's idea. He didn't look as bad as I was expecting. His eyes were swollen and bruised, there was a graze on his cheek. He couldn't tell how many people had attacked him, or even if it was more than one. They took nothing, just knocked him out. He didn't look at me once the whole time we were there.

I get up early. I haven't slept well; last night I'd seen the figure again, outside my window. It looked more real this time, it had more substance. I even thought I saw the glow of a cigarette, but once again, once I'd looked away to talk to Hugh then gone back, he'd gone. If he'd ever been there at all.

I'm blurry eyed as I go downstairs. I find my phone and see I missed another call from Adrienne last night. I feel guilty. She's been travelling; she wants to know if I got my present, a silver necklace I admired months ago when we were out shopping. 'Just let me know,' she'd said, in her last message. 'And let's meet up. I'm busy, as ever, but dying to see you! Call me back.'

I haven't done so, and I'm not sure why. Maybe because she knows me too well; she'd see straight through me if I tried to hide anything from her. Plus, there's the lie I told Hugh, about me falling on the escalator. I need to put a bit of distance between us. It's easier to avoid her, just for a little while.

Connor and I have breakfast in front of the television. When we finish I ask him what he wants to do today, and he says maybe we could go and see a film. 'Sure!' I say. I tell him to choose one. 'Whatever you like.' He picks the new *Planet of the Apes* film. I'm disappointed, but I'm careful not to let it show.

We walk to the cinema, across Islington Green. I realize it's been a long time since we did this, just the two of us. I've missed it, and wonder whether he has, too. From nowhere I'm filled with a deep sense of love, and of guilt. It hits me that now Kate's gone Connor is the only blood relation I have, the only person with whom I share DNA. I realize Kate was the link, to all of us. Our mother and father, me, her, and now Connor. She was the centre of it all.

I have to say something. The need is overpowering. 'You know I love you,' I say. 'Don't you?' He looks at me; his expression is inscrutable, as if he's slightly embarrassed. For a moment I see the vulnerable little boy inside him, the one trying to cope with the adult world in which he's finding himself more enmeshed with each passing day. But then it passes and something else flashes briefly on his face. It's pain, I think, followed a moment later by the resolve to conquer it.

'Connor? Is everything all right?'

He nods, raising his eyebrows as he does. It's a familiar gesture, meant to be reassuring but now too automatic for it really to mean anything at all. 'I'm good.' We cross the road, then on the other side we stop, both at the same time, as if we'd rehearsed it. 'Honestly.'

I put my arms on his shoulders; sometimes he doesn't like

to be hugged, and I guess that standing in the middle of Upper Street might be one of those times. 'You can talk to me, Con.' I remember how long it's been since I used to call him that. Did he ask me to stop, or did it just fade away? Perhaps that's what always happens between mothers and sons. 'Please remember that. I'm here for you. Always.'

I feel guilty as I say it. Am I there for him? I haven't been, recently.

'I know.'

'The last few weeks . . . months . . .' I begin, but I don't know where I'm going. I'm trying to build the connection between us, one that I should never have put in jeopardy. '. . . they've not been easy. I know that. For any of us.' He looks at me. I want him to forgive me, to tell me I've been there for him, that he's all right. 'I know they've been really shit for you, too, Connor. I want you to know that. I do understand.'

He shrugs, as I knew he would. He's silent, but he looks at me with an expression of gratitude, and something passes between us. Something good.

In the cinema Connor goes to the bathroom while I buy our tickets at the machine then queue for the popcorn I've promised him. When he returns we make our way to the screen. I'd thought it would be busy, but it's less than half full. People are dotted around – mostly couples – and I suggest that we head for an almost empty row about halfway back. Connor agrees and we settle ourselves. The film hasn't yet started and the room is filled with the symphony of bottles being opened, drinks being slurped through straws, bags of sweets or crisps being torn into. I pass our popcorn to Connor. 'Have you got everything you want?' I whisper, and he says he has. He's checking his phone and looks up guiltily. A message from his girlfriend, I suppose. Evie. He mentions her occasionally; he's said she wasn't at Carla's party, but he's evasive, still at that age where discussing a girlfriend with his parents is embarrassing. Without thinking, and to reassure him it's fine, I pick up my bag and check mine.

I have a message, from Lukas. I'm relieved; our last few conversations have been frosty, and since I last saw him I've thrown an accusation at him and told him I didn't want to see him today. I thought maybe he'd taken the decision to end things before I did, and to do it with silence. 'How's the shopping?'

I type my reply quickly.

'Boring. But thanks for caring . . .'

I press send. Part of me is hoping he won't respond, yet still I keep my phone in my hand in case he does. Sure enough, a moment later, there's a reply.

'I wish I was there with you.'

I smile to myself. He's no longer angry with me, if he ever was. I was being ridiculous.

'So do I.' Once again I press send then I switch off my phone.

The film begins. It's not my kind of thing at all, but I remind myself I'm here for Connor and when I look across at him I can see that he's enjoying it. I try to settle. I try to stop thinking about Lukas, try to ignore the temptation to fish my phone out of my bag and check whether he's replied. I concentrate on the movie.

A minute or so later Connor shifts his legs. Someone is pushing past him, murmuring, 'Sorry,' as he does so. It's odd, I think. This new arrival is alone, there are plenty of seats.

Why does he choose our row? I move out of the way, too, and he says sorry to me, though he's looking at the screen while he does it. I'm even more surprised when he sits in the seat right next to me. I consider pointing out that there are plenty further along, but then think, really, what's the harm? I go back to the film.

A few moments later I begin to feel a pressure on my leg. I'm not certain at first, but then it becomes definite. The newcomer is pressing his leg against mine; it feels deliberate, though I can't be sure. I look down – his leg is bare; he's wearing board shorts – then move my leg away, just an inch or so. It might've been accidental; I don't want to make any kind of fuss. I pretend to be engrossed in the screen, but then the man's leg moves to connect with mine again, more urgently this time, too deliberate for it to be coincidence.

I look over. The action on the screen is dark and I can't see much. I make out thick-rimmed glasses and a baseball cap, one of the ones that's rigid and sits tall on the front of the head. The man's staring at the screen, rubbing the lower half of his face with his right hand, as if in deep contemplation.

I move my leg again and take a deep breath, readying myself to say something, to tell him to pack it in or get lost; I'm not sure which. At the same time the stranger drops his hand from his face and turns to me, and as he does the action on the screen moves overground, to a scene of lit brilliance, bathing the theatre with light. It's then I see that the man sitting next to me is no stranger. It's Lukas. He's smiling.

I gasp, yet at the same time my stomach tips with desire. An abyss of fear opens in front of me and I begin to spiral towards it. What's he doing here, in this cinema? What the fuck is going on? It can't be a coincidence; it would be ridiculous. Yet how can it be anything else? He doesn't know where I live: I've never told him, I know that. I've been careful all the way through.

Yet here he is. He's looking back at the screen now. He's moved his leg away, as if he's now trying to avoid contact with me. I turn back to the movie, then a moment later glance at Connor, sitting on my other side. He's noticed nothing.

My heart is beating too fast; I don't know what to do. This is too far, I want to say. You've gone too far. Yet . . .

Yet he's pressing his leg against mine once again, and this time I haven't shifted away. His skin on mine is charged, I can feel every tiny hair, the warmth of his muscles. Even though my son is just inches away, I find I like it.

I close my eyes. My mind whirls in confusion. Just a few minutes ago he'd sent me a message, about the shopping I'd told him I was doing. He must have already known that was a lie, but how can he have known I was here?

I look over at Connor again. He's engrossed in the film, his hand dipping occasionally into the bucket of popcorn on his lap. After a moment I turn to look at Lukas, who appears to be fixated, too. He must sense my gaze. Slowly he turns to me, so that he's looking directly at me, as if he wants to make sure I know it's him. I look into his eyes and ask the question wordlessly, and he begins to smile. There's no warmth, and I feel a sick disappointment. I look back at the screen, then after a few moments at him again. This time he winks, still without warmth, then looks ahead once more, and after a few moments stands to leave. As he does he says, 'Excuse me,' and he pushes past my son with a 'Hey, dude . . .'

And then, as if he'd never been here, he's gone.

*

I sit. My mind won't be still, I can't concentrate on the film. I'm thinking of Lukas, I can't work out what he'd wanted, why he'd turned up.

Or how he'd known where I'd be.

My hand goes to the seat in which he'd been sitting, as if I might feel him there. It's still warm, I haven't imagined it. I begin to tremble. My mouth is dry and I take a sip of water from the bottle I'd bought with Connor's popcorn. Nausea rises within me. I must calm down. I take a deep breath, but the air is syrupy with the smell of half-eaten hot dogs and belched ketchup. I feel sick. I close my eyes. I see Lukas.

I have to get out. I have to get some air.

'Come on.'

'What?'

'We're leaving.'

'But Mum!'

'This is rubbish,' I say.

'Well, I'm enjoying it.' I'm aware we're making a lot of noise; from somewhere behind, someone tuts.

I stand up. I need to keep moving. 'Okay, stay here, then. I'll be back in a minute.'

I go to the toilet. I'm nervous as I push the door open; he might be in here, I think, and straight away my mind goes to the time we had sex in the toilet cubicle near his hotel. But he isn't. Just some girls, Connor's age or a little older, fixing make-up, gossiping. Someone was *fucking unbelievable*; someone else was apparently *gonna make him pay*. I ignore them and go into one of the cubicles. I lock the door and take out my phone. Nothing, just a message from Hugh. We've run out of milk. Can I pick some up?

I sit for a while, willing my phone to ring, or for there to be a message. A smiley face, a wink. Anything to reassure me that Lukas was just having a bit of fun. But there's nothing. I don't know what to think.

I call him. His phone goes straight to voicemail. I try again, and again, and again. And then, because there's nothing else I can do, I give up. I put my phone in my bag and rejoin my son.

Chapter Twenty-One

We get home. I'm numb, I can't think. I'd hoped Connor hadn't noticed Lukas, but as we walked home he said, 'Didn't you think that guy was weird?'

I was looking left and right, waiting to cross the road, but also looking out for Lukas. He was nowhere to be seen.

'Sorry?'

'That guy. The one who came in and sat right by us in a half-empty room?'

'Oh, *him*?' I tried to sound natural, but had no idea whether I was succeeding. 'People are odd.'

'And then he leaves, before the film's even over. What a freak!'

I wondered if that was it, part of the game. I wondered whether I was supposed to make an excuse to my son, follow Lukas, have him fuck me in the toilets. I wondered if, deep down, I'd really wanted to do just that.

Now, my mind spins. I don't understand how he's done this, much less why. Every time a possibility comes, a solution, I'm forced to reject it. If it was a coincidence, then why didn't he say hello? If it was a game, then why didn't he at least smile, let me know we were playing?

I keep returning to the same few thoughts. This shouldn't have been possible. He doesn't know where I live. He thought I was out shopping with Anna.

'You all right, Mum?' says Connor. I realize I'm still standing in the middle of the kitchen.

I force a smile. 'I think I'm getting a migraine.' Another wave of panic crashes in. I look at my son. He knows about you, now, I think. You're no longer safe. I feel myself begin to suffocate.

'Shall I get you some water?' he says. He goes to the sink and picks two tumblers off the drainer.

'Yes,' I say. 'Thank you.' I take the glass from him and sip; it's lukewarm.

'I think I'll go and have a lie down.'

I go upstairs. Lukas still isn't answering his phone, and there are no messages on mine. I open my computer and see he's online. My fury is doubled.

– What was that all about? I type. I hesitate before pressing send. I ought to walk away, I want to walk away. But I can't. There's no way out, now. Everywhere I turn, he's there.

His reply comes after only a moment.

– Did you enjoy it?

I gasp. He has no idea how I feel, what he's done.

– How did you know where I'd be?

There's no reply. For a long time, nothing. Damn you, I think. Damn you. And then, finally:

– I thought it would be a nice surprise.

A nice surprise? I'd laugh if my whole body wasn't humming with fear.

– How did you know?

– I had to get creative.

– Meaning?

There's an even longer pause.

– Don't panic. I was in Islington. There's an antiques shop

there I go to occasionally. I saw you across the street. I followed you.

Antiques, I think. Since when has he been into antiques? I don't know anything about this man.

– I thought it'd be fun.

– Fun? You scared me!

I read his messages again. I want to believe him, but I can't. He happened to be shopping in Islington? Some coincidence. And even if it were true, then surely he'd have just messaged me?

Instead, he'd followed me, sat next to me, winked at me in the dark. He'd spoken only to my son, not to me, and his expression wasn't that of someone giving someone else a nice surprise. It was the expression of someone who thinks they've found something out.

– Scared you? Why? What did you think I was going to do?

– I don't know.

Suddenly I realize. It's a moment of absolute clarity, when everything that had felt muddled and grey is as clear and colourless as ice-cold water. I'd become involved with him for the sake of my son, but now it was my son who was at risk. I have no choice. I'm going to have to end it.

I try to fix on the thought, but even as I do another, stronger, part of me is trying to push it away. Lukas sends me another message.

– What did you want me to do?

– What?

– In the cinema. Tell me.

I feel like screaming. How can I make him see this isn't a game? There are things at stake here, things that might be lost for ever.

– Not now, Lukas. OK?

I press send. I sit back. I want him to understand what he's done, how much it'd scared me. I want him to know there are lines we mustn't cross.

His reply comes a few seconds later.

– Tell me how you wanted me to touch you, it says. Tell me you were imagining it, right there in front of all those people.

– No, I say.

– What's wrong?

I don't answer. There's no avoiding it, and I don't want to have this conversation online. I can't make him understand what he's done, not here, not now. I don't want to see him again, but I have no choice.

– I want to see you. It's important.

– Whatever you like.

There's a long moment, then he sends another message.

– By the way, who's the kid?

'He's my son.' He's sitting opposite me, we're having lunch. My choice, even though now I'm here I wish I'd suggested somewhere more secluded. He'd wanted to meet in a hotel, but I knew that wouldn't be a good idea. We've come to a restaurant just near the river. We're sitting outside, under an umbrella. Commuters stream past on their way to the station.

I haven't even asked about his hunt for more of Kate's online profiles. I suspect he's given up. I doubt he was ever looking very hard.

'Your son?' he says. For a moment I think he doesn't believe me. 'You didn't tell me.'

'No,' I sigh. I have to be honest. It's time for that, at least. 'I wanted to keep him out of it.'

And I failed. Lukas knows everything, now, and it's too much. What had seemed manageable is now out of control, what had been in a box has now broken free.

I look at this man. It's almost as if he owns me, and I must claim myself back.

'What's his name?'

I flinch. It's a protective instinct; I'm angrier than I thought.

I look away. On the other side of the road a guy in Lycra remonstrates with a driver who must've almost knocked him off his bike.

'No.' I turn back. 'Like I said, I want to keep him out of it.'

'You don't trust me.'

'Lukas. It's not as simple as that. What we had, I wanted to keep it separate from my real life. I wanted to keep it apart. I didn't want to have to think about my husband, and certainly not my son.'

'What we had.' It's a statement, not a question.

'Sorry?'

'You said, "What we had." Past tense. So I'm guessing it's over?'

I don't answer; my choice of words had been uncalculated, my mistake Freudian. But it's made, and now a single word is all it would take. I could say yes, then stand up. I could walk away, change my phone number, never log on to those websites, then all this would be in the past. A mistake, but one that's easily undone. He's never been to my house, never even seen it; nor I to his. We're entangled, but not so much that one single decisive action wouldn't separate us, cleanly and for ever.

But is that what I want? On the way here I'd thought it was, but now I can't be sure. Sitting here now, I'm in two minds. Would he really hurt anyone? He seems so gentle, so loving. I think of the long nights of loneliness. I think of going back to the days when a new message on my phone would be nothing more exciting than Hugh telling me he'll be late again or Connor asking whether he can stay out longer.

'Look.' He shifts his weight, opens his arms to shrug his shoulders. I'm struck again by his presence, his flesh, right in front of me. It glows; it's in three dimensions, where everything else seems in two. 'I fucked up. In the cinema. I'm sorry. I really thought you'd like it.'

'I didn't.' I glance briefly over his shoulder at the argument that's only now beginning to lose momentum, then look back at him.

'It was a coincidence, that's all. I was in Islington. I didn't even know you lived round there.'

'Lukas . . .'

'You don't believe me?'

'What were you doing in Islington?'

He hesitates. It's just a fraction of a second, but long enough for it to sound like a lie. 'I told you. Shopping. I go quite often, when I'm in town.'

'So why were you in town?'

'I come in every Tuesday, if you hadn't noticed. Usually it's to see you. It was force of habit, I suppose.' He sighs. 'I missed you. My day felt kind of wasted without you, so I thought I'd come up to town anyway.'

'You expect me to believe that?'

'I was upset, I guess. I wanted to see you. It was our day. You cancelled on me.'

'So you were in Islington, completely randomly, where I was taking my son to the cinema?'

'Coincidences do happen, you know.'

I find myself beginning to wish I could believe him.

'You think I've been following you? You really *are* paranoid.'

'That's an unkind thing to say.'

'I'm sorry. Listen, I saw you. Honestly. Crossing the street. And I'd thought of nothing else but you for a whole week, so I followed you. Maybe it was a mistake—'

'It was.'

'But I'm going crazy. You're all I think about.'

'Lukas—'

'Tell me you've been thinking of me.'

'Of course I have. But—'

'So, what's the problem?'

'I don't know. I just . . . it freaked me out. It was . . . risky.'

'I thought you liked risk? I thought you liked danger?'

'Not like that—'

'It's what you've been telling me.'

I raise my voice. 'Not like that. Not when it involves Connor.'

Shit, I think. I've told him my son's name. It's too late now.

He says nothing. We're both silent for a moment. Neither of us has started to eat the food in front of us. A sandwich for him, a salad for me. It occurs to me we've never had a meal together, not properly. We never will.

'How did you know what film we were going to see? Or were you looking over my shoulder as I bought the tickets?'

He still doesn't answer.

'I want to trust you, Lukas.'

'Then trust me. I've never lied to you. I made a mistake, that's all. I'm not stalking you. I didn't attack your friend. I mean, after what you've been through?'

He looks angry, but also deeply hurt. It's this that comes closest to convincing me. Yet still I'm not certain. Not quite.

I came here wanting to end it between us, to get out, but now I'm not sure I can. Not yet.

'I'm sorry.'

'You have to trust me, Julia,' he says.

I look down at my plate. 'I find it difficult to do that with anyone, I suppose.'

He reaches out to take my hand. 'Connor,' he says, as if he's trying the name out for size, seeing how it feels, how it sounds. 'Why didn't you tell me you had a son?'

I look at the wedding ring he's wearing. You didn't tell me you had a wife, I want to say. Things start to add up. The ring, first, plus the fact he's never – not once – suggested we go to Cambridge, even though it isn't far away.

'You're married, aren't you?' I speak softly, quietly, as if I don't really want him to hear.

'I was. You know that.'

'I mean, you still are. Admit it.'

'No!' He looks angry. Shocked. How could I suggest such a thing?

'I told you the truth. I wouldn't lie about that. Ever.'

I watch as his anger turns to pain. It's visceral, unmistakable. The pain of loss, something I know only too well, and for a moment I feel guilty, and desperately sorry for him. I can't help it. I wish I'd let him in. I wish I'd told him about my son, right from the beginning.

'Promise me.'

He takes my hand between his. 'I promise.'

I realize I believe him.

'Look, my son – Connor – has been through a lot. I wanted to protect him—'

'You think I'd hurt him?'

'No. But it's not so much people I'm trying to protect him from, but situations. He needs stability.' I take a deep breath. 'It's complicated. Connor's adopted. He . . . his mother was my sister.'

I wait while he absorbs what I've told him.

'The sister who was killed?'

'Yes.'

A long moment.

'When did you adopt him?'

'When he was very little. My sister couldn't cope, so we took care of him.'

'He knows?'

I nod. He's silent for a moment, then says, 'I'm sorry.'

He looks at me. I have nothing else to say. I'm spent, empty. I begin to pick at my salad. After a minute or two he says, 'So, is this it, then?'

'Is what it?'

'That use of the past tense back there. This conversation. The fact you didn't want to go to a hotel. You want me to leave you alone.'

The answer should be yes, but I hesitate. I don't know why. I'll miss feeling desire; I'll miss having it reciprocated. I'll miss being able to talk to him about things I can tell no one else.

I want to keep hold of all that, even for just a few more minutes.

'I don't know.'

'It's all right. I had a feeling this was going to be one of those "I'm sorry, but . . ." conversations. You know. "I can't do this any more." That kind of thing.'

Have you had many of those? I think fleetingly. And, if so, how recently, and from which side? Dumping, or being dumped?

I look away. I think back, to everything that's happened. I realize the dark place my grief has taken me. I've become fragile. Paranoid. I see danger everywhere. There's a man standing outside my window, my lover has attacked someone when he doesn't even know their full name, much less where he lives. If I'm not careful I will push away everything that is good in my life.

I make my decision.

'I don't want this to be over. But what you did the other day . . . Don't do it again. Okay? I won't have Connor brought into this.'

'Okay.'

'I mean it. I'll just walk away.'

'Okay.' He looks anxious, and as I see this I start to relax. The balance of power has shifted, yet it's more than that.

I realize this is what I wanted, all along. I wanted to see him bothered, I wanted to know that he understood what was at stake, I wanted to see him frightened that he might lose me. I wanted to see my own insecurities reflected in him.

I soften my voice. 'No more games. Okay? All that stuff we've been talking about' – I lower my voice – 'the play-acting, the rough sex. It has to stop.'

'Okay.'

'I can't have you turning up unannounced. I can't go back home covered in bruises . . .'

'Whatever you say, as long as it isn't over.'

I reach across and take his hand. 'How can it be over?'

'What happens now?'

'Now? I go home.'

'Will I see you on Tuesday?'

'Yes. Yes, of course.'

He looks relieved.

'I'm sorry. About the games, and stuff. I guess I'm not so good at romance.' He pauses. 'We'll do something. Next time. Something lovely. Leave it with me.'

Chapter Twenty-Two

A week passes. Connor goes back to school, a year nearer to his exams, to adulthood and whatever comes with it, a year nearer to moving away from me. I've had his blazer dry-cleaned and taken him shopping for shirts and a new pair of shoes. He's not enthusiastic about going back, but I know that will only last a day or so. He'll be reunited with his friends, with his routine. He'll remember how he enjoys his studies. Hugh's right when he says he's a good kid.

On his first day back I go to the window and watch him walk down the street; by the time he's gone a few feet, barely past the end of the drive, he's loosened his tie, and just at the corner he waits for a moment. One of his friends arrives, they clap each other on the shoulder, then set off together. He's becoming a man.

I turn away from the window. I have another job tomorrow – the woman whose family I photographed a few weeks ago has recommended me to a friend – and another next week. The hole in my soul is closing, yet part of me still feels empty. Kate's death still haunts everything I do. When Connor goes, I don't know how I'll cope.

I try not to think about it. Today's Tuesday. I'm meeting Lukas. I have the morning to myself, hours to get ready. It's like the first time we met, all those weeks and months ago, back when I thought it would be a one-off, nothing more

than an opportunity to find out what happened to my sister.
How that has changed.

Yet I know it has to end. Sometimes I think about that
moment, when we separate, finally and for ever, and wonder
if it'll be something I'll be able to survive. Yet separate we
must; my relationship with Lukas has no happy ending. I'm
married. I'm a mother. I love my husband, and my son, and
I can't have everything.

When I leave the house Adrienne is pulling up in a car. It's a
surprise, not like her at all. I wave and she opens the car
door. Her face is grave, set in a hard line, and I'm nervous.

'New car?'

'Whatever. Darling, can I come in?'

'What is it? You're scaring me.'

'I thought I'd ask you the same question.' She points back
the way I'd just come. 'Shall we?'

I stay where I am.

'Adrienne? What is it?'

'You're ignoring me. Why?'

'Darling, I'm—'

'Julia. I've been trying to get hold of you for days.'

'Sorry. I've not been well.'

Another lie. I feel wretched.

'Is something going on? Dee says you're not returning her
calls either. And Ali said she invited you to a party and you
didn't even reply.'

Did she? I can't even remember. I feel something give, as if
something in my head has slipped, some kind of defence. My
mind begins to flood. Yes, I want to say. Something's going
on. I want to tell her everything, I want it all to come out.

But I know what she'll say.

'Going on? Like what?'

She shakes her head. 'Oh, darling . . .'

'What?'

'Bob's seen you.'

I flinch. It's not the enveloping fog of guilt, or shame. This is something else, razor sharp, a scalpel on my skin.

'Seen what?'

'You with some guy. He said you were having lunch.'

I shake my head.

'By the river?'

I tense. I'm flooded with adrenalin. I can't let her see. 'Last week?' I say. 'Yes, I was having lunch with a friend. Why didn't he say hello?'

'He was in a taxi. A friend? He said he didn't recognize him.'

I try to laugh. 'Bob doesn't know all my friends, you know!'

I see her begin to soften. 'A man friend. He said it looked pretty intimate. Who was it?'

'Just someone I met. I took a photograph of him and his wife.' I take a risk. 'She was with us.'

'He said it was just the two of you.'

'She must've been in the loo. What's this about? You think I'm having an affair?'

She looks right at me. 'Are you?'

'No!'

I hold her gaze.

'Adrienne, I'm telling the truth.'

'I hope so,' she says.

I don't look away. I *am*, I want to say. I want to plead my innocence.

But is that because I want it to be true, or because I want to wriggle off the hook?

'I'm really sorry, but I have to go. I have a shoot.'

I'm carrying no equipment. I see her notice.

'Later, I mean. I have to get some things first. Some shopping.'

She sighs. 'Okay. But call me. We'll talk properly.'

I tell her I will.

'Where are you off to? Do you want a lift?'

I tell her, 'No, no I'm fine.'

'Promise you'll call me,' she says, and then she's gone.

Now I'm in a taxi. I feel jumpy, anxious. Bob has seen me and Lukas. A lucky escape, I think, but next time? Next time it might be Adrienne herself, or even Hugh.

I've been neglecting him. I know that. I have to give Lukas up.

Either that or I have to start being more careful. I'm not sure which I want more.

I pull up to the St Pancras hotel and go into the lobby. It reminds me of the first time I came here. There's the same sense of danger, and excitement. The same notion that everything might be about to change.

I go to the reception desk and give my name. The woman behind the desk nods. 'For Mr Lukas?' she says.

'Yes, that's right.'

She smiles. 'There's a package for you.' She reaches under the desk, then hands me a parcel. It's a little bigger than a shoebox, wrapped in brown paper, sealed with packing tape. My name is scrawled on the front in black marker pen. 'And Mr Lukas asked me to give you a message,' she says. She hands me a slip of paper. 'Running late,' it says. 'There's champagne on ice behind the bar. Hope you like the gift.'

I thank her. I wonder why he's bought us champagne when he knows I don't drink. I begin to turn away. 'Oh,' I say, turning back, 'do you have some scissors?'

'Of course.' She hands over a pair. I stand at the desk and

slit through the tape. I think of Hugh as I do so; I imagine myself touching a scalpel to yellow-stained flesh, watching as the skin yields then gives with a swell of red. I hand the scissors back to her then take the box to one of the chairs nearby. I want to be alone when I open my gift.

I take a deep breath and fold back the flaps. A smell hits me – not unpleasant, stale air, a faint, floral trace of perfume. Inside, there's tissue, a sealed envelope. It's this I open first.

There's a postcard inside. It's plain, creamy white. I think back to the cards that were put through my letterbox, the ones I'd told him might have been from Paddy, but there's no woman in lingerie, no breasts, no pouting girl who looks not quite old enough to be holding the pose she's holding, wearing the expression she has on her face.

I flip the card over. On one side is a message.

'A little gift,' it says. 'See you soon. Wear this. Lukas.'

I put the note to one side. If he's crammed an outfit into the box, there can't be much to it. I lift out the bundle and tear through the tissue paper it's wrapped in.

It's a dress. Bright red. A mini-dress, short, with long sleeves and a low-cut back. I can already see how tight it's going to be, how it will hug my body, hiding nothing, only accentuating the curves of my flesh. I check and find he's picked the right size, but it's not the kind of thing I'd wear at all, which must be why he's chosen it. Beneath it there's a pair of shoes. They're black, high-heeled, almost four inches I guess, much higher than I'm comfortable in, with a tiny bow on the toe. I take them out; they're beautiful. They look expensive.

At the bottom of the box is one more thing. A padded jewellery case in soft red leather. My heart beats with childish excitement as I flip it open. Inside there's a pair of earrings. Gold drop with a four-leaf-clover design and, unlike the shoes, they look inexpensive.

I react instinctively. My heart thuds, I snap the box closed. They're similar to the ones Kate was wearing. It's coincidence, I think. It has to be. He's forgotten. It's like when Hugh casually mentioned that Paddy had been mugged but nothing had been taken. I'm over-sensitive. I have to pull myself together.

I find the bathroom. I'm nervous, unmoored. Something doesn't feel right. It's the dress, the shoes. The earrings. They're beautiful, but they're not gifts one buys for someone they care about. They're a costume. A disguise. This time he's making explicit what until now has been implied: this is unreal, a fantasy. I must become other. I must take off my wedding ring, even though he knows I'm married. I must pretend to be someone I'm not. This is a game, a masquerade. It's exactly what I'd told him I don't want.

So why am I getting changed? Why am I wearing the dress? I can't say; it's almost as though there's no other option. What's happening has its own momentum, a pull too powerful to resist. I'm heading into the unknowable, the foreign. I'm light, being drawn into the blackness.

I take the furthest cubicle from the door and lock it behind me. I take off the clothes I'm wearing then hold the dress up in front of me. It unfurls itself, a curtain of red, and I slip it over my head before shimmying the zip closed. I put the heels on the floor then step into them. The height lifts me into another space, a place where I am strong. I take off my earrings and replace them with the ones he's given me. The transformation is complete. I am other. Julia is no longer here.

I step out of the cubicle and go over to the mirror. My perspective has shifted; everything is different. I no longer know who I am, and I'm glad.

I smile at my reflection and a stranger returns my gaze.

She's beautiful, and utterly confident. She looks a little bit like Kate, though thinner, and older. The bathroom door closes behind me with a sigh.

At the bar I begin to relax. My heart slows to its normal pace, my breathing becomes deeper. Before I can stop him, the waiter has poured some of the champagne Lukas has left, but I ask for water as well. I look around. The bar isn't busy, just a few people dotted around. I put down my glass. I want to look comfortable when Lukas arrives. Composed. As in something that's made up, created. Something that's a fiction.

I drink the water slowly, yet still Lukas hasn't arrived by the time I finish the first glass. I pour myself another as I look again at the clock on my phone. He's very late now, and there're still no messages. I sip my drink and rearrange my dress. I wonder what's holding him up. I wish I were wearing my own clothes.

A moment later I realize there's somebody behind me, leaning on the bar. I can't see him but I know it's a man – there's a solidity to him, the space he occupies he does so confidently. Lukas, I think. I begin to smile as I turn, but I'm disappointed. It's not him. This man is larger than Lukas; he's wearing a grey suit, holding a glass of beer. He's alone, or appears to be. He turns and smiles at me. It's obvious, unsubtle and I'm not used to it. Yet it's flattering. He's young, attractive, with a beard, a strong jaw, a nose that's been broken. I smile back, because it would be rude not to, and look away.

He must take my smile as an invitation. He turns his body to face me, says, 'How're you?'

'I'm fine.' I think of Lukas, resist the temptation to tell him I'm waiting for someone. 'Thanks.'

His face opens. He grins, says, 'D'you mind?' He's indicating the empty seat between us but before I can tell him I'm saving it for someone he's already sitting down. I'm irritated, but only mildly so.

'I'm David.' He shakes my hand. His palms have a roughness not suggested by his clothes. I see his eyes sweep my body, travel from my neck, to my arms, to my ringless finger. It's only when they come to rest once again on my face that I realize he's still holding my hand.

I'm impatient. It's Lukas I want to be holding. His flesh, not this man's.

But he isn't here, and I'm annoyed, even if I don't want to admit it.

'I'm Jayne,' I say.

'You're alone?'

A breeze caresses the back of my neck. I think of Hugh first, and then Lukas.

'For now,' I say.

'Well, I'm very pleased to meet you, Jayne,' he says. He holds my gaze. He's reaching inside me. It's an offer, a proposition. I'm under no illusions, I know it's because of the clothes I'm wearing. I might not have even noticed it a few months ago; Lukas has sensitized me to it.

But I don't feel the same thrill that I did when I met Lukas – the thrill of being desired but also of feeling desire. This time it's slightly uncomfortable. Again I think of telling him I'm waiting for someone, or that I'm married, but for some reason I don't. That would be hiding behind a man. *You can't have me, because I'm promised to another.* It would make me weak. He shifts his weight on the stool so that his right knee is close enough to brush against my left and I get a sudden thrill, so intense it shocks me.

'Likewise,' I say. He asks me whether I'm staying in the

hotel, whether I'm here on business. I say no. I don't want to lead him on.

'How about you?' I say.

'Oh, I'm in finance,' he says. 'It's very boring.'

'Travelling?'

'Yes. I live in Washington DC.'

'Really?' I say.

He nods. 'What're you having?'

'I have a drink already,' I say. There's a look of mock-disappointment on his face. I smile, then glance at the time on my phone. Lukas is late and hasn't sent a further message.

'Then I'll have the same.'

There's a swell and fizz as the drink is poured. We chink glasses, but I don't drink. Dimly, I'm aware of how this will look when Lukas arrives, which surely can't be long now. It pleases me. I'd rather this than he sees me alone, desperate, waiting for him.

Yet at the same time I wonder how easy this guy – David – will be to get rid of.

'So,' he says, 'tell me about you. Where are you from?'

'Me? Nowhere, in particular.' He looks confused, and I smile. I won't tell him the truth, but neither do I want to make anything up. 'I moved around a lot as a child.'

'D'you have any brothers or sisters?'

'No,' I say. I don't want Kate in the room. 'It was just me.'

I look up, into his eyes. They're wide; the expression of sincerity on his face is so perfect it can only be fake. I realize we're sitting close. His hand is resting on his thigh, his knee still pressed against mine. It's intensely sexual. The room seems to be tipping, off balance. Something is very wrong.

'Excuse me,' I say. 'I think I'll just use the Ladies.'

I stand. I'm unsteady. It's as if I really have been drinking, rather than just bringing it to my lips and putting it down again. In the bathroom I look at myself in the mirror, trying to reclaim the confidence I felt earlier, but I can't. Julia is returning; she's just wearing someone else's clothes.

I take out my phone, dial Lukas; there's no answer so I leave him a message. I splash water on my face, take a few deep breaths and gather myself.

When I return David is still sitting on the stool, still leaning against the bar. He watches me approach. He smiles. His legs are spread to balance himself, I suppose, though I wonder if he's also offering himself in some primitive, animal way. I take my seat.

He smiles, lowers his voice, leans forward. For a moment I think he's going to kiss me, but he says, 'I thought we could take this upstairs. Somewhere more private?'

I can't help it. There's a tingle, an excitement. I realize I like the thought of Lukas being upset by me wanting someone else. Yet he doesn't know, and fear is also flooding in. This isn't what I came here for. This isn't supposed to happen. This man looks strong. He's not someone I could fend off, even if I had to. Plus, we're in public and I don't want to cause a scene. I play for time.

'Here?' I say. 'In the hotel?' He nods. I tell myself to concentrate. 'I'm sorry,' I begin, 'but . . .'

I shrug, but he doesn't stop smiling. I think of the girls at school, and what the boys called them when they didn't go as far as they'd unwittingly promised. 'Cock-teasers', they said.

He doesn't seem to get the message. He puts his hand on my knee, moves it a fraction up, towards my thigh. He leans forward. I can smell him, pepper and wood, leathery, like old books. He begins to stroke the inside of my wrist. I know he's going to try and kiss me, that in a moment he'll close his eyes and open his mouth, just slightly, and I'll be expected to do the same.

I cough, and look towards the bar. He touches my arm. There's another tiny crackle of static.

He whispers. 'I know who you are,' he says, as if he's read my mind. He smiles, baring his teeth, as if he's growling. He's still stroking my skin.

I look at his lips, his dark skin, the faint shadow of stubble that he's probably never quite without. 'What—?' I say, as panic begins to gather within me.

'Kiss me.'

I begin to shake my head. I try to smile, to look confident, but I can't, I'm not. I can't believe what's happening. Without thinking I reach for the glass of champagne.

Ride it out, ride it out, ride it out.

'I—' I begin, but he interrupts me again.

'Kiss me.'

I turn my head away from him and wrest my hand from his. I start to speak, to protest. We're in public, I want to say. Leave me alone; but my words tumble and fall. His mouth is inches away from mine; I can smell alcohol, and beneath it is something stale. Garlic, perhaps. Where's Lukas? I think. I need him. I want him.

I look over my shoulder. The crowd has thinned out even further; the few guests that remain are engrossed in their own conversations. No one has noticed what's going on, or else they've chosen to ignore it.

'How much?' he says. I gasp, a little grunt of horror, but he just shrugs. It's as if the answer to his question concerns him as little as do my protests.

'How much?' he says again. 'That's all I'm asking. Name your price.'

My price? My mind races. This man thinks I'll sell myself, we just have to negotiate a price.

'You've got it wrong.' My voice is unsteady now. Slurred not with alcohol but with dread.

'Have I?' He moves his hand further up my thigh; his thumb, his fingers, are underneath the hem of my skirt. Distantly, as if from a great height, I wonder why I haven't moved away. I imagine the whole room watching; somehow everyone knows what he's doing, can see that I'm not stopping him. I glance towards the nearest table: the couple sitting at it have halted their conversation to sip their drinks; the man behind them is speaking into his phone. No one has noticed us. No one is looking.

'Stop it,' I hiss.

'I will. If you kiss me. If you promise to come upstairs and then let me fuck you.' He licks his lips, as if he's hungry. The action is deliberate, it carries a message; if it'd been Lukas I'd be flattered, excited, but from him it's more like a threat. 'Like I know you want me to. Little slag . . .'

I turn in on myself. There's a rush, a swell of anger. Lukas is supposed to be here, not this man. I feel myself in balance, a perfect serenity that cannot last, and for a long moment I'm unsure what I'm going to do, which way I'm going to fall.

I steel myself. 'Look.' I've raised my voice, just slightly. I want to attract attention, though without yet causing alarm. I speak firmly, hoping my voice will have an authority I don't feel. 'I'm asking you, politely, just this once. Take your hands off me, right now, or else I'll break your fucking arm.'

Even as I say it I'm not sure how he'll react. Hurt perhaps, but surely he'll get the message? I expect him to turn away, mutter something under his breath, but it'll make no difference. I'll stand up, walk out. I'll hold my head up and walk away and I won't look back.

But he doesn't move. He's perfectly still, then without warning he grabs my wrist. I recoil, try to get away, but his grip is powerful. He digs in tight, twisting as he does. 'You want to go home? Is that it? Home to your faggot husband? Hasn't had you in weeks? Is that what you want, Julia?'

I freeze. I know I should cry out, but I don't. I can't. I'm paralysed.

He used my real name.

'What—?' I begin, but then he speaks again.

'What's his name? Your husband? *Hugh?*'

Fear floods me. I haven't mentioned being married, much less told him my husband's name. How does he know? This can't be right. The room begins to spin; for a moment I feel I might collapse, but then there's a voice. 'Is everything okay here?' I turn and it's him. Lukas. Relief rushes through me as instantly as if a tourniquet had been released. The sound of the bar rushes back, like blood cells closing in on a wound. I'm safe.

This other man, David, lets go of me. He holds up his hands, palms out, a gesture of submission aimed not at me but at Lukas. It's as if he's asking this other man for his forgiveness, saying he's sorry for touching his property, and it enrages me. What? he seems to say. I was just having a bit of fun. No harm done. At the same time Lukas steps in, putting himself between me and David. I can see his broad back, his hair, curly and unkempt. Finally I understand; the rush of excitement and fear I feel is so vertiginous that for a moment I think I might gasp aloud. I'd asked for this. *A stranger*, I'd said, during one of our chats. *In a bar. Someone who won't take no for an answer.*

He'd planned it. After everything I'd said, he'd planned this.

We go upstairs. The door slams behind me. Vaguely I'm aware that I'm the one who slammed it. Lukas turns to face me. I have the sense I shouldn't feel safe with him, yet somehow I still do and I realize that the feeling is familiar. It's the exact same feeling I used to have about heroin; how can something that feels this good ever hurt me?

'What the fuck are you doing? What the fuck—?'

'Don't be—' he begins, but I interrupt again.

'Where the hell were you? What the—?'

'I was late—' he begins, and I interrupt him, furious.

'Late! Like you not being on time is the important thing we're discussing here. Who was that guy? And how the hell do you know my husband's name?'

'What?'

'That guy, he called him Hugh. I've never told you my husband's called Hugh. Harvey. I've always called him Harvey . . .'

'Yes, why *did* you do that?'

'I've got every right to. But that's not the point! How did you—?'

'Relax. You slipped up. Just once. You called him Hugh. Weeks ago. You were upset, I guess. You called him Hugh, and I remembered.'

I try to think back, to remember, but it's impossible. I want to believe him, though. I have to. Not to believe him about this might mean I have to not believe him about other things, too. And then everything would come crashing down.

'Julia . . .' He takes another step forward.

'Don't come near me!' To my surprise he stays where he is. After a moment he turns, goes to the mini-bar.

'More champagne?'

I snort with derision.

'I don't drink.'

'Not with me. But you will with a stranger.'

I'm furious. 'You ordered that bottle!'

'And you drank it.'

I look away. I can't be bothered to argue, there's no point. I've been a fool. I don't know him at all. I've rejected every warning, failed to see what was going on at every turn. He's taken my deepest desires, the things I ought never to have told anyone, and turned them against me.

He opens a miniature – vodka, I think – and pours it into a glass. 'You told me your fantasy was being rescued. Or one of them was, at least.'

'You think that's what I wanted?'

'Didn't you enjoy it?'

'So you told him – that man – to be aggressive? To . . . to make me think . . . to behave like that? You shared everything I'd told you?'

'Not everything. Just enough. I kept some of it to myself.'

'I said no more games, Lukas! No more. Remember?'

I sit in the chair. He sits on the bed. I realize he's between me and the door; a fundamental mistake, Hugh would say, though I don't know why he's ever had to worry; his patients don't tend to be the aggressive type. I stand up again.

'I thought it'd be fun.' He sighs, runs his fingers through his hair. 'Look, you told me. Your fantasy. Being in danger. Being rescued. You did say that?'

'I said lots of things. That doesn't mean I want them to happen. Not really. That's why they're called *fantasies*, Lukas.'

Dread hits. I remember the other things I've told him I fantasized about. Being taken by force, not quite against my will, but almost. Being tied to the bed, handcuffs, rope. Is he also planning that?

I try to backtrack. 'Half of the things I said I wanted I only said to please you.'

'Really? Like how Paddy had forced himself on you?'

He's sneering. He looks as if he doesn't care about me at all. I mean nothing to him.

'Poor Paddy. Accused of all those things he didn't do. And look where it got him.'

I back away. Every part of me wants to reject what he's telling me is true. 'It *was* you!'

'It's what you wanted—'

'It was *you*!' My heart hammers. I tense, as if for escape. 'It was you, all along!'

'And the mysterious figure outside your window . . .'

'What?'

'It's what you want, isn't it? To be scared?'

I try to work it out. The first time I'd thought I'd seen someone watching me was before I even met Lukas. But the other night? It'd seemed more real, then. Could that have been him?

No. No, he doesn't know where I live. He's using my paranoia against me.

'You're crazy.'

He looks at me and I return his gaze. Something slips within me, like a lever that's been thrown. Somehow I see myself through him, reflected in his eyes. I see the clothes I'm wearing, the shoes, even the way I smell. I realize, as if for the first time, the place I'm in and how deep I've got.

I've been here before. In thrall to something that's destroying me. Unable to escape. I think of Marcus, and of Frosty.

I force myself to say it.

'I'm leaving now. This is over.'

The room is still. The words have escaped. I can't unsay them now, even if I wanted to. He closes his eyes then opens them again. His face breaks, he smiles. He doesn't believe me.

'You're not.' His voice is low and heavy; it sounds like it

belongs to someone else. All his pretence has gone, leaving in its place nothing but a heavy malevolence.

My eyes flick to the door. If he wants to stop me there's no way I can overcome him.

I draw breath, summon as much strength as I can.

'Get out of my way.'

'I thought we were having fun?'

'We were. But we aren't now. Not any more.'

His mouth hangs, half open, then he speaks.

'But I love you.'

It's the last thing I expect him to say. I freeze. I'm disarmed, utterly shocked. My mouth opens, but I have no words.

'I love you,' he says again. I want him to stop, yet at the same time I don't. I want to believe him, yet don't think I can.

'What?'

'You heard me. I thought I was making you happy. All this' – he gestures around the room – 'was for you. I thought it's what you wanted.'

I shake my head. It's another game. I know it is. 'No,' I say. 'Lukas, no—'

'Tell me you love me, too?'

I look at him. His eyes are wide, imploring. I want to believe him. Just this once, I want to know he's telling me the truth.

'Lukas—'

He reaches out to me. 'Julia. Tell me, please.'

'Okay,' I say. 'Yes. Yes—'

I freeze. His hands have dropped. He smiles, then starts to laugh.

'It's just another one of your fantasies, isn't it? Me loving you?'

Suddenly I'm empty. Defeated. It's as if everything has flooded out of me and, right now, I hate him.

'Fuck you.'

'Oh, Julia, come on. What's the big deal? Today? David? You want to be rescued, I want to rescue you. I wanted you to think you really were in danger.' He looks at me. He's trying to see if I'm softening, if the anger is burning off. It's not. Not really. 'Look,' he says. 'All I said was he should try and pick you up. That you might be keen, you might not. Either way, he shouldn't take no for an answer. Like you wanted.'

I take a step back. 'You're crazy.' I whisper it. To myself as much as to him, but he ignores me.

'Shall I tell you what I think? I think you're getting cold feet just as it's starting to get interesting.' He pretends to reconsider. 'Or maybe it's the opposite. Maybe you're enjoying yourself a little too much.' I begin to speak, but he continues. 'You're worried that you don't deserve it.' He finishes his drink, pours another. 'Look. It's a game. You know that. And yet you can't quite think of it like that. You still think of games as something that children play. Something you've outgrown.'

'No,' I say. My voice sounds cracked. I draw breath and say it again. 'No. You're wrong. It's not a game.'

He laughs. 'What is it, then?' I want to get out. I can think only of escape. 'Your problem,' he says, 'is that you're still too attached to the old you. You can slip away to hotels, you can dress up in all the gear, but you're still the little housewife, married to Hugh. You're still the person that does his shopping and cooks his food and laughs at his jokes, even though you've heard them a million times before. You used to despise people whose only ambition in life was a nice rich husband and an adoring son and a house in Islington with a patio and a garden. Yet that's exactly what you've turned into. You're still someone who thinks there's only one way to be married, only one way to have an affair.'

I'm enraged, now. Ripped open. I want to scream at him. I want to hurt him. It's as if he's seen inside me, then emptied me out.

'How does it feel to hate yourself?'

'Get out of my way!'

He moves. He's between me and the door.

'You know, I was watching the whole time,' he says. 'Today. In the bar.' He hesitates, then lowers his voice. 'And you loved it. Didn't you? The attention.'

He's right. I know it, deep down. He's right, and I'm ashamed. I despise him.

'Please, just let me leave.'

'Or else . . . ?'

'Lukas . . .' I say. I try to push past him, but he blocks me. I step back again. I look at him, this almost-stranger. He lowers his voice still further. He's threatening now. He has the power; he wants me to know it.

'You enjoyed it. Didn't you? You liked knowing he wanted you. A stranger.' He takes another step; this time I stay where I am. 'No strings . . . nothing to worry about . . .'

I try a different tack.

'So what if I did? What about if I'd decided I liked him? I was going to have him? This David? What then?'

'Then things might have turned out differently,' he says. 'Were you tempted?'

I don't hesitate. I want to see him hurt. More than anything, I want to see him feel some of the pain that he's inflicting on me.

'Maybe.'

He doesn't move. I don't know what he's going to do.

'Before he started to threaten you? Or after?'

'Hard to say.' I don't move.

'The fear added something. Admit it. That's what turned you on.' He's whispering now, murmuring. When I'm silent he moves forward, towards me. His mouth is inches from my ear. His hand goes to my waist, I feel it on me. I pull away, but he's strong. His flesh touches mine. 'Would you have gone upstairs with him?' He pulls me to him, I feel the warmth of his body, his hands on me, searching for my skin, moving firmly, grasping, kneading. It triggers something, a muscle memory, and without me wanting it to my body begins to respond. 'Alone? Or with me?'

I don't reply. Somewhere, deep within me, I know I should be crying out. I should be fighting, kicking. I should be screaming for help.

But I'm not. I don't do any of those things. It's as if my body has mutinied. It will no longer react to anything but his touch.

'Please,' I say. 'Lukas . . .'

He tries to kiss me. I begin to respond, my body's final betrayal. I gather my energy and force myself to speak.

'Stop! Lukas. This has to stop.'

He does nothing. He continues to push himself against me. Harder now. 'Stop me, if you want. If you really want.'

I feel his hands. They're everywhere. At the back of my neck, in my hair, at my crotch. He's pushing and grabbing, with more and more urgency. He tries to push me backwards, or turn me round. I flash on the time we'd had sex, in the cubicle, his hands around my neck; it'd been a game then, but it isn't now. I have to get away from him.

I lash out, aiming at his face, his eyes. It's only a glancing blow, but my nails draw blood. He wipes his hand across his face, wide-eyed and furious. He looks like he's about to hit me and I try to step away.

We square up against each other. I open my mouth to

speak but just then I hear the sound of the lock sliding open. Relief floods me. It'll be a maid, perhaps, someone with room service. They'll see what's going on, Lukas will have to stop. I can dust myself down, make an excuse, leave. He won't follow me. I won't let him.

We both look to the door. Too late I see that Lukas is smiling. 'Ah,' he says. 'I thought you'd got lost.'

Fear hits me, full in the gut. It's David.

I grab my bag. I run. I slam past David, out into the corridor. Tears are coming, I close my eyes, crash into the walls as I run towards the stairs, but I carry on running. I see myself as if from a great height. It looks like me, but it isn't me. She's not wearing the clothes I wear. She's not doing the things I do.

I run and run and run, and all at once I'm back in Berlin. I'm shivering, at an airport, not knowing how I'm going to get home. I'm phoning Hugh from a phone box in the departure lounge, then I'm waiting. Waiting to be rescued by the man I'll soon marry while the one I'd thought was my whole life lies dead in a squat on the other side of the city.

PART FOUR

Chapter Twenty-Three

I made it out of the hotel. My legs shook, I was sweating, my heart was hammering so hard I thought my chest might burst, yet still I managed to pretend to be calm as I walked through the lobby, on to the street. Once outside I walked and walked, and it wasn't until I was sure I was out of sight of the hotel that I stopped to check what direction I'd gone in. I hailed a cab, got in. 'Where to?' the driver said, and I said, 'Anywhere,' and then, 'The river,' and then, 'The South Bank.' We began to drive, and he asked me if I was all right. 'Yes,' I said, even though I wasn't, and when we reached the South Bank I found a bench overlooking the Thames and, because I knew Adrienne would say 'I told you so,' and I didn't know who else to call, who there was that I hadn't pushed away, I phoned Anna.

'How're you?'

I told her everything, blasting it out in a mess of non-sequiturs that must have been largely incomprehensible, and she first listened then calmed me down and asked me to try again. When I finished she said, 'You must go to the police.'

She sounded steely, determined. Absolutely sure.

'The police?' It was as if it were the first time I'd considered it.

'Yes! You've been attacked, Julia.'

I flashed on his hands on me, all over me, grabbing my flesh, tearing at my clothes.

'But—' I said.

'Julia. You *have* to.'

'No,' I said. 'No, they didn't . . . he didn't . . . and Hugh . . .'

I imagined telling Hugh, making the call to the police. What would I say?

I've heard the stories. Even if I had been raped, they almost certainly wouldn't take me seriously, and if they did it'd be me who'd be on trial, not David, not Lukas. 'And you went there for sex?' they'd say, and I'd have to say yes. 'Dressed in clothes that he sent you?' Yes. 'Having told him, more or less, that rape was a fantasy of yours?'

Yes.

And what would my defence be? *I didn't want it to happen, though. Not like that!*

I felt myself crumple. I began to cry again as I imagined what might have happened, what Lukas might've done and got away with.

I thought of Hugh, and Connor. I imagined them finding out where I'd been, how I'd ended up. I'd have to tell them, there's no way I'd be able to lie; I've done enough of that already.

'I don't even know where he lives.'

She paused. 'Is there anything, anything at all, I can do to help?'

There's nothing anyone can do, I thought. I just have to leave him, to walk away, to make the severance that, just a few hours earlier, I'd been dreading.

'No.'

I went home. I knew what I had to do. Let Lukas recede into the past, do my best to forget him. Not log on. Not check my messages. Not raise my hopes that there'll be flowers, apologies, explanations. Move on.

Mostly, I've succeeded. I've carried on working. I told Hugh I'd decided to stop seeing the counsellor but to start going back to my meetings. I've done so, and kept busy in other ways. I've called Ali and Dee and the rest of my friends, and spoken to Anna every day. I've spent more time with Connor, even tried to talk to him about Evie, to reassure him that he can tell me about his girlfriend, if he wants. 'I'd like to meet her, one day,' I said. His shrug was predictable, but at least I'd made the effort.

I've met up with Adrienne, too. Finally. She invited me to a concert and we had dinner afterwards. We chatted; the argument we'd had outside the house felt all but forgotten. Before we said goodbye she turned to me.

'Julia,' she said. 'You know I love you. Unconditionally.' I nodded, waiting. 'And so I'm not going to ask you what's going on. But I need to know. Are you all right? Is there anything I need to worry about?'

I shook my head. 'No. Not any more.'

She smiled. It was the nearest I'd come to a confession, and she knew I'd tell her, one day.

I've only been weak once, one Sunday afternoon a few weeks ago. I'd fought with Hugh, Connor was being impossible. I couldn't help myself. I logged on to encountrz, ignored the couple of new messages I'd accumulated, then searched for his username.

Nothing. *Username not found.* He'd vanished.

I couldn't help it. I called him.

His number was unavailable. It didn't even go to voicemail. I tried again – in case there'd been a problem, he was out of the country, there was an issue with the connection – and then again, and again, and again. Each time, nothing.

And then I realized where I was, what I was doing. I told myself I was being ridiculous. I'd promised myself complete cut-off; I'd told myself it would be easier, the best way.

And here it was. The severance I craved. I should be grateful.

I get in late. I've been out, taking photos, first portraits of a family that had been in touch through the website, then on the way home I'd stopped off to get some shots of people as they stood outside the bars of Soho – trying to get back to the subjects who really interest me, I guess – but now Hugh is already home. He asks me to come with him, he has something to tell me.

It sounds ominous. I think of the time I got home from the gallery, the police in the kitchen, the news that Kate was dead. I know Connor is fine, his light is on upstairs, it's always the first thing I ask when I arrive home and I've already done so tonight, but still I'm nervous. Tell me now, I want to say, whatever it is, but I don't. I follow him into the kitchen. I dump my bag on the floor, my camera on the table.

'What is it?' He looks serious. 'What is it? What's wrong?'

He takes a deep breath. 'Roger called. From the Foreign Office. They think they know what happened to Kate.'

I feel myself collapse. Questions tumble out – What? Who? – and he explains. 'There's a man, this guy who they arrested on something totally unrelated. Roger isn't allowed to tell us what, exactly, but he hinted it was something to do with drugs. A dealer, I guess. Anyway, apparently he's known in the area; they even questioned him about Kate but he said he'd seen nothing.' He takes a deep breath. 'When they searched his place they found Kate's earring.'

I close my eyes. I picture him ripping it off her, or her being forced to give it to him, thinking that cooperation might save her life when in fact it did no such thing.

A dealer. Was it drugs, after all? Not sex?

Suddenly I'm there, again. Me and Marcus. We'd go together, but I'd wait for him. At the end of the street, on the corner, outside the station. He'd meet our dealer, hand over the cash. He'd come back with what we both wanted. Smiling.

But Kate saw none of that. I made sure of it, even the one time she visited us, during the school holidays. She hadn't wanted to go home and be alone with Dad, she begged me to let her come for a visit. 'Just for a few days,' she said, and I relented. I scraped some money together to pay for her ticket, and our father put up the rest. She came for a long weekend and slept on the bed in our room while we slept on the couch, but I'm certain she saw nothing. It was a few weeks before Marcus died, and neither of us was using. I took her to the galleries, we walked the length of Unter den Linden, drank hot chocolate at the top of the Fernsehturm. I photographed her on the streets of Mitte – pictures that are lost, now – and we wandered around Tiergarten. I left her with Marcus only once, when I went to buy groceries, but he knew how much I wanted to keep her from drugs and I trusted him completely. When I got home they were playing cards with Frosty, the TV on in the background, showing cartoons. She saw nothing.

Still, shouldn't I have set a better example?

I begin to sob, a sound that turns into a howl of pain. Hugh holds my hands in his. I'd thought it might make me feel better. Knowing who'd killed my sister. Knowing he'd been arrested, would be punished. It should draw a line under everything. It should open up a future, allow me to move on.

But it doesn't. It feels so meaningless. So banal. If anything, it's worse.

'Julia. Julia. It's all right.'

I look at him.

'I can't bear it.'

'I know.'

'It's definitely him?'

'They think so.' I begin to cry properly, tears run in thick streams. My sister dead, her son devastated, over drugs?

'Why?' I say, over and over. Hugh holds me until I calm down.

I want my son.

'Have you told Connor?'

He shakes his head.

'We need to tell him.'

He nods, then stands up. He goes to the stairs as I go into the kitchen. I grab some kitchen roll and wipe the tears from my face, then pour myself a drink of water. When I go back into the living room Connor is sitting opposite his father. He looks up. 'Mum?'

I sit down on the sofa and take Connor's hand.

'Darling . . .' I begin. I'm not sure what to say. I look at Hugh, then back at our son. I dig as deep as I can, searching for the last reserves of strength. 'Darling, they've caught the man who killed Auntie Kate.'

He sits, for a moment. The room is perfectly still.

'Darling?'

'Who?'

What to say? This isn't the movies, there's no big plot, no satisfying resolution to the story, tied with a bow at the end. Just a senseless waste of life.

'Just a man,' I say.

'Who?'

I look again at Hugh. He opens his mouth to speak. Don't

say it, I think. Don't tell him it was someone selling drugs. Don't put that idea into his head.

'Auntie Kate was in the wrong place at the wrong time,' he says. 'That's all. She ran into an evil man. We don't know why, or what happened. But he's been caught now, and he'll go to prison and pay for what he's done.'

Connor nods. He's trying to understand, trying to come to terms with the lack of an explanation.

After a moment he lets go of my hand. 'Can I go back to my room now?'

I say yes. There's an urge to follow him, but I know I mustn't. I leave him for ten minutes, fifteen. I ring Adrienne, then Anna. She's shocked. 'Drugs?' she says.

'Yes. Did she—?'

'No! No. Well, I mean, she partied, you know? We all did. But nothing hard core.'

As far as you know, I think. I'm only too well aware how easy it can be to keep these things hidden. 'Maybe you just didn't know?'

'I don't think so,' she says. 'Honestly, I don't.'

We talk for a while longer, but I want to see my son. I tell Anna I'm looking forward to seeing her in a couple of weeks and she tells me she can't wait. We say goodbye, and then I tell Hugh I'm going up to see Connor.

I knock, he tells me to come in. He's playing music, lying on the bed, facing the ceiling. His eyes are red.

I say nothing. I go in. I hold him, and together we cry.

Chapter Twenty-Four

She's arriving today. I'm picking her up later, we'll have a coffee or something, but for now I'm alone. I have the newspaper spread out in front of me. I turn to the magazine, skim read something about some fashion designer, what she wishes she'd known when she was young, then turn the page. A real-life article, someone whose daughter became a heroin addict; I turn that page, too. I think of my own narrow escape – if that's what it was, if I really can be said to have escaped – and wonder for a moment whether they'd run a story about me and Lukas. I shudder at the thought, but my story isn't unusual. I got myself involved with a man who wasn't the person I thought he was, and things went too far. It happens all the time.

I close the magazine and empty the dishwasher, on autopilot. I pick up the dishcloth, the bottle of bleach. I clean the surfaces. I wonder if this is how my mother's generation felt; Valium in the bathroom cabinet, a bottle of gin under the sink. An affair with the milkman, for the adventurous. So much for progress. I feel ashamed.

When I've finished my chores I go up to see Hugh. He's in his office, despite the cold he's been fighting for almost a week. He's working on a statement; the case against him has progressed, the patient has relapsed and solicitors have been instructed. The hospital's legal team want to prevent it going to a tribunal. 'They've said I'm screwed if it does,' he told me. 'The fact is I didn't write down what I'd told them, so I might as well have said nothing.'

'Doesn't it make any difference that they'd have gone ahead anyway?'

'No. They just want some cash.'

It's Maria dealing with the family now. According to Hugh, if they were that upset they'd have sought their second opinion from a different hospital altogether.

I've asked him if he'll lose his job. He said no, no one's died, he hasn't been criminally negligent, but I can see the stress it's causing him. I knock on the door and go in. He's sitting at his desk. He has the window open, despite the draught, the cool air of early October. He looks pale.

'How're you feeling?' I say.

'Fine.' Sweat sheens his brow.

'Are you sure?' I say. It's good to care for him; it's been a long time since I've felt he needs me. 'Want anything?'

He shakes his head. 'No, thanks. How about you? What're your plans today?'

I remind him about Anna. 'I'm picking her up from the station.'

'She's not staying with us, though?'

'No. She's booked into a hotel. She's coming for dinner on Monday.'

'Where's Connor?'

'Out. With Dylan, I think.'

'Not his girlfriend?'

'I don't know.' Again I feel that sense of loss. I turn to Hugh's shelves and begin straightening things. I'm beginning to worry now. Connor is still upset after our discussion the other night, yet he won't talk to me. How can I be expected to protect him, to counsel him as he enters the world as an adult, if he won't let me in?

And that's my job. Isn't it? In the last few weeks the need to protect him, to keep him safe, has only increased. Yet I know I have to trust my son. To be old enough, mature enough. Not to get into any trouble – or not too much at least, and nothing with real repercussions. There's little point in me demanding that he lives a blameless, spotless life, after what I've done. He has to make his own mistakes, just as I made mine.

And he will make them; I just hope they won't be as catastrophic. Smoking in an alleyway, yes. A bottle of vodka or cheap cider, bought from the off licence by whichever of his friends is nearest to growing a beard. Weed, even; it's going to happen sooner or later, whether I like it or not. But nothing stronger. No accidents, no pregnancies. No running away from home. No getting mixed up with people when you should know better.

'Is he still seeing her?' I say.

'I'm not sure.' I'm momentarily relieved. I'm aware it's a contradiction; I want Connor to be close to Hugh but don't like the thought of him telling him things he won't tell me. 'What d'you make of it all?'

'What?' I turn back to Hugh. 'His girlfriend?'

He nods. 'They met online, you know?'

I flinch. I turn back to the shelves. 'Facebook?'

'I think so. She's a friend?'

'I don't know. She must be, I guess.'

'Well, *is* he still seeing her?'

'Hugh, why don't you ask him? He talks to you about this stuff more than he talks to me.'

He points to his screen. 'Because I have enough on my mind as it is.'

*

I arrive at St Pancras, order a mineral water from the champagne bar and sit down. From my seat I can see the statue at the end of the platforms where I met Lukas, all those weeks ago.

I sit facing it. Memories come back; there's pain, but it's dulled, bearable. I think of it as a test. He's won enough. I just have to get over him, finally and completely, and here is where I can start. I sip my drink as the train comes in.

I see Anna through the glass partition that separates the trains from where I sit. She walks down the platform, her phone pressed to her ear, with a case that's surprisingly large for the week she'd told me she was going to be in London. I watch as she ends her call then disappears down the escalators. She looks serious, as though something's wrong, but just a few minutes later she's in front of me, her grin huge and instantaneous. She looks delighted, relieved. I stand, and she envelops me in a hug.

'Julia! It's so good to see you!'

'You, too.' My words are lost in the folds of the silk scarf she's wearing. She squeezes me, then lets go. 'Is everything okay?'

She looks puzzled. I nod towards the platform she's just walked down. 'When you got off the train. You looked worried.'

She laughs. 'Oh! No, everything's fine. It was just my office. Some mix-up. Nothing major.' She looks at me. 'You look well. In fact, you look beautiful!'

I thank her. 'You, too.'

'Well . . .' she replies, and there's something about the way she smiles that makes me think her delight isn't just because of seeing me again. She has something to tell me, something she's been bottling up but can hold in no longer.

'What is it?' I'm excited, too, and intrigued, though already I wonder if I've guessed. I've seen the same expression before; I've even worn it myself.

She laughs.

'Tell me!'

She grins and holds up her left hand. A moment later I see it: a ring on her finger, catching in the light from the windows above.

'He asked me . . .'

I grin, but for the briefest moment all I feel is jealousy. I see her life, and it's one of excitement, of exploration and passion.

I hug her again. 'That's wonderful. Truly wonderful!' I mean it – my initial reaction had been unkind, but short-lived – and I look at the ring. It's a single round diamond in a gold setting; it looks expensive. She begins talking. He asked her just last week. 'He had the ring, he didn't quite go down on one knee, but . . .' She hesitates, clearly remembering. 'I wanted you to be one of the first to know—'

I force a smile. I'm jealous on Kate's behalf. It's as if her death has somehow set Anna free. She doesn't seem to notice, though. She squeezes my arm. 'I just feel very close to you, Julia. Because of Kate, I suppose. Because of what happened.'

I take her hand. 'Yes. Yes, I agree. I guess sometimes it's not so much about how long you've known someone, but about what you've been through together.' She looks relieved: we really are friends. I let go of her hand and pick up her bag before linking my arm in hers. 'So,' I say, as we begin to walk towards the car. 'Tell me what happened! How did he ask you?'

She seems to jump to attention, her mind was wandering, back into the memories, I guess. 'We went to the Sacré-

Coeur,' she says. 'I thought we were just going for a stroll, to look at the view, you know, or maybe get some lunch.' The words tumble out of her mouth, all exclamations and half-sentences. As they do I'm swept up in her enthusiasm and I feel bad about my earlier reaction. I wonder if it hadn't been jealousy but simple sadness. Sadness that this joy had been visited on her, and not Kate.

As she talks I think back to Hugh's proposal to me: we were in a restaurant – our favourite, in Piccadilly – and he'd asked me between the main course and dessert. 'Julia,' he said, and I remember thinking how serious he looked, how nervous. This is it, I'd thought, for the briefest of instants. He's brought me here to end it, to tell me he's met someone, or that now I'm better, now I'm cured, it's time for me to move on. But at the same time I thought it couldn't possibly be that; we'd been so happy, over the previous few months, so much in love.

'What?' I'd said. 'What is it?'

'You know I love you. Don't you?'

'And I love you . . .' He smiled, but didn't look particularly relieved. I think that's when I first realized what he was about to say.

'Darling,' he began. He took my hand across the table. 'Julia, I—'

'What, Hugh? What is it?'

'Will you marry me?'

The happiness was instant, overwhelming. There was no romantic gesture, no going down on one knee or standing up to announce his intentions to the other diners, but I was glad of that; it wasn't his style, and neither was it mine. He was a good man, I loved him, why would I say no? Plus, he knew me, had seen me at my absolute worst, knew everything about me.

Almost everything, anyway. And the things he didn't know were the things I'd never tell anyone.

'Of course!' I said back then, yet still some part of me hesitated, the part that felt I didn't deserve what Hugh was offering, what he'd already given me – this second life. But the relief that flooded his face told me I was making the right – the only – decision.

I realize Anna's stopped speaking. I force myself to snap back to the present.

'He sounds perfect!'

'Yes. You know, I think he is!'

'And he's from Paris?'

'No. He's based there. His family's from somewhere down in Devon.' She grins. 'This visit is a bit too rushed. I'm meeting them in a few weeks.'

We get to the car and I put her bag in the boot. Once we're buckled up and I've started driving she tells me again the story of how they met. 'Well,' she says, 'I told you about the dinner party?' She sighs, as if their meeting were an inevitability, a coming together of the fates. I say yes, even though I'm not sure she did. She goes on to tell me anyway, about how they clicked straight away, about how instantly perfect it felt.

'You know when something doesn't feel sensible, but just feels *right*?' she says.

'I do,' I say, turning the wheel. I sigh. 'I do.' She thinks I'm talking about Hugh, but I'm not. I'm thinking of Lukas. I've been trying to pretend to myself that I don't miss him, but I do. Or rather, I miss what I'd thought we could have had.

I believed he knew me; it felt like he'd cracked me open and seen through to who I really am. I'd convinced myself he was the only person who could still do that.

'. . . so we think we'll carry on living in Paris for a bit,' says Anna, 'and then maybe move back here.'

'Good idea. So, remind me when you met?'

'When? Oh, it was just after Christmas. It was a few weeks before Kate . . .' She stumbles, corrects herself, but the damage is done. '. . . Just before I met you.' I smile, but she can see I'm upset. I can talk about Kate, now. I can think about her. But such an explicit reference to her death, coming from nowhere, still throws me. 'I'm sorry,' she says. 'Me and my big mouth . . .'

'It's okay.' I don't want to dwell on it, and neither do I want her to feel guilty. Anna is the last person I should expect to avoid the topic of my sister. Nevertheless, I change the subject. 'But it all seems to have happened very quickly,' I say. I'm thinking of Lukas again, of how rapidly I'd fallen. 'I hope you don't mind me saying that? I mean, are you sure?'

'Oh! Yes, you're right! But no, I'm totally sure! We both are,' she adds. 'He says the same. Neither of us thought there was any point in hanging around, when we're so certain.'

She's silent for a moment. I can feel her looking at me as I drive, no doubt weighing up what to say, wondering how much happiness I can stand. 'You know, I think in a weird way it's all connected with Kate. With what happened. It just reminded me that life is for living, you know? It's not a rehearsal.'

'No,' I say. It's a cliché, but only because it's true. 'No, it isn't.'

'I think that's what Kate's death taught me.'

'Really? I feel it's taught me nothing.'

It comes from nowhere. I wish I could unsay it, but it's impossible.

'Don't say that.'

'It's true. All I've done is try to escape it.'

And look where it led me. I spent the summer obsessed with Lukas, a man ten years younger than me, falling in a love that I was stupid enough to think might be reciprocated.

I'd ended up running from a pain that I owed it to my sister to experience, and I'll never be able to repay that. It feels like a final betrayal.

'I'm just feeling sorry for myself. Ryan sounds wonderful. I can't wait to meet him.'

'You will! He might be coming over, this week. He's not sure. You might even meet him on Monday.'

'I didn't know he was in town. He must come to dinner.'

'Oh, no. He's not here yet. He had to stay behind to finish some work. I don't know when he'll be arriving, and . . . well, I'll ask him, anyway, if you're sure you don't mind?'

I shake my head. 'Of course not.'

'How're you and Connor getting on now?'

'Much better.' She nods. 'He seems to have got himself a girlfriend.'

'A girlfriend?'

I feel a flash of pride. 'Uh-huh.' I pull up at some traffic lights. In the wing mirror I see a cyclist weaving through the traffic, coming up too close. 'Though he won't talk to me about it, of course,' I add. 'He barely even admits that she exists to me, though he seems to talk to Hugh.'

'Is that usual?' She sounds genuinely interested. 'For him, I mean?'

I think of what Adrienne has told me. 'It's probably usual for all teenagers.' I sigh. The lights change and we pull away. We're almost at Great Portland Street. Nearly there. I'm happy Connor's growing up, sad that must also, inevitably, mean growing away. I remember talking to Adrienne about that, too, a few weeks ago. 'It's something they go through,' she'd said, then she hesitated, corrected herself. 'Well, not exactly *go through*,' she said. 'They don't really come out of it. This is the first stage of him leaving you, I'm afraid . . .'

I glance at Anna. 'He doesn't want to come out with us when we go out any more. He just stays in his room . . .'

She smiles. 'So you're sure it's a girlfriend?'

'Oh, yes. I think so, though he tells me to mind my own business, of course.' I don't tell her I insisted he showed me a photograph, this morning, after much discussion with Hugh. She looks a little older than him. I'm still convinced it's the girl from Carla's party, though he's certain she wasn't there. 'She's a friend of a friend of his. They met on Facebook.' She looks at me with a knowing smile. 'Hugh's spoken to him about her. They chat online, apparently, though she doesn't live far away.'

There's a long pause, then she says, 'And did you ever hear from that guy again? Lukas?'

'Oh, no. I haven't heard from him at all.'

I'm glad I'm driving; I can take my time to answer, decide what to say. I can pretend my silences are due to an increased need for concentration, rather than the fact that I'm finding the conversation difficult. I can fix my gaze on the road, disguise the expression on my face. I can skirt the truth as I tell her what's been going on. As much as I feel I can confide in Anna, I feel shame, too.

'So Hugh—?'

'He doesn't know any of it,' I say quickly. I glance at her. She's looking at me, her face impassive. I try to lighten the tone, to reassure her that I know I was stupid but it's over now. 'He'd never . . . he wouldn't understand.'

'Oh, God, I won't say anything to Hugh! Don't . . . I just wouldn't.'

'It was a bit of fun. You know? A distraction. Good while it lasted.'

'Oh, yes. Totally. Of course . . .'

Until it wasn't fun any more, I think.

'He's vanished, anyway.'

'You sound disappointed.'

'Not at all.'

There's a longer pause, then. I'm tense, embarrassed, because we both know how my affair with Lukas ended. The silence goes on; each of us waits for the other to break it. Eventually she does. She asks me what my plans are for the week, and I tell her. A bit of work, I might catch a movie. At last we reach the hotel.

'Ah, we're here.'

We pull up. The place is surprisingly nice, though nothing like as grand as the places Lukas was taking me to. 'Want me to come in?'

She shakes her head. 'It's fine. You probably need to get on.'

It's an excuse, and I smile. I'd like to catch up some more, but she looks tired; I've forgotten she's here to work, will probably want to have a rest before preparing for her conference in the morning. There's plenty of time for catching up when she comes round for dinner.

We get out and I get her case from the boot of the car. 'See you on Monday, then.'

She asks what time she should arrive. 'And what shall I bring?'

'Nothing, nothing at all. Just yourself. I'd better give you directions,' I say. She takes her phone out of her bag.

'Oh, I'll use this.' She swipes through more screens. 'It's so much easier. There. I've added you . . .'

I don't know what she means. 'I don't—' I begin, but she interrupts me.

'Find Friends. It's an app that shows where your friends

are in relation to you. On a map. It's standard. Check your emails.'

I do. There's a new message. 'Accept that invitation,' she says, 'then our profiles are linked. I can see where you are on the map, and you can see me. I use it all the time back home. After Kate died it was kind of reassuring to know where my friends were.'

She takes my phone and shows me. A map opens, showing where we're standing. Two dots pulse over each other. 'One for me, one for you,' she says.

I look at the screen. Underneath the map there's a list of people who're following me. Anna's name is there, but underneath is another. Lukas.

I feel like I've been slapped.

'Shit.'

Anna looks shocked. 'What is it?'

'Him. Lukas.' I try to keep my voice steady. I don't want her to hear the fear in it. 'He's been following me on here . . .'

'What?'

I hold out my phone. 'Look. How—' I begin, but she's already explaining.

'He must've linked your profiles. You didn't know?'

I shake my head. I can't believe what's happening.

'He must've found some way of sending you a request, then accepting it on your behalf. Easy enough, if you left him alone with your phone.'

All those times I was in the bathroom, my phone in my bag or on the bedside table. She's right. It would've been easy.

'Can we stop him following me?'

'Easy.' She swipes something on the screen, then hands the phone back to me. 'There,' she says firmly. 'Deleted.'

I look. It's just her name, now. 'He can't see where I am any more?'

'No.' She puts her hand on my arm. 'Are you all right?'

I nod, and I realize that yes, yes I am. I'm weirdly relieved. So this is how he'd known where I'd be. All that time. At least now I know. At least now I'm finally rid of him.

'You're sure?'

'It's a bit of a shock, but I'm okay. Honestly.'

'I'll see you Monday, then?' I nod. 'I'll let you know what Ryan's doing as soon as he knows himself.'

'Great. He's very welcome. I'm looking forward to meeting him.'

She kisses me, then turns to leave.

'He can't wait to meet you.'

At home I go straight to my computer. Seeing his name has awoken something. One last time, I tell myself. I open encountrz, search for his name, and again I get the same message, as stark and unambiguous as my disappointment.

Username not found.

It's like he never existed. He's vanished as completely as the bruises he caused.

I type his name into Google. There's nothing. No mention of him, or anyone that could be him. I try Facebook and find his profile is nowhere to be found, then ring his number again, even though I know exactly what dead sound I'll hear. Usually I'd circle back now, and do it all again. And again. But this time is different. This time I know it has to stop. I log back on to my own profile, the one on encountrz, the one I'd set up that afternoon in the garden. I navigate the menus until I find it. Delete profile.

I hesitate, breathe deeply, once, twice, then click.

Are you sure?

I choose yes.
The screen changes: *Profile deleted.*
Jayne doesn't exist any more.
I sit back. Now, I think. Now, finally, it's over.

Chapter Twenty-Five

I'm in the living room when Anna arrives. She's alone. Ryan had plans, she'd said, but will pick her up later. I call upstairs to Hugh and go to the door. Our guest is standing outside, holding a bottle of wine and a bunch of flowers. 'I'm early!' she says as I usher her in. 'Sorry!' I tell her it's fine and take the coat she's wearing, a red rainproof that's slightly damp.

'Is it raining?'

'A little. Just drizzle. What a lovely house!'

We go through to the living room. Her conference is going well, she says, though there's a lot to think about, and yes, her hotel room is fine. As she speaks she goes over to the picture of Kate on the mantelpiece and picks it up, looking at it for a moment before putting it back. She looks as though she's about to say something – we've spoken about the fact that they've found the man who murdered her, perhaps she wants to say something else – but then Hugh comes downstairs to say hello. They embrace warmly, as if they've known each other for years.

'Oh, I brought you these!' she says, handing over a bag. Hugh opens it: a box of macaroons, delicately wrapped. 'Great!' he says, then they both sit. I excuse myself to check on the food, happy that they're chatting. For a moment it feels as if I'm auditioning Anna as my new best friend and I feel first anxious about Adrienne, then guilty. Our friendship has been through a rocky patch and we're only just getting back on track.

Yet it's only natural that Anna and I would be friends, too. We've both lost Kate; the bond is recent but immensely powerful.

'Where's Connor?' she says when I go back in. 'I can't wait to meet him again!'

'He's out with friends.' I sit down on the sofa opposite Hugh, next to Anna. 'His friend Dylan, I think. He'll be back soon . . .'

I've told him he has to be. Maybe Hugh's right. I need to be firmer.

I shrug. You know what they're like, I'm saying, and she smiles, even though I guess she doesn't.

'Do you want children?' says Hugh, and she laughs.

'No! Not yet, anyway. I've only just got engaged!'

'You have brothers? Sisters?'

'Just a step-brother,' she says. 'Seth. He lives in Leeds. He does something to do with computers. I'm never really sure.'

'Is that where your parents live?'

She sighs. 'No. My parents are dead.' I remember Anna telling me about her parents, back in Paris, while we were sitting on her couch, having a drink. Her mother suffered with depression. She tried to kill herself. She'd survived, but required full-time care for the years she remained alive. Her father's drinking got worse, and after just less than a decade they died within six months of each other and she and her brother were left alone.

Hugh coughs. 'I'm sorry to hear that. You get on with your step-brother, though?'

'Brilliantly. We always have. He's everything to me. I don't know what I'd do if anything happened to him.'

I try not to react, but she must see my face fall.

'Oh, God, Julia, I wasn't . . . I didn't mean to . . . I'm sorry . . .'

'It's fine,' I say. It's the second time in only a few days that she's referred clumsily, if obliquely, to Kate's death. I wonder if she's already over it, has almost forgotten it. I don't for a moment think it's deliberate.

'Let's go and eat?'

It's a good dinner. I've made a chicken pie and it's turned out well. Connor arrives not long after I serve the soup and sits with us. He seems to bond with Anna particularly well. She asks him about school, about his football; she even gets out her phone at one point and he helps her with something with which she's been struggling. When we've finished the main course she helps me to carry the plates through into the kitchen, and when we're out of earshot says, 'He's such a lovely lad.'

'You think?'

'Yes!' She puts the plates down. 'You should be very proud. Both of you!'

I smile. 'Thank you.' Her approval feels important, somehow. Significant. She says she's going upstairs to use the bathroom. I direct her, then ask Hugh to give me a hand with the coffee.

He comes through. 'How're things?'

'Good.' I've made a pudding – a lemon syllabub – but now I'm wondering whether I should also put out the macaroons. I ask Hugh.

'Both, I think. Is Anna driving home?'

I know he's thinking about the dessert wine he has in the fridge. He's become awkward about alcohol since I had to lie and say I'd had a drink with Adrienne; he won't mention it, even though we still have it in the house. But he knows better than to try and manage my behaviour by pretending drink doesn't exist.

'No. Her boyfriend's coming to pick her up.' There's a tingle of resentment. Hugh's thinking of putting more wine out, but I can't have any. I acknowledge it, then let it go. He gets the packet of coffee beans out of the cupboard and scoops some out. 'How did you say she and Kate met?'

I tell him. 'They were friends at school. They lost touch for a while, then reconnected.'

Dimly, it occurs to me that I'm thinking about Kate, talking about her, and it's not painful. It's because Anna's here, I think. It's getting easier, as long as it's Kate's life I'm thinking about, rather than her death.

I take the syllabub out of the fridge. Hugh finishes making the coffee and I call through to Connor and ask if he'll fetch some dishes. He comes in almost straight away and the three of us carry the things through into the dining room, where we arrange them on the table. The family unity pleases me; part of me is disappointed that Anna isn't here to see it. I call upstairs and ask if she's all right. She shouts down, she's okay, she'll just be a minute, and when she appears she puts her phone on the table with a sheepish grin.

'Sorry. Ryan called.' She looks suddenly, radiantly, happy. 'He's on his way.'

'He should come for dinner,' says Hugh. 'How long is he staying for?'

'Not sure. Until next week some time.'

'And when do you go back?' says Hugh.

'Saturday.' She turns to me. 'That reminds me. Do you fancy lunch on Saturday? Before I get my train?'

I tell her that would be lovely.

'Okay, if you're sure?'

I tell her I am. 'You must invite Ryan in for a drink, too,' I say.

'Oh, no,' she begins. 'I wouldn't dream—'

'Nonsense!' says Hugh. 'He must come in!' He turns to me, and I say, 'Of course!'

Anna looks relieved. I pour her coffee. Connor asks if he can be excused and goes back to his room. We talk some more, sip our drinks, but the evening is winding down. After another fifteen minutes of chat we hear a car pull up outside. A door slams, there's the pip-pip of the alarm, and a moment later footsteps up the path and the doorbell rings. I look over to Anna, who says, 'He's early!' She looks electrified, like a little girl waiting for the postman to bring her birthday cards, and I feel a curious excitement, too; I'm looking forward to meeting this person, this man who has given Anna such transparent, uncomplicated happiness. Who has helped her grieve for Kate and move on.

I stand up. 'I'll go and let him in.' I walk through, into the hallway. I rearrange my hair, smooth down the front of my shirt, open the door.

It's Lukas.

I take a step back. It's as if I've been punched; the feeling is physical and intense, my skin burns with a hit of adrenalin as instant as if someone had just plunged a needle into me. I can't take my eyes off him. My body is reacting, my muscles tensed to fight or run. It's the memory of his attack, burned into my body. As I look he cocks his head, just slightly, and smiles.

'You must be Julia.' He's speaking clearly, his voice sounds loud, loud enough to be heard in the other room.

My mind is racing. All the panic and pain is coming back, wave after wave. Ride it out, I tell myself. Ride it out. But I can't. For a moment I think it's a game, another sick game. It's as if he knows I only just deleted my profile, resolved never to ring him again. It's as if he's teaching me that I don't get to decide when I let him go.

I feel as if I'm falling, the room behind me tips and spins.

'What are you doing here?' I say, under my breath, but he doesn't reply. I realize I'm gripping the door frame. Shaking.

The smile hasn't left his face. 'Well, aren't you going to let me in?'

I look away, look down, at the floor. Hugh, I think, in the other room. Anna, who's expecting Ryan.

Connor, upstairs.

I look back up, so that we're staring into each other's eyes. 'What the *fuck* are you doing here?' I hiss.

He doesn't answer, just stands there, smiling. I open my mouth to speak, to ask him again, for the third time, but then he glances over my shoulder and everything changes. It's as if a switch has been thrown; his face breaks, he beams widely, starts chattering. He takes my hand in his, shakes it, as if he's meeting me for the first time.

'What—' I begin, but then a moment later I realize Anna is right behind me. 'Darling!' she's saying, and I think she's talking to me, but then she reaches the doorway and goes to Lukas. He turns towards her, and then he has his arms around her and they're kissing. It takes only a moment, but it seems to last for ever, and when they've finished she turns to me.

'Julia,' she beams. 'Meet Ryan.'

Another wave crashes. A flush rises in my cheeks; I'm too hot. The hallway recedes; the sound of the music Connor's playing upstairs seems somehow diminished and deafening at the same time, as if I'm hearing it at top volume yet through a fug. I feel as if I'm fainting. I reach out – for the door handle, for anything – but miss.

'Honey?' says Anna. 'Are you all right?'

I try to compose myself. 'Yes. I just . . . I don't know. I feel a bit unwell . . .'

'You look a bit flushed—' says Lukas, but I interrupt him.

'I'm fine. Honestly . . .' And then a moment later the dynamic in the room shifts again. Hugh has appeared and I watch as he steps forward, saying hello. He's grinning, shaking Lukas's hand and saying, 'You must be Ryan?' He looks delighted to see him, to welcome him into our home. 'Good to meet you,' he says, and 'How're you?' They look like two guys together, two old friends. My stomach clenches. My husband and my lover. Together.

'Good,' says Lukas. 'Good. I'm a bit worried about Julia, though.'

Hugh turns to me. 'Are you all right, darling?'

'Yes,' I say, even though I'm not. The room has stopped spinning but still I shake with an anxiety so intense I worry I'll not be able to control it.

'I don't know what came over me.'

'Well,' says Hugh, 'come in at least, Ryan. Come in.'

Lukas thanks him. We go through to the living room, an awkward entourage. Hugh invites Lukas to sit on the sofa, Anna sits next to him, takes his hand. Hugh offers him a drink, but he shakes his head, says he's driving. I watch it all through a gauzy screen of fear, as if it's happening elsewhere, to other people, this scene of polite normality that no longer has anything to do with me. Wordlessly, I accept the drink Hugh gives me: a glass of water.

'Have this. You'll feel better.'

'Are you sure you're okay?' says Anna.

I sip and nod and say yes, then Lukas turns to me.

'It's so great to meet you. I've heard so much about you.'

I smile thinly. 'You, too.' I watch as he thanks me, then takes Anna's hand and squeezes it. 'Anna has told you our news?' He strokes her hand, looking into her eyes with an expression I recognize, one of love, of pure adoration.

'Yes. Yes, it's wonderful!'

'It is!' says Hugh. He's turned on the charm, is trying hard to impress. 'You're sure you won't have a drink? Just one?'

Lukas says nothing for a moment, then nods his head. 'Okay, then. Why not? One won't take me over the limit. Just a short. You're sure you don't mind me dropping in on you like this?'

'Not at all,' says Hugh. He goes over to the drinks cabinet and gets out the bottles of whisky, vodka and gin. 'What'll it be?' Lukas chooses a single malt, something I've never seen him drink before.

Hugh prepares the drink. Lukas turns to me. 'Anna tells me you're a photographer?' His face is open, his head tilted, as if he's genuinely interested. I look from him to Anna, back again. I can't work out what he's doing, whether I should say something, tell her now. I'm in shock, I suppose, though there's a kind of weird detachment. I need to figure it out. All this time, while I thought I was having an affair, he was already seeing my sister's best friend. I've been utterly betrayed. *I was* the affair.

But they met before Kate was killed, I think, so why did he choose me? It can't be coincidence. If it were, he'd have been shocked when I opened the door to him tonight. 'Julia!' he'd have said. 'What are you doing here? Where's Anna?' And then I guess I'd have told him how I knew his fiancée and we'd have agreed to keep quiet, to say nothing. He'd be trying to get out of here as soon as he could, not accepting a drink from Hugh, not settling in for a long chat, not asking questions he already knows the answers to.

I realize everyone is looking at me expectantly. The room is quiet, the air heavy and too warm. I've been asked a question and need to respond. 'Yes. Yes. That's right.'

I look from him to Hugh. One word, that's all it would take. Is that what he wants? To break me and Hugh up, to detonate the bomb that I've placed underneath my family?

'Sounds really interesting.' He leans forward. He really does look like someone who is fascinated. Absorbed. He asks me what kind of photos I take, and even though the pain and anxiety is almost physical, even though he's seen my pictures, even though we've lain naked on a bed together looking at my work, I tell him.

He nods, then after a moment he speaks again. 'By the way, I was so sorry to hear about your sister.'

You bastard, I think. *You're fucking enjoying this.*

I nod. I smile, but my eyes are narrowed. 'Thanks,' I say. I have to remind myself he didn't kill Kate, though right now I could hardly hate him more if he had.

He looks at me, straight in the eye. 'I never met her. I'm so sorry about her . . . passing on.'

Anger hits me, then. I can't help it, even though the last thing I want is for him to see how he's upsetting me. 'She didn't *pass on*. She was murdered.' You know that, I'm thinking. I look for a sign of remorse, of sadness, even of mischief, but there's none. I even think I might want him to laugh – then I can just hate him without being scared of him – but he does nothing. Nothing at all. Even his eyes betray no sign that we've ever met before; right now, he looks like his own twin brother.

The room is frozen. I'm aware I've raised my voice. I look defiant. I'm daring him to say something. Hugh looks from me to him, then back to me. The moment stretches; the only sound comes from Connor's room upstairs.

The tension thickens, then breaks. Lukas shakes his head. 'Oh, God, I've offended you. I'm so, so sorry. I never know what to say in these situations . . .'

I ignore him. I'm aware of Hugh, twitching, willing me to say something, but I don't. I hold Lukas's gaze. Anna looks from him over to me. She's expectant, and after a moment I relent. 'It's okay. No one ever knows what to say. There's nothing *to* say.'

He shrugs. He's staring at me. Hugh and Anna are in the room, watching. They can see it, I think. Surely. Is he crazy? Does he *want* them to see what's going on?

Or maybe he doesn't care. We're locked in combat, the power is flying wildly from one to the other. We're both blind to our partners, they're unimportant, relegated to the status of bystanders. We're potassium in water, acid on skin. We could burn each other, wreck everything and hardly notice, hardly care.

I open my mouth to say something – I still don't know what – but then Hugh speaks. 'Remind me what you do again, Ryan?' He's trying to diffuse the tension, and for a moment Lukas doesn't move. 'Ryan works in the arts,' says Anna, then Lukas turns to take her hand.

'I have my own company. In digital production.'

Not what he's told me.

Hugh nods. 'Based in Paris?'

'Yes. I've been there for almost five years now. I do a fair bit of travel, though.'

I look at my hands, folded into my lap. With each of his answers it hits again; it was me he was lying to all along, not Anna. Not his fiancée, the woman he's been seeing several times a week. I look up. I can't stop thinking about that last time, in the hotel room as David arrived. I can still feel his hands on me.

And now he's back for more. I can't bear it. Before I know what I'm doing I've stood up. But what can I do? What can I say? Anna is about to marry this man, and clearly knows nothing of what's been going on. I open my mouth, close it again. My mind reels.

And then, suddenly, I feel myself collapse inwards. It's as if I'm disappearing, reducing to nothing. 'Julia!' says Hugh. 'Are you all right?'

'Yes. Excuse me,' I manage, and then I'm heading upstairs, into the bathroom.

When I return Anna asks me if I'm okay. 'Yes. Fine.' Lukas is draining his glass, putting it on the coffee table.

'We should head off!' he's saying. He turns to me. 'We thought we'd go to Soho. Maybe a jazz bar. Ronnie Scott's. D'you know it?' They both turn to me. 'You should come.'

I say no. I'm numb. I just want all of this to stop.

'You go if you like,' says Hugh. 'I'm far too tired . . .'

I feel a wave of guilt as I picture the two of them there. What have I done to my friend? What might still happen?

'No. It's late. I should turn in, too . . .'

'Oh, come on,' says Anna. 'It'll be fun!'

'I really don't mind, darling,' says Hugh.

'No!' I speak a little too harshly, then turn back to Anna and soften my voice. 'Honestly. You go ahead.'

They stand and we all move into the hallway. Anna turns to me, smiles. 'Well . . .' she says. She holds out her hands, I step forward, into her embrace, while Hugh and Lukas shake hands. 'It's all been too quick!' says Anna. She can tell something is wrong. 'Promise me you'll come and see me soon. Bring Connor! Promise me! And I have to let you know about the wedding, as soon as we start to plan. You will come, won't you?'

I look over to Lukas. He's smiling, waiting for my answer.

'Of course I will. I'm seeing you on Saturday, anyway. But I'll call before then. Soon. Later. Okay?' She releases me. I want to hold on to her, to tell her to be careful, to warn her, but

I don't want to frighten her. In any case, Lukas is stepping forward.

'Well. It was great to meet you. I'm sorry about earlier. I didn't mean to upset you.' For the briefest moment I think he's talking about the attack, but then I realize he's talking about Kate.

'I'm not upset.' I hold out my hand. The last thing I want is for him to touch me, but it wouldn't be right for me to avoid him so obviously. 'You, too.' He takes my hand and pulls me towards him; I realize he means to embrace me, as if we've bonded, as if we're now best friends. I don't want to feel him, feel his body, and I resist. But he's powerful. He hugs me tight, then kisses me. First one cheek, then the other. I can feel the muscles of his chest; despite everything I can't help the barest fluttering of desire. He holds me for a moment, and I freeze. I'm hollow, scooped out. I'm aware that Anna and Hugh are saying their own goodbye, laughing about something, oblivious to what's going on.

He whispers into my ear. 'Tell her and I'll kill you.' I feel cold, paralysed, but then a moment later he lets go. He smiles at me once more, then takes Anna's hand and squeezes my arm.

'It's been so great to meet you!' he says, and then they both turn away and, with another flurry of smiles and waves, Hugh and I are on our own.

Chapter Twenty-Six

I close the door. I hear Lukas and Anna's footsteps as they walk down the path to the street, and then I hear them laugh. They sound so happy, so at peace with a life that they are living together. I can almost believe Ryan really is who he says he is, that the last half-hour has been imagined. I can almost convince myself that my affair with Lukas is a thing of the past, that Anna's engagement has just begun and these two things are totally unrelated.

But they aren't. His final words still ring in my ears.

I turn to Hugh. He's standing behind me, where he'd said goodbye to our guests. He hasn't moved. 'What on earth has got into you?' He's speaking quietly, so that only I can hear, but his tone is one of fury.

I can't let him know. I can't have him suspecting. 'I don't know what you mean.' I go into the living room.

He follows me. 'What was that all about?'

I pick up a plate, a glass.

'What?'

'I know it's annoying when people say "passed on", but these euphemisms are pretty common, you know. I hear them all the time. He meant well.'

I can't even begin to tell him the truth.

'I'm just . . . I just get sick of it. You know? She hasn't *passed on*, she hasn't *gone to a better place*. She was murdered. That guy hit her over the head, with God knows what, until her skull caved in and she bled to death on the ground in an alleyway in . . . in . . . fucking *Paris*.'

He takes a step towards me. I can see he's trying to calm down now, to be placatory. 'Darling, I know you're angry, but that was no reason to take it out on our guest. And think of Connor—'

'Hugh. For God's sake!'

I'm shaking, he can see how upset I am; I don't want him even to suspect what it's about. I don't want him to connect it with my behaviour in the hallway when Lukas arrived.

I take a deep breath, close my eyes. I try to take myself out of my anger.

'Look, I'm sorry.'

He smiles, but it's a sad smile.

'You're not all right, Julia.' I know where this is going.

'Don't start, Hugh!' I turn to face him, trembling with rage, my heart hammering as though it's about to explode.

'I just—' he begins and I turn round, slam out of the living room, storm up the stairs. I know Connor will be able to hear, but right now I don't care; I no longer even have the capacity to consider my son.

I get to the bedroom and close the door. I stand still, paralysed. I don't know what to do. I hear him follow me, stand at the top of the stairs.

I have to warn Anna. Even if it destroys our friendship. I have no choice.

'Julia?'

'I'm *fine*!' I shout. 'Just give me a minute. Please.'

I think again of what he said. *I'll kill you.* I feel the bruises on my back, my arms, my thighs; they begin to pulse again, as if they were still fresh. I remember what he did to me in that hotel room, how he made me feel. I feel used; used and then discarded.

But *kill* me? He can't have meant it.

I hear Hugh retreat. I try to calm down. I tell myself that Kate's killer is in custody but, over and over, the thought keeps coming back. He did it. They've made a mistake. They've got the wrong guy.

My mind will not be still, will not be rational. This is what he's done to me. This is how low he's brought me. I'm rejecting all sense.

My heart hammers. I remember logging on to Facebook, navigating to his page. I'd scrolled back to the photos of him in Australia, in Sydney, in front of Uluru. The dates tallied. I clicked on his friends, the ones he was with, and saw they'd posted more pictures from that holiday. One of him on a beach, another in which he's surfing, a third of him snorkelling off a boat. The evidence had been there.

If he had anything at all to do with Kate's death, then half of his friends must've been in on it.

I feel my breathing go back to normal. He's not a killer, just a nasty piece of work. Scaring me because he knew my sister had been killed. Maybe it's his revenge, for ending it, for running out on him. How he must hate me.

There must be a way to warn my friend. I pick my phone up from the bedside table and scroll quickly through to Anna's name. Without hesitating, I press call; I don't think as it rings out, but then it goes to voicemail. It's as if she's silenced it, and I wonder what they're doing. Maybe they've skipped Ronnie Scott's, or wherever they've gone instead, and are on their way back to the hotel.

I picture them. She'll be under him, kissing him as he enters her, running her fingers down the muscles of his back.

Or maybe she'll be cowering, in terror, a bruise already forming.

A wave of nausea hits me and I swallow it down. I have to believe he loves her. I have to. Their relationship is genuine; he's just someone who saw a photo of me – perhaps the one that Anna took when I was over in Paris – and decided he wanted me.

I imagine the conversation. Anna telling him she met me, showing him the snap. 'She's really nice,' she says, and he agrees. And then he comes for me, and I was only too willing to let him have me.

That must be it. He won't attack her.

But then my own memory surfaces again. The carpet beneath me in the hotel room, the burns on my wrists. I know what he's capable of. I have to warn her. She has to know before they're even married that he's prepared to do something like that.

I pick up my phone once more. This time I leave a message. 'Call me.' I try to control my voice, make it sound like I'm not nervous, not scared. 'It's urgent,' I add. 'There's something I need to talk to you about.' I lower my voice, even though Hugh is still downstairs and can't possibly hear me. 'It's about that guy I was seeing. It's about Lukas.' I wince when I say his name. 'Please call me.'

I put the phone back down. I get my computer out of my bag and with shaking hands navigate to the trashcan. The file I deleted the other day is still there, the messages I'd saved. I open a few, as if to check I'm right. He said he lived in Cambridge. No mention of a girlfriend, much less a fiancée.

I decide I should print one out, just in case I need it to persuade Anna, but the printer's upstairs, in Hugh's office. I pick up my machine and go up, flicking on the light as I do, barely even registering the paperwork that's begun to litter the floor since Hugh has had the complaint hanging over him. I select a message and print it out. On paper, it's solid, irrefutable. 'There's no one else I want but you,' it says. 'We were made for each other.'

Even so, all it proves is that I've been messaging someone called Lukas, and she knows that in any case. I wish I had a photo, one of the two of us, but I don't. I've deleted any I took, too scared that Hugh might find them.

I fold the page anyway and put it in my bag, then check my phone. She hasn't called, and I know what I have to do. I go back downstairs. Hugh's in the kitchen, loading the dishwasher.

'I'm just going out.'

'Where on earth to?'

I try to sound calm, breezy, even though I feel the opposite. 'I thought I'd go and meet Anna and Ryan, after all. In the jazz bar.'

'You're sure?'

'Yes. I feel awful, about over-reacting. I want to apologize. Anyway, it might be fun. And Anna's right. I don't see her very often.'

He looks puzzled, bemused. For an awful moment I worry he'll suggest coming with me, but then I remember Connor. 'I won't be late. Would you make sure Connor goes to bed?'

'Of course.' He picks up another plate.

'He has school tomorrow.'

'I know. You go. Enjoy yourself. Will you take the car?'

I know why he's asking. He wants to make sure I won't slip up and have a drink. He needn't worry; I won't go to Ronnie Scott's. I can't risk a confrontation in a noisy club, full of strangers. Instead I'm going to wait outside Anna's hotel.

'I will,' I say. 'And leave this, will you? I'll tidy the rest of the dinner things in the morning.'

He nods. 'Okay.'

I head straight to the hotel. When I arrive I park the car and call Anna again: still no answer; once again it goes straight to voicemail. I slam the steering wheel. I'm going to have to go in.

The lobby is large, impressive, but I barely notice it. I go into the bar and find a deep leather sofa, near the door. Through the glass partition I can see the main entrance. I won't miss them.

A waiter comes over to ask if I'd like a drink. 'Mineral water,' I say, and he nods, as if that's what he'd been expecting all along. He goes back to the bar and delivers my order with a whisper, a glance over his shoulder towards where I sit.

My drink arrives with a bowl of pretzels. The waiter hesitates for a moment, blocking my view of the entrance, then bends towards me. 'Waiting for someone?' he says as he wipes the table before setting my drink down and tidying the snacks and napkins. He's trying to sound casual, but his question has an edge of disapproval. 'Yes,' I say. My voice cracks with nerves. 'Yes, I am,' I say more forcefully.

'Very good.' I don't think he believes me. 'A guest?'

'Yes. She's staying here.' He doesn't move on. 'She's just got engaged. In fact, could I get a bottle of champagne? A surprise, for when she arrives? Two glasses?'

He nods, then stands up. 'Very good.' He turns to leave. When I look back into the lobby I see Anna. She must have arrived while I was talking to the waiter. She looks different somehow, sadder and more serious than when she'd left my house an hour or so ago, and it takes me a moment to recognize her. I begin to stand, but she's already heading into the lift. I could shout out, but the door between us is closed and she'd never hear me. Nevertheless, my heart lifts – for a moment I'm in luck: she's alone – but then it plummets. I see Lukas just a few steps behind her. I freeze, then watch as he waits to let a couple go ahead of him. By the time I've started moving again I can see that I'm going to be too late.

'Shit.' The lift doors are about to close, but then Anna sees me, over her fiancé's shoulder. She stares for a moment, she looks shocked, but before I can even smile the lift doors have closed and she's out of sight.

I head out of the bar and into the lobby. I run over to the lift, but it's already ascending. I watch, cursing silently, as it stops on the third, fifth and sixth floors; I have no way of knowing which is theirs, much less what room they're in. When it begins to come back down again I turn and head back to my seat, scrabbling for my phone, imagining their conversation.

'I'm sure I saw Julia in the lobby,' she'll have said. 'I wonder what she's doing here?'

'No,' he'll say. 'It wasn't her.'

They'll get to the room. 'Come here . . .' he'll say, and he'll kiss her, undress her, the way he had with me. She'll feel herself give in to him. Their hands, their mouths, will find each other. His prick will already be stiffening when she begins to undo his trousers.

I push the thought away. I have to stay focussed. My phone is already buzzing when I find it, and I answer it quickly. It's Anna.

'Is that you? Downstairs?'

She sounds happy, relaxed, if surprised. I can hear Lukas in the background. It sounds like he's pouring drinks.

'Yes.'

'I thought I saw you when I came in. Is everything all right?'

'Yes.' I realize there's no point in pretending. 'Actually, no. Listen, I have to see you. I've been trying to ring you. I left a message. I'll explain. Can you come down?'

She sounds hesitant. Intrigued.

'Why don't you come up here?'

'No. No, you come down. Please?'

I think of the printout I've brought with me. I don't want to show it to her, but I might have to. Will she believe me? Surely she'll have to, but still I'd rather not have to do that to her.

'Is Hugh with you?' she says.

'He's at home. Please come down. Please let me explain.'

I hear her cover the mouthpiece of her phone, confer with Lukas. It's obvious what he'll say. 'Anna!' I say. 'Anna . . .'

After a few moments she answers. 'We'll be down in a couple of minutes.'

'No!' I try to control my voice, but still I must sound desperate, panicked. 'No. It's better . . . could you come alone? Please?'

She hesitates. 'Give me five minutes.'

Even though it's late, she's changed into a pair of trousers, a sweater, trainers. The bar is less busy now; the few people there are finishing their nightcaps before heading upstairs. The bottle of champagne on the table in front of me looks out of place. 'Julia!' she says, once we've kissed. 'Is everything all right? You sound so worried!' She lowers her voice. 'Is everything okay with Hugh?'

'Yes.' I look over her shoulder; there's no one there, just the waiter, collecting glasses, checking the new arrival. We sit.

'Good. I was worried something had happened. Or, you know, Hugh had found out about *that guy*.'

She mouths the last two words silently, as if she thinks there are spies everywhere, eager to report back. 'No, not that,' I say. 'Nothing like that.'

'Good!' She raises her glass. I nod. Mine is still empty.

'What is it?'

'Have you listened to the message I left on your phone?' She shakes her head.

I can't speak. I don't want to tell her. I don't want to destroy her happiness, even if it is founded on lies. But then I think of all the things Lukas did to me, the things I asked for, and the things I didn't. I can't fail her the way, deep down, I know I failed my sister. I can't let her down, just to save myself from a difficult conversation.

'It's about Ryan.'

'Ryan?'

'Listen.' I take her hand. I tell myself it's what Kate would have done. 'I don't want you to think I'm . . . y'know . . . jealous . . .'

'Jealous? You're not making any sense!'

'Of you and Ryan, I mean.'

'Why would you be jealous? Julia, what's this about?'

I hesitate. I'm searching for the right words, but they seem just out of reach.

'It's just—'

'What?'

'Do you know if you can trust him?'

'Of course! Why?'

'It's just, you haven't known him that long, and—'

It sounds petty, lame, and already I know I've said the wrong thing. I see Anna's expression change to one of anger.

'I've known him long enough,' she says. 'What's this

308

about, Julia? I wouldn't expect this from you, of all people!'

I take a deep breath. I begin to speak. 'I don't think he's who he says he is,' I say. I close my eyes. 'Sorry—'

'What?' She sounds shocked. 'What on earth are you saying? What d'you mean?'

I tread carefully. I need her to work it out for herself. I need her to realize that the man she calls Ryan is lying about where he goes every week.

'What does he do? On Tuesdays?'

'He goes to work . . .'

'In Paris?'

'It varies. He travels a lot.'

'London?'

'Sometimes . . . What's this about, Julia?'

'The thing is,' I say, but then I stop. The atmosphere in the room has shifted, the door to the bar, swung open, has admitted a current of cool air. Over Anna's shoulder I see Lukas, scanning the room, looking for us. He looks utterly calm.

'Shit!'

'What?' She looks over her shoulder. 'Oh, hi!' She calls him across the few tables that separate them, and when he notices her he waves.

I grab her hand. 'Listen.' I talk quickly, I have to get it out before he gets here. 'You can't trust him, he isn't who he says he is. He's seeing someone else. You have to believe me—'

'Julia!' She's shaking her head. I feel a rising urgency; any moment it might tip into panic.

'*Just leave him!*' I've spoken too loudly. The waiter has noticed and no doubt Lukas as well.

She pulls her hand away and stands up. She looks at me with disbelief. Disbelief and anger.

'I'm sorry—' I begin, but a moment later Lukas arrives.

'What's up?' Anna's face relaxes. She turns to kiss him, then looks back to me.

'Julia was just leaving.' She smiles. 'Weren't you?'

'No. Listen to me . . .'

Lukas steps forward, puts himself between me and Anna. As if it's me who's dangerous. He looks angry, protective towards his future wife.

'What's this about?'

Anna turns to face me. 'I know what this is about.' She sounds upset but determined. 'You're jealous. Just because you and Hugh are falling apart and we're just coming together. Or is it about the money?'

'The money?' I have no idea what she's talking about.

'You know we're going to sort our wills out on Friday—'

'What?' My mind whirrs. I don't know anything about that. I cast my mind back, try to remember our last conversation.

'Anna, no. No, it's not that at all. That money is yours. Kate left it to you. I *want* you to have it.'

I think back to the conversation we'd had in Paris, all those months ago. I'd told her as much then.

'Listen,' says Lukas. He puts his hand on my arm and I flinch. 'I don't know what's going on here, but you two need to calm down.'

Anna is angry now. The bar staff have noticed; a man is coming over. 'Miss,' he's saying, to me, and then, 'Is everything all right here?'

'Fine,' says Lukas. 'It's fine. Nothing we can't handle.' He begins to steer Anna towards the door. She's looking at me with an expression of disbelief, shaking her head as if she can't believe the person I've become. I wonder what else she's thinking, maybe that Kate was right all along, I'm a jealous bitch who betrayed her, stole her child and wouldn't give him back. 'I think you'd better leave,' says Lukas firmly, turning to me, and at the same time I feel a hand on my arm. It's the barman, turning me around, escorting me in the opposite direction.

'He's Lukas!' I shout as they reach the door, but she's looking away and my voice is swallowed by the cavernous bar. The other patrons look at me – they think I'm drunk, a troublemaker, a jealous ex – but I'm not sure Anna heard me. It's only when I break free of the waiter's grip on my arm and turn round to say it again that I see I'm too late.

She's gone.

I pay and leave. There's nothing else to do, and I can't stay, not after the commotion I've caused. When I reach the car I open the window then light a cigarette from the packet I've started to keep in the glove compartment. I think of Hugh – he doesn't approve of smoking in the car – and wish I could be with him right now.

I screwed it up. I don't know what I could have done differently, but I screwed it up.

I exhale, sit back in the leather seat. I've parked on a sidestreet just off Portland Place and can see the doorway to the hotel framed in the wing mirror. Even though it must be after midnight now, people are still coming and going.

I wonder if Anna was right. Maybe it really is all about my sister's money, though not in the way she imagines. I imagine Lukas, hearing about Kate's death, moving in on me but then finding out my sister had left all the cash to her best friend.

But no, that makes no sense; he was definitely seeing Anna first, before Kate died. I'm back to square one.

Again the same thought forms, the one that's been haunting me. It grows, I can't shake it, can't hold it down. It's because I know he lives in Paris, now. It rises to the surface, inexorable, unstoppable.

It was him.

But it can't be. There's Kate's earring; they've made an arrest. Plus, we know the police checked everyone out, all Kate's online contacts. They're satisfied. It can't have been him.

So why did he target me, then? Or am I not a target at all – was it just sheer chance?

I finish my cigarette then toss it on to the pavement, through the half-open window. Straight away I feel the urge to light another; I fight it, but it seems pointless, futile. I have to calm my mind. I have to sort it out. I lift my bag off the passenger seat and begin to rummage inside it.

It happens quickly. I don't see him come out of the hotel, don't hear him approach, I'm barely aware of him opening the door. I look up and he's there; I've gone from alone to not-alone in an instant. My heart leaps with sudden terror.

'What the—?' I begin, but he turns to me.

'Surprise!' His exclamation is dry and humourless. His face is inches from mine; he smells of aftershave, the one I'm used to. The fragrance of wood – sandalwood, I think – mixed with something else, something medicinal. He looks paler than I remember, his features thinner. I try to tell myself that if I met him now I wouldn't look twice, but it's a lie.

'Lukas,' I gasp. My muscle memory kicks in once again; instinctively I shoot as far back in my seat as I can, move as far away from him as I can get without opening the door and running. I wonder if that is what I should be doing. Running.

'What d'you want?'

'Oh, sweetheart. Don't be like that . . .' His voice sounds thick, not like him at all.

'Where's Anna?' I have visions of her upstairs, pacing. I

wonder if she knows he's with me; it's possible he's told her he's just popped out for a walk, to get some air.

He smiles. It's bitter, resentful. 'Relax. I don't know what you think is going on, but let me tell you, you're wrong on every count.' He pauses. 'Anna's upstairs,' he says. 'I left her in the shower.' He grins. I wonder if I'm supposed to find his comment suggestive, sexual. Titillating. Is this the game he's playing? The three of us, upstairs, naked.

'She knows I'm here. She sent me. She's sorry about losing her temper. She wants you to come up and have a drink with us. Sort things out.' He shrugs. 'So how about it?'

I want to believe him, but I don't. How can I? Anna thinks I've met him for the first time tonight.

'Who are you? Tell me what you want.' He ignores me.

'No? Didn't think so.' He turns. 'Look. Anna's a big girl. She can look after herself. I don't know why you want to come and interfere.'

'Interfere?'

'Warning her away? Telling her I'm not who she thinks I am? Maybe I'm exactly who she thinks I am, just not who you thought I was.' He looks thoughtful. 'Maybe it's you who doesn't know anything about me. Not her.' He leans towards me. 'Anna trusts me, you know? She tells me everything . . .'

I think of the printout I have in my bag. I should've given it to her when I had the chance.

'Maybe, for now—' I begin, but he moves abruptly. He grabs my arm, twisting it as he does so. It's sudden, and brutal. I cry out, a scream of shock and pain, and then I'm silenced.

'You know,' he hisses, still holding my arm, still digging in his fingers, 'I don't like little tarts like you who come between me and my fun. So, this is what's going to happen . . .' He twists my arm further. I struggle, but he holds me. He's using only one hand yet still it seems easy for him. It feels as if he could snap my arm with hardly any effort at all, as if that's exactly what he'd like to do. I gasp once more; again I remember his hands on me, how once they'd caressed the very skin that now screams with pain. 'You're going to get the fuck out of my life,' he says. 'You're going to leave Anna alone, and you're not going to interfere. Get it?'

I gather all my strength. I turn to him; finally I manage to wrench my arm from his. 'Or what? I saw you, you know. Earlier. Getting into the lift. You didn't look that in love to me. I don't know what you're doing, but she doesn't deserve it. She's done nothing to you. She really thinks you love her.'

I feel his resolve waver, just slightly. I've hit a nerve. But then he speaks. 'It makes no difference to me what you think you saw.' His smile is sickly, thin. 'And you *are* going to leave us alone.'

He seems so certain. Dread fills me.

'Or what?'

'Or I might just make my private archive a little bit more public . . .'

I don't understand what he's saying, yet I feel myself tense. It's as if my body has already worked it out while my mind lags behind.

'Your what—?'

'Yes,' he says. 'I've got some very interesting photos in my collection. Videos, too. Want to see?'

I feel myself falling. He seems so totally confident. I'm no one, nothing. He could destroy me, without even having to try.

I shake my head. He pulls his phone out of his pocket and scrolls through some screens. 'Ah. This is a good one.'

He selects a photograph, and the glow from the screen

briefly illuminates the dark interior of the car, then he angles the screen so that I can see the picture. It's a woman, taken from the waist up. She's naked.

It takes me a moment to realize it's me.

I gasp. 'This is . . .' I begin, but the words catch in my mouth and I can't get them out.

'This is from that first time . . .' he says. 'The first time you turned your camera on. D'you remember?'

I do. I'd been in my studio, the door locked. I'd angled my camera, stood up. I felt stupid, at first, but then I'd become swept up in it until there was just me, and him, and the rest of the world had faded to nothing.

The betrayal seems absolute. I can't look at it any more, but neither do I want to look at him.

'You took it . . . you *kept* it?'

'I like having an archive.' He shrugs, as if it's nothing. 'For when I'm bored, you know?'

'How dare you!' Fury is rising in my chest, but something else, too. A new fear, cold and hard and piercing. If he has this, I think, then he'll have more.

He begins to scroll through his phone. 'I have plenty of others,' he's saying. 'This, for example? Or this?'

He shows me image after image. A rerun of the past few months, the edited highlights. Almost every time I'd stripped for him, because he was bored, or horny, and I missed him and wanted to please him. With each picture I sink lower, until I feel I'm drowning. The water is closing over me, invading me, until I can't breathe.

'Oh, and this.' This one is different, taken in the hotel after we'd had sex. In it I'm standing up, smiling at the camera; he's caught me as I was dressing. I remember the day he took it. I'd been flattered at the time; he wanted a memento, some reminder of the day.

I'd been glad, yet I remember I'd asked him to delete it. 'I just feel uncomfortable,' I'd said. He told me I was beautiful, that he wanted a picture. 'Please, Lukas,' I said. 'Delete it?'

Clearly, he hadn't. Now, as I look at it, I'm horrified. It's like one version of me looking at another. Julia, looking at Jayne. I'd thought I could keep them separate, in boxes, locked away, but I was wrong. Things have a habit of escaping.

Another wave of despair hits. None of it was real. From the beginning it was based on a lie, an illusion of love.

'Anyway, you get the general idea.'

'You bastard . . .' I whisper. Even this word feels wholly inadequate, after what he's taken from me.

'Oh, come on now. These pictures are great! You should know. It'd be very selfish of me not to share . . .' His hand goes to his pocket again. When he takes it out he's holding a memory stick. He holds it up. 'Here's your copy, for example.' I stare at it but refuse to take it from him. 'No? You might as well have it. There are plenty more . . .' He smiles, then puts it between us on the dashboard.

'But you're in half of these photographs. Why would you share them?'

'I'm in some of them, yes. But not all. And, in any case, I don't have a child. I'm not married to a surgeon. I think I'd just about get away with it.' He smiles. 'Just think . . .' He shakes his head, tutting. 'Imagine what the press would say. The *Mail*? TOP SURGEON'S WIFE IN SEX SCANDAL? It might even go viral. Don't you think?'

I don't reply. He's right. The future collapses in slow motion. On top of the complaint against Hugh, it would be too much. I see the scandal, our friends turning away from us. Maria, Carla – all of his colleagues. I imagine myself walking down the street, feeling people's eyes burning into me, not knowing what they'd seen, what gossip they'd believed.

He's won, I think, and there's nothing I can do. He has Anna, he will get his hands on my sister's money, and then he'll abuse and mistreat Anna the way he has me.

He hasn't finished, though. 'There's Hugh's boss at the hospital, too. All his colleagues. Can't be good for business. For his reputation. There's Connor's school, all those parents. I can't imagine it'd be too difficult to get hold of their email addresses. Oh,' he says, as if something's just occurred to him, 'I just remembered. There's all those porn websites I can upload these to. "Hot amateur."' He looks at me, watching for my reaction. '"Older woman fucks young stud."'

It happens suddenly, comes from nowhere. I slap him, as hard as I can. It's as if all the energy I've been clamping down has erupted. I want to kick and scream and fight.

Yet his only response is to laugh quietly, almost under his breath, and I realize he's pleased.

He looks at me. His eyes are expressionless. I wonder if he's capable of experiencing pain.

'So, as I was saying, you're going to stay away from me and Anna.'

I feel myself begin to cry. I tell myself I won't let the tears come, I won't give him the satisfaction, but they burn behind my eyes.

Yet at the same time I'm almost relieved. When everything's gone, there's no more pain, nothing else to lose.

Staying away from him and Anna – it might be difficult, but it can be done.

'Plus,' he says, 'why not have a think about how much these pictures might be worth to you. I mean, I know your sister left a bit of money to Anna, but I understand there's a lot more that's gone to your son . . .'

'You bastard,' I say again.

He turns to open the door. The temperature in the car seems to drop as he moves away from me and the rest of the world rushes in. 'I ought to be going,' he says. 'Anna will be wondering where we are. Plus, I guess you've got a lot to think about. I'll tell her you were still upset, you had to get home to Connor. Something.'

I want to give up, to let him go, but then I think again of Kate and I know what I have to do. I'm strong enough; this year has taught me that, if nothing else. I'm stronger than I think.

'Wait.'

He pulls the catch, but doesn't step out. He turns to me, instead. 'What?'

'Anna trusts me.' Now I've made my decision, my voice is strong, defiant. 'She'll never believe you. Not if I tell her what you're doing.'

He closes the car door.

'Tell her whatever you like. The truth is, Anna is beginning to think you're a bit crazy. Sick. She thinks your sister's death might have sent you off the rails. That perfect life you had . . . and now . . .' His hand goes to his pocket. 'She thinks you're a little bit unpredictable. A tiny bit jealous, perhaps. Which of course you are, though she doesn't know why.'

I think back to the time I spent with Anna in Paris, to all the conversations we've had over the months. He's wrong.

'You're lying. Whatever—?'

'Makes her think that? I guess this doesn't help . . .' He holds his hand up, between us. He's holding something; it must've been in his pocket. It takes me a moment to realize it's a knife.

I'm overcome with panic. I try to back away but the car is cramped and there's nowhere for me to go. It happens in an instant. He grabs my hand with both of his, so that he's holding me tight. The knife is exposed, sticking out towards me, in his hand though it looks as if it's in mine. I struggle to free myself, thinking he's trying to stab me, and he begins swinging my hand, left, right, back again. It's as if we're struggling, as if he's trying to get the knife off me, even though he's the one holding it. I hear a voice, shouting, and at first I think it's coming from outside the car, but then I realize it's me and I see it all. It's as if I'm watching from the street, peering into the car. It looks as though I'm trying to stab him as he tries to hold me off with both hands. He relaxes for a moment, and just as I think he's about to drop the knife he does it. With sudden ferocity he pulls both hands towards his face and the knife he's holding catches against the skin of his cheek. 'Fuck!' he says, and then a moment later there's a dull gush of blood.

'You silly bitch.' He smiles. He shoves my hands away as if I repulse him and drops the knife. It falls into my lap and I see it's just a kitchen knife, one I'd use for preparing vegetables, and was never going to do much damage. Yet still it's sharp, it's cut him, the blood is beginning to run down his cheek.

'You tried to stab me!' He scrabbles, as if he's trying to get away from me, then he's stumbling, out of the car. I'm speechless, dumb. There are a couple outside the car, a man and a woman. They peer in, trying to see what's going on. My mouth opens and closes, pathetic. I can see the wound on his cheek is a scratch more than anything, but still the blood pours. It's over his mouth now, running off his chin, dripping on his white shirt.

I think of Anna's reaction when he gets upstairs. There'll be blood everywhere by then, it'll look like a frenzied attack. It'll look like he's had a lucky escape and she'll believe whatever he tells her. That I'm jealous, crazy. That I'm trying to split them up out of spite, because I have no one of my own.

'Still think she's going to trust you?' he says, then a moment later he's gone and I'm alone – even though there are cars and people, I'm alone – and all I can hear is the beating of my heart and a dog, way in the distance, howling into the dark.

Chapter Twenty-Seven

I have no choice. I go home.

It's late; the house is quiet, in darkness. It ought to feel safe, a place of refuge, but it doesn't. Hugh and Connor are upstairs, asleep. Completely unaware of what's happening, of where I've been. I'm separate from my family. Separate and alone.

I go into the lounge and turn on a table lamp, then sit in its warm glow. I turn the memory stick over and over in my hands. It's so small, fragile. I could destroy it easily, crush it under foot, melt it over the flame from my lighter. For a moment I think I will, but I know it's futile. I put it down, pick it up again.

I fetch my computer, switch it on, slide the stick into the port. I know I shouldn't look, but somehow I can't help it. Once, maybe even just a few weeks ago, I'd have still been hoping it might all turn out to be a joke, that he'll have loaded the device with one of those tacky e-cards I used to hate but now send routinely when I've forgotten someone's birthday. I'd have half expected the file to be an animated cartoon. Dancing monkeys, my face superimposed, singing a song. *Fooled you!*

But not any more. I can't even pretend to myself now.

There are a dozen or so files, some pictures, some videos. I make sure my machine is muted then choose one at random.

It's a video. The two of us. On the bed, naked. I'm underneath him, but my face is in the frame. I'm recognizable.

My eyes are closed, my mouth open. I look faintly ridiculous. I can bear it only for a second or two. I feel a sort of detached horror; detached because I could easily believe the woman on the screen has nothing to do with me, horror because this most intimate of acts is here, recorded without my knowledge, preserved for ever.

Exhaustion wipes me. How did he film this? Did he set up his laptop, angle the inbuilt camera towards the bed? I would've noticed, surely?

Maybe it was something more sophisticated, then. A hidden camera, disguised as a drinks can, built into the cap of a ballpoint pen. I know they're available, I've even seen them in the department stores – John Lewis, Selfridges – when I've been looking at cameras. At the time I wondered why anyone would want one. They were for professionals, surely, private investigators. They belonged in the realm of James Bond. I guess now I know.

I shiver. These videos and pictures go right back to the beginning of our affair; he must have been planning this, all along. A wave of nausea breaks. I breathe as deeply as I can, long, slow breaths that don't help at all, then slam my machine closed before ripping the memory stick out of the port and throwing it across the room. It bounces off the wall and clatters to the floor at my feet.

I stand up. I can't leave it here. I imagine Connor picking it up, taking a look. What would he say? What would he think? I find it and go upstairs. I put it in my drawer; tomorrow I'll take it out, throw it in the canal or under the wheels of a bus. I want a drink, yet am aware it's the last thing I ought to do. Once I start I might not be able to stop. I run a shower instead, as hot as I can bear it. Still my skin has never felt less alive. It's only when the water is so hot it nearly scalds that I feel anything at all.

For the next two days I don't sleep. I call Anna, over and over, but she doesn't answer. I'm on edge. I startle at every noise, wondering if it's Lukas. I dread every call or message, every package in the post. I'm not sure what to do. I call Adrienne, but I can't tell her what's wrong. I just say I'm not well, I have a virus, I'll talk to her next week. She's going to be away for a few days anyway, she says. Bob's taking her to Florence.

I decide I'll turn up for lunch with Anna, at her hotel as we arranged. He might be there, of course, or she might not want to speak to me, but I have no other option. In any case, I decide a severance might actually be better; I could go back to my own life, then, concentrate on Connor and Hugh.

Still I can't settle. I want to leave the house but can think of nowhere to go. I want to switch my phone off, but daren't in case I miss a call from Anna. By Thursday Hugh has noticed; he tells me I need to get out, to do something to take my mind off Kate. 'You've just taken a step backwards,' he says. He thinks the grief has returned, and in a way he's right. There's the grief he knows about, and also the grief he doesn't.

I take Connor out for supper. I choose a bun-free burger and a salad, though when I look over at Connor's meal, all melting cheese and twice-fried chips, I wonder why I'm bothered. My life is falling apart, my affair about to be exposed in the worst possible way. Why do I care what I look like, what I eat?

Perhaps Kate had the right idea. Eat, drink, fuck who you like and never mind the consequences.

And then die.

I reach over and grab a couple of Connor's fries. He looks up from his phone, his brow furrowed, his face a picture of mock-indignation. 'Mum!' he says, but he's laughing. It's a tiny moment of pleasure, seeing him happy. I wonder if it's the first time since we told him they'd caught Kate's killer.

I nod at his phone. 'What're you up to?' I say.

He puts his phone back on the table. Within reach, face down. It buzzes almost straight away.

'It's just Facebook. And I've got a chess game going.'

'With Dad?'

'No. Hugh only likes to play in real life.'

'Hugh?' I'm shocked, momentarily.

'He said I could call him that, if I wanted. He said he didn't mind.'

It bothers me. He's growing up, but also pushing away from us. The first is inevitable, but like every parent I'd hoped to avoid the second, for a little while longer at least.

But in a way it's good to be upset by this. After the horrors of the last few days, the worry about Anna and the pictures Lukas has on his computer, this is something mundane and easily sorted. It feels normal. Family stuff.

'Just don't ask to call me Julia.' I'm Mum, I want to add.

'Okay.'

I smile. I want him to know I understand, that I remember being a teenager; that desperate hunger for adulthood and responsibility. I want him to know I'm part of his world, that I love him. He takes a huge bite of his burger; juice runs down his chin. He wipes it with the back of his hand and I pass him a napkin. I can't help myself. He takes it from me but doesn't use it. I pick at my salad, casting around for something to talk about.

'How's football?'

'I was picked for the team again. I'm playing next Saturday.' He pauses, then says, 'Oh! Did I tell you?'

I put down my fork. The noise in the restaurant seems suddenly to increase. He's looking at me, expectantly, his eyebrows raised, and I shake my head.

He takes another bite of his burger, a few fries.

'Well . . .' he begins. I'm about to tell him to please finish chewing before beginning to speak but something, some kind of premonition, stops me. 'You remember when we went to see *Planet of the Apes*?'

I feel myself tense. 'Uh-huh?'

He reaches for the mayonnaise. 'Well, you remember the creepy guy? The guy who came in and sat right by us and then just left?'

I try to sound as though I'm struggling to recall. 'Oh, yes,' I hear myself say. I don't recognize my own voice; it sounds filtered, distorted, as if it's coming from some distance away. 'I'd completely forgotten about him,' I add. There's a catch in my voice and it sounds false, even to me. Yet he doesn't seem to notice. I watch, silently, bile rising to my throat, waiting for him to continue as he squirts mayonnaise on to his plate, then goes for the ketchup. As he speaks he mixes the two to a marbled pink mush. I want him to hurry up with whatever he's got to tell me.

'Last night I saw him again,' he says. 'You remember I went bowling? With Dylan and Molly and the others? Well, he was there. Over in the next alley.' He picks up a handful of fries, dips them in the pink sauce. 'I noticed him first of all 'cos it looked like he was there on his own. Y'know, no kids or anything. We thought he was waiting for someone, but nobody turned up. He just stood there bowling by himself. Then he left. Weird, eh? I mean, who does that? Molly thought he looked like a paedo.'

My head begins to spin. I flush, as if all the blood in my body were rushing to my head and neck, then a moment later everything – Connor, the rest of the restaurant – begins to recede, as if disappearing down a tunnel.

'Mum?' says Connor. 'Are you okay?'

I reach for the glass of water in front of me. It's cool to the touch; I bring it to my mouth. The movement is mechanical, I do it without thinking. I sip, and some spills from the over-full glass. I barely notice; it's as if I'm watching myself from the other side of the room.

'Mum?' says Connor, more urgently. He looks worried, but I can do nothing to allay his fears.

My head spins with images of Lukas. I should've known. I should have protected my son. I've let him down, just like Kate and Anna. I force myself back to the present.

'Yes?' I realize water is dripping down my chin. I wipe it. 'I'm fine. Sorry? Go on . . .'

'Well, that's it. He just turned up and bowled and—'

Another rush of panic hits. 'How did you know it was him?'

'Oh, y'know?' He picks up another couple of fries. I grab his hand.

'Connor. How did you . . . are you sure?'

He looks at my hand on his arm, then up to my face. 'Yes, Mum. I recognized him. He was wearing the same cap. Remember? The Vans trucker? It was a classic patch—'

I don't know what he's talking about. I must look puzzled; he seems to be about to describe it to me when he changes his mind. 'Anyway. He had the same cap on.'

'You're sure?'

'Yes!'

'Did he say anything to you?'

'Not really . . .'

Anger begins to displace the panic. Anger with myself, with Lukas, with Connor. 'Not really? Is that not really yes, or not really no? Which is it, Connor?'

My voice has risen, in both pitch and volume. I fight to control it.

'He just said sorry.' Already he sounds resentful, sulky. He's looking at me as if I've gone crazy. I can see he wishes he hadn't mentioned it. 'He spilled his beer over me. That's all. It was an accident. Anyway . . .'

It's clear he wants to change the subject, but I ignore him. 'So what did this guy say?'

He sighs. 'He said, "Hey, dude, I'm sorry." That was it. That's one of the ways I knew it was the same bloke, 'cos that's what he'd called me in the cinema. Dude. No one says it any more.' He sips his milkshake. 'Can you let go of my arm?'

I hadn't realized I was still clutching him.

I release him and sit back. Anger is burning within me now, a rage. Yet it has nowhere to go, nothing to burn, and so it sits, deep and poisonous. I'm trying to keep my face neutral, my features calm. I'm failing. I tense, I'm chewing my bottom lip.

A question comes to me, with an awful, sickening lurch: I now know Lukas has been following me on the iPhone app, but how did he know where my son would be? How did he get to Connor?

I sit forward. 'Who knew you were going bowling?' I say, trying to keep the panic out of my voice. 'Who did you tell?'

'No one. Why? Mum?'

'Don't be ridiculous!' I'm almost shouting. 'You must've told someone!'

'Mum—?'

'Molly, and Dylan? They knew, for a start! Who else was there with you?'

He looks at me. His expression is odd; almost fearful. 'Dylan's dad took us.'

'When?' The questions come thick and fast. 'When did you arrange it? Who did you tell, Connor? Who knew you were going?'

'Jesus, Mum! Some of the guys. Y'know? We invited Sahil, and Rory, but they couldn't come. Oh, and I guess Molly might've invited a few people. And I guess Dylan's dad might've told Dylan's mum. Just possibly . . .'

His voice has a new note, one I haven't heard in him before. Sarcasm.

'There's no need for that attitude—'

He ignores me.

'. . . and I probably told Evie, and I suppose I just might've posted it on Facebook, so there's all the people who follow me there, and—'

I interrupt him. 'Who follows you on Facebook?'

'I dunno. Friends. Friends of my friends. People like that.'

Something begins to coalesce in my mind. All the way through, Lukas had always known more than I thought I'd let him know. I now know he was tracking my location, moment by moment, but I've never worked out how he knew the other details. The fact we were planning on going to a cinema at all, what film we were going to see. Hugh's name, when I'd only ever called him Harvey.

And now I think I know. If he was following Connor's posts, and Connor was posting everything . . .

An awful thought occurs. Could that be how he'd figured out Paddy's last name, too? And where he lives? I can see how it might be. Connor might've mentioned our guests by name, and from there a quick search – Maria, Hugh, surgeon – would lead to a surname. He could then easily look at Paddy's Facebook page, or LinkedIn, or whatever else he might use.

'Give me your phone.'

'Mum—!' he begins, but I silence him.

'Give me your phone, Connor. Now.'

He passes it over and I tell him to unlock the screen, to open his Facebook profile. I can see he wants to fight, to protest, but he knows he's not old enough to stand against me, yet. I hold my hand out for him to give me the phone back, but he tosses it on to the table.

I pick it up. I scan through his updates. Most days he's posted several; there are too many to check, and many of them I don't understand. Messages to his friends, in-jokes, gossip, chat about the football or things he's watched on TV. I go back, rewinding through the year, to the summer, and I see what I'm looking for. 'Off to Islington Vue,' says one. 'With my MOTHER.' I scroll back further, to older messages, realizing as I do how used I am to reading things in backwards chronology. A few messages later I see, 'Family trip to the cinema tomorrow. Planet of the Apes!'

'Who are you friends with?' I hand the phone back to him. 'Show me.'

He begins to protest, but I interrupt. 'Connor! Show me, now!' He hands back the phone. There are hundreds of people following his updates, some whose names I recognize, but many I don't. I scan them quickly, and after a moment I see it. David Largos. Without warning I flash back on my first conversation with Lukas, back when things had felt simple, manageable. The surname is the same as his username back then. Whatever hope I'd had – that I was mistaken, that I was wrong – collapses.

I hold the phone out to him. 'Who's this?' I shout. 'Who's David Largos?'

'I don't know, Mum.' He raises his voice. 'Just somebody. Okay? That's the way it works. I don't know *everybody* who follows me. Yeah?'

I select the username and a picture appears. It's a picture of a dog, wearing a baseball cap with the word 'Vans' written on it. There's no other information, but it's him.

That's it, I think. That's how he knew. That's how he knew everything.

First Anna, then me. And now I know it. Connor is involved as well.

'Delete it.' I give him his phone back. 'Delete your profile.' I'm shaking, but he doesn't move.

'No!' He looks horrified, as if what I've asked him to do is utterly unreasonable. I wish I could tell him why it's so important, but I can't. I wish I could tell him how much his ridiculous and almost constant sense of being hard done by infuriates me, but I don't.

'I'm not joking, Connor. You have to delete your profile.' He begins to argue, a barrage of buts and can'ts and won'ts.

I ignore him. 'Connor!' I've shouted. There's a momentary hush – a stillness – in the restaurant and I know that if I were to look around I'd see people staring at us. There's a young couple on the table next to us, he, wearing tracksuit trousers and a hooded top, she, in a mini-dress, and on the other side a woman with someone I imagine is her daughter, a pram parked between them. I don't want to be their entertainment for the evening, but neither do I want them to know I'm embarrassed. I lower my voice but keep my eyes fixed on my son.

'This isn't a game. I'm telling you. Delete your profile. Now. Or else I'll take your phone off you and you can go back to using your old one . . .'

'You wouldn't!'

'Watch me.'

His jaw drops. He's incredulous, it's outrageous, he doesn't believe I'd even consider such a thing. He stares at me, and I stare back.

I hold out my hand.

'Your phone, Connor. Give it to me. Now.'

He snatches his phone out of my reach and stands up. At first I think he's going to say sorry, or make some other plea to my better nature, but he looks furious and, sure enough, does no such thing. Instead he hisses at me, 'Fuck you.' A moment later he's turned and is heading for the exit, leaving me open-mouthed with shock.

I stand up, too; my napkin slides to the floor. 'Connor!' I say, as firmly as I can, but he ignores me. 'Get back here!' People stare, there's a hush. I'm losing control, everything's receding. It's as if I'm hurtling down a tunnel, trying to get back to a reality that's slipping away from me as quickly as I am from it. I try to follow Connor as he shoulders past people at the door and goes outside. I have to catch up with him, and I force myself back to reality.

'I'll come back,' I say to the waiter, who looks as though he's seen this sort of thing before. I squeeze past the tables – people move their chairs out of the way, turning their faces away from me as they do, as if I'm best avoided – but by the time I get outside Connor has gone. I glimpse him in the distance, running along Upper Street in the opposite direction from home, and without thinking any further I begin to give chase.

Hugh's waiting for me when I get in. He comes to the door as I open it. I'm flustered, fumbling with my keys. I drop them as I take them out of the door. He bends over and picks them up, then gives them to me.

'What's going on?' I shrug off my coat.

'He's here?'

'Yes.'

He must've doubled back, or gone through the backstreets.

'Where is he?' I say.

'Upstairs. What's going on, Julia?' He's raised his voice but appears largely unflustered.

I push past him. I'm furious. I'd had to go back to the restaurant; people had stared at me as I'd asked for the bill and paid it. A woman had tilted her head, half smiling, in a way that I suppose was meant to convey sympathy and understanding but in fact made me want to slap her. I'd then left in a hurry, forgotten the bag I'd stashed under my seat, had to go back for it.

'He made me look an absolute bloody idiot.'

He tries to interrupt, but I don't let him. I go upstairs, towards Connor's room. What I can't let him see is that I'm scared, as well as furious. Lukas has got to my son, as well as to me, as well as to my friend. He's stalking him now, and I don't know why. I can only hope it's to intimidate me, to let me know he has the power to do that. I can only hope that he's made his point now, and that's all it is.

But maybe he's got a taste for it. For scaring me, for proving just how deeply he's infiltrated my life. I realize that I'm going to have to see him again, somehow confront him. I can't let him get away with it.

I'm at the top of the stairs when Hugh calls me back. 'Julia! What the hell is going on?'

I turn to face him. 'What's he told you?'

'Some argument about his phone. The internet? He said you were being totally unreasonable.'

I could tell Hugh, I think. I could tell him everything. Lukas would have no power over me then.

But it would end our marriage. And Connor wouldn't be able to cope with that, not on top of his mother's death. I might lose him, too, if it all came out.

I have to protect him. I promised Kate I'd put him first, always. I told her that he was the world to me, when we first had him, and then again and again when she was trying to take him back. To let him down now would be the final betrayal, the ultimate failure.

'He's grounded.' It's a punishment – for leaving me in the restaurant, for using Facebook to tell the whole world about my life – but then I realize it would also be a protection. If he can't go out, Lukas can't get to him.

'I mean it.'

Hugh stands still. He shrugs, as if to say it's up to me, but then says, 'Is it really that important?' It enrages me even further. He thinks he's protecting Connor, but he doesn't understand. I turn to go into Connor's room; by now my fury is stoked, throbbing. Dimly, I'm aware that it's an anger that would be better directed at Lukas, but that's not possible, and it must be discharged somewhere. And so, here we are. 'And I'm taking his phone,' I say, adding, 'That's all there is to it,' as if he were about to argue.

Connor has closed his door, of course. I knock, but it's perfunctory; I'm opening the door before I've even finished telling him I'm coming in. I don't know what I expect to see – him lying face down on his unmade bed perhaps, wearing headphones, or lying back to stare grimly at the ceiling – but what I do see surprises me. The room is even more untidy than usual, and he's standing at his bed, frantically stuffing the contents of his chest of drawers into the sports bag he has open in front of him.

'Connor!' He looks up, his face grim, but says nothing. I ask him what he thinks he's doing.

'What the fuck does it look like?'

'Don't you use language like that with me!' I'm aware of Hugh arriving at my side, though he hangs back slightly; this is my argument, and he won't take sides until he's sure which one he should be on. The room is silent for a moment, thick with venom and animosity.

Connor mutters something. Again it sounds like 'Fuck you', though that might be my imagination finally refusing to give him the benefit of the doubt.

'What did you just say?' I'm shouting, now. I can feel my heart in my chest, too fast. Preparation for the fight.

'Julia—' begins Hugh at the doorway, but I silence him.

'Connor Wilding! Stop what you're doing right now!'

He ignores me. I go over, snatch the bag off the bed and toss it to the floor behind me. He raises his hand, as if he's about to strike me, and I look in his eyes and see that he'd like to. I grab his wrist. For a moment I think about Lukas grabbing mine, and I'd like to twist my son's in the same way, hurt him in the same way. Instantly, I'm ashamed. Distantly, I get the impression I'd never think this with a son of my own, one I'd given birth to; the thought of causing him pain wouldn't cross my mind, not even fleetingly. Yet I'll never know, and in any case I don't get the chance. He wrenches his arm out of my grip; I'm surprised at his strength.

'You stupid little boy!' I can't help it. I can feel Hugh bristle behind me; he takes a step forward, is about to speak. I get in ahead of him. 'Where d'you think you're going to go? Running away? At your age? Don't be so ridiculous.'

He looks wounded.

'You think you'd last more than five minutes?'

'I'm going to see Evie!' he yells, his face inches from mine. His spittle falls on my lips.

'Evie?' I start to laugh. I'm regretting it already, but

somehow powerless to stop speaking. 'Your *girlfriend*?'

'Yes.'

'Your girlfriend who you only talk to online?'

His face falls. I can see I'm right.

His voice cracks. 'So?' I experience a moment of triumph then feel utterly wretched.

'Are you even sure she's who she says she is?'

I mean it to be a genuine question, yet it comes out as a sneering accusation.

'Julia . . .' Hugh's taken another step forward, is by my side now. I can feel his heat, the faint aroma of his body after a day in the office. 'Enough,' he says. He puts his hand on my arm and I shrug it off.

There's a long silence. Connor stares at me with a look of absolute hatred in his eyes, then he says, 'For fuck's sake, of course she's who she says she is!'

'That's enough of your language,' says Hugh. He's picked his team. 'Both of you, just calm down—'

I ignore him. 'You've spoken to her? Have you? Or are you just *Facebook* friends?'

My tone is supremely condescending, as if I find him pathetic. I don't. It's me I'm really talking to. I did exactly that, fell for someone on the internet. It's myself I'm furious with, not him.

I try to calm down, but I can't. My anger is unstoppable.

'Of course I've spoken to her. She's my girlfriend.' He stares right at me. 'Whether you like it or not, Mum.' He pauses, and I know what he's going to say next. 'She loves me.'

'Love?' I want to laugh out loud, yet manage to stop myself. 'As if you –'

'Julia!' says Hugh. His voice is loud. It's an attempt to shock me into silence, but I won't be silenced.

'– as if you have *any* idea about love. You're fourteen years old, Connor. *Fourteen*. How old is she?'

He doesn't answer.

'How old, Connor?'

'What does it matter?'

Hugh speaks again. 'Connor! Your mother asked you a question.'

He turns to his father. Go on, I think. I dare you. Say 'Fuck you' to him.

He won't, of course. 'Eighteen,' he says. He's lying, I know it. I snort. It's through nerves, through fear, but I can't help it.

'Eighteen?' I say. 'No, Connor. No way can you go and see her. No way—'

'You can't stop me.'

He's right. If he were determined enough, then there'd be nothing I could do.

'Where does she live?'

He says nothing.

'Connor,' I say again. 'Where does she live?'

He remains silent. I can see that he won't tell me. 'I'm guessing from the bag that it's not up the road,' I say. 'So how're you going to get there? Eh?'

Connor knows he's beaten. He can't survive without me, not yet.

'I want to go and see her!' His voice rises, it takes on a pleading edge, and I'm taken back to when he was a child, to when he wanted an ice cream or another bag of sweets, to stay up late to watch some show on TV. 'Everything else this year's been shit!' he says. 'Except for her! And you know why, Mum!' It's an accusation, hurled; it hurts because it's true, and he knows it. It crosses my mind he did see the kiss I shared with Paddy after all; he's been storing it up, it's now when he'll tell his father. I shake my head. I want him to cry, to turn back into the child I know how to comfort, but he remains resolute. He's determined.

'I hate you. I wish you'd never taken me. I wish you'd left me with my real mother!'

It breaks. Whatever I'd been holding in check, it finally breaks. I slap him, hard, across the face.

'You ungrateful little *shit*.' I hate myself as soon as it's out of my mouth, but it's too late. His eyes are smarting, but he's smiling. He knows he's won. I've lost my temper. He's become the adult and I'm the child.

I hold out my hand. 'Give me your phone.'

'No.'

'Connor.' Still he doesn't move. 'Your phone.'

'No!'

I look round, at Hugh. My head is tilted, imploring. I hate having to make this request for him to step in, but this is a battle I can't afford to lose. He hesitates; there's a long moment when I'm not sure what he's going to say or do, then he speaks.

'Give your mother your phone, Connor. You're grounded for a week.'

Hugh and I sit on the sofa. Together, but separate. We're not touching. Connor is upstairs. Sulking. He's surrendered his phone, dug out his old model from one of his drawers, which we've told him he can keep. It has no internet connection; he can make calls, receive texts, take pictures. But that's it. No Facebook. No Twitter. We've left his computer in his room, but I've told him he has to delete every friend he doesn't know in real life. He complained, but I told him it was that or I'd take away his computer altogether. He's behaving as if we've cut off a limb.

'So . . .' I begin. Hugh looks at me with something like pity. There's a calmness in the room, despite the music

Connor has insisted on playing loudly upstairs. In an odd way it's refreshing that Hugh and I are united on something.

'It'll blow over. I promise you.'

Shall I tell him? I think. I could, even though it would end it all. My marriage, this life I've built, my relationship with Connor. All of it would go.

Yet still I imagine it. I'd take his hand, look him in the eye. 'Hugh,' I'd say. 'There's something you need to know.' He'd know, of course, that something was wrong, that it was something bad. I wonder what he'd think: I'm ill, I'm leaving him, I want to move out of London? I wonder what his deepest fears are, where his mind would race. 'Darling,' he'd say, 'what is it?' And then I suppose I'd say something about how I love him and always have and that hasn't changed. He'd nod, waiting for the blow, and then, eventually, once I've prepared the ground, I'd tell him. 'I met someone. I met someone and we've been having sex, but it's over. And it turns out that he was already engaged, to Anna of all people, and he has pictures and now he's trying to blackmail me.'

What would he do? We'd row. Of course we would. Things might be thrown. He'd blame the fact that I'd had a drink, I guess. And my duty would be to let him explode, to let him be angry and accuse me of whatever he wanted, to duck the crockery and to remain silent while he blows off his rage and Connor hears it all.

And then, if I'm lucky, we might be able to figure out what to do, how to stay together. Or – just as likely, if not more so – that would be it. I've betrayed him. I know what he'd say. He'd tell me I could have let him help me cope with Kate's death, but instead I'd run. First, in Paris, I ran to the bottle, back here I ran to the internet, then to bed with a stranger. I've no doubt he'd help me to sort out whatever mess I'm in, help Anna, but that would be it. Our relationship would be over.

And he'd want to take Connor, and Connor would want to go with him, and I'd be powerless to stop them. My life would be over. Everything gone. Even the thought of it is utterly unbearable.

'This Evie,' I say.

'The girlfriend?'

'You know he's never met her? Hugh? Doesn't that bother you?'

'It's just what they do. Isn't it?'

'Do we even know she is who she says she is?'

'What?'

'You hear stories, these days.' I'm treading carefully. This is a story he can't know I'm part of. 'All kinds of things,' I say. 'There are horror stories. Adrienne's told me. Kids being groomed . . .'

'Well, Adrienne can be a bit melodramatic at times. He's a sensible boy.'

'It happens, though.'

I picture Lukas, sitting at a computer, talking to my son.

'We don't even know she's a girl.'

'You're the last person I'd have thought would have been bothered about that!'

I realize what he means. 'No, I'm not talking about him being *gay*.' I could cope with that, I think. That would be easy, compared to this, at least. 'I mean, do we even know this Evie is the person Connor thinks she is. She might be older, a bloke, anything.'

I realize I'm closer than I thought to telling him. It'd be easy, now. I could just say it. I think I know who it is. I think it's this guy. I'm sorry, Hugh, but . . .

'Well . . .' He draws breath. 'I've spoken to her . . .'

339

A mixture of emotions hits at once. Relief, first, that Connor is safe, but also annoyance. Hugh has been allowed into a part of our son's life to which I've been denied access.

'What? When?'

'I can't remember. She called. The night you went out with Adrienne, I think. She wanted to speak to Connor.'

'And . . . ?'

'And what you're asking is if she's a girl? Yes. She is.'

'How old?'

'I don't know! I didn't ask. She sounds about – I don't know – seventeen?'

'What did she say?'

He laughs. He tries to sound flippant. He's trying to reassure me. 'She said she'd tried his mobile, it was just ringing out, he must have it on silent or something. She asked if he was there. I said yes, we were halfway through a game of chess—'

'I bet he loved that . . .'

'What d'you mean?'

I shrug. I don't want Hugh to know that none of Connor's friends knows he plays chess with his father. 'Carry on. What happened?'

'Nothing. I gave the phone to him, he took it into his room.'

I'm angry, yet relieved.

'You should've told me.'

'You've been very distracted,' he replies. 'There never seems to be a moment to talk. Anyway, he's growing up. It's really important that we allow him his privacy. He's had a really tough time. We should be proud of him, and we must tell him that.'

I say nothing. Silence hangs between us, sticky and viscous, yet familiar and not altogether uncomfortable.

'Julia. What's wrong?'

If only I could say. Life is spiralling. I see danger every-where, I'm paranoid, hysterical.

I don't speak. A single tear forms.

'Julia?'

'Nothing,' I say. 'Nothing. I . . .'

I let the sentence disappear. Again I wish I could tell him, but how can I? All this has happened because I tried to take more than I was owed. More than I deserved. I had my second chance, my second life, and it wasn't enough. I wanted more.

And now, if I tell my husband, I'll lose my son.

I go upstairs. There's a message on my phone, one that I suppose I've been expecting.

It's from Lukas. My heart leaps, though now my response is Pavlovian, meaningless, and as soon as it forms it disap-pears and turns to terror.

You've won, I think. Okay, you've won.

I want to delete it unread, but I can't. I'm compelled, driven. I marvel at Lukas's timing, almost as if he knows exactly when I'm most vulnerable. I wonder if Connor's somehow back on Facebook already, broadcasting to the world.

I click on the message.

There's a map. 'Meet me here.' It's just like the old days, except this time the message continues.

'Noon. Tomorrow.'

I hate him, yet I look at the map. It's Vauxhall, a place I don't know well.

I type quickly.

– No, I say. Not there. Forget it.

I wait, then a message appears.

– Yes.

I feel hate, nothing but hate. It's the first time my feelings for him have been wholly, unambiguously, negative. Far from giving me strength, for the briefest of moments it saddens me.

A moment later an image appears. Me, on my hands and knees, in front of him.

Bastard, I think. I delete it.

– What d'you want from me?

– Meet me tomorrow, he replies. And you'll find out.

There's a pause, and then:

– Oh, and surely you don't need me to tell you to come alone?

Chapter Twenty-Eight

I don't sleep. Morning comes, my family eats breakfast. I claim a headache and more or less leave Hugh to make sure Connor gets ready for school. I feel nothing. I'm numb with fear. Unable to think of anything other than what I have to do today.

I take the tube. I'm thinking back to Lukas's last message. Who would I bring, anyway? Does he think I know someone who could be trusted with this? Anna still isn't answering my calls, and even if I felt I could confide in Adrienne, she's away until next week. I realize again how grief has overwhelmed me, has taken everything, and in its place there's nothing but emptiness. And so I'm here, facing Lukas, alone.

I emerge from the tube station into the clear light of a sunny day. There are people everywhere, on their way to lunch, pushing prams, smoking on office steps and outside the station. Ahead of me there are blocks of flats, silver and glistening after a misting of rain, and beyond them the river. I follow the map on my phone and walk through a tunnel, lit with neon, as trains roll overhead, and emerge to traffic and more noise. There are alleyways, graffiti, refuse bins everywhere, but the area has a strange beauty. It's rough, it has edges. It's real. In different circumstances I would have wished I'd remembered my camera; as it is, I couldn't care less.

I check my phone again. I'm here, more or less, the corner of Kennington Lane and Goding Street. The Royal Vauxhall Tavern stands alone; beyond it is a park. I wonder if that's where Lukas intends us to go. I tell myself I'll refuse, if so. It's too dangerous.

I light a cigarette, my third of the day. I guess this means I've started smoking again. I inhale. Hold. Exhale. Its rhythms calm me, even in these desperate circumstances; I can't believe how much I've missed it. I look at my watch.

I'm late. He's even later, I think, but then I feel his gaze burning into me and I know. He's here, out of sight, watching me.

Suddenly I see him approach. He's in front of me, wearing a blue parka jacket. He's walking slowly, his head up. I'm aware my hands are shaking. Instinctively I put my hand in my pocket, feel for my phone, just as I've been practising. By the time he's level with me I'm ready, composed. For a long moment we stare at each other, then he speaks.

'Hello, Julia.' He glances at what I'm wearing: jeans, a sweater, my Converse trainers. I tell myself not to react. I mustn't let him make me angry. I'm here to find out exactly what he wants, to make him stop.

I notice the red mark on his cheek. I open my mouth to speak when he lunges for me. He grabs my arm, I yelp.

'What the—?' I begin, but he silences me. His grip is strong, and then he kisses me on the cheek. It's rough, unpleasant, yet brief. Even so, every part of my body reacts powerfully, reflexively. I pull away.

'For old time's sake. Come on.'

He tries to direct me down Goding Street, towards the arches under the railway. A street of bike shops and store-rooms, the shuttered rear entrances of the bars and clubs of the Albert Embankment. I resist. 'What's down there?' I say, my voice high and anxious. 'Where are you taking me?'

'Somewhere quiet,' he says.

I have visions of being found, my neck broken, bleeding, gutted like one of Hugh's patients. I have to remind myself again that he didn't kill Kate, that I mustn't let him see my fear. Whatever else he did, he didn't do that. I repeat it like a mantra.

I shake my arm free. I could run, I think. Into the pub, though its shuttered windows suggest it might not be open.

'Relax. I'm not going to hurt you.'

'Just stay away from me.' I'm shaking with fear, my voice is unsteady. 'We can talk here—'

'You want *me* to stay away from *you*?' He looks incredulous. 'I want *you* to stay away from *me*, and from Anna.' I begin to protest, but he continues. 'You're the one who's messaging me non-stop, who's ringing me up day and fucking night, over and over. I had to change my fucking number, just to get rid of you.'

I stare at him. We're both totally still, as if locked in stalemate, then I speak. 'No,' I say. 'No.'

'So, you're the one who won't leave me alone.' He points to his cheek. 'I mean, look at this. Crazy. You're crazy.'

The wound has healed, more or less. It's superficial. Soon it won't be visible at all.

'You did that.'

He laughs. 'Are you mad? I brought the knife down with me to protect myself, not so that I could stab myself! I didn't know you were going to lose it and try to grab it out of my hand . . .'

'No. No, no . . .' I take a step back. I remind myself why I'm here. To protect Connor. 'You're stalking my son!'

'What?'

'The bowling alley. He told me.'

He laughs. 'You're crazier than I thought! So keep away from me, okay? Or else—'

'Or else what?'

'Haven't you worked it out yet? I can do anything. Anything at all . . . Hugh? Anna? I can destroy them both. Unless there's a way you could make it worth my while not to . . .'

'You're wrong.' I try to keep my voice steady. I want it to have a strength I don't feel. I want him to think I'm telling the truth. 'You think I care, but I don't. Hugh and I are only staying together because of Connor. I've already told him all about you. He understands. So,' – I shrug – 'what you're trying won't work. Show those photos to anyone you like . . .'

'Anyone?'

I nod.

'Really?'

'Yes.'

'How about Connor?'

I try not to recoil, but I can't help it. He sees it.

'Connor's grounded. You won't get near him again. Coincidentally or not.'

'Oh, don't worry. Me and Connor? We have history now. We're virtually friends.'

I feel a chill. What does he mean? Is there something else, something I don't know about? Again the fear comes, that he's got something to do with Evie. I have to remind myself that Hugh's spoken to her, in real life. He's heard her voice. It can't be Lukas. I have to remember that.

'You don't scare me.'

'Don't you get it? You and me? It was fun while it lasted. But now I just want what's owed to me. You have to back off. I'm having my fun with someone else. You have to get it into your stupid head that it's over.'

I'm shocked. 'Anna? Anna? You make her sound like an object, but you asked her to *marry* you!'

'There are lots of different types of games, you know . . .'

He's a few feet away, a little further than arm's length. It might not be close enough. I step towards him. I raise my voice.

'What're you doing with Anna? Really? I know you're using her. You don't love her, like you didn't love me.'

He's smiling. It's an answer in itself, but I want to hear him say it.

'What are you doing with her? I know this is about the money, my sister's money, but why involve her?'

He leans in. 'How else was I going to get close to you?'

I remember why I've come here.

'You don't love her? You've never loved her?'

I'm careful to phrase it as a question. It takes him only a moment to reply.

'Me? Love *Anna*? Look, we have a nice little arrangement going on, but I don't *love* her. The sex is great, that's all. And you know what? I like to think of you as we do it.'

I take a deep breath. There, I think. I have it. I almost smile. It's my turn to feel smug now.

'Oh, by the way, don't even think about contacting Anna again.'

I can't help but reply: 'You can't stop me.'

'How so?' He hesitates, he's enjoying this. 'Oh,' he says. 'You think you're having lunch with her tomorrow?' His smile is chilling. 'I guess she hasn't told you? She's changed her ticket. Some family emergency, I think. Or something at work? I can't quite remember. Maybe it's just that she thinks you're absolutely crazy and wants to get as far away as possible. In any case, you won't be seeing her tomorrow. In fact, I reckon she'll be leaving the hotel,' – he looks at his watch – 'around about . . . *now*.'

My eyes narrow. I have to make him think he's beaten me. 'What?'

'You heard me. Anna thinks you're crazy. She's on her way back home, and I'm joining her in a few days. So why don't you just toddle off home? Go back to your husband and be a good little wife for him? Eh?'

I don't react. I can't. I don't want him to see how scared I am. I haven't won, not yet. Not until I can speak to Anna. I have to make him think I'm going to do exactly as he says. Go back home.

I shake my head. 'Fuck you,' I say, and turn away from him.

His gaze burns into me as I retrace my steps. I don't run, I have to look unconcerned. I daren't turn round, I don't want him to know how much I hope he's not following. Everything depends on him leaving me alone, just for a couple of hours. Everything depends on me getting to Anna before she boards her train. I turn the corner and am out of sight. Then, I run.

I head through the bus station, on to the main road. I look behind me, but he's nowhere in sight. Why would he hang around? He's won. A taxi pulls up, at the lights. It's available and I hail it. 'St Pancras,' I say, then get in.

'Okay, love,' says the driver. She must sense my urgency. 'Traffic's bad today. What time's your train?'

I tell her I don't know, I'm meeting someone. 'Please hurry,' I say again. The lights change and she pulls away. She says she'll do her best. I take my phone out of my pocket, where it'd been the whole time, the voice memo recorder already running, and press done. I'd hit record as soon as we met. With any luck I've recorded our entire conversation.

I look over my shoulder. Lukas is still nowhere to be seen.

We're in luck. Our route through Lambeth is pretty clear, the lights are in our favour. I listen back to what I've managed to capture. It's muffled, recorded as it was from the pocket of my jacket, while the two of us were moving around. Some of it is okay – in places my voice is loud but it's Lukas's reply I need and it's barely registered on the recording – but a good deal of it is usable. I can hear him saying 'For old time's sake' after he kissed me, and he'd also raised his voice to say, 'You're crazier than I thought.' But that's not good enough. It isn't what I'm looking for. I fast forward, desperate to find a section that is incontrovertible proof of what I need Anna to know; that he's not who he says he is, that she's in danger and that we need to help each other.

It's there. The part I'd hoped for. Luckily, I'd stepped towards him, he'd been close; plus, my plan to raise my voice in the hope that it would encourage him to raise his had worked.

I rewind. Play it again. At first it's broken: '. . . using her . . . love her . . .' but then there's a gap and the next sentence is clear. 'I know this is about the money, my sister's money, but why involve her?'

Lukas's answer is clear, too.

'How else was I going to get close to you?'

Then it's me. I must've shifted on my feet as I spoke; the first part of the sentence is lost as something rubs against the microphone of my phone's recorder. I recognize my own voice, but what I'm saying is all but lost. Only one word is audible: 'her'.

It shouldn't matter, though. I know it's his response I need next; I remember what he'd said, but the whole recording is meaningless unless it's audible.

Luckily, his answer is perfectly clear. I play it twice, just to be sure.

'Me?' he's saying. '. . . Look, we have a nice little arrangement going on, but I don't *love* her.'

I close my eyes, as if in victory, then rewind and listen to it a third time. It should be enough to convince my friend, I think. I just need to get there in time now.

I freeze. It occurs to me, as if for the first time. I don't have to do this. I could just leave it, just walk away, go home. Lukas has demanded I leave them alone, so why not?

I think of his hands on me. I think of the places he's taken me. Can I abandon my sister's best friend to that? What kind of person would that make me?

From nowhere I think back to Anna's reading, at the funeral. 'To the angry I was cheated, but to the happy I am at peace.'

She thinks she's happy, but it won't last. I can't abandon her now and live with myself, knowing I've betrayed her. I can't.

I glance at the time and shift forward in my seat. It's just after one o'clock. The traffic is bad, but we're moving; already we're over the river and skirting the city. If only I knew what time her train was, I think, then I'd be able to work out whether I have time, or no chance at all.

I look on my phone, navigate to the Eurostar webpage, to the timetable. It's grindingly slow – I need to press refresh two, three times – but it makes me feel like I'm doing something, at least. Eventually the page appears. There's a train just after two, and she'll be checking in at least half an hour before it.

I look up. We've got as far as Lambeth North. It's a twenty-minute trip, I'd guess, then we'll have to find somewhere to pull in. I'll need to pay the driver, then I have to find my friend. I'm desperate, yet helpless. I will the traffic to move, the lights to change. I curse as we get stuck behind a cyclist, as someone steps out on to a pedestrian crossing and we have to brake.

I'm not sure we're going to make it, plus Lukas may ring her and tell her I'm on my way. It's hopeless.

It's almost one thirty when we pull up outside the terminal; I'm numb, certain I'll have missed her. I pass my fare over to the driver – far too much, but I tell her to keep the change – and then I start to run. She shouts, 'Good luck, love!' but I don't answer, don't even turn round. I'm already frantically looking for Anna. I run in, towards the gates to the terminal, past the coffee shops and ticket offices, remembering as I do the times I'd met Lukas here. The images assault me, in Technicolor. I think of the second time we'd met, just after he'd lied to me and told me he lived near London after all. Back when I felt almost nothing for him, by comparison to what came later, at least. Back when it would've been easy, relatively, to walk away. Back when I was worried he had a wife, when really he was about to ask someone else to marry him.

Not just *someone*, I think. Anna. And now, I realize with increasing panic, I'm here rushing to try to save her.

The station is crowded; I can't see her. I stop running. 'Find Friends,' I think she'd called it. We'd linked our profiles. I scrabble for my phone, drop it, pick it up again. I open the map, but there's only one dot. Mine.

She's disconnected her profile from mine. She hates me. I'm about to despair. She'll go back home; all is lost. I could try to call her, yes, but she probably won't answer the phone, and even if she does how will I make her believe me? I need to be there, in front of her. I need to make her understand.

I see a flash of red in the crowds, and somehow I know it's her coat. When the crowd clears I see I'm right. She's at the gate itself, pulling her case behind her with one hand, with the other already fumbling her ticket over the automatic scanner. 'Anna!' I shout, but she can't hear me and doesn't respond. I start running again. My words are lost in gasped breath, caught up in the noisy chaos of the station, rising and echoing in the vault of the ceiling. I shout again, louder this time – 'Anna! Wait!' – but by the time she looks up and sees me I'm too late; the automatic gates have registered her ticket, swung open and she's gone through.

'Julia!' she says, turning back to face me. 'What're you . . . ?'

I stop running. We're on either side of the gates, a few feet apart. There's a security booth just beyond her, and beyond that the waiting rooms and restaurants of the international terminal. 'I met Lukas.' She looks momentarily confused, then I remember myself. 'I mean, Ryan. I saw Ryan.'

She looks at me, her head tilted, her mouth turned down. It's pity. She feels sorry for me. Again I'm reminded that Lukas has won.

'I know. He called me.'

'They're the same person, Anna. I swear. Ryan *is* Lukas. He's been lying to you.'

She seems to well up. Something she's so far been holding in check erupts to the surface.

'I thought you were my friend.'

'I am.' But then my mind goes to the scar on Lukas's cheek, just beginning to crust. I can only imagine what he's said to her.

'Whatever Ryan's told you, he's lying.' I look her in the eye. 'Believe me . . .'

She shakes her head. 'Bye, Julia.' She turns to leave.

I grip the barrier. For a second I think I could jump it, or push through, but already we're attracting attention. A staff member is watching us, he's stepping forward, as if he expects trouble.

I call instead. 'Anna! Come back. Just for a minute. Let me explain!'

She looks over her shoulder. 'Goodbye, Julia.' She begins to walk away.

'No!' I say. 'Wait!'

The guy in the uniform is standing right by us, now looking from one to the other. Anna doesn't turn round.

I cast about for a way to convince her. I'm desperate. I need something that proves I know him as Lukas, have slept with him. Then I remember.

'He has a birthmark. On his leg. His thigh. His upper thigh.'

At first I don't think she's heard me, but then she stops walking. She turns, then slowly comes back towards the barrier that separates us.

'A birthmark.' I point to my own body. 'Just here.'

At first she says nothing. She shakes her head. She looks hurt, devastated. 'You . . . *bitch*.'

The last word is hissed. Of course she hates me, and I hate myself for having to do this to her.

'Anna! . . . I'm sorry . . .'

She's standing just on the other side of the barrier now. If either of us were to reach over we could touch each other, yet she is utterly unreachable, as if the barrier between us were impenetrable.

We both remain utterly still, just staring. A moment later a voice cuts in with a jolt.

'Is there some kind of a problem here?'

I look over. It's the guard. He's standing just beyond Anna.

We both shake our head. 'No. It's fine.' Dimly, I'm aware that I'm blocking the barrier, a queue is forming behind me.

'Could you move along, please?' He sounds so calm; his politeness clashes with what's going on.

I put my hand out, palm up, as if offering something. 'Anna, please.' She looks at it as if it's an unknown object, dangerous, alien. 'Anna?'

'Why are you doing this?' She's crying now, tears pouring down her cheeks. 'I thought we were friends . . .'

'We were.' I'm desperate, insistent. 'We still are.' I wish I could make her understand, let her know I'm doing this because I do love her, not because I don't. I get out my phone. 'He's not the person you think he is. Ryan, I mean. Believe me.'

'You have everything. From the moment I told you we were engaged you haven't been able to even *pretend* to be happy for me. I feel sorry for you. D'you know that?'

'No—' I begin, but she interrupts me.

'I've had enough.' She turns to go, and I try to grip her arm. The guy watching us steps forward; again he asks us to move along.

'Give me a second, will you? Please?'

I have to make Anna understand, before she gets on the train and disappears back to Paris and everything is lost. Otherwise she'll marry this man and ruin her life. It hits me that, even if I succeed, Lukas will carry out his threat, send Hugh the pictures. Whatever happens I might lose everything.

I feel myself slip back into the blackness, but I know I can't. This is my last chance to do the right thing.

'Wait a minute. I need you to hear something.' The rest of the station disappears; I can think of nothing else. It's just me and her. My words come out in a rush. 'He's . . . I know him as Lukas . . . he's the one I met through the website you told me about . . . he . . . he's . . . he's got to Connor. He's been following him . . . following me, too . . . he's flipped, I swear . . .'

'Liar.' Over and over again she says it. 'You're a liar. A liar.'

'I can prove it.' I hold my phone in front of me. 'Just listen to this. Please. And then—'

'Miss. I'm going to have to ask you to move out of the way. Now.'

He steps between us. My desperation turns to anger; the world comes back in a furious rush. The station seems noisy and I don't know whether Anna will be able to hear my recording. A small crowd has now gathered, on both sides of the barrier, staring at us. A man has taken his phone out and is taking pictures.

'Please! This is important.' I'm fumbling with my phone, unlocking the screen, opening the file. 'Please, Anna? For Kate?'

She stares. It's calm, suddenly, and then the guard asks me again to move away. This is my last chance.

'Just give her this. Please?'

'Miss—' he begins, but Anna interrupts him. She's holding out her hand.

'I'll listen. I don't know what you want, but I'll listen.'

I hand the phone to the man standing between us, and he passes it to Anna.

'Press play. Please?' She hesitates, then does so. She stands, her head craned forward. The section I'd selected is ready. My voice, his voice. Just as it'd been in the taxi. She's too far away and I can't hear what she's listening to, but I know it by heart: '. . . a nice little arrangement . . . I don't *love* her.' She plays enough, just a few moments, then it ends. She crumples. It's as if all the tension of the last few minutes has caused her to snap.

'I'm sorry.'

She looks at me. She's crushed. She seems diminished, empty. All emotion is squeezed out. I wish I could reach out, comfort her. I can't bear the thought of doing this to her and then sending her on her way. Back home. Alone.

Then she speaks.

'I don't believe you. It doesn't even sound like him. Ryan's right.'

I see the doubt on her face. She's not sure.

'Listen again. Listen—'

'It's not him.' Her voice falters, broken. 'It can't be.'

Her free hand goes to my phone, though. She presses the play button, tries to turn up the volume.

'Love Anna? . . . I don't *love* her.'

'Anna. Please . . .' There's a hand on my arm, someone tugging at the sleeve of my jacket, trying to drag me away.

'Anna?'

She looks up at me, then. The expression on her face is chilling, her eyes wide with disbelief and pure horror. It's as if I'm watching all of her plans evaporate, taking flight like nervous birds, leaving nothing behind.

'I'm sorry.'

'We need to talk.' It's so quiet I can barely hear her. The crowd around us senses the breaking tension and begins to move, to go back to their day. The bubble of drama that had formed in front of them has burst. Anna turns to the official standing between us and says, 'Can you let me back through? Please? I need to talk to my friend . . .'

Time seems to speed up. The world has been on pause, held in the thrall of her fury, and my desperation. But now it's all been released; it crashes in. The noise of the station, the bustle and chatter, the old piano that's been installed on the concourse and which somebody is playing badly, the same phrase, again and again. I take her arm and she doesn't resist; together we go, up the escalator, supporting each other. We're silent. I suggest a coffee, but she shakes her head, says she needs a drink. I need one, too, I tell myself I could, just this once, but I force the thought away. Anna is crying, her voice cracks as she tries to speak. She fumbles for a tissue and we go upstairs to the bar. I feel wretched, my guilt is almost overwhelming. All I can think is, *I've done this. This is my fault.*

We sit under the umbrellas. Behind me the door leads to the hotel, to the room in which Lukas and I first had sex. Memories of our affair are everywhere, and I look away, trying to ignore them. Anna is murmuring something about her train. 'I'm going to miss it,' she says, stating the obvious. 'I want to go home.'

I hand her a tissue. 'Don't worry. I'll help. You can stay with me, or—'

'No. Why would I want to do that?'

She looks angry. It's as if things are finally coalescing for her, the hurt she feels condensing, becoming easier to comprehend. I want to do something, make some small gesture, however meaningless.

'Then I'll pay for you to go on the next train. But Anna, you have to let me explain. I didn't want any of this to happen . . .'

'I can pay for my own ticket.' She's defiant, but then she looks down at her lap. I imagine she wonders how she could ever have got herself into this situation, how she could have let herself trust Ryan. And also how she could have ever trusted me. The waiter comes over and I order some water and a glass of white wine. He asks which we want, whether we'd like to see the list. 'Anything. Just the house white is fine . . .'

Anna looks up once he's moved away. 'Why?'

'I don't know. Believe me. I never knew . . . I didn't know that that man, Lukas was seeing you. If I had, I'd never have dreamt—'

'You mean he didn't tell you? He didn't tell you he was engaged? To me?'

'No.' I'm emphatic. 'Of course not.' I want to make her understand; right now it's all that seems to matter.

'And you didn't think to ask?'

'Anna, no. I didn't. He was wearing a wedding ring—'

She interrupts me, shocked.

'A ring?'

'Yes. He told me he'd been married, once, but that his wife had died. That was it. I thought he was single. I didn't . . . I wouldn't have seen him if I'd known he was involved with someone else. Least of all you . . .'

Even as I say it I wonder if it's true. Am I kidding myself? My relationship with Lukas had developed incrementally, had started off with my search for the truth, developed into chatting online, and from there had turned into what it became. Even if he had been married, or engaged, at what point would I have stopped it, said, no, this far but no further? At what point *should* I have done that?

There's a point when an online dalliance might become dangerous, but who can really say when it is?

'I swear.'

'And I'm supposed to believe that?'

I feel a flicker of anger, of injured pride, but her face is impassive.

'He pursued me, Anna. You might not want to hear that, and I'm sorry, but you need to know. He came after me.'

She blinks. 'You're lying. He wouldn't.'

Her words are a slap. They sting. Why not? I want to say.

Why wouldn't he? I'm aware again of the way he'd made me feel. Young, desirable. Alive.

'Because of my age?'

She sighs. 'I'm sorry,' she says. 'I didn't mean that. I just meant . . .' The sentence dissolves, her head sags to her chest. She looks exhausted. 'I don't know what to think.'

'Anna—'

She raises her head. She looks defeated, she's searching for help, for somewhere to turn. 'Tell me what happened. I want it all.'

And so I do. I tell everything, in great detail. She's silent as I talk. Five minutes. Ten. The waiter comes with the glass of wine and my water, but I push my drink away and keep talking. There are things she's heard before, and things she hasn't, yet this is the first time she's known the story is not about me and a stranger but about me and her fiancé. I find it hard enough; for her the pain must be unbearable. Every time I ask her if she'd like me to stop she shakes her head. She says she needs to hear it. I tell her about Lukas's first approach. I tell her that we'd started to message regularly, that I thought he lived abroad, in Milan, that he told me he travelled a lot. I explained that he'd asked me to go and meet him, in real life, and because I'd thought it could only happen once and might lead me to the truth about my sister I'd done so.

'And you had sex?' Her lips are set in a hard line. I hesitate. She knows we did.

I nod.

'What was it like?'

'Anna. Please . . . I'm not sure it's a good idea—'

'No. Tell me.'

I know she wants to hear that it was disappointing. That we didn't click, that it was obvious his heart wasn't in it. She wants to be allowed to think what they have is special, and that what happened between me and him was a one-off, nothing.

I can't lie, but neither do I want to make her feel any worse than she already does.

I look away. Unwittingly, my eyes are drawn to the statue across the platforms. 'It was . . . all right.'

'All right. So you never saw him again, after that one time. Right?'

Her sarcasm is caustic. She knows I did.

'I never intended for it to become an affair. I never intended any of it.'

'And yet here we are.'

'Yes. Here we are. But you must understand, Anna, I didn't know he even *knew* you. I promise. What can I swear on?' I whisper. 'Connor's life? Believe me, if that's what it takes I will.'

She looks at the wine in the glass in front of her, then back up to me. She seems to make a decision. 'Why? Why is he doing this?'

'I don't know. Money?'

'What d'you mean?'

'He knows Kate left money to you, and to Connor. Maybe he was hoping to get his hands on Connor's share as well as yours—'

'He isn't going to *get his hands on* mine!' She sounds shocked, affronted. 'We're getting married!'

'I'm sorry. You know what I mean.'

'And how would he get his hands on yours, anyway?'

Once again I look away. 'He has pictures. Pictures of us. Of me . . .'

'Having sex?' She sounds devastated, the words are seeping out.

I nod. I lower my voice. 'He's threatened to show them to people. To Hugh.'

I see Hugh's face, sitting at the dining table, looking at the pictures. He looks confused, then shocked, then angry. 'How could you do this?' he's saying. 'How could you?'

'He's asked you for Connor's money?' says Anna. I think about blackmail. If I let it start, it'd never stop. He'd just demand more and more and more.

'Not yet. But he might.'

She looks down again. Her eyes seem to lose their focus. She slowly nods her head. She's remembering, piecing things together.

'That recording,' she says eventually. 'He says he doesn't love me.'

I reach across the table and take her hand.

'None of this is your fault. Remember that. He could be anyone. He's probably not called Ryan or Lukas. We don't know who he is, Anna. Neither of us does . . .' I take a deep breath, this is painful. I'm trying to support her when I have no strength left myself.

But I have to do this.

'Anna,' I say. I hate myself for asking her, but know I must. 'Has he ever hurt you?'

'Hurt me? No. Why?'

'During sex, I mean?'

'No!' She answers a little too quickly, and I wonder whether she's telling me the whole truth.

'I just wanted to make sure—'

She looks horrified. 'Oh my God. You still think he killed Kate?'

'No,' I say. 'I'm certain he didn't. He can't have—'

'You're crazy,' she says, but at the same time I see horror

flash on her face. It's as if I can see her faith, her belief in her fiancé, disappear.

'He killed Kate,' she says.

'No. He can't have—'

She interrupts.

'No! You don't understand,' she says. She's speaking quickly, caught up in the whirring cogs of her own fantasy. I'd done it myself, not long ago. Tried to make his behaviour fit into a pattern I could recognize. 'He might've met her, online, then found out about the money. He might've got close to me just to get to her, then killed her, and—'

'No. No, it's coincidence. Lukas was in Australia when Kate died. And anyway—'

'But we don't know that! He might've lied to both of us . . .'

'They've caught the man who killed her. Remember?'

She still looks unconvinced. I go on. 'Anyway, there're photos. They show him, in Australia. They're dated from the time that Kate was killed . . .'

'Is that conclusive? I mean, can't you alter those things?'

I don't answer. 'But the main thing is they caught him, Anna. They caught the man who killed her.'

It seems finally to sink in. 'I don't believe this,' she says. A low moan starts in her throat; I think she's going to scream. 'How could he do this to me? How could he?'

'It'll be okay. I promise.'

'I have to end it, don't I?' I nod. She reaches for her bag. 'I'll do it now . . .'

'No! No, you mustn't. He can't know I've told you. He said if I told you he'd show Hugh those pictures. Anna, we have to be clever about this . . .'

'How?'

I'm silent. I know what I want her to do. To wait for a

while, to pretend to the man she calls Ryan that she's still in love with him. And then to end it, in a way that seemingly has nothing to do with me.

Yet how can I ask her to do that? I can't. The idea is monstrous. She has to realize it for herself.

'I don't know. But if you end it now he'll know I had something to do with it.'

She's incredulous. 'You want me to carry on seeing him?'

'Not exactly—'

'You do!'

'No, Anna. No . . . I don't know . . .'

Her face collapses. All her defiance rushes out, replaced by bitterness and regret.

'What am I going to do?' She opens her eyes. 'Tell me! What am I going to do?'

I reach out to her. I'm relieved when she doesn't push me away. Sadness fills her face. She looks much older, nearer to my age than to Kate's.

'It's up to you.'

'I need to think about it. Give me a few days.'

I'll have to live with the uncertainty. But next to what she has to live with, that's nothing.

'I wish this had never happened. I wish it could be different.'

'I know,' she says.

We sit for a while. I'm drained, without energy, and when I look at her I see she is, too. The station seems less crowded, though that might be my imagination; the lunchtime rush can hardly make any difference to somewhere so perpetually busy. Nevertheless, a quietness descends. Anna finishes her drink then says she has to leave. 'There'll be another train soon. I need to go and get a ticket . . .'

We stand. We grip our chairs for support, as if the world

has tilted to a new axis. 'Do you want me to help? I really don't mind paying—'

'No. It's fine. I'm fine. You don't have to do that.'

She smiles. She knows I feel guilty, that the offer of money is my attempt to assuage that guilt.

'I'm so sorry,' I say again. I desperately need to know I have her friendship, but for a long moment she doesn't move. Then she's melting into me. We hug. I think she's going to start crying again, but she doesn't.

'I'll call you. In a day or so?'

I nod. 'You'll be okay?' I'm aware of how trite the question sounds, how meaningless, yet I'm exhausted. I just want her to know I care.

She nods. 'Yes.' Then she lets go. 'Will you?'

'Yes.' I'm far from certain it's the truth. She picks up her case. 'Go. I'll get this. And good luck.'

She kisses me again. Wordlessly, she turns to leave. I watch as she crosses the concourse, heads for the stairs that lead down to the ticket offices. She rounds the corner and goes out of sight. I feel suddenly, terribly, alone.

PART FIVE

Chapter Twenty-Nine

Monday. Hugh is due to have a meeting about his case today; he'll find out whether his statement has satisfied the chief executive, the medical director, the clinical governance team. If it has, they'll refute the claim; if not, they'll concede that he made a mistake. 'And then they'll close ranks,' he said. 'It'll all be about preserving the reputation of the hospital. I'll probably be disciplined.'

'But you won't lose your job?'

'Doubtful. But they're saying I might.'

I couldn't imagine it. His job is his life. If he were to lose it the repercussions would be catastrophic, and I'm not sure I'm strong enough to cope with something like that hitting our family. Not with everything else that's going on.

Yet I'd have to, there wouldn't be a choice. I clung to the word 'doubtful'.

I have to be strong.

'Are you all right?' I said.

He took a deep breath, filling his lungs, tilting his head back. 'I am. I have to be. I have to go into theatre this morning. I have to operate on a woman who'll most likely be dead within weeks if nothing is done. And I have to do that with a clear head, no matter what else is going on.' He shook his head. He looked angry. 'That's what really pisses me off. I haven't done anything wrong. You know that? I forgot to warn them that for a few weeks their father might forget where he'd put the remote control. No' – he corrected himself – 'I didn't even do that. I forgot to *write down* that I'd warned them. That's what this amounts to. I was too busy worrying about the operation itself to write the details of some trivial conversation down in the notes.'

I smiled, sadly. 'I'm sure it'll be fine. You'll call me?'

He said he would, but now the phone is ringing and it's not him.

'Anna?'

She's hesitant. When she does speak she sounds distant, upset.

'How're you?'

'Fine,' I say. I want her to tell me what she's decided. For two days I've been convincing myself that she's reconsidered, or hasn't believed me at all. I've imagined her talking to Lukas, telling him that I'd caught up with her at the station, recounting what I'd said.

I daren't imagine what his next move would be then.

'How are you feeling?'

She doesn't answer. 'I've been thinking. Ryan's away for another week. He's staying in London. I need a week after he gets back.'

I'm not sure what she means.

'A week?'

'I need to finish it with him. But I need to make him think it has nothing to do with you at all. I've already told him I haven't seen you since the other night at the hotel, that you haven't been in touch. I told him I thought you were a freak, and that I didn't want anything else to do with you. When he comes back I'll just have to be busy, I'll pretend I've got a lot on at work or something. I can manage it for a week, I think.'

'And then?'

'Then I'll end it.'

She sounds defiant. Absolutely certain.

'I'll get the pictures – the ones he's got of you – and delete them from his computer. I'll find a way, I have a key to his flat, it shouldn't be too difficult. Then, even if he does suspect, it'll be too late to do anything about it.'

I close my eyes. I'm so grateful, so relieved. It might work. It has to work.

'You'll be all right?'

She sighs. 'Not really. But I suppose I kind of knew, really. There was always something about him, I just couldn't put my finger on what it was. He'd always be travelling, at short notice. I should've known.'

I'm not sure I believe her. It sounds like justification after the fact.

She carries on. 'Maybe when all this is over we can get together and go out for a drink. Not lose our friendship because of it.'

'I want that, too,' I say. 'Will we stay in touch? Over the next couple of weeks, I mean?'

'It wouldn't be good if Ryan finds out we're speaking.'

'No.'

'I'll try and call you, when I can.'

'Okay.'

'You'll have to trust me,' she says.

We talk for a minute or so more, then she says goodbye. Before we end the call we agree to reconnect on Find Friends. Afterwards I sit for a moment as relief floods me, relief and fear, then I call Hugh. I'm not sure why. I want to hear his voice. I want to show that I support him, that I haven't forgotten what he's going through today. His secretary answers; he's still in his meeting.

'Will you ask him to call me when he gets out?'

She says she will. Almost on a whim I ask if I can speak to Maria. I want to know that Paddy's okay, that he's recovered.

I think of the steps. I've made my moral inventory now; without even being conscious of it, I'm working on making amends.

'She's not in today,' she says. I ask if she's on holiday. 'No, some problem at home.' She lowers her voice. 'She sounded very upset.'

I put the phone down. I'm uneasy. Hugh has always said that Maria can be relied upon; she's never sick, never late. I can't imagine what might be going on. An illness? Paddy, or her parents, perhaps? They're not elderly, but that rules nothing out, I should know that as much as anyone.

I almost call her at home but then decide against it. I have plenty going on as it is, and what could I say to her? We're not friends, not really. I haven't seen her since we visited Paddy, weeks ago. Hugh hasn't invited them round, or maybe he has and they haven't come. I wonder if that was Paddy's decision, and if so what excuses he may have given his wife.

I spend the afternoon working. Connor arrives home and goes upstairs. Doing his homework, he says, though I'm not sure I believe him. I suspect he usually spends hours online – with his friends, Dylan, his girlfriend – and even now, every time I go up, to check if he wants a drink, to try to persuade him down for dinner, to make some sort of a connection, he seems to make a point of being cool towards me. He's still angry over the grounding, I guess; even though it's only for a week, it seems to be taking a long time to wear off.

Maybe it's something else. He's still upset that the arrest of the man who killed Kate hasn't brought him the relief he'd hoped. He's looking elsewhere, now. 'Do you know who my real dad is?' he said the other day, and when I said no, he said, 'Would you tell me, if you did?' Of course you wouldn't, he seemed to be saying, but I tried to stay calm. 'Yes,' I said. 'Yes, of course I would. But I don't know.'

I want to tell him it won't change anything. I want to say, Your father – whoever he is, whoever he was – was probably very young. He abandoned your mother, or more likely didn't even know she was pregnant. 'We're your family,' I said instead, but he just looked at me, as if that was no longer enough.

It's upsetting, but I tell myself it's normal, he's a teenager. He's just growing up, away from me. Before I know it he'll be sitting exams, then leaving home. It'll just be me and his father, then, and who knows if he'll even come back to see us? All children go through a phase of hating their parents, but they say adopted children can find it all too easy to break away. Sometimes the severance is permanent.

I'm not sure I could cope with that. I'm not sure it wouldn't kill me.

I'm in the kitchen when Hugh gets home. He kisses me, then goes straight to the fridge and gets himself a drink. He looks angry. I ask him how it went.

'They're making them an offer. Out-of-court settlement.'

'Do they think the family will take it?'

I wait while he empties his glass and pours another. 'Hope so. If it goes to court I'm fucked.'

'What?'

'I'm in the wrong. It's unequivocal, to them at least. I made a mistake. If it goes to court we'll lose, and they'll have to make some kind of example of me.'

'Oh, darling . . .'

'Next week I have to go on a course.' He smiles, bitterly.

'Record keeping. I have to cancel surgery to go and learn how to write a set of bloody notes.'

I sit opposite him. I can see how injured he is. It seems so unfair; after all, no one is dead. It's not as if he made a mistake during surgery.

I try to look hopeful. 'I'm sure everything will be okay.'

He sighs. 'One way or the other. And bloody Maria didn't turn up today.'

'I know.'

'You know?'

'I called. They said she wasn't in. What's going on?'

He takes out his phone and makes a call. 'No idea. But I hope she's intending to come in tomorrow.' He puts the phone to his ear. After a few rings it's answered, a faint hello. Maria's voice. 'Maria? Listen . . .' He glances at me, then stands up. 'How're things?'

I don't hear her reply. He's turned away and is walking out of the room, his attention completely focussed on his colleague. I go back to preparing the meal. Hugh, Connor, Anna. I just hope everything will be all right.

Two days later Paddy calls. It's the first time I've heard his voice in weeks, and he sounds different, somehow. I wonder if something's happened to Maria, but he says no, no she's fine. 'I just thought you might want to meet up. Lunch, or something?'

Is that what all this is about? Does he want to make another attempt at seduction?

'I'd better not—'

He interrupts. 'Please? Just a coffee? I only want to talk to you.'

It sounds ominous; certainly it's not casual. How can I say no?

'Okay.'

*

That evening I tell Hugh. 'Paddy?' he says. I nod. 'But what does he want to see you for?'

I tell him I don't know. I ask him why he wants to know; we're friends, after all, it shouldn't be that shocking.

He shrugs but looks worried. 'Just wondered.'

It crosses my mind that Connor did see something that day. Maybe he's told his father but Hugh has decided to say nothing as long as things don't progress.

Or maybe he's worried that we'll go to a bar, that I'll be persuaded to drink alcohol.

'There's nothing going on between me and Paddy Renouf,' I say. 'We're just going for a coffee. And it will be a coffee. I promise.'

'Okay,' he says. But he still doesn't look convinced.

We arrange to meet in a Starbucks in town. It's cold, raining, and he's late. I'm sitting with a drink by the time he arrives. The last time I saw him he was bruised, his face swollen, but that was weeks ago and he looks back to normal now.

We kiss awkwardly before sitting down. A friendly kiss, a peck on each cheek. I think of the time we kissed in Carla's summer house. How different that had been. It crosses my mind that it would have been better if I'd slept with him, rather than Lukas. But then that might have turned out worse. How do I know?

'How are you?'

I sip my drink. 'I'm all right.' The atmosphere is heavy, awkward. I hadn't known quite what to expect, but it hadn't been this. It's obvious he's here for a reason. He has something to tell me.

'Is everything okay?'

'I just wanted to tell you I'm sorry.' It's a surprise, him apologizing to me.

I look down at my drink. A hot chocolate, with whipped cream swirled on top.

'For what?'

'What happened, over the summer. You know. At Carla's party. And then—'

I interrupt. 'Forget it.' But he continues:

'—and then not ringing you. All summer, I've wanted to apologize. I'd had too much to drink, but it was no excuse. I guess I was embarrassed.'

I look at him. I can see what this honesty is costing him, yet I can't reciprocate. For a moment I'd like to. I'd like to tell him everything. I'd like to tell him he has nothing to apologize for because, next to mine, his transgressions are insignificant.

But I don't. I can't. These are things I'll never be able to tell anyone.

'Honestly. It's fine—'

'I haven't been a good friend.'

It's been an odd time, I want to say. I haven't been a good friend either.

But I don't.

He looks at me. 'How're you doing now?'

'Not bad.' I realize it's mostly true; my grief hasn't gone, but I'm beginning to see a way I can live with it. 'You know they caught the guy who killed my sister.'

He shakes his head. Hugh must not have told Maria, or else Maria hasn't told her husband. I tell him the story, and in doing so realize that the fog of Kate's death is lifting. The pain is still there, but for the first time since February it's no longer the prism through which everything else is refracted. I'm not stuck, wading through a life that's become thickened with grief and anger, or else ricocheting out of control, and I'm no longer angry – with her for getting herself killed, with myself for not being able to do anything to protect her.

'It still hurts,' I say. 'But it's getting better.'

'Good.' He pauses. We're building up to something. 'You have friends around you?'

Do I? Adrienne, yes, we've spoken in the last couple of days, but there's still some way to go to reverse the damage done. 'I have friends, yes. Why?' He looks oddly relieved, and I realize the reason he's here involves me, somehow.

'What is it, Paddy?'

His face is expressionless for a few moments, then he seems to make a final decision.

'I have something to tell you.'

I try to focus, to pull myself into the present. 'What is it?'

I don't breathe. The air between us is as thick as oil.

'Maria told me she slept with someone.'

I nod slowly, and then I know what's coming. Some part of me – some buried part, some reptilian part – knows exactly what he's going to say.

He opens his mouth to speak. It seems to take for ever. I say it for him.

'Hugh.'

His face breaks into relief. Still part of me hopes he'll contradict me, but he doesn't. I wonder when he'd known.

'Yes. She told me she slept with Hugh.'

I can't work out how I feel. I'm not shocked; it's like I've known all along. It's nearer to numbness, an absence of feeling. I take a deep breath. The air fills my lungs. I expand, I wonder if I could keep breathing in until I'm bigger than the pain.

'When?' My voice echoes off the walls.

'In Geneva. She says it was just once. Apparently, it hasn't happened since.' He stops speaking. I wonder if he's waiting for me to say something. I don't have anything to say. Just once? I wonder if he believes his wife. I wonder if I do.

'Hugh hasn't told you?'

'No.' So that's why Hugh hasn't invited them round for months. It has nothing to do with what Connor may or may not have seen in the summer house.

I feel cold, as if I'm sitting in a draught. Hugh and I have always told each other the truth. Why hasn't he told me this?

But then, look at what I haven't told him.

'I'm sorry.'

I look at him. He's in more pain than I am. He looks empty, hollow. I can see he hasn't slept.

Then, I realize. That's why he kissed me. He knew, or suspected at least. I was his revenge.

I don't blame him. I ought to reach out and hold him and tell him it'll be all right, the way I tell Connor things will be all right. Because I have to. Because it's my job, whether I believe it or not.

But I don't. I keep my hands on the table.

'Thank you for telling me.'

'I thought I ought to. I'm sorry.'

We sit for a moment. The space between us seems to expand. We should be able to help each other, but we can't.

'No, you did the right thing.' I pause. But did he? It's not so clear cut; sometimes there are things it's better off not knowing. 'What're you going to do?'

'I don't know. I haven't decided. Maria and I have some talking to do, but I know that. I suppose we all make mistakes.' He's talking to himself, not to me. 'Don't we?'

I nod. 'We do.'

*

On the way home I call Hugh. I feel different, in some way I can't quite determine. It's as if something has shifted within me, there's been some violent rearrangement and things haven't yet settled. I'm furious, yes, but it's more than that. My fury is mixed with something else, something I can't quite identify. Jealousy, that Hugh's affair has been short-lived and uncomplicated? Relief, that my husband has a secret of his own, one that almost matches mine, and now I don't have to feel quite so bad?

His phone rings out. I'm still not sure what I'm going to say to him when we speak and I'm relieved when it clicks through to voicemail.

I hear myself speak. 'I just wanted to make sure you were okay.' I realize that's all I'd really called for. To hear his voice. To make sure he still exists, and hasn't been swept away by the tidal wave that has threatened everything else. 'Phone me back, when you get the chance.'

I end the call. I wonder how I'd feel if he didn't ring back, if he were never to ring back again. I imagine a car smashing into him, a terrorist bomb, or something as mundane as a heart attack, a stroke. I imagine trying to live with myself, knowing during the last months of his life I'd been resenting him, suspecting him, looking elsewhere so that I could avoid confronting myself. As I try, I realize I can't. He's always there. He always has been. I still remember getting off that flight – the one he'd paid for, the one that brought me home. He was waiting for me, not with flowers, not even with love, but with something far simpler, and far more important back then. Acceptance. That night he took me to his home, not to his bed, but to the spare room. He let me cry, and sleep, and he sat with me when I wanted him to and left me alone when I didn't. The next morning he set about getting me help. He demanded nothing, not even answers to his questions.

He promised to tell no one I was there, until I felt strong, until I felt ready.

He was there for me in the most real, the most honest, way possible. And still he's the person I go to, the person I trust. The person who I want the best for, and want to be the best for, as he does for me.

I love him; finding out he's slept with someone else – even boring Maria – has somehow made that feel more real. It's reminded me he's desirable, capable of passion.

I close my eyes. I wonder if they really have slept together only once. Either way, he's had an affair that goes some way to countering my own. One of the holds Lukas thought he had over me is shrugged off, as simply as that. Anna will erase the photos and get him out of her life, and mine. For the first time in months I imagine emerging into a future without Lukas, clean and pure and free.

Hugh comes home. He's late; a case had overrun. 'Sorry, darling,' he says when he comes into the kitchen. 'Nightmare day. And Maria let me down again, at the last minute.' He kisses me. Again I'm relieved. 'Some crisis at home.'

So she hasn't told Hugh that Paddy knows everything. I wonder why she told her husband, what prompted her confession. Guilt, I guess. That's what it always boils down to, in the end.

'How was your coffee with Paddy?'

It occurs to me that if I'm going to tell Hugh, this would be the moment. I know about you and Maria, I could say. Paddy told me. And I have something I want to tell you.

'Hugh?' He looks at me.

'Uh-huh?'

I pause. I'm serving dinner. I wonder what would happen, if I went ahead. If I told him about Lukas. I wonder if he'd understand, if maybe he's already guessed. I wonder if he'd forgive me, as I realize I've already forgiven him.

I change my mind. The secret I now know he's keeping makes Lukas's hold over me feel somehow diminished. I love Hugh, and I don't want to give that up. Two wrongs don't make anything right, but maybe they make things more equal.

'Call Connor down, would you?'

He does, and a few minutes later our son comes downstairs. We eat together, sitting at the dining table. As we do, I watch my family. I've been a fool, an idiot. I've come close to losing everything. But I've learned my lesson – what good would a confession do now?

That night we go to bed early. I tell him I love him, and he tells me he loves me too, and we mean it. It's not automatic, a call and response. It comes from a place of truth, deep and unknowable.

He kisses me, and I kiss him back. We're truly together, at last.

Chapter Thirty

It's the day Lukas is due to go back to Paris, to Anna. I'm working when Hugh calls, photographing a family who contacted me through the Facebook page I set up. Two women, their two little boys.

It's going well, it's a distraction. We're near the end of the shoot, or else I'd have let the call go to voicemail. 'D'you mind?' I say, and the taller of the two women says, 'Not at all. I think Bertie wants to go to the loo anyway.'

I direct them to the downstairs bathroom at the back of the house and then answer the call. 'Hugh?' I say.

'You busy?'

I step outside into the cold autumn air and close the shed door behind me. I'm jumpy today, on edge.

'Just finishing a shoot. Is everything okay?'

'Yes, fine.' He sounds upbeat. The fear that had begun to grip loosens its hold. 'I just wanted to let you know.'

'Yes?'

'They've accepted the offer of an out-of-court settlement. They're dropping their complaint.'

My shoulders sag with relief. I hadn't realized how much tension I'd been holding in my body. 'That's great, Hugh. That's wonderful.'

'I thought we should celebrate. Dinner, tonight? The three of us? You're not busy, are you?'

I tell him I'm not. It'll help me to relax, I think, it'll take my mind off whatever might be happening in Paris. For a week I've been wondering what Anna is thinking, trying to resist the temptation to call her, worrying that she'll change her mind and decide to stay with him. What would happen then, if she does? A demand, I guess, for money. I never believed all he wanted was for me to leave Anna alone.

And even if it were, I couldn't do that. I couldn't leave her to a man prepared to lie in the way Lukas has. She's my friend. My sister's best friend. I owe it to her.

But all that is to come, I tell myself. Just one more week, and then it'll be over.

'I'd like that,' I say to Hugh.

'I'll book somewhere. You'll tell Connor?'

It's just before lunchtime when I finish the shoot. I tell the couple I'll email them when the shots are ready and they can choose which ones they like. They thank me, we say good-bye, then I put my equipment away, take down the lights. I'm thinking about what Anna will have to do. I imagine her, having the conversation. *It's not you, it's me. I'm not sure I want to marry right now.*

Would it work? Will Lukas believe that it has nothing to do with me, that I've stayed away?

She should do it in a bar, I think. Somewhere neutral, where he can get angry but not violent. I should have suggested she change the locks first.

I wonder if I should go over there, to be with her. But that might make things worse. For now, she's on her own.

I finish tidying and go inside. I open the fridge; there's some salad for lunch, some smoked mackerel. I take them out and look at the time; Connor will be at lunch. I take my phone and ring him. I tell him we're going out tonight. He complains, 'But I'm meant to be going out with Dylan!' His voice implores, he's looking for me to tell him it doesn't matter, he should spend the evening with his friend, but I don't.

'It's important, Con. To your dad.'

'But—'

I swap the phone to my other ear and take a plate from the cupboard.

'I'm not arguing, Connor. After school, you need to come home.'

He sighs but says he will.

I finish preparing my lunch and eat it in the kitchen, then go back to my studio. I look at the pictures I've taken and begin to think about the edit, making notes of which have worked best. At about two in the afternoon the phone rings.

I jump. It's Anna, I think, but when I answer it the voice is unfamiliar.

'Mrs Wilding?'

'Yes?'

'Ah.' The woman on the other end of the line sounds relieved. She introduces herself: Mrs Flynn, from Connor's school. 'I'm just ringing from Saint James's. It's about Connor.'

I shiver, a premonition. 'Connor? What's wrong?'

'I just wondered whether he was at home?'

The world stops; it tilts and shifts. The room is suddenly too cold.

'No. No, he's not here. He's at school.' I say it firmly, with authority. It's as if simply by saying it I believe I can make it so.

'I rang him at lunchtime.' I look at my watch. 'He's there. Isn't he?'

'Well, he wasn't in for afternoon registration.' She sounds

unconcerned, in complete contrast to the panic that's beginning to grow within me, but it feels forced. She's just trying to reassure me. 'It's not like him, so we just wanted to check he was at home.'

I begin to shake. He's been *not like him* a fair bit lately. 'No. No, he's not here.' I don't know whether I'm supposed to be apologizing for him or not. I'm both angry and defensive, and behind all that the swell of fear is about to break. 'I'll call him. I'll find out where he is. He was in this morning?'

'Oh, yes. He was in as usual. I'm told everything seemed fine.'

'Okay.' I tell myself to stay calm. I tell myself that there's nothing to worry about; he's sulking, I've made him come home rather than seeing his friends, he's teaching me a lesson.

'He just hasn't come back from lunch.'

'Okay,' I say again. I close my eyes as another wave of panic washes on the shore. Have I been worrying too much about what's happening in Paris, not enough about what's in front of me?

'Mrs Wilding?'

'Thanks for letting me know,' I say.

She sounds relieved I'm still here.

'Oh, it's fine. I'm sure it's nothing to worry about. I'll be having a word with him about it on Monday, so it'd be great if you could talk to him over the weekend.'

'I will.'

'You will let me know when you find him?'

'Of course.'

'It's just there are procedures. If he disappears from the school grounds, I mean.'

'Of course,' I say again. 'I'll let you know.'

We say goodbye. Without thinking, I call Connor. His phone rings out then goes to voicemail, so I try Hugh. He answers straight away.

'Julia?' I can hear a discussion in the background; he's not alone in the office. Vaguely, I wonder if he's with Maria, but I hardly care.

My words tumble over each other, my voice cracks. 'Connor's gone missing.'

'What?'

I repeat myself.

'What do you mean, *missing*?'

'The school secretary rang. Mrs Flynn. He was in school this morning, but he hasn't gone back this afternoon.'

As I say it I see an image. Lukas, bundling him into a car, driving him off. I can't shake the feeling that something dreadful is happening, and that Lukas is behind it, somehow. I thought I'd escaped, but he's still there, a malevolent force, a siren pulling me into a nightmare.

I tell myself I'm being ridiculous, though I don't believe it.

'Have you called him?'

'Yes. Of course I have. He didn't answer. Has he phoned you?'

'No.' I picture him shaking his head.

'When did you last speak to him?'

'Calm down,' he says. I hadn't realized how panicked I sounded. He coughs, then lowers his voice. 'It'll be fine. Just calm down.'

'He's run away.'

'He's just bunking off school. Have you tried his friends?'

'No, not yet—'

'Dylan? He's been hanging round with him a fair bit.'

I imagine the two of them in the park, drinking from a cheap bottle of cider, my son getting hit by a car as he crosses the road. Or maybe they're messing about on a railway bridge, daring each other to go over the edge, to dodge an oncoming train.

'Or Evie. Can't you call her mother?'

Of course I can't call her mother, I want to say. I don't know who her mother is.

Again I see Lukas, this time standing over Connor. I blink the image away.

'I don't have her number. You think he's with her?'

'I don't know.'

I think back to the other day, after he left me in the restaurant. He'd been packing his bag. *I'm going to see Evie!*

'He's with her.' I begin to head up the stairs, towards his bedroom. 'We need to find her.'

'We don't know that—' says Hugh, but I'm taking the stairs two at a time, already ending the call.

I hesitate in the doorway of my son's room, looking helplessly for some kind of clue. His bed is unmade, piles of clothes sit unhappily on his desk and chair, an empty glass is by the bed, a plateful of crumbs. He's become more private in the last few weeks, I guess worried I'll find a stash of magazines or a semen-encrusted T-shirt thrown under his bed, not realizing that the more private he becomes the harder I find it not to look.

I take a step in, and then stop. I call him again, but this time his phone is switched off. I try a third time, and a fourth, and this time I leave a message: 'Darling, please call me.' I try to keep my voice even, to keep everything from it but my concern. I don't want him to hear anything he might mistake for anger, even for a moment. 'Just let me know you're all right?'

I go further into his room. I know why he's doing this. I'd stopped him from running to Evie that day; now he's showing me that if he wants to do something he will. There's nothing I can do about it.

I look in his wardrobe first, then under his bed. Piles of clothes, old trainers, CDs and video games, but the bag isn't there. He must have taken it to school, already packed. '*Fuck!*' I say to myself. I stand in the middle of the room in the fading light of the afternoon. I'm drowning, helpless.

I open his computer and navigate first to his emails. There are hundreds, from Molly and Dylan and Sahil and lots of others, yet none from his girlfriend. I try Skype next, and then Facebook. He's back online, of course. In the search box at the top of the screen I type 'Evie'.

Her name appears, next to her photograph. It's a different picture to the one he's shown me; she looks a little older and is smiling happily. It's not the girl at Carla's party, I realize, though they don't look dissimilar.

But in the background is the Sacré-Coeur.

I feel another tug downwards, another sickening plunge.

It's nothing, nothing at all. I hear myself talking out loud. Lots of kids have been to Paris. The Sacré-Coeur is somewhere to visit, absolutely on the tourist trail, something to have your photograph taken in front of. It's just coincidence that it's also where Lukas proposed to Anna. It has to be.

A moment later the machine pings and a box appears in the bottom of the screen. It's a new message. From Evie.

– You're online! it says. Immediately, I'm back in the middle of my affair with Lukas. So many conversations that started with those words, or similar. So many times I let myself be drawn in.

Yet I'd wanted it, at the time. Hadn't I? I'd wanted it all.

I push the thoughts away. I have to focus. I have to answer Evie's message.

I remind myself she thinks she's talking to my son. I could

tell her she's wrong, or I could find out what's going on.

– Yes! I type.

– On your phone?

For a moment I don't understand the relevance of her question, but then I realize. She's assuming he's not at his computer, not at home.

– Yes.

– I love you.

I don't know what to say. Again I'm being slammed backwards, into the past, with a ferocity that leaves me breathless.

– Tell me you love me, too.

I have to focus on Connor. This girl thinks she loves him, or tells him so at least.

– I love you, I say.

– You got out of school okay? Are you on your way?

So it's true. He's bunking off, he's gone to meet this girl. I'm about to reply when my phone rings. It sounds way too loud and I startle before snatching it up. 'Connor?' I say, but it's not him. It's Anna.

'Julia,' she says. She sounds hurried, breathless with anxiety, but I can't deal with her right now. Next to Connor she seems utterly unimportant.

'I can't talk now. I'm sorry.'

'But—'

'Connor's missing. It's complicated. I'll call you right back, I promise. I'm sorry.'

I end the call before she can reply, then type again.

– Yes. I'm on my way.

– I can't believe I'm finally going to get to meet you! I can't believe we've found him!

I feel myself contract, my skin pulls tight. Found who?

– Just imagine! After all this time! Your dad!

The trapdoor opens. I plunge.

So this is what he's been doing? Trying to find his father.

Succeeding.

But how?

I force myself to stay in the present. I have to. I force myself to imagine what my son might write.

– I know! It's going to be amazing! Where shall I meet you again?

I press send. A moment later she replies.

– At the station, where we arranged! See you there!

I lean forward to type, but a moment later her final message arrives. Three kisses. And then she's gone.

Fuck, I think. Fuck. Maybe I should have told her who I am, that I'm furious, that she'd better tell me right now where she plans to meet my son.

But now it's too late. The green dot next to her name has disappeared. She's offline, and there's no way of contacting her. I'm stuck, with no idea where my son has gone. *The station*. It could be anywhere.

The whirring cogs of my mind engage, the engine catches. I can't afford the descent into despair. I have to stay focussed. I have to find him. Which station, where? There has to be a clue. There's a pile of papers and magazines on the desk and I riffle through these, then I open the drawer. Nothing. Just pens and pencils, a copy of *The Hitchhiker's Guide to the Galaxy* that Hugh gave him for his birthday a few years ago, a hole-punch and a stapler, a pair of scissors, Post-it notes, the detritus of study.

I stand up, turn round. I take in the football poster above his bed, the scarf over the back of his door. No clue, nowhere obvious to look.

And then I have an idea. I turn back to his computer and a moment later have pulled up his browser history. The first thing I see is a new Twitter account he must have created. @helpmefindmydad. But before I can even absorb what this means, I see, at the top, the last website he looked at. This morning, before school. Eurostar.com.

When I click on the link it takes me to a map of Gare du Nord.

He's on his way to Paris.

Chapter Thirty-One

I try to tell myself it's a coincidence, it has nothing to do with Lukas.

But I can't believe it. Not today of all days. The day he's due to return to Paris; it can't be a coincidence that my son is going there, too.

Even if Hugh has spoken to Evie, even if he is sure she's a girl.

Anna answers after the second ring. 'Thank God,' she says.

My mouth is dry, but I'm desperate.

'Anna, listen—'

'Thank God,' she says again. I can hear relief in her voice, but there's something else. She sounds awful. Out of breath, almost stricken with panic. 'I'm so sorry.' Her voice drops, almost to a whisper, I can barely hear what she's saying. It's as if she doesn't want to be overheard. 'I tried to tell him. I tried. I'm so sorry. I'm so sorry.'

She sounds terrible, and her fear infects me. 'Anna, what's wrong? Where's Lukas? Is he there?'

It's as if she hasn't heard me. 'I couldn't wait. I tried to tell him. Today. I tried to tell him it was over, that he had to go—'

'Where is he? Anna!'

'He's stormed out. But he'll be back any second. I went

into his computer, Julia, like we agreed. To look at those files.
I found something else.'

There's a tremor in her voice. An uncertainty I haven't
heard before.

'What? What did you find?'

'There were these files. There was the one called "Julia",
but there was another.'

I know what she's going to say.

'It was called "Connor" . . .'

My world shrinks to nothing.

'There were all these pictures.'

I'm frozen, a tiny point. I feel like I haven't breathed for
days. I force myself to speak. My voice is a whisper.

'What sort of pictures?'

'Just . . . you know. Pictures of him—'

'What sort?'

'Ordinary pictures. He's just smiling at the camera.'

'Jesus—'

'Do you think he was using me, just to get to Connor—'

'No. No, no.'

I wonder if my certainty is only because I can't face the
thought of it being true.

'Connor's run away.'

'Run away?'

'He's gone to see Evie. His girlfriend. But he's gone to
Paris. They're meeting Connor's father.'

'His father, but how—?'

'I don't know. Online, I think.'

'Wait. What did you say his girlfriend's name was?'

I close my eyes. Fear builds, infecting me. My skin is
crawling. I force myself to speak.

'Evie. Why?'

She sighs. 'Julia, I found this list. On Ryan's computer. All these usernames and passwords.' She speaks hesitantly, as if she's unsure, or is figuring something out as she goes. 'At least that's what I think they are.' There's a long pause. 'One of them's Lukas, but there are loads more. Argo-something-or-other, Crab, Baskerville, Jip. And there are all these names. Loads of them, God knows what he's been doing.'

I know what she's going to say, even before she says it.

'One of them's Evie.'

Something gives within me. I'm sure, now. 'Oh God,' I say. I've had weeks to understand. Months. I just haven't wanted to.

'How do you think he knows her? How does he know Connor's girlfriend?'

'Anna. He doesn't *know* her. I think he *is* her.'

'But—'

'Is his computer there now?'

'Yes . . .'

'Go online. Look on Facebook.'

I listen as she goes into another room. I hear as she picks up a machine, there's a swell of music as she wakes it from sleep. A few moments later she says, 'I'm in. He's left it logged on. What . . . ?'

And then she stops.

'What is it? Anna, tell me!'

'You're right. The photo he's using is a young woman,' she says. 'And the name . . . it isn't Ryan. You're right, Julia. It's Evie.'

It all hits me at once. All the things I've ignored, not wanted to see. All the things I've left unexamined. I go over to Connor's bed. I sit on it; the mattress gives, the duvet smells of him. Of my boy. My boy, who I've put in danger.

'Anna,' I say. 'You have to help me. Go to the station. Gare du Nord. Find my son.'

*

Downstairs, I call a taxi first and then Hugh. There's no time to go round to his office, to explain face to face. I have to be on the next train to France.

He answers on the third ring. 'Julia. Any news?'

I still don't know what I'm going to say to him.

'He's on his way to Paris.'

'Paris?'

He's shocked. I want to tell him. I have to tell him. Yet at the same time I don't know how.

'I can explain—'

'Why Paris?'

'He's . . . he thinks he's on his way to meet Evie.'

'How d'you know?'

'I spoke to her.'

'Well, I hope you told her how ridiculous this is. He's fourteen, for goodness' sake. He shouldn't be skipping school, taking off for Paris.' He draws breath. 'What did she say?'

I try to explain. 'It's not that simple. We were talking online. I logged on to Connor's machine. She thought I was him. It's how I know where he's headed.'

I stop speaking. My cab is here, I can hear it idling on the street outside the front door.

'I have to go,' I say. I haven't had time to pack a bag, but I have my passport, and the forty euros I brought back last time and left in a pot on one of the shelves in the kitchen is in my purse.

'Where?'

'To Paris. I'm going over there. I'll get him back.'

'Julia—'

'I have to, Hugh.'

There's a moment of silence as he decides what to do.

'I'll come, too. I'll get the first train I can. I'll meet you there.'

I sit on the train. I'm numb, I can't focus on anything. I can't read, or eat. I've left safety behind and don't know what's ahead of me.

I concentrate on being as still as possible. I look at the people around me. An American couple sitting across the aisle are discussing the meeting they're obviously heading back from; they sound clipped and professional, I decide they're not lovers, just workmates. Another couple, opposite, are sitting in silence, she wearing earbuds and nodding along to music, he with a tourist guide to Paris. I realize with sudden clarity that we're wearing masks, all of us, all the time. We're presenting a face, a version of ourselves, to the world, to each other. We show a different face depending on who we're with and what they expect of us. Even when we're alone it's just another mask, the version of ourselves we'd prefer to be.

I turn away and look out of the window as we tear through the city, the countryside. We seem to be building momentum; we hit the tunnel at speed. The noise we make is a dull thud, and for a moment everything goes black. I close my eyes, and then see Frosty, putting her drink down – red wine, and as usual she's drinking it through a straw. She's fully made-up, even though it's the middle of the day and her wig is still upstairs.

'Honeybunch,' she's saying. 'Where's Marky?'

I look up. She looks terrified, and I don't know why. 'Upstairs. Why?'

'Come on,' she says, then she's running out of the kitchen, and even though I'm following as quickly as I can we still move in slow motion, and we're going up the stairs, up those dark, carpetless stairs. When we get to the bedroom I shared with Marcus the door won't open. He's propped a chair against it, and Frosty has to shoulder it open.

I shake the vision away. I check my phone again. There's supposed to be a signal down here now, but I have none. I lean over to the American couple, and ask if they're picking anything up. 'Not me,' says the woman, shaking her head, and her colleague tells me he's already asked a member of staff and no one is. 'Some problem with the equipment, apparently.' I force a smile and thank them, then turn away. I'm just going to have to wait.

My mind goes to what Anna told me. Lukas's usernames. Argo-something-or-other, I know. Crab, Baskerville, Jip. They're related, I'm sure of it, though I can't work out how.

Baskerville is easy, I think. There's the typeface, of course, but the only other reference I can think of is Sherlock Holmes, The Hound of. Slowly it comes: Jip is from *David Copperfield*, as well as *The Story of Dr Dolittle*, and Crab is from Shakespeare, though I don't remember which play. And Argos is from *The Odyssey*.

They're all dog's names.

I see it all, then. A burst of realization. A few years ago, when Connor was nine or ten, the three of us went on holiday to Crete. We stayed in a hotel, near the beach. One night we were at dinner, discussing our names, where they'd come from, what they meant. Later Hugh had looked them all up online, and at breakfast he told us what he'd found. My name means 'youthful', his means 'mind' or 'spirit'.

'And mine?' asked Connor.

'Well, yours is Irish,' said his father. 'Apparently, it means "lover of hounds".'

The truth I've been dodging is no longer avoidable. Right

from the beginning, from the very first time Lukas had messaged me, calling himself Largos86, it'd been about Connor.

All along.

Chapter Thirty-Two

We emerge from the tunnel into dusk. I grab my phone but there's still no signal, and as I wait I look out of the window.

The French landscape looks unreal, shrouded in a thin gauze. I see the desolate hypermarkets, their huge car parks without a sign of the shoppers who've driven there. The train seems to have a different rhythm now, as if the mere fact of travelling to a different country has caused the world to shift, just slightly. I put my watch forward by an hour; my phone has set itself automatically. A minute later I see three bars in the display and a second after that my phone beeps with a waiting voicemail. It's from Anna.

I listen to it. 'Julia!' she begins. Already I'm searching for clues; in the background I can hear what sounds like the bustle of the station, and she sounds excited. Good news? Can it be? She goes on.

'I've got him! He was just getting off the train as I got here.' Her voice is muffled, as if she's holding her phone against her chest, then, 'Sorry, but he won't speak to you.' She lowers her voice. 'He's embarrassed, I think. Anyway, we're just sitting here having a milkshake, and when we've finished we'll head back to my place. Ring me, when you get this, and we'll see you there.'

Relief mixes with anxiety. I wish she'd sit with him, where she is, or take him somewhere else. Anywhere but back to her flat, I want to say. She doesn't understand the danger she's in.

I call her back; the phone rings out. Come on, I say to myself, over and over, but she doesn't answer. I try her again, then a third time. Still nothing. It's no good. I leave a message, it's all I can do, and then I try Hugh.

No answer there either; his phone goes straight to voicemail. I guess he's on a train behind me, with no reception. I leave a message, asking him to call me. I'm on my own.

I sit where I am. I concentrate on my breathing, on staying calm. I concentrate on not wanting a drink.

I try to work out why he's doing it. Why he's pretending to be my son's girlfriend, why he's luring him to Paris.

I think of the dogs. Largos86.

Finally my mind settles on the last truth it's been avoiding. Lukas is Connor's father.

The elements begin to slot into place. He must've befriended Kate, first, maybe Anna around the same time. It's possible neither knew of the existence of him in the other's life; perhaps he was friends with Kate online only. He'd have been the one persuading her to try to get Connor back, and then, just when it looked like it might be about to succeed, she'd been killed.

And so he came after my son using the only other route open to him. Through me.

Why didn't I see it? I think of all the times I'd suspected that there was more to our relationship than I knew, all the things I'd glimpsed, and then avoided.

I wonder what Lukas thought would happen. I wonder if he'd hoped I'd end my marriage to be with him, that we'd all become one big happy family.

I think back to those times. Kate, calling me. *I want him*

back. He's my son. You can't keep him. I wish I'd never let you take him from me.

Now I know it was him. Lukas, telling her what to say. Lukas, who'd come back for his son. My son.

'I want Connor,' she'd said, over and over, night after night.

Deep down, I know she'd still be alive if I hadn't said no.

We reach Gare du Nord and I step off the train and get a taxi. It's dark now, rain falls on the silvered streets of Paris as we glide towards the eleventh arrondissement. I've called Hugh and given him Anna's address; he said he'll meet us there. Now I try Anna again. I have to speak to my son.

The screen shows that she's online, available for a video chat. I press call and a few moments later a window opens on my screen. I can see Anna's living room, the same furniture I'm used to, the same pictures on the walls. A moment later she appears.

'Thank God. Anna—'

I freeze. She looks distressed, her eyes are wide, tinged with red. She looks terrified.

'What's wrong? Where's Connor?'

She leans in close to the screen. She's been crying.

'What's happened? Where's my son!'

'He's here,' she says, but she's shaking her head. 'Ryan came back. He was angry—'

I interrupt. 'But you had Connor with you!'

'No, no. Connor was waiting outside. But . . . I couldn't stop him. The pictures on his computer . . . I think he's going to send them to Hugh. And . . . and he hit me.'

She looks numb, almost as if she's been anaesthetized.

I think of the time with David, the incident in the car, the knife.

'He was angry.'

'That's no excuse! Anna, you have to get out of there!'

She leans in, close to the machine. 'I'm okay. Listen' – she looks over her shoulder – 'I haven't got long. I need to tell you something. I have a gun.'

At first I think I've misheard her, but her face is grave. I realize I haven't, and she's serious.

'What . . . ? A gun? What d'you mean?'

She begins speaking quickly. 'When Kate died . . . a friend of mine . . . he said he could get me one. For protection. And I said no, but . . .'

'But what?'

'But then, this stuff with Ryan. I was scared. I . . .'

'You said yes.'

She nods. I wonder how it came to this, and whether there's anything she's not telling me about Ryan. About what he might've done already.

'But . . .' I say. 'A gun?'

She doesn't answer. I see her look over her shoulder. There's been a noise, and then it comes again. A thudding.

'Listen . . .' She's speaking quickly, whispering. I struggle to make out what she's saying. 'There's something else. Hugh made me promise not to tell you, but I have to—'

'Hugh?' His name is the last I expected to hear.

'—it's about Kate. The guy. The one they found with the earring. It wasn't him.'

I shake my head. No. No, this can't be.

'What do you mean, it wasn't him?'

'He had an alibi.'

'Hugh would've told me. He wouldn't let me go on thinking . . .'

The sentence peters out. Maybe he would. For the sake of peace.

'I'm sorry, but it's true. He said—' There's a noise at her end, loud. It sounds like a door slamming, a voice, though I can't make out what's being said.

'I've got to go. He's back.'

'Anna—!' I begin. 'Don't—'

I never finish the sentence. Over her shoulder I see Lukas. He's shouting, he looks furious. There's a flash of something in his hand, but I can't tell what it is. Anna stands, blocking my view. I hear him ask who she's talking to, I hear the words 'Who the fuck?', and 'kid'. She gasps, and the screen goes dark. I realize he's pushed her into the table, she's fallen against the laptop and blocked the camera. When the image returns the computer is on the floor and through its camera I can see the floorboards, a rug, the edge of one of the chairs.

Yet I can hear what's going on. I can hear him saying he's going to kill her, and her, gasping, crying, saying 'No!', over and over. I call out her name, but it's no use. I hear a thud, a body against the wall, or the floor. I'm unable to take my eyes off the screen. Anna's computer is knocked, the image changes. Her head appears, flung to the floor. She gasps, and then a moment later is jerked violently backwards. There's a thud as his fist connects with her, a sickening crunch. I call out her name, but all I can do is watch as her head is jerked back again and again until, eventually, she's silent.

I stare at the screen. The room is quiet. Empty. And still there's no sign of Connor. Terror descends.

Desperate, I end the call. In terrible French I ask the driver how long we're likely to be, and he says five minutes, possibly fifteen. I'm frantic, every nerve hums with energy that won't be contained. I want to open the car door, to leap out into the traffic, to run to our destination, but I know even if I could it would be no quicker. And so I sit back and will the traffic to clear, the cars to go faster.

I dial Hugh. Still no answer.

'Fuck!' I say, but there's nothing I can do. After a while I begin to recognize the streets. I remember walking here, back in April. Consumed by grief, burning in a fire that I'd fooled myself into thinking I had managed to avoid. How simple things had been back then – all I had to do was get through it, survive the pain – yet I hadn't even seen it.

Finally we arrive in Anna's street. I see the laundrette, still closed, and opposite there's a *boulangerie* where, last time, we bought fresh bread for our breakfast. I need to be cautious.

I ask the driver to stop a few doors down from Anna's building; it might be better if I surprise them. He does so, and I pay him. A moment after he pulls away my phone rings.

It's Hugh. 'I've just arrived in France. Where are you?'

'At Anna's,' I say. 'I think Connor's here.'

I tell him what I've seen, ask him to call the police.

'Anna was attacked,' I say. 'I'll have to explain the rest later. And Hugh?'

'Yes?'

I don't want to ask him, but I know that I must.

'The guy they arrested. What happened?'

'What do you mean, what happened?'

Tell me the truth, I think. Tell me the truth, without me demanding it, and maybe we still have a chance.

'You told me they charged him.'

He's silent, and I know what Anna told me is right, and Hugh knows I know it, too.

I hear him cough. 'I'm sorry.'

I don't speak. I can hardly breathe, but I have to stay calm.

'I thought I was doing the right thing. Julia?'

I tell myself everything will be fine. Hugh will call the

police, they'll be on their way soon. I try to tell myself that whatever he's done, Lukas is Connor's father. He might take him somewhere, but he won't hurt him.

I should tell him. I should tell Hugh why we're here. But I can't. Not like this.

'Just call the police and get here. Please.'

I run up to Anna's building, then try the handle. I'm in luck. The digital entry lock is broken, as she told me it often is. The door opens and I step inside, closing it softly behind me.

I don't turn on the light but climb the stairs. On the first landing I see Anna's door, just as I remember it. A dull light shines through the glass panels, but when I stand beside it and listen I hear no sound. No voices, no shouting. Nothing. I go over to the writing bureau and, as softly as I can, pull out the drawer, praying that the key Anna stowed under it hasn't been removed, and that she hasn't changed her locks since I was last here.

My luck holds. It's there, taped to the underside. I take it and stand once again outside Anna's door. Still no sound. I let myself in. The light in the hallway is on, there's a vase of dead flowers on the side table. I step forward, the creak of my shoes sounds improbably loud in the silence.

The apartment seems much larger in the dark. It takes all my willpower not to shout out, not to ask if anyone's there. I realize I don't know which I'm hoping for more; that someone is, or that the place is empty.

I search the apartment. One room at a time. The TV is on in the living room – some news channel, but muted – and in the kitchen I see that a chair is overturned and the sticky brown remains of a meal smear the walls. My foot crunches underfoot; when I look down I see the remains of the striped blue bowl that must have once contained it.

I carry on. I look in Kate's bedroom then move on to Anna's. I hesitate outside. I wonder what I might find in there. I picture Kate, with her head staved in, her hair matted with blood, her eyes open and limbs twisted.

I take a breath and swallow. I push open the door.

The bed glows blood red in the dim light, but when I flick on the light it's just the duvet cover, slipped off the end of the bed. The room is as empty as the rest of the apartment.

I don't understand. I take out my phone, switch on Find Friends. The purple dot still blinks, now superimposed on mine, right here, right where I'm standing. She should be here.

I press call. For a second I hear the international tone, and then there's a buzzing, low and insistent, from somewhere near my feet. I bend down. A phone is rattling across the floor under the bed, flashing as it goes. It must've fallen to the floor, been kicked under there. I get on to my hands and knees and grab it, and at the same time see that there's something else under there, too, something shiny and metallic. The gun.

I freeze. I don't want to touch it. I wonder how it got here, under the bed. I imagine her and Lukas fighting, Anna going for the gun, trying to threaten him. Maybe it was kicked under here in the struggle. Or maybe she never got that far. Maybe she kept the gun here and didn't even have the chance to go for it.

But where's Connor?

I feel the world collapsing, begin to disintegrate. I breathe deeply and tell myself I have to stay calm. I sit on the bed, the gun beside me. Anna's phone shows my missed call, but there's another message, a text that has been sent to the phone from a number I don't recognize. 'Julia,' it says. 'If you want to find Connor, return this call.'

I hesitate, but only for a moment. I have no choice. I swipe the screen and the phone connects.

It's a video call. After a moment, it's answered; the outline of a face appears. It's Lukas, he's sitting in darkness, in front of a window. His body is blocking what little light comes in from the street outside, throwing him into silhouette. For a second I'm reminded of those true-crime TV shows, the victim unrecognizable, her voice disguised, but then my mind goes to the times we've chatted on video before.

'You found the phone.'

I take a deep breath, try to muster as much courage as I can. I put my hand on the gun beside me; it gives me some kind of strength. 'What d'you want?' My voice still cracks. I'm aware of how impotent the question sounds.

He leans forward. His face is illuminated by the glow from his screen. He's smiling.

He's unchanged, yet I don't recognize him at all. The Lukas I knew has gone completely.

'Where's Connor?'

'I have no idea.'

His words are loaded with threat.

'Let me see him.'

He ignores me. 'Like I said, I've decided I want Connor's share of your sister's money.'

I know he's lying. His words are flat, and unconvincing. Even if I didn't know the truth, I'd be able to tell.

'This isn't about money. I know who you are.'

'Really?'

I close my eyes. Hatred pours into me; my mind will not be still. How long has this man been talking to my son? His father, pretending to be his girlfriend.

For a moment I feel huge, unstoppable, as if my hatred is limitless and I could transcend the hardware that links us, the fibre optics, the satellites, and destroy him simply by willing it.

Yet I know I can't. I force myself to refocus on the screen. Lukas is still talking, but I can't hear him.

'Let him go,' I say. 'Let them both go. What have they ever done to you?'

He doesn't answer. He ignores me. He holds up the memory stick. 'I told you what would happen if you didn't leave me and Anna alone . . .'

An image swims into view. Me and him, in a hotel room, fucking. I have one hand on the headboard; he's behind me. I feel sick.

'Don't do this. Please. Let me see Connor.'

He laughs. 'Too late. I told you I'd tell your family the truth.'

He stands up, holding his camera phone in front of him so that his face remains static. It looks as though it's the background that's wheeling violently, a ship upturned. A bare light bulb spins into view – dead, I guess, or not switched on – and then a glass-panelled doorway, beyond which must be another room, and next to it a cooker.

'Julia . . .' he says. The image spins again, then freezes; he's standing still, as if deep in thought. Over his shoulder I can see a window, through it the street. 'I want Connor's share of your sister's money. It seems only fair, as I won't be getting Anna's any more.'

I can't understand why he's doing this. 'I know this isn't about the fucking money!' I'm shouting, my anger coursing through me, a boiling intensity. 'I know who you are, you creep!'

He ignores me. 'Don't forget those pictures. Tell you what. Why don't you stay there tonight? Make yourself at home, I'm sure Anna won't mind. Then tomorrow, first thing, I'll come round. You can give me the money, and then you can have this.' He holds up the memory stick once again. 'Or else I can give it to your family. It's up to you.'

I'm silent. I have nothing to say, nowhere to turn.

'Right. Until tomorrow, then.' He laughs. I'm about to answer when he says, 'And if you like we can have one last fuck, just for old time's sake.'

And then he's gone.

I stand up. My rage is volcanic, yet impotent. I want to lash out, to smash and destroy, but there's nothing I can do. I look down at the gun and pick it up. It feels heavy in my hand.

I don't have time to think. The police haven't turned up yet, but they might be here soon. A wasted journey for them, but I've effectively broken in. I'm holding a gun, they'll ask questions. I have to get out. I pick up the pistol and rummage through the chest of drawers over by the window. I pull out a lemon sweater and wrap the gun in it, then put it in my bag. I close the door behind me as I leave, then slam down the stairs.

Lukas has made a mistake. When he turned his phone round in the kitchen I'd caught a glimpse through the window to the right of his shoulder, on to the street outside. It hadn't been for long, but it'd been enough. Through the window I'd seen a street, a row of shops, a neon sign reading 'CLUB SANTÉ!' with a jaunty exclamation mark and a logo of a runner formed out of a curve and a dot. Above it was one word. 'Berger'.

When I'm out of sight of the apartment I search on my phone, typing the words into the browser, praying that there'll only be one branch. My heart sinks as two appear – one in the nineteenth, the other the seventeenth – but both have maps attached and one looks to be on a busy road while the other is opposite a park.

It must be the nineteenth, which I guess is a couple of miles away.

I have to go there. I have to get Connor back, and maybe I can force Lukas to give me the memory stick, scare him into letting Anna go and leaving us all alone.

I hail a cab. I give the address, then get in. 'How long?' I say to the driver, in English. It takes a moment before I realize my mistake and say it again: '*Combien de temps pour y arriver?*'

He looks at me in the rear-view mirror. He's indifferent, largely. He shrugs, says, '*Nous ne sommes pas loin.*' A plastic tree hangs off the mirror, and on the dashboard there's a photo: a woman, a child. His family, I guess, mirroring mine. I look away, out of the window, at the streets as they slide by. Rain has begun to fall; it's heavy, people have put up their umbrellas or are dashing with newspapers held over their heads. I rest my head against the cool glass and close my eyes. I want to stay like this for ever. Silent, warm.

But I can't. I take out my phone and call my husband.

'Hugh, where are you?'

'We're just getting into Gare du Nord.'

'Did you call the police?'

He's silent.

'Hugh?'

'Yes. I called them. They're on their way.'

'You need to call them back. Please. I went to Anna's. She isn't there. The place is deserted. She and Connor . . . I think something terrible has happened.'

'Terrible?'

'Just meet me here,' I say. I give him the address. 'As soon as you can.'

'Why? Julia? What's there?'

I close my eyes. This is it. I have to tell him. 'Hugh, listen. It's where Connor's gone. This Evie, she doesn't exist.'

'But I spoke to her.'

'It's just a name he's used to lure him here.'

'Who? You're not making any sense, Julia.'

'Hugh, listen to me. Connor's found his father. His real father. He's here to meet him, but he's in danger.'

There's a silence. I can't begin to imagine what my husband must be feeling. In a moment he'll ask me how I know, what's happened, and it will all come spilling out. I take a deep breath. I'm ready.

'Connor's father . . . I know him. He didn't tell me who he was, but—'

Hugh interrupts me.

'But that's not possible.'

'What?'

I hear him sigh. 'I'm sorry, Julia. Kate told me—'

'What?'

'Connor's father is dead.'

I'm silent. 'What? Who is he then? That's ridiculous.'

'I can't tell you now. Not like this.'

I hear an announcement in the background. His train is pulling in.

I begin to shout. 'Hugh? Tell me!'

'We're here. I've got to go.'

'Hugh!'

'I'm sorry, darling. I'll be there soon. I'll tell you everything.'

Chapter Thirty-Three

We slow to a crawl, then stop in traffic. There are lights ahead, a busy junction where a railway bridge spans the road. Hugh is wrong, he must be. Connor's father isn't dead, he's here, and he's lured his son here, too.

'*Nous sommes ici*,' says the driver, but he's pointing forward. I peer through the rain; ahead I can see the place. Berger. It's still open, its doorway looks warm, inviting. A woman comes out, almost collides with a guy going in. I watch as she stands, lights a cigarette. I can't sit still any longer; I have to get moving. The driver grunts as I tell him I'll get out here; I pay him and then I'm on the pavement. The rain hits, instantly I'm soaked through. The woman with the cigarette is walking towards me; she nods as we pass, then I'm outside the gym. Lukas's apartment should be just on the other side of the road, yet now I'm here I don't know what to do. I glance over the road, past a stack of prefab offices covered in spray-painted graffiti. The building opposite is grey, its windows monotonously regular. It looks institutional; it could be a prison. I wonder which flat is his, and how I'll get in. Further up the street a train thunders along rails and I see a row of bollards strung like sentinels along the pavement. Just beyond them is a kiosk, bright blue, advertising *Cosmétiques Antilles*, and just this side of it an alleyway arcs off the road, unlit, towards who-knows-where.

I know, then. I'm sure. I've seen this place before, on my computer. I hadn't recognized it at first, not in the dark, but this is the place. I run past Berger to the mouth of the alleyway. I'm right.

This is where my sister died.

I run into the alleyway. It's rain-soaked, in almost total darkness. I can't believe it. I'm here. This is it. This is where my sister's body was discovered, where her life bled out on to the cobblestones. This is where the nightmare that has been the last few months began.

My mind races. I've been a fool. All along. Lukas wasn't on holiday in Australia, or at least he wasn't when Kate was killed. It wasn't a drug dealer who killed her.

Kate wasn't mugged for a cheap earring, or attacked while buying drugs, or killed in a random attack on her way home from a bar. She'd come here to see him, to meet the father of her son.

I try to picture it. Was he hoping for a reconciliation? I see Kate rejecting him, telling him she wanted nothing to do with him, that he'd never see Connor again. They argue, insults are hurled, a fist is raised.

Or maybe it was his plan all along. To bring her here. To punish her for sending Connor away and then failing to get him back.

I take out my phone. I want Hugh. I need his help, I want to find out how far away he is, but it's more than that. I want to tell him he's wrong, that whatever Kate said, she lied. Connor's father is alive, and he killed her. I want to make him understand, and tell him how I found out, and that it's my fault and I'm sorry. I want to tell him I love him.

But his phone goes straight to voicemail. Once again, I'm alone.

I feel curiously calm, like stone, yet underneath it my stomach begins to knot and I'm aware it's the first sign of an incoming tidal wave. I have to stay focussed, remain still. My hand goes to the gun in my bag, yet this time it doesn't give me confidence. Instead it reminds me of the impossibility of what I have to do. For a moment I want to run, not to the police, but away. Away from everything, to a time when all this had never happened, and Kate is still alive and Connor is happy.

But that's not possible. Time grinds forward, inexorable. And so I'm stuck; there's no escape. I want to sink to the wet ground and let the cold rain wash over me.

All of a sudden there's a noise, a shriek. I startle. A train is passing, overhead. It's come from nowhere. I look up; it's yellow and white, travelling so quickly it's almost a blur. Still I can make out the passengers, all looking downwards, unsmiling. Reading newspapers, no doubt, working on laptops, using their phones. Had none of them seen what happened? Did no one happen to glance down to see my sister, fighting with Lukas?

Or maybe they did, and thought nothing of it. Just a row, an argument. They happen all the time.

The wheels squeal, the train passes, as quickly as it'd come. I look back to the end of the alleyway, where it joins the street.

And he's there. Even though he can't possibly know that I'm here, that I've worked out where he lives, he's there. Standing at the end of the alleyway wearing the same blue parka he'd had on the other day. Lukas.

Something is released inside me. The wave builds and I take a step back. 'What—?' I begin, but I already know how he found me.

'You think it was an accident? Letting you see over my

shoulder? You're a clever girl, Julia. I knew you'd work it out. Plus, I knew you wouldn't want to leave it until tomorrow—'

'Where's Connor? Where's my son?'

'I don't know what you're talking about.'

Damn him. I begin to move. My hand goes to my bag, then inside it. I feel the weight of the gun, its hardness. I wonder if the rain will affect it, then remember it doesn't matter. I have no intention of using it. I have to scare him. I have to make him think I'm capable of killing, something I now know he himself has done.

No. I stop the thought dead. Connor's face comes into view. I can't afford to think of Kate. Not now. I have to focus. I have to make him give me my son back, and then admit what he did, somehow get him to turn himself in.

I raise my face to him. Defiant. The rain hits.

'I know what you did.'

'What I did? To Anna? And what's that, then?'

'Here. I know what happened here. You were chatting to Kate, online. You . . . you *enticed* her here. You killed her . . .'

He shakes his head.

'I know you're Connor's father. No matter what she told Anna, or me, or Hugh. You're Connor's father.'

His eyes narrow. 'You're even crazier than I thought. I didn't even know Kate.'

'Liar.' I try to steady my voice and say it again. 'You're a liar.'

'Don't be absurd. I didn't—'

I lift my hand up out of my bag. The sweater drops away. He sees the gun, his eyes go wide.

'Fuck!'

I feel it coming. The boiling anger, the rage. The wave is

413

breaking, but I can't give in to it, not yet. I have to keep my head clear.

'You killed Kate!' My fury is molten lava; it burns and will not be contained. I wipe the rain out of my eyes with the back of the hand holding the gun. 'You killed my sister!'

He takes a step forward. 'Julia,' he says, 'listen to me . . .'

A look of fear flashes on his face and his swaggering bravado drops away. He's Lukas again, the man I once knew. My mind goes to the time I'd been angry with him, told him I wasn't sure what was happening between us or whether I wanted it to continue. He'd looked frightened, then. I thought that was because he loved me, when really it was because I was close to escape.

I raise the gun. I point it at his chest. I think of pulling the trigger, seeing the red bloom on his shirt. For an instant I wish I could do it.

'Stay away from me!'

He freezes. I see him try to work out what to do. He probably thinks he could rush at me, grab the gun. He probably thinks I wouldn't pull the trigger.

'I said stay away!'

He takes a step back. He looks less certain now, he doesn't know what to do. He glances back to where he came from, then up to his apartment, as if the answer will be there.

'This is what's going to happen.' I hesitate; I'm trying to calm down. 'We're going to go up to your apartment. We'll let Anna go, and then—'

'Listen.' He looks at me, imploring, and for a moment I want to believe he's innocent, that none of this is real. 'You've got this all wrong. I didn't kill your sister. I never even met her. Anna said she knew you'd inherited some money and she thought we could get it . . .'

I stab the gun towards him. 'You're lying.'

'No, listen. Anna's just a casual thing, you know? I met her online. Just like you. A few months ago—'

'Shut up!'

'—we're not getting married. She said we should blackmail you.'

I take a step towards him. My finger rests on the trigger. 'Stop pretending this is about money!'

I close my eyes, open them again. I want to believe him. I want to believe that this has nothing to do with Connor.

But it does. My son is missing. Of course it does.

'Where's Connor?'

'It was just part of the game. I don't know anything about your son. You have to believe—'

I shout. 'Where is he?' My voice echoes off the cold walls of the alleyway. He shakes his head. 'My son is missing. My sister was killed right here, right where we're standing, and you expect me—'

'What?'

He looks genuinely confused.

'She died here.'

He shakes his head. 'No. No.'

Again, doubt creeps in. Maybe I'm wrong, maybe this is a mistake.

I level the gun. I won't let him convince me again. Over his shoulder I can see down the alleyway; there's a figure, crossing the road, coming slowly towards us. A passer-by? There haven't been any of those, not since we got here.

It looks like Anna. I don't want him to turn and see her.

'Stop lying to me.'

'Julia. Believe me. How can I have killed your sister? I was in Australia. You know that . . .'

I ignore him. The approaching figure is under the street lamp now. I'm right, it is Anna, and even in the dim light I can see that she looks awful. Her face is bruised, there's a dark patch on her white shirt that might be blood. I gasp, I can't help it. 'Anna!'

Lukas looks round but doesn't move. She runs past him and joins me.

'Julia, whatever he's saying, he's lying.' She's out of breath, but speaks quickly, furiously. 'Listen to me . . . he killed Kate . . . I found out . . . it was over Connor . . . but he made me lie . . . he made me . . .'

My last shred of hope falls away. I look into his eyes and remember that I loved him – or thought I did at least – and he had killed my sister.

'It *was* you.'

'Don't be absurd. Don't believe her! Julia! I didn't kill your sister. I swear—'

'You killed her.' I'm almost whispering; my words are swallowed by the rain. 'And then you made me fall in love with you.' I hesitate. The words won't come. 'I loved you and you killed my sister. You used me to get close to Connor.'

'No!' He steps forward. The rain has plastered his hair to his forehead; it drips from him, soaking him. 'I didn't kill anyone, I swear.' He looks from me to Anna. 'What are you doing?' He reaches for her but I wave the gun and he backs off. 'How can you say you lied for me? I lied for you!'

I lift the gun up.

'Tell her!' he says, then. He's speaking to Anna. 'Tell her I was abroad that night!'

She shakes her head. 'I'm not lying for you again.' She sobs. 'I lied to the police, but I'm not doing it again. You told me you were abroad, but you weren't. You killed her, Lukas. You did it.'

'No!' he says. 'No!' But I can barely hear him. All I can hear is Anna. *You did it.*

'Listen,' he says. 'I can explain—'

My hand begins to shake. The gun is heavy, slick with rain. 'Where's Connor?'

No one speaks.

'Where is he?'

Anna looks at me. 'Julia,' she says, and I can see that she's crying. 'Julia. Connor . . . is upstairs. I tried to protect him . . .'

I look at the blood on her shirt.

'I couldn't. We need an ambulance. We have to get him to a hospital—'

Everything collapses. It's automatic, impulsive. A reflex. I don't even think. I look at the gun in my hand and, beyond it, Lukas.

I pull the trigger.

What happens next isn't supposed to. There's an instant – an almost imperceptible moment – of something that resembles stillness. Stasis. I don't feel as if I've made an irreversible decision; for a moment it's as if I can still take it all back. Turn away. Become something else, or follow a path that leads to a different future,

But then the gun fires. My hand leaps up with the kick; there's a flash and the noise hits. It's intense; my whole body reacts as the gun's blast echoes off the walls of the alleyway. A second later it's gone, replaced by a deadening numbness. In the silence I look in horror at the gun in my hand, as if I can't believe what I've done, and then I look at Lukas.

He's spinning, away from me, his hands at his chest. Even as he turns I can see that he's wide-eyed, terrified; within a second or two he's lying on the ground against the opposite wall of the alley. Stasis returns. There's a whistling in my ears, but all else is quiet. I look at the gun. There's a faint smell, dry and acrid, like nothing I've known before. Nobody moves. Nothing happens. I can feel my heart beat.

And then a red smudge blooms on his shirt, the world of sound crashes back in, and everything happens at once.

I step back, feel the cold wall against me. Lukas speaks; it sounds unnaturally loud now that my hearing has returned, yet still it's little more than a thin, reedy noise in his throat. 'You stupid bitch! You fucking shot me!'

My courage has gone, my bravado has disappeared. My hand goes to my mouth.

He's panting, looking down at the blood that's beginning to seep through his fingers. He cries out. I can't make out what he's saying, it's little more than a rasping moan, but he looks from his bleeding chest to Anna and there seems to be a name in there. It sounds like 'Bella'.

The word seems familiar, vaguely, but I can't place it. I look over at Anna. Help me, I want to say. What have I done? But she's looking at me. Her face is cold. Her eyes wide, as if in shock, yet at the same time she's wearing half a smile.

'Bella,' he says again.

'Shut the fuck up,' she says. She takes a step forward. She moves slowly. She is utterly calm.

I look at her. I'm incredulous. I don't know what to say. My mouth opens, closes. She looks at me.

My world is imploding. I can't work out what is happening. Everything seems too bright, as if I've been staring into the sun. I can only make out outlines, shadows. Nothing is solid, nothing seems real.

'Where's Connor? Where is he?'

She smiles, but says nothing.

'Anna? What's this about? We're friends . . . ? Aren't we?'

She laughs. The name begins to float to the surface. I've heard it before. I know I have. Bella.

I just can't yet place it. I look to the body at my feet, desperate for help. 'Lukas?' He looks up at me. He's gasping, pale. His eyes close, open again. 'Lukas?'

He tries to take another deep breath, to speak, but the words fracture and fail.

Anna speaks. It's difficult to tell, but it looks as though she's begun to cry. 'The police will be here soon, Julia.'

I look at the gun in my hand, at the man I've just shot. The truth begins to emerge, yet still it's distorted, not yet in focus.

'I didn't mean to kill him.'

'You never do—'

'What—?'

'Yet people still keep dying . . .'

I don't know what she means. 'What? Anna—!'

'Oh, Julia. You still haven't worked it out, have you?'

I begin to sob. 'It's your gun. Yours. You're the one who told me about it.'

'But I'm not the one who pulled the trigger.'

'He killed my sister!'

She smiles, then, and steps forward into the light. 'No, he didn't.'

Her voice is utterly cold, her words sharp enough to sever flesh.

'What?'

'It was me she was meeting that night. I said we needed to talk. But not here.' She looks at Lukas, lying silently on the floor. 'At his place. He said we could use it.'

'What?'

'But she was late. She stayed for one more drink. So I bumped into her here. Right where we're standing.'

'Kate?'

She nods. 'I told her it was time. We'd tried everything, but you still wouldn't give Connor back. So I said we ought to tell you the truth.'

A wave of dread wraps itself around me, around my throat. I fight for breath.

'It *was* you? Persuading her . . .'

'Yes. I said we should tell you about Connor's father. Tell you that he had family, family that would look after him. Not just Kate—'

Again I look at Lukas. 'Him?'

'Don't be so ridiculous. He was just some bloke I was fucking.' She shakes her head. 'I mean me.'

I take a step back. The gun drops to my side. I don't believe what I'm hearing.

'But—'

'She wouldn't listen. She said she wasn't telling you. It would hurt you too much.' She shakes her head. 'As if you getting hurt matters in the slightest, after what you did. We fought.'

'What . . . ? Who *are* you?'

'I didn't mean to push her over.'

'*You* killed her!'

She looks at me. She raises her chin, defiant. Her hate is almost physical; sticky and cloying. It penetrates deep within me. She looks at me and I can see that I disgust her.

'I pushed her over. She hit her head. I was angry, I wanted to stop, but . . .' She shrugs. 'I didn't know she was dead when I left her. But yes. I left her here and I went round to his place' – she looks again at Lukas – 'and then the next day I found out she was dead. And I was glad. You know that? Glad I left her here, alone.'

My sobs turn into scalding tears. They run down my face. I raise the gun.

'I'm glad because that's exactly what you did to my brother.'

'What . . . ?' I say, but an image comes. The last time I'd stood over a body, a dying man. And then finally it snaps into focus. I remember the name Marcus had had for his sister.

'Bella . . . You're Bella.'

I see it now, the thing I've failed to see all this time. In certain lights, from certain angles. She looks a little like her brother.

Suddenly I'm back there. I see him that night, his face ashen, bloodless, yet filmed with sweat. He looked unreal somehow, made of rubber. Spittle fringed his mouth; there was vomit on the floor. 'Go!' said Frosty.

'No. I can't.'

She looked up at me. She was crying. 'You have to. If they find any of us here—'

'No.'

'—it'll be over for all of us.' She stood up, she held me. 'There's nothing we can do for Marky now, honey. He's gone. He's gone—'

'No!'

'—now you have to go, too.'

And then I'd seen it. The truth. The people's lives I'd ruin by staying behind with a man it was too late to help.

'But—'

'I promise I'll let them know he's here.' She kissed me, the top of my head. 'Go, go now. And look after yourself.'

And then she went back to Marcus and, with one final glance at his body, I turned away and left him behind.

I look up at the woman I'd thought was my friend Anna. At the woman who's been pretending to be my son's girl-friend. 'You're Marcus's sister.'

No response. My hands shake.

'Look. I don't know what you think—'

'Marcus was coming home. You know? We were going to look after him. *We* loved him. His family. Not you. You weren't even *there*. You left him.'

'He overdosed, Anna! You might not like that, but it's true. He'd been clean for weeks, he took more than he could cope with. It was nobody's fault.'

'Is that right?' She shakes her head slowly, her eyes narrowed with bitterness. 'You were selling your photographs, buying him drugs. I know that—'

'No. No.'

'And then when he couldn't take it any more, when he overdosed, you left him to die.'

'No! I loved him. I loved Marcus . . .' I'm sobbing now, my body convulsing, my tears mingling with the rain that runs down my face. 'I've never loved anyone like I loved him.'

Her cold gaze locks with mine.

'You don't even know what happened. He was dead already. I had to leave. Marcus had . . . we were . . . I just had to go.'

'You left him there, dying on the floor. You ran away. Back home to start your new life, with your lovely little house and your oh so fucking successful husband. And your son. Darling Connor.'

'Connor. Where is he?'

'You took everything from me. My mother hanged herself—'

I point the gun at her. 'Where is he?'

'Then my father went, too. You should have gone to prison for what you did.' She pauses, her head tilted. Over the driving rain I can hear sirens. 'And now you will. They're coming for you.'

I scream. '*What have you done to my son?*'

422

'Connor? Nothing. I'd never hurt Connor. He's the only thing I've got left.'

It hits me then, finally. 'Marcus? Marcus was Connor's father?'

She says nothing, yet as much as I don't want to believe it, I know it's true. I see it all. It must've been when Kate came to visit. Just before Marcus died.

She nods. 'I didn't know he'd had a child. But then last year Kate told me all about Connor. How she'd got pregnant when she visited her sister in Berlin, and her sister still didn't know. I had no idea she was talking about Marcus, but then she showed me that picture of the two of you. I nearly told her that Marcus was my brother, but I decided not to. You know why? Because, finally, it all made sense. After all these years I now knew who the bitch was who'd left him to die.' She looks me in the eye. 'It was you, Julia. And here I was, living with your sister.' She shakes her head. 'That photo. I started to see him everywhere . . .'

'If you've hurt my son—'

'He's my nephew, and I want him, Julia. He can't stay with you. Look at you. Look at what you've done. You're not fit to be his mother. I proved it. I sent the videos to Hugh, to everyone. They'll all know what a cheap slut you are now.'

So that's it. It had been about getting Connor back, all along. Not the money.

I look at Lukas. Lukas, who thought he was blackmailing me for money. He's lying, motionless, his unseeing eyes wide open.

I hear a car pull up, a door open. I daren't turn round. I look at the gun in my hand. It's as if it has nothing to do with me.

He's dead. The man who is the proof of what's been going on, is dead. And I killed him.

'A slut,' says Anna. She takes a step towards me. She's

almost close enough to touch. I can hear footsteps, close by. I risk a quick glance over my shoulder. Two police cars have pulled up and Hugh is getting out of the first, along with three or four officers. They're all shouting, a mix of French and English. Hugh's voice is the only one I can make out. 'Julia!' he's saying. 'Julia! Put the gun down!'

I look at him. In the car behind him I can see another figure and with a jolt of relief I realize it's Connor. He's looking at me. He looks lost, bewildered. But he's alive. Anna was lying. He's safe. Hugh must've found him, wandering Gare du Nord, just as Anna had pretended to. Or perhaps he finally relented and turned his phone on, to call his dad.

'Julia!' says Hugh again. He skids to a halt. The police are ahead of him, they've crouched on the ground. There are guns pointing at me. I look at Anna.

'She killed Kate!' I say.

Anna speaks, too quietly for anyone but me to hear. 'You're a junkie and a slut and a murderer.'

I'm still looking at my husband. I remember what he'd said, on the phone on the way here. *Connor's father is dead.*

He'd known. Kate must have told him. And he'd kept it to himself.

I look back at Anna. I know she's telling the truth. She's sent the pictures to Hugh.

She smiles.

'I took it all. I've ruined your life, Julia, and now you'll lose your son.'

'No—' I begin, but she silences me.

'It's over, Julia.'

I raise the gun. The police shout, Hugh says something, but I can't make it out. I know she's right. Whatever happens, it's over now. There's no way back. I've loved someone, someone who isn't my husband. I've loved someone and I've shot him. I can't go back from this. My life – my second life, the one I escaped into when I ran from Berlin – is over.

'I should kill you,' I say.

'Then do it.'

I close my eyes. It's what she wants. I know it is. And if I do she's won. But I don't care, now. I've lost Hugh, I'll lose Connor. It's irrelevant.

My hand is shaking, I don't know what I'm going to do. I want to fire the gun, and at the same time I don't. Maybe it's not too late, maybe I can still prove it was Bella who killed my sister, that she tricked me into shooting Lukas. But I can't work out what difference it will make; Lukas may have been many things, but he was no murderer. I've killed an innocent man; whether deliberately or not hardly seems to matter. I can't live with myself either way.

I open my eyes. Whatever happens next, whether I shoot or not, it's over.

Acknowledgements

Very special thanks to Clare Conville, Richard Skinner and Miffa Salter. For practical advice on the world of photography, my thanks go to Annabel Staff and to Stuart Sandford. Thanks to my editors around the world, in particular Larry Finlay, Claire Wachtel, Michael Heyward and Iris Tupholme. Thanks to my family and friends, in particular to Nicholas Ib.

The character name 'Paddy Renouf' was supplied by its original owner, who won the right to have his name featured in this book during a charity auction to raise funds for Kelling Hospital, Norfolk. The character is entirely fictional.

ABOUT THE AUTHOR

S J Watson's first novel, *Before I Go To Sleep*, is a phenomenal international success. A bestseller around the world, it won the Crime Writers' Association Award for Best Debut Novel and the Galaxy National Book Award for Crime Thriller of the Year. The film of the book, starring Nicole Kidman, Colin Firth and Mark Strong, and directed by Rowan Joffe, was released in September 2014.

S J Watson was born in the Midlands and now lives in London.